CHARITY NORMAN

After the Fall

ALLEN&UNWIN

First published in Great Britain in 2012 by Allen & Unwin

First published in Australia in 2012 by Allen & Unwin
(under the title Second Chances)

Allen & Unwin
c/o Atlantic Books
Ormond House
26–27 Boswell Street
London WC1N 3JZ

Phone: 020 7269 1610
Fax: 020 7430 0916
Email: UK@allenandunwin.com
Web: www.atlantic-books.co.uk

A CIP catalogue record for this book is available from the British Library.

ISBN 978 1 74331 096 0

Internal design by Lisa White

Printed and bound in Great Britain by the MPG Books Group

10 9 8 7 6 5 4 3 2 1

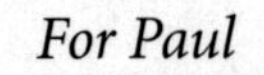

For Paul

Hawke's Bay Today
Local News

In the early hours of this morning, the Lowe Corporation rescue helicopter was scrambled to airlift a five-year-old boy from a coastal address north of Napier. He was flown to Hawke's Bay Hospital where he underwent emergency surgery for extensive internal injuries.

It is understood that the child was injured as a result of a fall from a first-floor balcony. However, hospital staff declined to speculate on the circumstances of the incident.

'I can confirm that a small boy with life-threatening injuries was admitted earlier today,' said a spokesperson. 'At this stage it would be inappropriate to comment further. Police and child protection agencies have been alerted, and comprehensive enquiries are ongoing. I am not in a position to release any details until that investigation has taken its course.'

The injured child remains in the hospital's intensive care unit, where his condition is reported to be critical. His name has yet to be released.

One

Finn fell.

I don't think, if I used a million words, I could call up the horror. It isn't a matter of words.

My son plunged headlong, tiny hands clutching at nothing. He never made a sound. I can see his pyjamas disappearing into the greedy dark. Mr Men pyjamas, from his Christmas stocking. I can see his pirate doll, cartwheeling out of reach.

No moon yet. In films, tragedy always strikes during a torrential storm amid lightning and thunder, and the heroine's hair is plastered to her tear-streaked cheeks—though she's wearing waterproof mascara so no harm done. But it was a calm night, when Finn fell. A starry winter's night, and the hills were gentle swells against a singing sky. There was only the screech of a plover in the fields; the mother-in-law bird, bossy and reassuring. A calm New Zealand night.

And then the world exploded. I can still hear the swish of bushes. I can feel the thud as my baby hit the ground. Really, I can feel it. It shook the house. It shook the hills. It shook the heavens. I hurled myself down the stairs, trying to outrun this unholy terror.

Something lay lifeless beside a lemon tree, a dark little mound in the garden of my dream house. I thought my boy was dead. I touched the white face, feeling the miracle of his pulse, bargaining with a God in whose existence I'd never believed. You will, too. Oh yes you will, if ever your own nightmares come alive. You will pray with all your heart, and all your soul, and with some part of your brain that you've never used before, never even knew was there. Believe me, you will. At such a time, atheism is a luxury you can't afford.

It took so long for them to come. *So* long, while Finn hung suspended over the abyss of death, and fear pressed us both into the black earth. Buccaneer Bob sprawled close by. Where Finn goes, his pirate goes too. At last I sensed the throb of rotor blades beating through the pitiless dark, the rhythm of rescue; brilliant lights rising over the hillside. The Heavenly Host. They landed in our front paddock in a hurricane of sound, sprinted towards my waving torch—two men in red coveralls, not a choir of dazzling angels—and worked with urgency and few words: fixed a line into Finn's arm and a brace around his neck, muttering together about his spine as they lifted him across the lawn and into the helicopter.

Neither asked how it happened. Not yet. They knew—as I knew—that this could be Finn's last journey. He's in trouble, they were thinking. Head injury, internal bleeding, God knows what else. In all likelihood, this one isn't coming home.

We were gone within minutes, Finn and I, lifting tail-first into the future.

Even as we landed, people and equipment appeared out of nowhere, mobbing us in an efficient scrum. Through a fog of panic I heard that Finn's blood pressure was falling, that heart and respiration rates had increased. Figures were called out—eighty–forty; sixty–thirty—with increasing insistence. They cut away his favourite pyjamas and covered him with a worn flannel blanket. Now he was anonymous.

I was with him when they began a blood transfusion, when they fed a plastic tube through the gentle mouth and into his airways, when his lonely body moved through the massive complexity of the CT scanner. I couldn't hold him, I couldn't care for him. I was useless. Soon they took him away, wheeling him rapidly through impassable doors to where surgeons' knives were waiting.

I know someone led me to this quiet cubicle and tried to explain what was happening. They've done their best, but my mind has seized. I'm hunched in a plastic chair, my fingers wrapped around a white mug that has inexplicably appeared in one hand. I clutch Buccaneer Bob's floppy body to my chest. We're trying to comfort one another.

Finn is alone under vicious white lights and the eyes of adult strangers. They'll be discussing the weather as they cut my baby open. Hardest frost on record . . . nearly two metres of snow up at Ruapehu, going to extend the ski season. We're losing him, says the anaesthetist.

A woman ambles past. Another patient's mother, I imagine. She has wide hips and a comfortable bread-dough face, and she reminds me of Louisa. I'd give anything to see my sister's matronly form in a flowered skirt, swinging solidly up the hospital corridor with her arms held out wide and love in her smile. I'd give anything to see an old friend, someone who likes and trusts me because we go back a lifetime. I've no old friends here. In this whole country, this whole hemisphere, there's not one person outside my family—no, including my family—who truly knows me.

I curl my legs onto the sharp plastic of the chair, knees pulled up. I know I look a sorry sight, a bag lady on a bad day. A passing nurse obviously thinks so because she turns into my cubicle, tugging on the curtain. She's a tidy creature with a curling fringe. When she speaks, I dully register a familiar accent. Liverpool, I'd say.

'How're you doing?' It's made-in-China sympathy, but better than nothing.

I shake my head, driving my teeth into my knees. I'm rocking.

'Whoops! You're going to spill that.' She takes the mug from me, resting it on a stainless-steel trolley. 'What a horrible thing to happen. He's getting the best possible care, that's the main thing.'

Then she asks the question. She's the first, but I know she won't be the last.

'How did he come to fall?'

Honesty is the best policy! hisses Mum, right in my ear. Makes me jump. She's long dead, my mother, but that doesn't stop her and her clichés. Don't misunderstand me; I'm not having auditory hallucinations, nor—so far as I know—am I a medium. My mother's personality was so assertive and censorious that she took up residence in my head when I was about three. I've been trying to evict her ever since. Sometimes she disappears for months at a time, but always pops up to twist the knife when the going gets tough.

The truth sets us free! she whispers now.

I think about the truth. I really do. I turn it over and over with a sense of horrified disconnection. I look at it from every angle, like a 3-D image on a computer screen. And on that screen I see police, and a courtroom, and a prison cell. I see disaster.

Finn's a sleepwalker, I tell the kind nurse. Always has been. It's funny because his twin brother never does it. Funny peculiar, not funny ha-ha. I should have locked their door. It's my fault.

That last part is true, at least.

'Nah. Could have happened to anybody,' she croons, in comfortable ignorance. She isn't really listening. People don't. 'It's an accident waiting to happen when they mess about in their sleep. I've got one who did it till he was thirteen. We lost him in a resort in Fiji, two years old!'

'Awful.'

'Worst ten minutes of my life. Lucky he wasn't floating face down in the pool.'

'Lucky.' I think of Finn, whose luck ran out.

'So what brought *you* out here?' she asks.

It's a perennial question. This country is home to many immigrants, and every one of us has our story. I wonder how many tell the whole truth.

'My husband,' I say. 'He fell in love with the place years ago, always wanted to come back. You?'

'Married a Kiwi. Broke my mum's heart, but what can you do?'

I try to answer, but Finn is falling. He's falling, and I hear the thud. The nurse pulls some tissues from a box, handing them to me with a sisterly rub of my shoulder.

'Sometimes you have to wonder, don't you?' she muses, smoothing the breaking wave of her fringe. 'You have to wonder *why* these things have to go and happen.'

Clattering feet, the rumble of a trolley. A baby's fretful wail.

'Got to go,' she sighs, giving my shoulder one last pat. 'No rest for the wicked.'

Ah, I think, as I watch her twitch back the curtain and hurry duck-footed to the latest emergency. There's the question. Not how. *Why.*

I'm haunted by that question as the night wears on.

Why, why, and why.

Two

If I had to stick a pin in the map of space and time, marking the start of our journey, I'd choose a Bedfordshire village on a Friday in June. Our village. Our house.

I remember driving home from work through a brief summer downpour. For ten minutes I skulked in the car by our garden pond, while the cooling engine tick-tick-ticked, summoning the will to go into the house. Finally I dug out my phone. Delaying tactics.

How did physics go? xx

Immediately, the screen flashed and buzzed. *dunno xxx*

Very informative, I thought resignedly as I hauled myself out and up the path. My daughter was coming to the last of her fifth-form exams, and I had no idea how she'd done. I stood for a long moment in the porch, steeling myself. Then I opened our front door.

The change struck me as soon as I stepped into the hall. That morning, I'd escaped a house pervaded by the cold draught of Kit's despair. Now I caught the cheerful whiff of toasting crumpets and his mellow voice, accompanied by the twins' merry discordancy.

Jack and Jill went up the hill

To fetch a pail of water

I followed these sounds of revelry to the kitchen. Kit stood ironing a shirt while his sons lumbered on the tabletop among the plates. Charlie paused to give me smacky crumpety kisses, but Finn was reaching an ear-splitting crescendo, shaking matted dark locks:

Jack fell down and broke his crown

And Jill came tumbling af-ter! Hello, Mummee!

Inevitably, he stood in the butter dish.

'Yuck!' he squawked, hopping on one narrow foot while holding the buttery one up in front of him.

'Butter toes,' said Kit, and flashed me a vivid smile.

Charlie pointed a chubby forefinger, delight on the cartoon-round cheeks. Fair-curled and sturdy, he was the elder by half an hour. 'Butter toes, butter toes.'

I gave Finn a piggyback to the sink, dumped him on the draining board and doused his foot. Then I stood close behind Kit, running my hands around his waist and basking in his buoyancy. When he was on top of life, we could cope with anything at all. Sacha's dog slithered out of her basket to headbutt my knees. Muffin has a lot of Old English sheepdog in her and a touch of something smaller, and wanders through life with an air of genial absent-mindedness, like a professorial teddy bear.

'Hey, Muffin,' called Finn from the sink. 'D'you want to lick some lovely butter?'

'You're ironing a shirt,' I said, watching Kit turn a crumpled rag into something crisp and immaculate. 'Why are you ironing a shirt?'

'Think I've had a bit of a break.' Steam hissed from the iron. I could smell washing powder. 'I'll be taking the train to London in an hour. I called Stella Black today—remember, from way back? Graphic designer, I've worked with her on a couple of projects—she reckons her boss might have some consultancy work for me.'

'That would be wonderful,' I breathed, rubbing my cheek into the warmth of his shoulder. Consultancy work would be more than wonderful. It might even be a lifeline.

Kit was taut with hope and nerves; I could feel them jangling through his skin. He always had a deceptively lazy, understated way of moving—never seemed to pick up his feet—yet I sensed a frantic excitement that day. He finished the shirt, kissed me enthusiastically and strode off to the shower. Our house was one of the oldest in the village, the stairs steep and uneven. I sat halfway up, fretting, while the boys plotted mischief in the kitchen. My chest seemed to be squeezed in a vice, as though it was I who had the vital meeting. There was so much at stake. I had to force myself to exhale.

That's where Sacha found me. She paused in the hall, grinning, schoolbag swinging from one shoulder. 'Mum! You on the naughty stair?'

My daughter inherited the syrup-and-caramel ringlets from me. I can't seem to grow my hair beyond shoulder length and it sticks out like a string floor mop, but hers is glorious, rippling exuberantly down her back and around her face. She has the Norris family hooked nose, too. I've always thought—as her adoring mother—that her high forehead and imperfect nose are what make Sacha truly beautiful.

'I put myself here,' I said. 'It's my place in life. Now gimme the lowdown on that exam, and if you say "dunno", I'll tan your hide.'

She held up innocent palms. 'Well I *don't* know, do I? I think I did okay. Bastards never asked about electromagnetism though, after all the swotting I did. That was scummy.'

'Kit might have some work,' I blurted, and she promptly dumped her bag and sat on the stair beneath mine, resting her forearm on my lap while I told her about his trip to London.

'How bad *are* things, Mum?' she asked seriously. 'You can come clean, now GCSEs are almost over. I know you two have been trying to cover up.'

She was right, of course. We'd been shielding her from the worst. I reached down to plait her hair, comforted by the heavy skein of it under my fingers.

'Our lifestyle—this house, everything—it all came from Kit's income, from the heyday of his agency before the economy melted down. My salary isn't nearly enough. I don't earn much more than his PA did! Pretty galling, but there we are.'

'So we'll have to sell this house if he doesn't get another job?'

'Maybe,' I agreed cautiously.

'And I'll have to shift schools, won't I?'

'We'll see.'

'That means yes.'

I shrugged, wishing I could deny it.

'Um . . .' She began tapping a syncopated rhythm on my knee with her palm. 'I know Kit's drinking again.'

'You do?'

'I have eyes, Mum, and I have ears. Last Friday the twins told me they locked themselves out in the rain and got soaking wet while he was asleep on the sofa. Charlie said he'd "gone funny again". Poor little beanies! No prizes for guessing what went on there. And I heard on the grapevine that you had to collect him from the pub.'

'They don't want him back,' I confessed.

That call was excruciating. Our local landlord, concerned and embarrassed: *I've had to take his car keys off him again . . . might be best if he doesn't come here for a while.*

'Losing the agency was his worst nightmare,' I said now, needing to defend Kit. 'Letting people down, when they had mortgages and school fees too. The past few months have been really rough and—well, endless knockbacks and money worries have finally worn him down. Alcohol's a sort of self-medication.'

'Poor Kit.' Sacha wrinkled her nose. 'Banned from the local? That's pretty screwball.'

Charlie appeared in the kitchen doorway, lighting up at the sight of his sister. 'Come and see,' he squeaked, beckoning. 'We've made a slide on the kitchen floor.'

'A slide? How?' Sacha sounded suspicious.

'With loads and loads of butter. It's *really* slippy.'

Sacha's jaw dropped, but I flapped a hand in defeat. 'Leave it for now. There are worse messes than butter.'

I found Kit in our bedroom, shrugging into a jacket and looking every inch the successful advertising guru. He had a way of wearing clothes as though they didn't matter; it was peculiarly stylish.

'You still scrub up good,' I murmured, taking his arm in my hands and watching us both in the wardrobe mirror. When the man in the mirror smiled back at me, I saw the old spark dancing in his eyes. After eight years of marriage, and all our troubles, Kit's smile still made me feel happy. I turned him to face me, took hold of his lapel and began to fuss with it. 'The picture of civilised man,' I said, brushing my knuckles along the firm line of his jaw. 'Good luck.'

He caught my hand and pressed it to his mouth. I felt a small tremor in his fingers, and ached for him. 'I've run out of doors to knock on, Martha. If this doesn't come off, I'll have failed you.'

Sacha hurried in, pretending to do a double take. 'Wow, Kit! You look like James Bond. Well, except for that zany black mane, which is more Mumbai street urchin.' While her stepfather made a dutiful attempt to tame his hair, she plonked newly shined shoes at his feet. 'I gave these a quick polish for you. Found them by the back door. They're the right ones, aren't they?'

'You're a princess,' said Kit fervently. 'How was the exam?'

'Murder.'

'Oh, bugger. Really?'

'Nah, not too bad. Only one left—and then it's party time!'

'I'll bet you've sailed through,' predicted Kit, sitting on the bed to tie his laces. 'Jesus! Look at the time.'

Minutes later he'd hopped into his car and was roaring away towards Bedford. Sacha and I stood at our gate, watching that bright green blur threading between the traffic. It seemed terribly significant somehow, the only coloured dot on a sombre landscape.

'I really hope he gets it,' said Sacha.

I held up two sets of crossed fingers, blinking hard, overwhelmed by the strain of the past weeks. I felt Sacha's arm around my neck.

'Don't worry, Mum,' she whispered, kissing my cheek. 'Whatever happens, it'll all come out in the wash.'

She and I spent the rest of the evening eyeing the clock, begging fate to give Kit this break. The phone rang twice. We jumped both times, but it wasn't him. The first call was from Sacha's boyfriend, Ivan, wondering how she'd done in physics. The next was male too, with a Dublin accent.

'Gerry Kerr,' he said, and instantly I remembered. One of Kit's art college cronies, Gerry had become a dealer and swanned around the States for a few years before buying a gallery in Dublin. I had a mental image of the man at our wedding reception—an urbane figure, cornering me to swear that Kit McNamara was a fucking genius and I had to get him painting again, he didn't care how much filthy lucre he could make in advertising.

Kit's career was rocketing when we were married, and then the twins arrived and took up every spare second. There was never enough time to indulge his passion, unless you counted the enchantment he'd created for his family. In the boys' bedroom it was Palaeolithic cave paintings: exquisite stags and bison chased one another all around the walls and over the ceiling, to the envy of visiting children. For Sacha he'd conjured a bewitching mural of mermaids.

'Gerry!' I cried now. 'How are you? Kit's out at the moment.'

Just touching base, Gerry said, wondering how we were doing. He'd heard about the agency going under.

'Ad agencies are falling like ninepins,' I explained. 'Kit hung on for grim death but . . . well. Advertising budgets are the first thing to be slashed.'

Gerry sounded genuinely concerned. 'Poor old McNamara. Still, look on the bright side. That man of yours is wasting his talent. This is a wake-up call.'

I looked at the sitting-room walls, where I'd hung a trio of Kit's paintings from college days. They were strange portraits: mud-brown, impish people with angular faces. I couldn't make head nor tail of them. I much preferred the mermaids and bison.

'He hasn't really painted for years,' I said doubtfully.

'Bloody crime. The man's got something, Martha, and he knows it.'

'Yes,' I retorted, laughing. 'You're right. He's got a family to support. And he knows it.'

I tried calling Kit after that. His phone promptly trilled from under a box of cereal in the kitchen. Forgetting his phone was a habit of Kit's.

By eight the boys were fast asleep, tangled among mounds of soft toys. At nine, I persuaded Sacha to turn in too. I could tell she was shattered. Much, much later, the house phone rang.

'Martha,' said Kit, and my hopes plunged. His voice was flat.

He was calling from Euston station. Stella's company had lost a crucial contract that very day and was reeling. Kit had spent the evening in a bar in Soho, consoling Stella and the boss who were now battling to stay afloat themselves. They wanted to help, he'd be top of their list if something came up, but they had nothing for him now. Sorry, mate.

'So that's that,' said Kit. I could hear the alcohol clouding his voice and his thoughts. 'I'm bloody useless.'

'Are you coming straight home?' I wanted us to face this together. 'Please don't . . . you know. Just come home. Take a taxi from the station.'

'Soon,' he said quietly, and rang off.

Bed was out of the question. I'd lie there rigidly awake, anxiety ricocheting around my head like a stray bullet. Instead I grabbed the in-tray—hair-raising bills screamed from its papery depths—and sat in front of the computer. I'd have to juggle everything somehow, and buy us time to get the house on the market.

Sacha had been messing about online. She must have been distracted by Ivan's call, and forgotten to log off. There were several websites left open: YouTube, eBay. Ah, and here was her Facebook page; never anything sinister on that. I was about to close it when a warning siren blared, somewhere between my ears.

Looking for my real father!! Name is Simon apparently, passed thru Bedford 16–17 years ago. Brwn hair brwn eyes, tall. Wld be 35–40 by now? Mum swears that's all she knows but I'm not so sure. Anyone—any ideas??? Wld really lve to trace my dad.

I sat stunned, a rabbit gaping into the harsh glare of the screen. Her Facebook friends had plenty of ideas, of course.

Have u checked ur birth certificate?

Hi sash, ask everyone in your family and all your mum's old friends, someone knows something, lock them in a room until they spill

My dads called simon LOL we might be sisters!!! I will ask him did he shag yor mum

cld try private detective

It's an icy shower, the moment you realise your child is an independent being who questions family mythology. Whenever she asked about her father I told Sacha the story of Simon, a pleasant young man who couldn't be traced. Now, it seemed, she'd started digging. One day her spade would hit a landmine, and we'd all lose limbs in the explosion.

See? Mum popped up, her voice gleeful. *Those chickens are coming home to roost! One girl's sordid secret is another girl's father.*

I staggered into the kitchen and filled the kettle, as though a nice cup of tea might somehow save us all from ruin. I couldn't face those bills, now. The latest copy of my occupational therapy magazine lay half-read on the kitchen bench, smothered among charitable appeals. I leafed vaguely through it as the kettle boiled. Techniques in the classroom, wheelchair fitting. Several recruitment agencies advertised regularly. Jobs in Australia . . . Canada . . . New Zealand. Kit had been to New Zealand as a student, and raved about the place. Carrying the magazine back to the computer with my mug, I typed in the website address. Just for fun, I told myself. Just to pass the time until he came home.

Seductive thing, the World Wide Web. Within an hour I'd educated myself on work, education and costs of living on the other side of the world. I was scrolling my way through visa information when the little carriage clock on the mantelpiece whirred, sighed and struck midnight. The tinny chime sent fear tapping on the door of my mind, though I tried to be rational. He'd roll up any minute, and I'd give him a royal bollocking.

By the time it struck the half hour I was pacing, literally wringing my hands. Kit was wrapped around a tree—oh my God, *why* did I let him take the car?—brilliant eyes blank and staring, blood trickling from the corner of a mouth that would never laugh again. Perhaps he was dying alone in the rain, pulverised by thugs, his vitality flowing away down the drain. Maybe he'd thrown himself into the river.

Inactivity was unbearable. Grabbing my handbag, I scribbled a note for Sacha. *Sorry gone to look for Kit. Love M x*

The phone rang as I was opening the front door. *Thank God.* I lunged for it, expecting to hear my husband's familiar tones—depressed, slurred, contrite. Light-headed with relief, I drew breath for a first-rate fishwife impersonation.

It wasn't Kit.

'Mrs McNamara? Barry Prescott, Bedfordshire police.'

The room darkened. I stared in terror at one of Kit's paintings, and the imp smirked back at me. This was it, then: the voice of doom. I was a widow. I felt the first jolt of grief.

The voice of doom sounded matter-of-fact. 'We've got your husband here. In the cells. He's, erm, you might say he's a little bit the worse for wear.'

'You mean he's drunk,' I croaked furiously. Not wrapped around a tree, then; not pulverised by thugs or under the waters of the Great Ouse.

'We picked him up off the High Street. Lucky he didn't get himself run over.'

They were really quite nice about it down at the police station, though I expect they'd all been having a good laugh. Sergeant Prescott seemed positively avuncular as he led me to the cells, jingling his keys. He was well past middle age, bushy-browed and seen-it-all. 'Your bloke's a bit of a mess,' he warned. 'Bet he'll be in hot water once he's slept it off.'

I've never been so humiliated in my life—for myself, for Kit. It was like collecting a mangy dog from the pound. My beautiful husband lay sweating on a concrete bench, his once-immaculate shirt grubby and torn, reeking of vomit. Hair hung lankly over his face. At Prescott's good-natured urging he swung his legs to the floor and sat up, pressing his head into his hands.

'Sorry,' he groaned. 'Oh God, Martha, what the hell is happening?'

I needed to be out of that place; I needed to get my man home and clean and human. Prescott swiftly processed the paperwork and gave me back Kit's wallet. Then he steered him outside and into my car.

'Next time we find him in this state, we'll have to charge him,' the policeman said, and he wasn't smiling any more. 'You do appreciate that, Mrs McNamara? We can't have people rolling around in the gutter.'

I dimly recall rain-soaked streets, the lights of McDonald's, a black cat streaking across the road with a flash of luminous eyes—did that mean we were in for good luck or bad? Kit half lay with his head against the window, whispering hoarsely—*sorry, sorry . . . Christ, I'm such a fucking fool*—and I knew the morning would bring a thudding head, crippling guilt and even deeper despair. He'd try to pull himself up by the bootstraps, swear off the drink for a week, maybe three, and then the whole miserable cycle would begin again.

'I've heard it all before,' I said wearily.

'Me too. I'm sick of myself.'

I swerved into our driveway and yanked at the handbrake. 'This is bloody ridiculous. Okay, so your business went down. Okay, you can't find work.'

'And we're broke.'

'And we're broke. It's been hell. But it's happened, and now it's time—'

While I ranted, Kit was fumbling at his door. 'I can't get out,' he said. I walked around and opened it from the outside.

'There,' I declared coldly. 'You're a free man.'

'Am I?' He put his arms around me, leaning his head against my waist. 'I don't think I want to be.'

'C'mon. Bed.'

It was a struggle, because he didn't have the will to move. I manhandled all six foot of him into the house and up the steep stairs. We'd almost made it when he sat down heavily on the top step, his head drooping as though it was made of stone.

'Don't wanna go to bed,' he muttered. 'Leave me here.'

'Rubbish!' I balanced on a lower step, bending to hook my elbows under his armpits. 'Couple of Alka-Seltzer, good night's sleep, you'll be right as rain.'

His voice rose to a bellow. 'Jesus, Martha! Leave me alone, will you?'

'Shh!' I was furious now, pushing and pummelling, trying to drag him to his feet. 'For God's sake, pull yourself together!'

I really, truly don't believe he intended what happened next, though he called me a fucking smug bitch as he shoved me away. I remember thinking, as I fell—clutched at the handrail, missed—and rolled and hit the bottom step, that he had a deal of strength for someone so shambolically drunk.

I was still crumpled and dazed in a heap when I felt shaking hands on my face. Kit sounded stricken, breathy with panic and almost sober. 'Martha? Look at me. Come on, Martha, *look* at me! Can you hear me?'

His face loomed close to mine, sheet-white, eyes wide and bloodshot as he searched my pupils for signs of concussion. I'd landed on my shoulder, not my head, but I felt as though I'd been run over by a truck. Kit abruptly pulled me to his chest and wrapped his body around mine. His voice was pitched higher than usual.

'Christ Martha, Christ Martha, please be okay.'

'Bloody hell,' I moaned, feeling the slick warmth of blood seeping from my nose. 'How much worse can things get?'

Then my self-control crumpled, and I began to cry, out of pure misery. Kit sprawled on the bottom step, his back against the wall, cradling my head and saying sorry, sorry, sorry.

It was there at the foot of our stairs—at rock bottom—that we finally began to talk, and to listen. We talked about our marriage, our past and our future. We faced the facts of our crisis: mortgage, school fees, frozen bank accounts. We worried about Sacha and about the boys. We seemed unable to stop talking, faces close together, whispering anxiously through the early hours. Then we began to look for a way out.

By the time we disentangled our limbs and stood up, our future was utterly changed. I felt stunned by the decisions we'd made, yet quietly elated. Kit brought me a cup of tea, gently wiping the blood from my face with a warm flannel.

'Jesus, I'm an idiot,' he murmured.

I laid my finger on his lips. 'Enough,' I said. 'Enough regret. I need you whole, Kit.'

The midsummer dawn was a silver gleam at the window. A new day.

Three

My sister sat pole-axed, her eyes over-bright. 'For God's sake, Martha! *Why?*'

I'd been dreading this confrontation. My glass shook, splashing wine in a red worm over my wrist. 'It's not been easy,' I said feebly.

Louisa had a baby shoved up her jersey, as usual. Well, not quite a baby; we were there to celebrate Thundering Theo's first birthday. He had teeth. He could walk. Call me old-fashioned, but should children who wear orange Kickers still be breastfeeding? She always takes things to excess, does my sister. She had four children in five years. Excessive, I call that.

'Martha.' She shut her eyes. 'Tell me you're not serious. You aren't going to sell your house, ditch your career and move halfway around the bloody world?'

'Well—'

'This is Kit's idea, isn't it?'

'Not really, although he's been really low about the agency.'

'I thought he was sick of the advertising game. Claimed to despise everything it stands for.'

'Perhaps, but it was *his* game.'

One-handed, she pretended to play a violin. 'I love Kit, but he's just a moody bastard. All glittering blue eyes one day, waltzing you around the kitchen, brooding Beethoven the next. You can't uproot your family on his whim.' She fixed me with a suspicious glare. 'Oh God! I get it. He's hit the bottle again, hasn't he?'

'No, no.'

'If he's laid a finger—'

'Christ's sake.' I swatted at the buzzing implication. Lou was going to get the sanitised version: I wasn't letting any skeletons out of closets; certainly not for my effortlessly competent sister. I'd even been too proud to tell her just how desperate our finances were.

'We can't all run away from our problems,' she huffed. 'How about a career change—I thought he was a frustrated artist? Those murals are extraordinary.'

'Aha! Nail on the head. He's going to have a shot at painting.'

The birthday boy popped up, looking smugly moon-faced while Louisa fiddled distractedly with the strap of his dungarees.

'Kit says New Zealand is beautiful,' I ventured. 'Like Ireland, but better weather and no relatives.'

'Huh. He's been watching too much *Lord of the Rings.*'

I sighed. 'It's actually me you have to blame. I was sitting in front of the computer one night, freaking out about the mortgage.'

'Join the club.'

'I couldn't resist having a little peek at this recruitment agency's website. I found five great jobs straightaway, so I started researching—Lou, it was like riding on a magic carpet! With a couple of clicks it flew me—*whoosh*—out of my gloomy sitting room and off to a promised land. Forests, mountains, pristine white beaches, all stunningly lovely. No traffic, no queues. People swimming with dolphins. Skiing. Surfing. Kayaking on crystal-clear rivers—hey, d'you know what their advertising slogan is?'

Lou looked as though I'd invited her to see my gallstones.

'*One hundred per cent pure,*' I announced, with a flourish.

She stuck out the tip of her tongue. 'How twee. And what else did you visit on your magic hearthrug?'

'The estate agent. A dream house in the hills—ten dream houses in our price range, mortgage free. Places for Kit to paint and me to keep chickens.'

'Like Beatrix bloody Potter.'

'And finally the government website. We'll get visas if one of us has an essential skill and—hey, presto!—occupational therapists are on the list.' I lifted the baby from her lap and pressed my nose to his. I was going to miss him.

'Have you talked to the witch doctor?' Lou meant our father, and she was playing her ace card. She knew the children idolised him.

'I'll do it tomorrow—and don't you dare get in first.'

'Kit's family?'

'Not yet.'

She buttoned her shirt, lips clamped into a line. I'd known Louisa thirty-seven years; she was a three-year-old tyrant when I was born, and the only person I ever met who could stare down our mother. She really hadn't changed in all that time, and I loved her as much as ever.

'What it comes down to is that you've let a daydream get out of control,' she said.

'What it comes down to is that we want a different life for our children. Oh, yuck, Theo! You're supposed to throw up on Mummy, not me.' I set him down on the Kickers, and he thundered off.

Handing me a bit of white muslin, Lou swayed across the kitchen in her flowery skirt. My sister is opulent, like a peony. The plumper she grows, the better she looks. I'm sure she posed for Botticelli in another incarnation. She might be his Venus, with twining tendrils of caramel hair, a slightly hooked nose and arching brows. Apparently she and I are strikingly similar—could be twins, they tell me—but I slightly resent the suggestion. Lou would never in a zillion years get into my jeans.

Upstairs, Finn and Charlie were having a barney. Howls of rage culminated in a smash, then Charlie's agonised wailing.

'Trouble?' asked Lou, reaching for her cigarettes. She and smoking had a love-hate relationship. She was always trying to give up.

'It's not serious; I can tell from the engine note. Anyway, Sacha's with them.'

Lou flicked her lighter.

'Sacha's got a new boyfriend,' I said, hoping to distract her. 'Did she tell you?' She shook her head sulkily, but I persevered. 'Ivan Jones, the garden gnome. Plays the timpani in her orchestra. He looks uncannily like something you'd find cross-legged on a lily pad.'

'Does he wear a hoodie?'

I opened my hands, mystified. 'Nope! No ponytail, no tattoos. Not so much as an earring. Nothing *remotely* rebellious. What a codswalloping yawn. He won't get her pregnant or hooked on heroin, but what's he got to offer a girl like Sacha?'

'Perhaps he's fascinating, if you happen to be sixteen.'

'Can't see it, myself. He's got a silly little beard and a pink VW Beetle.'

Lou shrugged. 'Well, there you are, then. Wheels.'

'He's hypnotically boring, Lou. Sits there piggling at his fingernails.'

'Why worry? He'll be gone by next week.' She balanced her cigarette in an ashtray and began to chop onions for tomato salad. 'I wish I had a Sacha—cheerful, competent and permanently available for babysitting.'

'Ah, but you wouldn't have enjoyed telling Mum you were pregnant at the age of twenty-one, and not a father in sight.'

'My virginal bridesmaid, rolling along in that vile maternity dress. The *shame*!'

I forced a laugh. It wasn't a happy memory. 'She'd have put me in one of those Irish laundries if she could have.'

Slamming down her knife, Lou began to massage her temples. 'Martha, don't go. Why are you doing this? Aren't we enough for you?'

I'd never refused my sister anything. I could feel knots tightening in my stomach.

'You'll never go through with it,' she said suddenly. 'You haven't told Dad or the McNamara clan. It'll never happen.' With a sharp little nod of denial, she held out her salad. 'C'mon, enough nonsense! Grab this. I'll go and find Philip.'

I didn't move. 'I've signed a contract,' I said sadly. 'It's a private rehab unit just outside a city called Napier. Head injury and spinal. I had an interview with an agency in London. I've . . . Lou, I've already given notice at work.'

She froze for a second before ramming the bowl into my midriff. 'I wish I knew what you're trying to prove,' she snapped, and flounced off.

I trailed outside. It was only just beginning to sink in, what we were doing. The enormity of it left me dizzy. Finn and Charlie ran past me to join their cousins who were splashing in and out of a paddling pool, dicing with hypothermia.

Kit was lounging against the barbecue where Louisa had sent him, one hand in a pocket, sizzling sausages. 'How'd she take it?' he asked, and chuckled sympathetically when I imitated the face from *The Scream.*

As if on cue, Lou swept from the house, followed by her husband. 'Philip's appalled,' she said, her voice brassy with hurt.

My brother-in-law threw me one reproachful glance as he lowered himself into a deckchair and proceeded to scuba dive in the merlot. Philip was a young man when I first knew him, with copper eyelashes and a Captain Kirk grin. We go back too far; met while I was training and had a practice placement in the unit where he was a psychologist. I introduced him to Lou, God help me. Seventeen years on there's half the sandy hair, double the chins and plenty of regret. He works in industry, doing isometric testing on ostensibly sane people. Must be pretty depressing.

'So.' He made his fingers skip along the chair's arm. 'The rats are scurrying from the sinking ship.'

'Rats, are we?' Kit laughed. It was a long time since I'd seen him so carefree. His eyes seemed almost electric blue. 'Don't beat around the bush, Philip. If you're not entirely impressed, why not say so?'

'Your scheme is hare-brained. What are your children going to be—Irish? English? New Zealanders?'

'Happy,' retorted Kit. 'Untroubled. Unhurried. Uncrowded.'

'Uneducated and uncultured.'

'Ooh, you old snob!' I wrapped a towel around Charlie, who'd bumped his nose and was screaming loud enough to rouse my mother from her grave. 'Shh, Charlie . . . They don't wear grass skirts over there, Philip. They have excellent schools. Rutherford was a New Zealander. You know, the atom man.'

'Well, hurrah.'

'You're jealous,' proclaimed Kit, hitting the bullseye.

'Bollocks, man!'

Philip's disgust merely widened Kit's smile. Sparks quite often flew between the two of them. Kit thought Philip was pompous and self-absorbed, which was undeniable; but it wasn't the whole picture.

'We're off to Hawke's Bay,' said Kit, 'where that wine you're drinking comes from. While you're shivering in your thermal undies, we'll be wearing t-shirts and taking little dips just to cool off.'

'What gives you the right to run away?' Philip turned to me. 'Martha, where's your bloody loyalty?'

I sighed. 'Look. We're really going to miss you, but we rats just want out of the race.'

'Sacha!' he exploded, slapping his knee. 'You're surely not going to turn that wonderful girl's world upside down?'

'She can't stay at her present school, anyway. We can't afford the fees.'

'So move her. Don't cart her off to a third world country.'

'Philip! It's not a . . . Look. I've sussed out the schools where we're going, and there's a choice of several good ones. Their academic year starts in February so she'll be able to settle in before the sixth form.'

'It's all a question of balance,' said Kit. 'Ouch.' He'd burned his fingers on the barbecue, and sucked them. 'We have to balance everybody's interests.'

Philip snorted. 'You mean it's all right to sacrifice Sacha's wellbeing if it suits you?'

'No, that's not what he means,' I interrupted firmly, before Kit could reply. 'We think she'll love it. Skiing, surfing, riding. It's . . . well, it's Eden.'

'*Eden.*' The deckchair groaned as Philip leaned back. 'Didn't turn out too well for poor old Adam and Eve, did it? One temptation too many, as I recall. Bit of a cock-up.'

Kit rolled his eyes.

'Lucky for you she's got no father,' persisted Philip. 'Might jam a spanner in the works. He might even want what's *best* for his daughter.'

That was below the belt, and everyone knew it. There was a moment of charged silence. Louisa froze in the act of lighting another cigarette, her gaze swivelling towards Kit, but he was unruffled.

'She *has* got a father,' he responded affably. 'Me.'

'Where is she, anyway?' Philip looked around. 'Where's my favourite niece? She's the only one of you with two brain cells to rub together. Sacha! You coming out?'

Answering voices floated from the house. There was a moment's cessation of hostilities while we waited. Lou lived underneath the flight path to Heathrow and all day long jets floated majestically overhead, trailing white chalk scribbles on powder blue.

Fast, light footsteps. Lou's six-year-old, Lily, whirled out and showed us her sparkly fingernails before charging into the pool. Sacha followed her out of the house, wearing jeans and a t-shirt with a slogan scrawled across the bust: *ALL THIS, AND BRAINS, TOO!* She was curvy, maybe even carrying an extra pound or two, and it suited her just as it did Lou. Nor did she see the point in pretending she was a modern, androgynous beauty. Around her head dangled several braids, beaded in fluorescent pink. Theo clung to her hip like a baby baboon.

Instantly the garden was brighter, the sun warmer. No really, it was. Bubbly, dazzling Sacha, my best friend. Only she was refusing to talk to me at the moment.

She focused cross-eyed on one of the braids. 'Lily did my hair.'

'Sacha.' Philip patted the empty chair beside him. 'Sit. We need a bit of sanity.'

Putting Theo down, she flopped gracefully into the seat, long legs stretched out—I envied her those legs—glowing with youth.

'That's unusual.' Lou leaned across and fingered a silver oval that hung around her niece's neck.

'My boyfriend gave it to me. It's an antique locket. There's his picture, and mine—see?'

Lou made enchanted noises. Privately, I thought it was all a bit nauseating. I mean, what modern youth gives a girl a Victorian locket with their photos? What's wrong with an MP3 player, or maybe a pair of funky bed socks?

'I know what you've been talking about.' Sacha shot me a glance of disgust. 'Mum and Kit's epic pioneering scheme. All aboard the *Mayflower*!'

Lou tutted in mutinous sympathy. 'There's a big orange FOR SALE sign by the front gate,' Sacha continued. 'And *what's* for sale? My home!'

'Already on the market?'

'Oh, yes. If we so much as put a mug down, Mum grabs it and starts fussing about with a tea towel. Crowds have been streaming through all week, led by a geek called Dave from Theakston's Realty. Poking about in *my* bedroom, raving on about how much they love my mermaids. Loud-mouthed kids climbing the twins' apple trees. We should start doing Devonshire teas.'

Lou laid a hand on Sacha's knee. 'We don't want you to go, darling.'

'Yeah, well. Mine not to reason why.'

'I don't believe all this, you know,' said Lou, scowling as she looked from Kit to me. 'This press release about the mortgage and lifestyle, and Kit's career. It's all shit.'

Her outburst was oddly shocking, because my sister never swears when there are children within earshot. *Coarse language*, Mum said once, when I was ten and she padded up the stairs and caught me cursing. *Only those with an impoverished vocabulary resort to profanity.*

'You've given us a whole stack of reasons.' Lou downed her glass. 'A mile-high pile of excuses. And not one of 'em was the real one.'

Four

Dad was working when I tapped on his open door. He handed me a mug of something he called tea, and pottered back to his patient. Today it was his old friend Flora. She ran the garden centre and kept putting out her spine.

Dad lives on the outskirts of Bedford, three streets away from the house where I was brought up. In spite of being on the wrong side of seventy, my father is still a great chiropractor. In fact, he's the only man I know who can manipulate my neck and stop a migraine in its tracks. Kit tried, once. Big mistake. Nearly wrenched my head off. I couldn't reverse the car for a week.

I waited in the kitchen, listening to the rise and fall of voices and dutifully drinking the undrinkable: one of Dad's herbal brews. It tasted like an infusion of silage. Bernard, the rusty black cat, sat neatly on a rag rug by the stove like a small, curved vase.

My dad's eccentric, I'll admit. The kitchen walls were painted in blurred gradations of gentle colour, and bunches of herbs hung from the ceiling. There were crystals and an oil burner lined up along the dresser. And all this new-age mumbo jumbo worked, that's the beautiful thing. It did the trick. Dad's kitchen always felt serene. Wacky, but serene. I loved it in there.

He's into the Steiner thing; didn't discover it until middle age. Now he's quite a big cheese in the movement. I never argue with him about it. Mum did though, and eventually—once Lou and I were grown up and off her hands—she left him for Vincent Vale, a widower who owned an upmarket country pub. Vincent, she said, was reassuringly dull. He made her happy for the last ten years of her life, so perhaps she was right to go.

Once Flora had limped out, Dad stood by the stove, stretching the kinks in his own spine. He doesn't look like a witch doctor; he's more of a fox terrier—wiry and tough, with curly grey hair and eyes that miss nothing. 'And what brings you here on a Monday?' he asked.

I told him. He didn't respond at all, at first. Didn't recoil in horror or fire off a round of reproach; just crouched down and riddled the stove, which banged and sputtered. I watched a twirl of vapour rising like a genie from his oil burner.

'Well,' he said finally. 'I see. It makes excellent sense.'

I'd never felt so grateful. Having Dad's blessing changed everything. 'You'll come and visit?' I asked.

'Hope so, if I can square my conscience with the carbon output. In the meantime, let's organise one of those terrifying video internet things. Then I'll be able to see the boys' cheeky grins, and my Sacha becoming the woman who's going to save the world.'

'Our house is on the market.'

'I know.' Dad plonked the kettle onto the stove, and crystal spheres bounced across the cast iron. 'I saw a bloomin' great orange sign.'

'You saw . . . when?'

'Um, let me see . . . Thursday last week? I dropped by. There was nobody in.' He bent to stroke Bernard's smooching little body, and the cat licked his hand. 'So I've been waiting for you to visit.'

I felt terrible. We should have fronted up days ago but initially it hadn't seemed real; more like a computer-generated cyber adventure.

'How are the children?' asked Dad, sitting down opposite me. 'Excited?'

'Sacha's not.'

'No.' He smiled gently. 'She's sixteen, never known any other life.'

'But New Zealand is a teenager's paradise! Beaches, mountains, athletic young hunks who surf and play rugby and generally live life to the max.'

'Perhaps she'd rather have Ivan.'

I harrumphed. 'Have you *met* Ivan?'

'I have, actually. She brought him here. A steady young man, I thought.'

'Steady! Yes, that's a good, limp-wristed word, Dad. I like that. It encapsulates everything about Ivan Jones.'

Dad tapped the table. 'You should be grateful for *steady*, Martha. You're much too quick to dismiss people. It isn't wise. Be careful what you wish for.'

I forced back another mouthful of his brew, making a face. 'This is vile.'

'Dandelion root. Marvellous for your liver.'

'Yeuch. Look, Ivan is a nice lad. I bear him no ill will. If he was my babysitter I'd break out the chocolate Hobnobs. But he has all the charisma of a supermarket trolley and he does *not* figure in Sacha's future.'

Dad just chuckled.

'I caught her smoking the other day,' I said. 'She came back from Lydia's house smelling like a hobo. I found some cigarettes in her pocket.'

'You searched her pockets?'

'Kit thinks I should turn a blind eye. He says Sacha has never rebelled before and a little bit of acting out is a good thing—we don't want her to be a prig.'

'Smart lad! I'd add my sixpence to that and ask you, Mrs Goody-Two-Shoes McNamara, to explain what you were doing in my potting shed at the age of fourteen.'

'I don't know what you're talking about.'

'Martha, you used to sit in my deckchair and puff away like a dark satanic mill. I know for a fact you took a cup of cocoa so you could drop your fag in it if anyone came along.'

'Says who?'

'I took a swig one time. Not a mistake I'd make twice.'

I grimaced. 'Okay, fair cop. Did Mum know?'

'Don't be silly. Why would I tell *her*? When did you give up?'

'Pretty quickly. Couldn't afford it.'

'There you are, you see? If I'd burst in like the drug squad, it wouldn't have made a scrap of difference. You had your waltz with nicotine and moved on—unlike Louisa, admittedly. Sacha will do the same if you leave her be. Probably has already.'

I sighed. 'God help her if she turns out like me. What a blueprint.'

We fell into companionable silence. A blackbird warbled, out in the rain. It was a wonderfully English sound. Bernard's tail flicked.

At length, Dad stirred. 'Had any interest in the house?'

'Some.'

'Offers?'

'Nope. Sacha must be telling everyone the place is haunted.'

'Martha.' He regarded me carefully. 'D'you want this?'

'Kit—'

'I didn't ask what Kit wants.'

'I'm terrified,' I confessed, sagging. 'I've worked in the same unit for ten years. I'm team manager, I've got my friends and my little power base. I know everyone around here and they know me: the lady in the post office and the GP and the man at the fuel station who's only got one arm. In a crisis there are twenty people I could call on. I'm so *comfortable* here.'

He listened without comment, head tilted, grey eyes fixed on mine.

'On the other hand, that's just the point,' I said. 'We've had it good. Too good. I hate smug people who can't see that their world is very small. I think we all need a shake-up.'

'Right.' He nodded. 'Right. But Martha, don't go if it's only because you're running from something.'

'What would I be running from?'

'Everyone has their demons.'

'Not me.'

'You can't run away. They follow.' Dad's got X-ray vision, I reckon. He sees everything. 'Incidentally, Sacha's been asking me about her father. I gather she collared your Aunt Patricia, too.'

I felt my face redden. 'There are no monsters under my bed, Dad.'

'Good. Go for positive reasons, or else stay put. That's all I'll say on the matter.'

Bernard began to wind around our ankles. His purr was filled with creaky miaows, silkily insistent. I was wondering who else Sacha had hassled.

'I'm going to miss you lot.' Dad reached down to scratch his friend in that soft place all cats have, just behind their ears. 'Hell, yes. It's going to be quiet around here. My Sacha, and those boys . . . can't imagine not hearing the racket as they run up to the front door. They always tussle over who's going to ring the bell.'

'But neither of them can reach it.'

Dad smiled, sadly. His face was like a ploughed field.

'The housing market's dead,' I said, lifting Bernard onto my knee. 'You never know, this move may never actually—' I hadn't even finished the sentence when my phone sang from the depths of my handbag. Bernard pounced on the sound, tail high as a flag.

I dug out the phone. Flicked it open, and gaped at the message.

'Our poor house,' I said.

It wasn't anything special, really; but it was picturesque, and it had been home since Sacha was a seven-year-old chatterbox with corkscrew curls. She never stopped smiling in those days, and Kit used to say she never would. We got married from that house; I remembered Dad handing me into the wedding car. We planted two apple trees when the twins came along. Their first wobbly steps were in the kitchen, chasing after Muffin. Every clang of the plumbing, creak of the stairs or rattle of the front door was profoundly familiar. When the wind blew, it made exactly *that* kind of droning sound through the Expelair in the bathroom. In the mornings the dust beams whirled in front of *those* windows in the hall. The dimensions, acoustics and smells were ingrained in our subconscious. It was our friend. We were traitors.

'The estate agent,' I said, reaching tremulously for my silage tea.

'An offer?' Dad was craning his head to see.

Hi. Gd news. The Simpsons have made an offer at asking price. Pls phone or call in at your earliest convenience. Dave

'Whatcha going to do?' asked Dad.

I didn't know. My brain was making a run for it.

'Do you go forwards?' Dad leaned back, eyeing me. 'Or do you hightail it home to your warm, dry burrow?'

I shut the phone, swinging it like a pendulum between my fingers. 'The point of no return,' I said.

*

English rain. A pink Beetle was parked beside the FOR SALE sign, and I felt a twinge of irritation. I'd worked all day, broken the news to Dad, collected the twins from nursery and been elbowed twice in Tesco. I'd also sold my beloved home. I didn't feel kindly disposed towards gnomes.

While I lifted out shopping bags, Finn sat Buccaneer Bob in a booster seat, singing as he clicked the seatbelt around his old friend. Bob was a gift from Kit's Great-Aunt Sibella, whose portrait hung in our hallway. He's a rag-doll pirate dressed in black, with a rakish eye patch and a red parrot on his shoulder. They've been friends since the day Finn was born. The family live in fear of losing the wretched thing. On one cataclysmic occasion, Finn left Bob in the Reading motorway service station. He was inconsolable. Breaking into a cold sweat, I drove straight back—a four-hour return run—and prostrated myself tearfully before the extravagantly pierced youth in Burger King. Pierced Youth regarded me unemotionally, chewing the cud like a cow in the queue to be milked. Then he reached behind the counter and produced Bob. I could have kissed the boy. Actually—if I'm going to be honest—I *did* kiss him. He was mortified. I saw him using antibacterial handwash on his face as I skipped away.

Now, his pirate safely buckled in, Finn snapped into his customary high-velocity state and sprang out of the car, leaping two-footed into a vast puddle.

'Brilliant,' I grumbled, as sludge splashed over both of us.

He grinned unrepentantly and stamped in the water, uttering bloodcurdling battle cries. Keen-eyed and lawless, the child was a miniature version of his father. I recognised Kit's intensity in the fine-boned face, Kit's laughter and passion. Sometimes the look in Finn's blue eyes was a little too knowing.

Charlie was both kinder and more cautious. He did his best to copy Finn's giant leap for mankind but lacked his brother's agility. Predictably, he slipped and sat down—legs stuck out, jeans and red wellingtons submerged. Even his fair curls were sodden by the swell of muddied water that sloshed over his jersey. He sat looking up at me, bug-eyed, waiting to see whether I would go into orbit.

Shaking my head, I gave him the thumbs-up. Then I scanned the garden for Ivan. There he was, perched with half a buttock on the swing, rocking himself on gawky legs.

'Ivan!' I forced a grin that actually hurt my facial muscles. 'How nice. But Sacha isn't here, I'm afraid. Just me and two feral boys.'

He cleared his throat. 'Can I have a word, Mrs McNamara?'

I ground my teeth. First, I had asked him fifty million times to call me Martha. Second, *Can I have a word?* I mean, for God's sake. Only policemen in really bad television dramas say that.

'Come on in!' I threw open the front door.

Finn and Charlie were happily engrossed in their water world, squatting down and commentating animatedly. Ivan tottered awkwardly behind me, fingering his little beard. I threw a despairing glance up at Great-Aunt Sibella as I passed her in the hall. She was never one to suffer fools.

'Tea?' I switched on the kettle with an irritated jerk before opening the back door for Muffin, who was gazing through the glass, her nose button-black beneath the shaggy fringe.

Ivan seemed completely tongue-tied. Perhaps, I thought, he'd come to murder me and feed me down the waste disposal unit. Now that *would* show hidden depths.

'Milk?' I persisted. 'Biscuit?' He managed to nod. Then he started piggling at his fingernails. 'Sit down, Ivan,' I barked, pointing at a chair. He sat. Poor boy, it takes a lot of misery to puff your eyelids like that.

'Mrs McNamara,' he said. 'Um . . .'

'C'mon. What's on your mind?'

He was clearly summoning his courage. 'Sacha says you're fantastic at your job. Your clients dote on you. All your colleagues come to you with their problems.'

I raised my eyebrows. I had never heard Ivan string more than two sentences together. He rubbed the reddened eyes. 'She feels as though the only person you're *not* listening to at the moment is her.'

'Well, she's quite wrong.'

'I thought she was joking when she first told me you're emigrating. I actually laughed until I saw she was crying. I didn't believe for one minute you'd do that to her.'

'Ivan. When you're older . . .' My voice petered out. I was being patronising, I realised, in self-defence. I needed to stop that.

'I know Mr McNamara lost his business. I know that's shit. It's totally shit to be still young and feel like you're a waste of space. My dad was laid off.' Ivan fiddled with his mug. 'He was in pieces, too. He works at the petrol station now.'

'I didn't realise.'

'Not the guy with one arm. Dad does nights.'

Thinking hard, I remembered a tidy shadow in a blue shirt and tie, muffled behind reinforced glass, joking bravely about the weather.

Ivan cracked his knuckles. I sensed he was getting ready for the big push. '*Emigrating?*' He shook his head. 'It's too much. Sacha will be paying for the rest of the family's happiness, and it'll cost her an arm and a leg.'

'This must be hard for you, Ivan. I know that, and I'm sorry. But I really do believe it's the best thing for Sacha.'

'She's paying,' he repeated doggedly. 'She'll lose her friends. Her school. Her grandpa. Her cousins.' He took a mouthful of tea and swilled it from one cheek to the other before swallowing. 'Oh, and *me* . . . but that's not very important because we wouldn't be together for long anyway.' He meant that, I think. He said it simply, artlessly. It was a statement of fact. 'I've never known anyone like Sacha, but she's going places I can't follow. And I *don't* mean New Zealand.'

The twins began giggling outside. I got up and stood at the window. They were plotting something, their heads close together. 'We've had an offer on the house,' I said.

'Shit.' Ivan drummed long, ragged fingers on the table.

Finn and Charlie suddenly tugged down their jeans, glee in every furtive movement. The next moment they were merrily peeing into a puddle.

'Those little blighters will never be lonely,' said Ivan from behind me. 'Wherever they go, they'll always have a ready-made Best Mate, piddling into their puddle.'

'That's true; but Sacha will make friends wherever she goes.'

Finn turned, trying to direct his stream down Charlie's wellingtons. Fortunately his aim wasn't very good. I rapped smartly on the window and they both waved, so overcome with mirth that they had to hold one another up.

'She thinks the world of you,' said Ivan. 'She says you used to be like sisters.'

'We still are, really.'

'Well, then. I'm begging you to think again. Refuse the offer, get that sign down and find Mr McNamara a job. They're a waiter short at the Beefeater.'

Kit, waiting at the Beefeater. That *would* be the mighty, fallen. I had a horrible vision of him with his hair standing on end, thunder rumbling on his brow, deliberately pouring beer into people's laps. I pulled my face straight as I turned around. 'What did your father do, before he lost his job?'

'Nuclear physicist.'

'W-wow,' I stammered, wondering how I hadn't known this. 'That's, um . . .'

'Unexpected?' Ivan pushed back his chair. 'Nah, pulling your leg. He drove the mobile library. Might not sound very exciting, but he loved it. The council closed it down. Not cost effective, they said. But . . . thing is, that library wasn't just a bus filled with books. It was the highlight of the week for some people.'

I saw my young visitor out. He stopped by the front door, watching the twins, who were on their hands and knees as they tried to lap water out of the pond.

'Mrs McNamara—Martha. Can I offer you a deal? Change your mind, and I promise I'll piss off and never have anything to do with Sacha again.'

Touched, I squeezed him on the arm.

'I mean it,' he insisted.

'I believe you, Ivan.'

'The rest of you will be okay. I can see that.' He cocked his head at the boys. 'It's an adventure for those little nutters. For you, it's . . . I dunno, an escape? For Mr McNamara it's a dream. But what about Sacha?'

'I think it's a wonderful opportunity for her,' I maintained stubbornly.

He walked to his car and wrenched at the door. 'I've had my say. I just wish you'd think again.'

The pink Beetle was pulling out onto the road when Mum stuck her oar in.

For Sacha, it's a disaster.

Five

It all happened so fast, once we sold the house. There wasn't time to take a breath.

Logistics and practicalities devoured our energy: packing, organising, discarding. Clothes to Oxfam, toys to Lou. Selling cars, renewing passports, applying for visas. Everything we did became charged with an awful significance because it was the Last Time. That Last Time Waltz was ghastly. I never want to do it again. The word goodbye became meaningless. Yes, we'll keep in touch! Yes, lots of sheep in New Zealand. Yes, ha-ha, if you went any further you'd be clean off the planet. Mm, hilarious. In the end we stopped wanting to see people, especially the ones we most loved. We longed to be teleported away. Scotty, beam us up.

They threw a party for me at work, with all the flags and bunting. Flattering speeches, a natty little video camera and a truly mammoth card signed by everybody, including people I never remembered having met and at least one who heartily disliked me. Kisses, hugs, pretending to wonder how they'd manage. I was touched and nostalgic, but the truth is I'd already left them. My mind was focused on the future.

Some people thought we were making a mistake and felt constrained to say so. Many seemed to interpret our leaving as a personal insult—what, did we think we were better than them? Three, with ghoulish satisfaction, predicted that we would be back within the year.

The one-armed man at the fuel station sucked on the matchstick he always held between his teeth. 'Tedious spot though, isn't it?'

'Oh, I don't think so.'

'Dull as ditch water. Like Switzerland.'

'Is it really? I didn't know that.'

He nodded gloomily. 'Nothing but mountains and smug folk in hiking boots.'

'Do you know New Zealand well, then? Or Switzerland?'

'Tears before bedtime,' he predicted, in his Eeyore drone. 'Never a good idea. Not in my opinion. Gambling with your family's lives, really, aren't you?'

'Got to go,' I said, hastily snatching back my credit card. 'I'm collecting my daughter from school.'

The final bell had gone, and girls were pouring out to begin their summer holidays. Abandoning the twins in the car, I raced up to the fifth-form common room to find a Greek tragedy being re-enacted. Mascara streamed down stricken faces. Ties were loosened, hair crazed in distracted grief. They were all signing Sacha's school shirt with indelible marker pens while munching on the giant cupcake she'd made for them.

Their lavishly coiffured class tutor, Belinda Rothman, caught my eye and wiggled her fingers. I went to this same school with Belinda. She used to be a total bitch, actually, but that's another story. I don't know what possessed the board when they made her deputy head. She minced over on ridiculous kitten heels.

'Mass hysteria,' she sighed. 'I've had to stop one of them mutilating her arms with a compass.'

'You're joking . . . aren't you?'

'Tanya's a bit of a drama queen. But we're *all* devastated to be losing Sacha.'

'Sorry.'

'You're public enemy number one in the staffroom.'

I murmured something lame, and the silly woman patted my arm. 'I do hope this move won't disadvantage her academically. She wants to do medicine, doesn't she? And what about her flute lessons? Ooh!'—holding up a finger—'I've got something for you to read!' She skipped over to her French shopping basket, looking smug. Actually, Belinda Rothman's been looking smug for twenty-five years, ever since she stole my part in the school play.

'As it's been an emotional day, I asked all the girls to express their feelings in a poem, essay or poster. Here's Sacha's. She doesn't mind you seeing it.' Belinda was holding out a piece of A4 refill, blackened with angry scrawl. 'You've got a bumpy ride ahead of you!'

Sacha emerged from the wailing chorus with her best friend draped around her shoulders. Dopey little Lydia was off to Tenerife the following day, so this truly was goodbye.

'I'll phone,' Lydia promised. She had chestnut boy-hair and never looked more than half awake. I'd known her all her life; her mother and I were in the maternity unit together. She'd eaten at my kitchen table a thousand times over the years, and swapped awful knock-knock jokes, and was rude about my cooking. 'I'll be on Facebook every single night.'

Sacha burst into tears. 'Night's morning over there,' she sobbed. 'It's all upside down.'

'Get her out,' hissed Belinda from the corner of her mouth. 'Before they become blood sisters. They've still got their compasses.'

Getting out of the building—past teachers, girls and the janitor—took twenty heartbreaking, horrible minutes. We needed a couple of those hunky bodyguards in black suits and mirrored shades. The car was a blessed sight.

Charlie and Finn hadn't throttled one another, thank God, and no passing do-gooder had called the NSPCC to report neglected children. They were listening to a Mr Men story tape.

'Hey, Sacha. Whadya call a Smartie in a combine harvester?' asked Finn as we got in.

'Shredded sweet!' crowed Charlie, and both boys fell about.

'Listen to your story,' I warned them, 'or I'll put on Radio 4.'

Sacha and I travelled in a loaded silence as it began to rain. I didn't ask how she felt; didn't try to jolly her up. I was tired of her anger. I was tired of feeling guilty. I was tired, full stop. And all the while my mind was scurrying in exhausted circles, fizzing dyspeptically with lists—things to do, things to remember, things I'd just remembered I'd forgotten to do.

Oh, bugger. Muffin. She was going to Dad's until we were settled, but there was a mile of red tape before she could join us in New Zealand. Must get her to the vet's for a microchip. Oh my *God*, I hadn't phoned the lawyer back about that wretched easement. Maybe Kit had done it? No, I'd said *I'd* do it because Kit had flown across to Ireland.

Oh bugger bugger *bugger*—the goldfish! Perhaps the nursery school would like them? The tank was so encrusted with slime that I hadn't actually seen a fish in weeks. From time to time a flicker of piscine movement would stir, like Jaws, in the green gloom. I'd have to clean it.

'If anyone cares, that was the worst day of my life,' announced Sacha.

I braked for a lollipop lady, my mind on the fish. And the dog. Oh God, and the easement. 'I'm sorry to hear that, doll.' *Bloody hell, what if the sale falls through?* 'You're feeling sad about leaving your friends.'

'Do me a favour,' snarled Sacha. 'Listen to yourself.'

'Sorry?' I drummed my fingers on the wheel, wondering if I should just drop in at the solicitor on the way past.

'Turn off the professional busybody language, Mum.'

My mobile rang as we were pulling away again. With one eye on the road, I checked the number.

'It's the removal people,' I moaned. 'Oh God, what's gone wrong now?'

Sacha's hand whipped out. She snatched the phone out of my fingers and held it to her ear. 'Yes? . . . Oh, hello. Yes, speaking.' She sounded calm, mature and utterly charming. 'Yes. No. Actually, you can cancel the whole thing because we're not going after all. Yes, I'm afraid you *did* hear right. Cancelled. Sorry for the short notice, but it can't be helped. Change of plan. Thank you. Goodbye.' She switched off the phone and tossed it over her shoulder.

'Ouch!' yelped Finn. 'That bloody phone bashed me in the ear.'

'Sacha Basher, Sacha Basher!' sang Charlie.

I pulled into a bus stop. We sat side by side, staring at the windscreen wipers.

Swipe, swipe.

'Pick it up,' I hissed. '*Now.*'

Sacha began to fiddle with her own phone, texting.

'That wasn't a request,' I said. 'It was an order. Just phone them back, Sacha. Tell them you were joking.'

'But I wasn't joking. You're acting in breach of my fundamental human rights. I've asked a lawyer. We're going to apply for an injunction.'

She pressed *send* as a snorting bus loomed in my rear window. Harassed, I pulled into the road only to be hooted at by a harridan in an Audi. The whole world hates me, I thought. The world, including my own daughter.

'The lawyer is *also* going to find my father,' said Sacha. 'She says I have a right to a genetic and cultural heritage.'

'For God's sake!' I slapped a hand to my brow. 'How many more times?'

'Yeah, yeah, yeah. You shagged a bloke after a party, and you didn't even ask his surname?'

'Yes, actually! I didn't ask for a name or address or phone number because I thought there was time for that. Your father was the love of my life for about five hours, until he staggered off to the shower and never came back. I'm sure he was a decent boy, and I've forgiven him. He left me the most precious gift in the world.'

'Did he also leave a glass slipper?'

I screeched in frustration, but she wasn't moved.

'Some married man, I'll bet. MP? Doctor? Vicar? You've stolen *my* identity to protect *his*.'

'Have you really seen a lawyer?' I asked, but she'd begun typing another text. These were her friends, these people who flashed upon her screen with their indolent spelling and acronyms.

'Have you seen who?' chirped Finn, from the back. 'Who, Sacha? Who, who, who?'

'Look at that sporty car with no woof,' cried Charlie. 'They're getting wet!'

Sacha twisted in her seat. 'One day, you two little loonies will have a sporty car with no woof. You'll share it. The boy with the hottest chick gets to use the wheels.'

'We'll take you for rides,' Finn promised kindly, while his brother made a variety of sporty car noises.

Sacha hadn't been to a lawyer. I knew she was winding me up, once I'd thought about it calmly. I turned in at our gate, thinking uneasy thoughts about Sacha's father. I wished he knew he had such a daughter. I wished she knew she had such a father. They both had much to gain, and much to lose.

I really didn't want to read the bit of paper that Rothman tart had given me.

In the good old days at primary school, Sacha's class used to waste their Monday mornings, week after week, writing *What I Did at the Weekend.* It's an inane exercise. When I am dictator, it will be banned in all schools.

But I still kept those little exercise books. Sometimes, when clearing out the attic or packing to emigrate, I flicked through them. They recalled those halcyon days through a soft-focus lens. It was like living in a chocolate box.

At the weekend my Mum and me went to a caffay. I had hot choclat with white and pink mashmalos. We sat at a tabel by the fire. It raned outside but we were cosy. It was luvly.

At the weekend my Mum took me rideing. My pony was calld Wendy. Mum showed me how to feed Wendy appels. She sed Wendy likes me.

At the weekend I got stung by a be. My Mum cuddled me and put speshal creem on from her hambag. It made me beta.

At the weekend my Mum got marryd. I was the brides made. I had a yelow silk dress, white shoes and gorjus flowers in my hair. Mum lookd like Cinderella at the ball and everywon wanted to kiss her. She said she still loves me most in the wurld. I said I love her more.

Compare and contrast:

You know what? My mother has no humility. She thinks she's perfect. People don't realise this simple fact about her.

When you're small, your mother's a goddess. But when you grow up you realise she's anything but. My friends reckon she is cool. Some of the guys even think she's hot, which is just plain sick. People think she's so HUMAN. She laughs about her legs and her double chin. Well, she's safe to go on about those things, isn't she? Because there's nothing wrong with her legs, or her chin. Nothing at all. What she doesn't giggle about are things that really are MORTAL SINS. Like sacrificing your daughter to the great god Emigration!!

She is ruining my life. Everyone says this about their parents, but in my case it is actually true. My mother IS ruining my life. My feelings don't seem to come into it any more. She's selling my happiness to buy a dream. I'm just a commodity.

She's always trying to hint that I'm jealous of Kit and the boys. But this isn't one of those wicked step-parent things. Yes, Kit's got his faults and he can be scary when he's drinking. But we get on brilliantly. It's great the way he says things that are really funny, really crack me up, but he doesn't laugh. And he stands up to Mum when she's being ridiculous. He doesn't let her perform. It was terrible when the agency went bust. It hit him really hard. It must have felt as though he was no use to anyone. He looked bent over, as though he'd been kicked in the guts. I never said this to anyone, but I was afraid I'd come home from school and find him swinging from the banisters.

And how could I be jealous of the twins? They're my little brothers! I'd kill anyone who hurt them. I truly would. I wish I was four years old too. You've no worries at that age. They think they can pop back for tea with Grandpa every Sunday, like they do now.

So NO, this isn't about Kit and the twins taking Mum away from me. This is about Mum putting them first, which is a completely different thing.

This is about me losing everything.

I'll be leaving Ivan, and he makes me feel safe. He's kind and gentle and he truly cares about me.

I will never, ever again have friends that I have known since we were tiny little kids.

I will never again have friends who laugh at the same things as me.

I will never have friends that I can truly trust.

All the things I know are being torn out of my hands. I'm trying to hold on but I'm losing everything. It feels as though there's an earthquake in my life.

I am so scared.

*

I walked into Sacha's room uninvited. She was making an album of photographs, hampered by tears and a running nose. Pictures of friends and family lay scattered on the desk. Muffin sprawled across her mistress's feet.

I sat down on the bed. 'Need any help?'

'No thanks.'

'I read your essay.'

'Huh.'

'This feels like the end of the world, doesn't it? But it's not.'

'Yes, it is.'

'Hey, maybe you could have your own horse. You've always wanted a horse! It's going to be an adventure.'

'I don't need an adventure.'

'We'll all be together, that's the main thing. The five of us. Actually, six—even Muffin's coming.' At the sound of her name, the soppy animal sighed blissfully.

Sacha was trying to cut out a photo of Ivan but seemed unusually clumsy. Mermaids frolicked all around us in the calm water of Kit's sea. When Sacha was small I often found her lying half-asleep, gazing at the scene as though her bed was adrift on the silvery blue. When she got older, Kit offered to paint it out and give her something more adult, but she refused point-blank.

'Ivan loves me,' she said now. 'He's special. How can you do this?'

'Listen,' I urged. 'Your friends will always be your friends. It's easy to stay in touch nowadays on the internet. And it needn't be forever—you could even come back to university here.'

'Oh yes, great!' Sacha dropped the scissors with a clatter. 'You'll make me choose between my family and my country. That's the thing, you see? You're splitting me in half.'

I sagged. 'Yes. Yes, I see that.'

'Grandpa,' she cried, dissolving. 'How will we ever manage without Grandpa?'

'He'll come and visit. Look,' I added in desperation, 'please will you just give it a couple of years? If it isn't working, I promise we'll come home.'

'We won't have our home! *This* is my home.'

'Doll, please. I'm actually begging you. The thing is . . .'

'Yeah. I know, I know. We've got money troubles, gotta sell the house and live in a cardboard box. You want a better life for us children, and Kit needs to indulge his midlife crisis.'

I looked down at my hands. I didn't want her to despise Kit, but surely she had a right to know more. 'Remember that last trip to London? Well . . . I had to fetch him from the police station that night.'

'*What?*'

'He was in a cell. He was . . . well, they'd scraped him off the High Street. They said they'd charge him next time. It was awful. I've been really worried about him, Sacha. I know you have too. You said as much in that essay.'

She chewed her lip, thinking about it.

'We've made a deal,' I said. 'He is not to binge ever again. We're going to give it two years—he feels that's a fair crack of the whip, and without a mortgage we can scrape by on my income. Then, if the painting isn't going anywhere, or if we hate it out there, we'll think again.'

'So you slave away while he's a kept man? Marvellous.'

'That's really unfair. This house was bought with Kit's money, much of it made before I ever met him. For the past nine years we've been bank-rolled by his income. He's been a father to you in every way, school fees and all, never quibbled. Maybe it's my turn to be the main breadwinner. Marriage is a partnership: you take, and you give.'

She was silent, blinking tearfully up at her mermaids.

'I've had enough,' I whispered. 'I want my man back. You and I both know he's worth this risk. A filthy old lag in a police cell, laughed at by a bunch of coppers—that isn't our Kit, is it? *Our* Kit's beautiful. He's got an artistic temperament, okay, but he's brilliant and kind and fun. He's . . . well, he's Kit. I love him, and I want him back.'

'Me, too.' She dropped her forehead onto the desk. 'Okay. I'll come quietly, but I hope you know what you're doing, because I've never been so scared in my whole life.'

I hope you know what you're doing, too, needled Mum. *But I doubt it.*

I was on my way out of the room when Sacha held up the photo album. 'This is just about finished.'

'Well done.'

'I've left a blank page at the end. I'm saving that for photos of someone, but I've still got to take them. Someone special.'

Caught off-guard, I waltzed straight into the trap. 'A special someone! Who's that, then?'

'My dad. My actual, factual, biological father. Because sooner or later I'm going to find out who he is.'

Mum laughed. Bitch.

Late in July we said a sad farewell to our home, closed the front door for the last time, and went to stay at Dad's.

Muffin came too. We spent those last few days stroking the old dog's gentle face and wondering if we'd ever see her again. Muffin had been a fixture since Sacha was four, when I stopped our car for a quivering fluff ball abandoned beside the A5. One floppy ear was dark grey, the other white. The little creature immediately clambered onto the back seat, whining and licking bleeding paws. Girl and dog grew up together.

On our final morning our friend was anxious, troubled, shambling round and round Dad's kitchen table. She leaned her head against each of our knees in turn, graphite tail miserably sweeping the floor.

'Don't worry, Muffin. You're coming soon,' said Charlie, kneeling with his arms around her neck. The other children joined him, showering her with kisses. Kit and I exchanged glances. Muffin was twelve years old and shaggy as a polar bear; her eyesight was dodgy, her joints arthritic. Secretly, we thought it might be best if she ended her days peacefully with Dad.

Suddenly, time ran out. Kit looked at his watch, then at me. I stared around the kitchen, my chest constricting, longing to stay for just one more hour, one more cup of tea. Dad had given us lots of homeopathic pills for jetlag and a home-brewed recipe for stress, but he couldn't give us a homeopathic version of himself, which was what we really needed.

'C'mon, guys!' Finn shouldered his miniature backpack and tugged at the front door, flinging it wide. 'We're goin' to New Zealand!'

Sacha settled Muffin in her bed by the stove, and Bernard curled beside her. Then Dad drove us to Heathrow in a borrowed van. Lou and the family weren't coming to see us off. Too sad, she'd said. They were going to wait in their garden and wave at every plane that flew overhead.

I remember those final moments so vividly; that last, worst goodbye. The boys were wired, rocketing around the terminal as though they'd drunk a gallon of Coke each. They were intrepid explorers, and each carried his most precious treasure for the voyage. Buccaneer Bob travelled in Finn's pack, his knitted head sticking out so that he could see everything. Charlie had stuffed Blue Blanket up his jumper. This priceless rag used to be satin-edged and luxurious, but by now it was quite disgusting because I never dared to wash it. What if it shrunk? Throughout his toddlerhood Charlie dragged it along like Linus in *Peanuts*; towed it through muddy farmyards and chewing-gummy streets. When tired or bewildered, he held it against his cheek. In contemplative moments he would pull off pieces of blue fluff and stick them up his nose.

Dad and the twins played paper-scissors-rock in the check-in queue until Finn fell over the luggage and screamed like someone who's been bitten by a rattlesnake. Deflated, Charlie sat down and sucked his thumb. He looked forlorn, a curly-headed evacuee child. Kit knelt on the floor to comfort his boys while I tried not to meet the sidelong glares of other passengers. I could tell what they were thinking, and I didn't blame them: *Please don't be on my plane, family from hell.*

Sacha had plugged herself wordlessly into her iPod, unbrushed hair jammed into a messy knot. She was wearing a red t-shirt Lydia had given her, and the slogan said it all: *EMIGRATION SUX.* Her flute was in her carry-on bag; we hadn't dared trust it to the shipping container. She was texting all her friends and crying quietly.

'How much does a jumbo jet weigh?' asked Finn, pulling at Kit's ear.

'Dunno. A million tons?'

'Well anyway,' Charlie took his thumb out of his mouth, 'it'd really hurt if you dropped it on your toe.' The thumb went back in.

There was a heaving, chaotic queue for security. It was like dying a slow death, waiting with Dad, shuffling our bags forward a few inches at a time. In the end I suggested he should get going.

'I'll go back to Muffin,' he agreed reluctantly. 'It'll be easier for you once I've left. You'll be able to concentrate on shoving your toothpaste into little see-through bags.'

So that was that. Suddenly, it was time to say goodbye. Dad pulled a box out of his pocket. 'For you,' he said, handing it to me. 'It was your grandmother's.'

'Grandma Norris?'

He dipped his head. 'It still works, and I've had it serviced and cleaned.'

I opened the box to find a delicate gold watch. It was painfully familiar. I'd seen it on Grandma's wrist thousands of times: an exquisite thing, with all the craftsmanship and elegance I'd expect of my grandmother.

'Dad,' I whispered, blinking.

'Don't imprison it in a box,' he said, lifting it out of the velvet case and wrapping the gold band around my wrist. 'Wear it. Better to wear such a lovely thing and lose it than keep it hidden away.'

Lost for words, I hugged him frantically as though it was for the last time. Kit did much the same. Then Dad turned to Sacha, arms held wide. 'This is a great adventure,' he told her. 'Grasp it with both your hands, my beautiful girl. Grasp it. *Grasp* it!'

Sacha's generous mouth twisted. She threw her arms around his neck and hung on. I had to prise her away. As I watched him take his leave of the twins, their cheerful ignorance almost broke my heart. They didn't—couldn't—comprehend that they might never see their grandpa again. They behaved as though they were just off to Wales for the week, on a jolly jaunt. Dad caught hold of one under each arm and lifted them clear off the ground. Closing his eyes, he squeezed his grandsons to his chest. It made them giggle and wriggle.

Finally, he straightened. He saluted smartly, winked at me and turned his back. Swallowing hard, I watched my father walk away. I watched until he'd disappeared down the escalator.

Long after he'd gone I kept scanning the space where I'd last seen him, hoping for another glimpse. I was still watching when Finn hit Charlie over the head with a water bottle and all hell broke loose.

*

Three hours later, flight NZ001 began its ponderous run-up to the ultimate high jump. We sat stunned in a roar of sound, vibration and bereavement. Sacha's face was turned to the window. The boys were cheering. Kit reached across the high-fiving twins and fiercely laced my fingers through his.

With a final jerk we felt England fall away beneath us, and then a grind and shudder as the landing gear was lifted.

We'd left our country.

Six

The hospital night wears on. Hours pass, but there's no news of Finn. No call from Kit either, and he isn't answering his phone.

I float in a pall of dread, staring in nauseated fixation at the covers of old magazines. Every time I hear footsteps, I brace myself. Finally I'm on my feet, haunting the hospital corridors with Buccaneer Bob against my chest. The pirate doll looks sad. We are restless ghosts, he and I. We don't exist.

Finn is five years old. Just five. He fell silently in his Mr Men pyjamas. Mr Happy. Mr Tickle. Mr Bounce, who bounced too much.

Sometime during these nightmare hours, the police pay me a visit. Two broad young men, pacing sombrely down the disinfected corridor on their shiny shoes. They're too big for the place. They have thick stab-proof vests and murmuring radios, and they walk in step. Perfectly matched, like bookends. Like twins.

I see my Charlie walking alone through life with an empty space at his side; alone at the school dance, the graduation, the wedding. Not a ghost of his other half. Not even a shadow. Just an empty space. Perhaps Charlie will walk alone forever. You might as well cut off his arms.

Just routine, say the twins in uniform, pulling out reassuring nods and notebooks as they sit down. Sorry to intrude at this difficult time. Now, er, what happened, exactly?

I tell them how Finn wandered out of his room and climbed onto the rail, and then he fell. And I saw him falling, and I ran, but I couldn't save him.

One of the policemen scratches his nose, glancing covertly at his watch. But the other—actually, he's older than I thought—gazes into my face without so much as a blink. He's losing his hair. He has pale eyes. 'Did anyone else witness the accident, Mrs McNamara?'

'No, they were all asleep.'

'Your husband?'

'Kit's on his way back from Dublin.'

Martha! yells my mother, arriving unannounced and uninvited. *How can you?* But I chase her out. I chase her right out, and I slam the door on her. Mentally dusting off my hands, I look the man in the eye. 'I haven't been able to contact him.'

They offer to help. What flight is Kit on? He can be met.

'Thanks,' I say firmly, 'but he'll contact me once he's landed. He'll turn on his phone and see all the texts. I must tell him myself.'

The older one seems to think for a moment, and I stop breathing. Then he asks me who else was in the house when Finn fell.

I rub my eyes. 'My daughter, Sacha.'

'Age?'

'Sacha? Seventeen. But she was out for the count. Been off school with flu. Then there was Charlie, Finn's twin. He was fast asleep too—well, obviously, it happened at midnight.'

His pen circles above the notebook. 'Nobody else?'

He's watching my mouth now, as though lies might come sidling out with labels on. *He's onto you*, hisses Mum, with her echoing sibilance. Minimum words, maximum damage; that's always been her special skill. *He knows you weren't alone on that balcony.*

'Nobody else,' I whisper, and tears slide from the corners of my eyes. 'I was too slow.'

The policemen shut their notebooks. They have other things to be doing, I'm sure. More pressing jobs: criminals to catch, reports to type, cheeseburgers to eat. The pale-eyed one gives me a leaflet with his name scribbled on it.

Once they've disappeared around the corner, hospital noises begin to blur in my inner ear. Sleep deprivation, I suppose, and the unreality of disaster. Squeaks of trolley wheels, murmuring of voices, shoes softly thudding on lino; all muffled in white cloud.

Missed an opportunity there.

'No. Yes. No. I don't know what to do.'

You can't sweep this one under the carpet.

'You don't really exist, you know. You're just an embodiment of my conscience.'

This has gone too far, Martha!

'Mum, I'm desperate. If I make the wrong decision my family will be obliterated. How about a bit of unconditional love?'

I hear her sniff. Honestly, I swear she sniffs. All those years being dead hasn't sweetened the bitter tang of her.

'Okay,' I concede. 'Perhaps not *unconditional* love. But do you think you could manage forgiveness, after all this time?'

Finn may die, she retorts. *Who will you be forgiving then, Martha Norris?*

She has a point.

Seven

That was a long, long journey.

Twenty-four hours in a metal cylinder with Finn and Charlie, and anyone would need to lie on a psychiatrist's couch. I'm sure the four hundred or so other passengers all suffer from post-traumatic stress to this day. They probably have recurrent flashbacks of cabin-fevered fiends—one blond and cherubic, the other dark and diabolical—pelting up and down the aisle, upsetting the trolleys and howling like tortured banshees just when everyone had finally put on their eye masks and nodded off.

Mercifully, jetlag has somewhat blurred the memory. Also faded, like dreams, are the August days we spent in Auckland, struggling to stay awake during the day and sleep through the upside-down nights. We'd left our beloved English summer, hay bales in the rain, and landed slap-bang in the middle of Antipodean winter. We stocked up on warm clothes, opened bank accounts and bought a people carrier from a car shark. It all seemed fresh and hazy at the same time, like a bracing swim on a hangover. After four days as tourists in the City of Sails we headed for Hawke's Bay.

I often think our new life began in a single moment, as we crossed the Napier-Taupo hills. Kit had taken over the wheel and was having a wonderful time on the hairpin bends, slamming the gear stick across and making very childish rally-car noises. I'm surprised nobody was carsick.

We'd considered filling up with fuel as we left the lakeside town of Taupo but decided to press on. Since then we hadn't passed a single petrol station. Indeed the hills seemed uninhabited, save for isolated dwellings with paint-peeling porches and murderous-looking hounds. I expected tumbleweed. You could almost hear the strumming of the banjo. The only human beings we saw were the drivers of monstrous logging trucks whose brakes hissed like man-eating pressure cookers.

'You wouldn't want to break down out here,' remarked Kit blithely. I leaned past him to check the fuel gauge. It didn't look too healthy.

For miles the road wound through New Zealand's native bush: subtropical rainforest complete with giant ferns, creepers and cabbage trees that looked like palms. Every bend brought another sharp-intake-of-breath view of raw-boned mountains and white waterfalls. These weren't quiet English hills. They were angular and rock-strewn, like a Chinese painting; jagged peaks and drifting swathes of cloud.

'It's the jungle,' murmured Finn, clutching Buccaneer Bob to his cheek and stroking his left ear. 'Jungle bells, jungle bells, jungle all the way.'

'Are there snakes?' Charlie's voice was muffled by Blue Blanket.

'No snakes!' yelled Kit gleefully.

'Does Bagheera live here?' The twins had watched *The Jungle Book* on the plane.

'There he is!' squealed Finn, pointing into the shadows. 'Bagheera—I seed him looking at me from out of a tree.'

Soon after that, all three children were asleep. It was night-time in Bedfordshire. The boys lolled in their booster seats, soft legs dangling, baby jaws slack. Sacha was holding Finn's hand. The locket Ivan had given her—the one with both their photographs inside—was tangled around her hair. She never took it off.

Gradually, native bush gave way to forestry and farmland. As we crossed the last summit, Kit swerved onto a verge and cut the engine. In the sudden silence, he and I stepped out and stood leaning against the bonnet.

Above and around us rolled an immense pine forest, but the valley ahead opened its arms as though welcoming us to the coast. In the distance lay the Pacific, glittering in a mist of opal light, beckoning all the way to Chile. On the coast, as unexpectedly lovely as a mirage, we glimpsed a little city.

'Must be Napier,' I said, squinting at the map. 'Hastings is beyond, but I don't think we can see it from here.'

From our height, distance and state of jetlag Napier seemed a Greek village. White houses jumbled up the slope of a hill that rose straight out of the sea, like the shell of a giant turtle.

'We've made it,' said Kit. 'This is home.'

We based ourselves in a motel and tried to hit the ground running. Napier was a small city—about fifty thousand people—with a Mediterranean climate, a thriving port and Pacific beaches. That much we knew from the guidebook. What we hadn't expected was its picture-postcard beauty. Flattened by a catastrophic earthquake in 1931, it had risen phoenix-like from the ashes. The result was an art-deco town with wedding-cake buildings and a seafront boardwalk. On our first morning we had breakfast in a café by the marina. We sat out on a wooden deck in the winter sun, gazing across the clinking masts of yachts to snow-capped hills. I couldn't quite believe it was real.

An affable estate agent called Allan, who knew we'd brought sterling and sensed an obscenely large commission, devoted himself to showing us what he called 'lifestyle blocks'. Allan looked about sixty, with hair that swirled into a shining chocolate peak like a walnut whip. I think he had the wrong idea about us at first, and we hated everything he showed us. Modern monstrosities they were, on over-manicured subdivisions; not at all what we'd expected of this enterprising, militantly nuclear-free country. This was the land of the All Blacks and the *Rainbow Warrior*; this was Mordor and Rivendell. We weren't ready for electric garage doors and ludicrously phallic gateposts. Anyway, they cost too much; the exchange rate had been hopeless. We rejected them all, but Allan had the patience of Job.

'Impress your friends!' he crowed, throwing open the doors to yet another stone-grey kitchen. We trooped in, making awed noises about the view—which, incidentally, was stunning: orchards, basking in golden sunshine. Then Kit and I exchanged despairing glances.

'Not your cup of tea, is it?' Allan looked baffled. 'Homes of this calibre at this price rarely come on the market, you know. The discerning buyer—'

'Look, Allan,' said Kit, holding up his hands. 'It's still more than we can afford. And anyway, I couldn't live in a house that's designed purely to impress. This place is just a monument to somebody's ego.'

'Kit!' squeaked Sacha, rolling her eyes. 'You are so *embarrassing*.'

'We don't have any friends to impress,' I explained sheepishly. 'Not within twelve thousand miles, anyway. C'mon, Allan. Isn't there anything a bit . . . I don't know . . . older? Less, um, *tidy*?'

Kit pointed out of the window. 'Like that, over the valley—see? Bit small, that one, but you get the idea. Those old weatherboard things.'

'Ah. Yes. You're looking at the traditional New Zealand construction method,' said Allan, following Kit's gaze towards a white wooden cottage wreathed in foliage. I bet there was a rocking chair on the front porch.

'They're lovely,' I said.

'They're a pain in the backside. Millstone around your necks. You have to paint them every five years or the wood rots away. They're draughty. Dark. No indoor–outdoor flow.'

'They're still lovely,' I insisted. 'Find me one of those.'

'Sorry.' Sacha smiled up at Allan from the floor, where she was tickling Charlie's tummy. 'Sorry to waste your time. My family are idiots.'

Allan twinkled at her and rubbed his chin. 'Okay,' he mused. 'I'm thinking . . . you need at least four bedrooms, ideally more, bit of land, some kind of space for Kit's painting . . . and you'll be working north of Napier, Martha?'

'That's right. Capeview Lodge.'

'D'you mind living in the Wop-wops?'

'The *where*?'

'The Bundu,' said Allan, helpfully. 'The back of beyond.'

Finn had been watching the estate agent with goggle-eyed interest. If he stood very straight, the tip of his sticking-up hair was on a level with the man's waistband. 'Will I ever talk like him?' he asked, jabbing a thumb.

'No, silly.' Charlie leaned down from Sacha's lap, spinning a Dinky car across acres of concrete floor. 'We'll nevereverever sound like *them*. They talk in baby language.'

Sacha yelped and clapped her hand over his mouth, but Allan bent to ruffle Charlie's curls. I think he genuinely liked children. 'There's a Grand Old Lady with the acreage you're looking for. It's way up north, in tiger country. *Much* longer commute than I'd like, but you Poms are probably used to that, and it's on a school bus route. Needs, erm . . .' He faltered a little, looking for a euphemism. 'Needs a bit of TLC. Home handyman's paradise. Might suit you.'

I grabbed the car keys from Kit's pocket. 'Lead on!'

'It's quite a long way,' warned the estate agent.

He never spoke a truer word. After a lifetime of following Allan's truck down deserted country roads through banjo country I'd begun to doubt the man's sanity. Perhaps we'd pushed him over the edge; he was leading us into the wilderness and a slow death. Maybe he was going to tie us all to trees and use us for target practice. The road meandered through landscape that was a little like Scotland, and a little like a Pacific Island, and a lot like nowhere else on earth. There was pine forestry with wisps of cloud rising like steam; there were ravines, and black cattle, and glimpses of rocky coast. I was groping for the map, last seen under my seat among two weeks' worth of rotting chips and sweet wrappers, when Allan flicked an indicator and turned up a farm track.

A rusting letterbox squatted by the gate. It proclaimed, in faded paint: *6001—Patupaiarehe.* And in a different script, HAWKE'S BAY TODAY, which I knew was the local newspaper. It all sounded vaguely intrepid.

We crossed the cattle grid with a satisfying rumble. Our people carrier—suddenly puny and low-slung—tilted unhappily, jolting as we negotiated boulders in the drive. Charlie, who'd taken off his seatbelt when we turned off the road, was bounced so high that his hair actually touched the roof. Allan's rugged four-wheel drive crunched ahead, throwing up a festive swirl of dust. We ground our way uphill past grazing sheep, willows and stands of scrubby cypress trees before turning along a ridge. Then Allan swung around a hairpin bend and up an even wilder incline.

'He has to be *joking*,' I clucked, spinning the wheel with both hands. Stones and dust slid beneath our tyres. Terrifyingly far below, a river sparkled cheerily as it wandered in a lazy blue arc between limestone cliffs.

'Oh my God,' gasped Sacha. 'We're all going to die.'

I pictured our car slipping, sliding backwards down that rocky precipice. I could hear the screaming of the twins as we plunged into the cold water. Sweating now, I changed into first gear, revving the accelerator and letting out the clutch with a shaking foot.

'Christ,' breathed Kit beside me. It was a prayer rather than an oath. I'm fairly sure he crossed himself. He's never a better Catholic than in times of peril. Useful trick, that: instant faith at the touch of a button, but no nagging guilt when life is going well.

'I want a four-wheel drive,' I whimpered. 'Right *now*.'

Abruptly, the ground levelled out and looked as though butter wouldn't melt in its mouth. The drive—suddenly pretending to be regal and gracious—widened into an open space under the shade of a wise old tree before disappearing into the canopy of native bush on the far side. The house was waiting patiently, watching us from under heavy lids. I had an impression of cream weatherboard, of wide verandahs and magnolias. It reminded me, immediately and irrevocably, of Kit's Great-Aunt Sibella.

'I recognise this place!' I cried happily, craning my neck for a better look. I'd seen it from my magic carpet as I floated in the dark. Perhaps, without realising it, I'd been looking for this very house ever since we came to Hawke's Bay. Arriving was like sinking into one of those really comfortable sofas you can't get out of gracefully.

We passed a couple of sheds and pulled up next to Allan under that gnarled grandfather of a tree. It was a walnut, I later discovered, and it had seen a bit of life. Jubilant to be free, the boys leaped out and began to swing like gibbons on tyres that hung from the ancient boughs.

'Look at that,' said Kit, staring past the house and across an overgrown lawn to where the ground dropped sharply away. He reached for my hand. 'Martha, will you look at that.'

The house stood at the head of a valley which flowed down to the glimmering haze of the Pacific. One peak after another billowed away from us, sheep-grazed and bare. Inland, forest swayed and jostled to the edge of the drive.

'Patupaiarehe Station,' announced Allan.

Kit blinked. 'Who?'

Allan said it again, more slowly. 'Patu. Pay-a-ree-hee.' He stressed the *ree*. 'Probably pronouncing it wrong. That's the name of this farm. It was a massive station originally but it got cut up into smaller blocks. Some of it's in forestry now, and there's a native bush reserve. You're looking at the original homestead. It's a Maori name, obviously.'

We practised the word. It sounded mystical and melodic.

'I know there's a legend involved; blowed if I can remember the details.' Allan slapped himself on the back of the hand. 'Must do my homework next time.'

'It's so *quiet*,' whispered Sacha, shoving her hands into the back pockets of her jeans. We all listened. It was like no silence I'd heard before. There was, quite literally, not a man-made sound to be heard. None.

Then a haunting little melody drifted out of the cathedral gloom of the bush. A pipe, you'd swear it. Answering music burbled from the branches above our heads, ending in a whistle, playful and mischievous. Leaves rustled.

'Tui.' Allan began fishing in a plant pot, pulling out keys. 'There's fantails, bellbirds, kereru—that's our native wood pigeon. Morepork, which is a kind of owl. You'll get them all up here. When your dog arrives, do keep it under control; they're trying to introduce kiwis not far away.'

'Muffin's too old to chase anything,' said Sacha. 'She just sleeps.'

'Best kind of dog. This opens into the kitchen.' Allan unlocked a wood-and-glass door. 'The front of the house faces northeast down the valley. Comes with eight hectares: pasture and a block of native bush.'

'What's that in English?' asked Kit.

Allan squinted skywards, calculating. 'About twenty acres—I'll show you the boundary later. It's leased to your neighbours and they're happy to carry on the arrangement if you don't want the malarkey of running stock yourselves. There's a dam—that's a pond to you. Yards and a woolshed up here. They're pretty run-down, but the house has been reroofed in the last five years.' He smacked his hand against the doorframe. 'It's solid.'

He watched unsurprised as a hen—feral, presumably—scurried out from behind a scrubby bush and sprinted under the house. The twins shrieked and tore after it, but Allan didn't even comment. 'The original station ran all the way to the sea.'

He stood back to let us in. Charlie and Finn abandoned their chicken hunt and hurtled into the cool interior. I heard the demented clattering of feet on stairs. Sacha followed, her arms crossed tightly over her chest.

The place made me think of *Gone with the Wind*: high ceilings, wooden panelling and prehistoric plumbing. It had polished floors and a wide staircase for flouncing down in a red taffeta frock. The back door led into a kitchen with grim 1970s lino, a pantry and a laundry. Upstairs, three of the five bedrooms opened onto a balcony that ran right along the front, looking out to sea. The boughs of a spreading magnolia touched this balcony, even scraping the roof. Directly below, a deep verandah edged two sides of the house. It called for wicker chairs and potted ferns; for sundowners and a gramophone playing into the night.

'Cold,' warned Kit, resting his hand flat on the kitchen wall. 'It's just made of wood, really. No central heating.'

'No insulation either,' said Allan, who clearly thought us off our rockers. He hadn't given up hope of selling us a concrete cake tin in suburbia. 'This stuff on the wall is called scrim. It's not even plaster. You're looking at building materials from the eighteen hundreds.'

We heard the squeak of the twins' jeans as they slid down the banisters. 'We've bagged our bedroom,' declared Finn.

'Did you see those smaller trees right beside the verandah?' asked Allan. Crouching down to the boys' height, he cupped his hand and spoke in a stage whisper. 'Be covered in lemons later. Great for fights. And the best thing—don't tell Mum—is you have to pee on 'em sometimes! They love the nitrogen.'

The conspirators sniggered and sneaked outside to fertilise the lemon trees. I followed Allan across the hall and into a large sitting room. Sacha was standing in a bay window, one knee resting on the red velvet cushions of a window seat. The room was dominated by a heady cacophony of scents: a century of wood polish, wet grass and a strong, exquisite fragrance that turned out to be daphne bushes in flower.

'The parlour,' said Allan. 'In the early days they would have kept this for best.'

Sacha looked thoughtfully across a bedraggled orchard, piling her hair up on her head. 'Horses,' she said. 'There, see?'

Following her pointed finger, I spotted five horses way up on the northern side of the valley, grazing peacefully beside a stand of Lombardy poplar.

'Why all the imported trees?' I asked Allan. 'Walnut, beech, poplar.'

'Those early settlers were homesick. They brought as much of the Old Country with them as they could. Mind you, most of it should have been left at home. Gorse and blackberry—to say nothing of rats, cats, dogs, ferrets, rabbits . . . Tragic, really.' I reckon Allan was a bit of an eco-warrior under his Jimmy Neutron hairdo. He jabbed his chin at a fence. 'Tennis court over there. Seen better days, but nothing a bit of white paint won't fix.'

Sacha let her hair go, and caramel ringlets cascaded around her face. 'The boys would love it here.'

'What about you, though?' I asked her. 'It's miles from town, from friends, clubs and things. You'll have a long bus ride to school.'

'I'm used to taking a bus to school. That doesn't bother me.' Sacha's gaze took in the horses, the tennis court and the distant sweep of the sea. 'Actually, I think I can see us living in this house.'

'Most rural kids drive themselves around,' said Allan. 'You're sixteen, right? Well, get your learner's licence now and in six months you can be driving on your own. Gives you a lot more freedom.'

We found Kit on the verandah. He was wearing that ragged corduroy jacket of his, I remember. The late afternoon light was a spray of gold, falling slantwise upon the hills so that every contour was accentuated. His hands were in his pockets, jingling coins, and his shoulders were up. I knew he was planning his first painting.

'There's the dam,' said Allan, pointing down the valley at a shimmer of water. 'By the cabbage trees, see?'

'You mentioned a school bus?' asked Kit, without taking his eyes off that view.

I swear I heard the cash register going ker-*ching!* in Allan's brain. 'Goes past the road gate. Dead convenient.'

*

We stopped at the beach on the way home. Allan had said he'd show us around Torutaniwha, which we gathered was the local village, and led us to a dirt car park behind some sand dunes. We could hear the rhythmic sighing of surf, and a salty breeze brushed our faces.

'Where's the village?' I asked, shielding my eyes against the glare.

Allan climbed down from his truck. 'Well, you saw the dairy; that's our name for a convenience store. They run a tearoom and sell fuel. There's a marae—Maori meeting place—further along the road. Then at the far end of the beach there's some holiday baches but they're mostly empty through the winter.'

'Baches?'

'Cottages.'

'Ah. But the . . . you know. The *village*. Houses. People.'

Allan chuckled indulgently. 'Martha, you're in New Zealand! We have a *lot* of space. There isn't a village as such.'

'But where does everyone live?'

'Believe me, there's a community. You've got the dairy and the marae. There's the Torutaniwha Tavern half a mile back, but I wouldn't take the kids. It's pretty rough, you get gangs riding out from the towns—they had a stabbing a while back.' He pointed at some nearby buildings. 'Here's the primary school. It'll take the little fellas up to Year Eight.'

Kit whistled. '*That's* a school?'

We moved closer. Torutaniwha school was built of white weatherboard, with deep porches. It looked vaguely colonial—an African hospital, perhaps, from the 1950s, tucked neatly under the hillside in sheep-nibbled pasture. There were picnic tables below the trees, and a fort complete with flying fox.

'They've got a swimming pool!' exclaimed Sacha.

Allan nodded. 'Most country schools do. In the summer term the kids'll be in and out of that three times a day. We get long, scorching summers, here in the Bay. Want to take a look at the beach?'

A path of duckboards led us through the dunes. We emerged at the southern end and wandered woozily down to the water. The beach was perhaps half a mile long, fringed by rugged hills. Sacha found a piece of driftwood, bent down beside her brothers and began to etch their names in sand letters three feet high. She was wearing low-slung jeans and a ribbon as a choker, like a hippy chick. The boys raced around her, in and out of the waves, shouting out the spelling.

I was distracted by the distant sight of two riders galloping along the beach. They kicked up a sandstorm, heads high, broad-brimmed hats flying behind them. Kit hummed spaghetti-western music, puffing Clint Eastwood's cigar.

'Cool,' said Sacha, as the riders slowed to a walk, rode into the waves and began to swim their horses. The breeze nudged her hair, striking fiery sparks in the evening sun. Then she smiled, really smiled, and I felt a great weight lift off my chest.

'Do S!' yelled Finn. 'Do S, S, S! S for Sacha!'

She handed him the stick. 'You have a go. Start up here . . . uh-huh . . . then it's like a *s*slithery old *s*snake.'

The glittering sea lapped gently, flashing with reflected light, and the moving figures of my children became silhouettes against a backdrop of rippling mirrors.

'Will you look at it,' muttered Kit. '*Look* at this place. It's . . .' he searched for the right word, '*clean.*'

Eight

Our dream house.

We got a survey, of course. We weren't so head over heels with Patupaiarehe that we didn't check for dry rot and subsidence; but as Allan had promised, it was sound. The vendors even threw in a lawnmower and quad bike. We were cash buyers, and the place was empty. It was ours before you could blink.

We'd been in New Zealand less than a month when we stocked up on the bare necessities—mattresses, bedding, crockery—checked out of a rather comfy motel, and drove to our old homestead on the hill. It was late August; nearly spring, in this topsy-turvy world. A drift of daffodils, unexpected and nostalgically English, greeted us like old friends as we navigated the drive.

But winter wasn't finished with us just yet. Within two hours of our arrival the sea disappeared and the landscape blurred under the shroud of a southerly storm. As a kind of reception committee, bolshy adolescent winds tore straight off the icy wastes of Antarctica and pounded the old house, whose wooden walls bulged inwards with each gust. The rain lashed horizontally; we pitied tiny lambs who huddled by their mothers, clearly wondering what kind of a world this was. In the distance I spotted a farmer—a woman, head bowed against the wild weather—driving among them on a quad bike. The barking of her dogs sounded faint on the wind. It wasn't what you'd call a tropical scene.

All afternoon we draped ourselves over the wood-burning stove in the kitchen, blowing optimistically and coaxing flames with bits of wet wood. I thought longingly of our heated motel room as we watched DVDs on Sacha's laptop—*Mary Poppins*, because we all needed a comforting nanny just then—and wondered what in God's name had induced us to buy this icebox. Why not one of those concrete palaces, with their insulation and draught-proof aluminium joinery and heat-exchange systems?

When we ran out of milk, I volunteered to drive the twins down to the dairy. My windscreen wipers squeaked and sloshed as I edged along the unfamiliar road. Rounding a corner, I was forced to brake smartly for a mob of sheep and lambs. They milled all over the road and up the verges, snatching mouthfuls of grass despite being harried by several dogs. Seconds later a red sports car skidded to a halt behind mine, wheels shrieking on the wet bitumen. The driver was female; I spotted a supersized bob hairdo.

'Look!' screeched Charlie from the back seat. 'A cowboy!'

There was indeed a cowboy, in a real cowboy's hat, apparently untroubled by traffic or downpour. He sauntered alongside his flock, sitting easily on a giant piebald horse and wearing a long stockman's coat with the collar turned up. Dripping hair curled around his neck. I could have gazed for an hour, but the driver of the red car clearly had no eye for picturesque masculinity. Engine revving, she inched forward until the red menace filled my rear-view mirror.

'One, two, three . . . four! Four dogs,' marvelled Finn. One seemed to bark all the time, while the others worked with silent efficiency.

Suddenly, the red car's driver pulled around me and drove into the sheep, trying to scatter them with a long blast on her horn. At first I was shocked, but what happened next had me laughing out loud. Neither the shepherd nor his horse seemed to notice her, but the man turned his head and spoke briefly to his dogs. They sprang into enthusiastic action, charging around the mob and pushing it right onto the red car. The four of them seemed to be laughing, too. Within seconds the woman was caught in a sea of bleating mayhem and could do nothing but sit and fume. I could see her gesticulating arms.

'Bloody townies,' I sneered, having lived in the countryside for a full three hours.

When we came to a wider stretch of road, the shepherd pulled his animals off to one side. Mrs Bob Hairdo roared crossly northwards with a final burst of her horn, to which he mockingly tipped his hat. As I passed, he nodded to me. I glimpsed a proud nose in a long, furrowed face.

As Allan had promised, the dairy was also a café. Its tables were giant cotton reels around a lily pond. The owner wore her hair twisted like a croissant on the back of her head. She was middle-aged and well upholstered, tucked into a tie-dyed skirt with tinkling bells around the hem and, when she discovered we were new residents, she threw in chocolate cake on the house. The rain had taken a breather, so Finn and Charlie pottered outside. I could see them chatting to some creatures in a hutch.

'You're the family that's moving in up at Patupaiarehe?' the woman called from her kitchen. Her skirt jingled.

I warmed my hands beside a glorious glass-fronted fire. 'Mm. We only arrived this morning, and I've never—*ever*—been so cold in my life.'

She laughed. 'It'll blow through by tonight.'

I asked her about the shepherd on the road.

'Tall bloke? Big black and white horse? That's Tama Pardoe.' She shook her head. 'He's a law unto himself. Hang on, I'll just get my daughter.' She nipped into the back of the building and reappeared with a chunky young woman jiggling a bald baby. 'I'm Jane, by the way. This is Destiny and Harvey. Say hello, Harvey.'

Her grandson grinned toothlessly, and I cooed on cue. Destiny wouldn't have been long out of her teens. She was blessed with wide eyes and flawless skin but—frankly—a bus-sized rear that should not have been squeezed into those leggings. She offered to get out her rabbits for Finn and Charlie.

'She left her boyfriend,' whispered Jane, once the girl was out of earshot. 'Stashed Harvey and her rabbits in the car and drove away. His mother kept coming round all the time, interfering, nagging, telling them how to run their life. Destiny warned him, time and again, "It's me or your mother," and—you've guessed it—spineless weasel chose his mother.'

'Fantastic name,' I said.

'Destiny?' Jane unloaded a tray with drinks and cake. 'I was a bit of a free spirit when she was born. Used to travel around in a wooden house bus with her father. Canary yellow, it was, like Mr Toad's caravan. He sold crystals. I did a bit of tarot reading. Now I'm just a dumpy grandma. Comes to us all.'

Jane was right about the storm. Maybe she'd read her tarot cards. Weather patterns can move with startling suddenness in New Zealand, and by sunset the front was passing away to the east. It left in its wake a limpid sapphire band that gleamed across the Pacific horizon. Sacha took the boys out to explore their new territory. The three had scarcely disappeared into the trees when Lou phoned, wanting to hear how we were settling in. I was delighted to hear my sister's voice, but she sounded indecently pleased to discover we'd spent our first day huddling over the fire.

'I thought you'd be wearing t-shirts and taking little dips to cool off?' she crowed.

'It's still winter, Lou.'

'No, it's not. It's the end of August.'

'But our seasons are reversed. You have to add six months, remember? So August here is the equivalent of . . . um . . . February there.'

'Well obviously. I knew *that*,' she said testily, but I'll bet she'd forgotten. You can't tell my sister anything.

'How's Phil?' I asked, and she harrumphed even more.

'You've unsettled him. He's getting itchy feet, talking about going back into clinical—oh my God, Theo! Coming darling, you're all right, that's it, brave boy . . . Sorry, Martha, got to go. Theo's fallen down the stairs.'

I made two cups of coffee and went to look for Kit. He was lounging on the verandah steps, staring down the valley with his sketchbook and a travel set of watercolours on his lap. I rested my head on his shoulder while the setting sun put on a fireworks display, just to welcome us.

'So,' he murmured. 'How d'you feel?'

'I feel . . .' I thought for a moment. 'I can't believe this is our home.'

'This light's so intense,' he said. 'So clear. Strong, vivid colours. I've never come across anything quite like it.'

'Not in Ireland?'

He narrowed his eyes, squinting at the angular peaks and flickering inverted triangle of the sea. 'Not even there.'

*

We'd been at Patupaiarehe about twenty-four hours when we had a visit from our neighbours. I heard a vehicle on the cattle grid and looked out as a blue farm truck stopped under the walnut's spring foliage. The next moment a vigorous woman sprang out, wearing untrendy jeans and limp hair in a grey pudding-basin cut. Her four limbs seemed slightly too long for her, but she had the posture of a ballet teacher and the stride of a sergeant major.

'Welcome to Torutaniwha,' she announced briskly. 'Pamela and Jean Colbert. We're your nearest neighbours. We're also running stock on your land at the moment so we thought we'd better drop by and say hello!'

I hurried to meet her. 'I saw you braving the storm yesterday. Where we've come from, our nearest neighbour lived five yards away.'

'Well. We're just over two kilometres as the crow flies or the quad bike buzzes. Quite a lot longer by road. Our boundary's the river.'

Pamela, I guessed, was in her fifties. I felt disconcerted by her fixed gaze: slightly vacant, like a seagull. I saw her eyes whisk over my spare tyre—I sucked my tummy in, but it was too late. However, I was prepared to overlook all that because she'd brought a tray with scones and jam and an interesting concoction that seemed to involve cream cheese, sweet chilli sauce and Mexican corn chips.

'Jean!' she called over her shoulder. 'Did you remember the wine?'

Jean was a relief: shorter than his wife, unashamedly balding and faintly paunchy. He trotted across from the truck, cotton trousers rolled up to the ankle, clutching a couple of bottles to his chest.

'From our own vineyard,' he puffed in a marked French accent, kissing me on the cheek in a delightfully Gallic gesture. Funny thing: after a month down here in the Antipodes, I suddenly felt fiercely European. At home, to be a part of Europe meant straight bananas and unelected bureaucracy and insufferable attempts to control the City of London; but here, Jean seemed a kindred spirit with centuries of shared experience and cultural understanding. He crouched down and made faces at Finn and Charlie, who were noisily spying on us from under the house. The boys wore nothing but torn shorts, and they were caked in mud and chicken mess.

'We have boys also,' chuckled Jean. 'Four crazy bruisers. But they grew up. They no longer make dens under our house.' He straightened and moved close to Pamela, taking her arm.

Sacha emerged from the kitchen door and leaned her elbow on my shoulder. She was taller than me by a couple of inches, most of them in her legs, and her hair fountained out of a high ponytail.

'Hello,' she said, extending a graceful arm. 'I'm Sacha Norris.' I was proud of her. She almost made up for my filthy sons.

Jean shook her hand. 'And how do you like your new home?'

'It's lovely here,' replied Sacha, with her wide, wonderful smile. 'But I'm afraid I'm rather homesick.'

We showed them around to the verandah, which was a suntrap. Close by, the magnolia was coming into bloom, white flowers skittering in the breeze. Sacha asked the visitors about themselves. Jean was originally from Normandy. He'd visited New Zealand in his twenties, met Pamela and never looked back. Pamela was Hawke's Bay born and bred. Her ancestors arrived on one of the first boats, back in the nineteenth century.

'Where will you be going to school?' Pamela asked. 'There isn't anywhere terribly convenient.'

'I'll be catching the bus into Napier,' said Sacha, and mentioned the name of the co-ed we'd chosen. It had good reviews—excellent for music—and was fifteen minutes from Capeview Lodge, so we could share a car sometimes.

'Where did yours go to school?' I asked.

Jean sighed. 'They boarded. In many ways we regret that, but it seemed the right thing at the time.'

I was still holding the two bottles the Colberts had brought: red wine, dusty and with no labels, which made them seem very chic. I sent Charlie off to find a corkscrew, and Finn to drag Kit out of his studio. Sacha excused herself and disappeared inside to finish an email to Lydia.

'Well,' said Pamela. 'We hope you'll be very happy here.'

We could hear Finn mimicking her accent as he trotted off. 'Virry hippy here, virry hippy here,' he was chanting, quite audibly. 'Virry, virry, virry, virry hippy.'

I giggled feebly, wondering how many more times my children would humiliate me before I grew too old to care. 'Sorry,' I said, flapping my hands. 'It's all new to them.'

Pamela didn't smile. Actually, she didn't seem overburdened with a sense of humour. In an attempt to lighten the mood a little, I reached for one of her scones. 'These are *fabulous*!'

'She makes the jam herself,' said Jean, piling cream on his. 'Her own strawberries. She gets up at dawn, just to keep on top of the garden.'

'Really? I could no more make my own jam than I could tap-dance.' I was spitting crumbs as well as sycophancy.

'Don't worry,' said Pamela consolingly. 'You'll learn! I'll give you the recipe.'

I thought then that Pamela Colbert and I would never, ever understand one another. I was alien. I would never care about baking scones or cutting a fabric on the bias. I would never swap recipes. I would never spring out of bed at five to tend my garden. I would never be a real pioneer. I was a fraud.

Jean winked at me. 'Be assured, Martha. After fifty years, you will be a domestic goddess.'

'No need.' Kit was loping along the verandah with his hands in his pockets and ebony hair rumpled. 'She's got me.'

I was delighted to see him. He saved the day, settling himself beside Pamela, chatting as he uncorked their wine. Pamela seemed captivated. Her features came to life, and I had to admit she had good bone structure. It turned out that she was a pretty competent watercolour artist herself, which I suppose was inevitable. She was interested in botanical studies and sold them out of galleries in Napier. She seemed to think the same shops might promote Kit, which was a leap of faith since she hadn't seen any of his work.

'Is this your first visit to New Zealand?' she asked.

'No,' said Kit, his eyes widening as he tasted the wine. 'Hey—this is pretty good! No—I travelled around as a student. I've always longed to come back.'

'And here you are,' declared Jean, raising his glass in welcome.

To my delight, the Colberts were gossips. There was nothing and nobody in the area that escaped their notice, and they could go back several generations. They gave us the low-down on Jane at the dairy. Apparently her ex was a skunk who physically threw her and ten-year-old Destiny out of the canary-yellow bus before roaring off into the sunset. Then we asked about our neighbour on the northern boundary, whose horses we could see flicking their tails at a haze of insects.

'Tama Pardoe,' said Pamela.

'Aha!' I exclaimed. 'I've come across him, then.' As I described the scene with the red sports car, a fond smile tugged at the corner of Pamela's mouth.

'Yep, sounds like Tama. He's running Glengarry—four hundred hectares, sheep and beef—entirely from the saddle. It's less common nowadays but it makes sense because there's some steep country at the back of his land.'

I looked at the hills that reared to the north. They could almost have been Scottish highlands. 'What's he like?'

'Tama? Nobody's fool. His grandfather was a Scots immigrant who married into one of the local Maori families. Tama never saw eye to eye with his father—I knew old man Pardoe well, stubborn brute—so he left home at fifteen. He took a job as a shepherd on one of those immense stations way up in the hills. Thousands of hectares. He'd be on horseback twelve hours a day, seven days a week, training his own dogs and horses. Fifteen years old.'

Kit whistled. 'Younger than Sacha.'

'Didn't come home for years, not until his father was safely dead. He carried the coffin in the morning, got on with docking the same afternoon.'

'Is there a Mrs Pardoe?' I asked.

Again, that indulgent smile. 'Tama's had no shortage of applicants for the post, and women have moved in from time to time. But I think he prefers horses to people.'

When Pamela insisted on seeing Kit's new studio—a crumbling black-and-white-tiled conservatory that had just the right light—Jean and I set out for a stroll. My neighbour's command of English was impeccable; quite a lot better than mine, in fact. His delivery was deliberate and measured. I wondered about trying out my schoolgirl French on him, but thought better of it.

'So you are English, and Kit is from Ireland?' he asked as we followed the drive along the edge of the bush. 'How did you meet?'

'At a funeral, of all places.'

'But he was not an artist then?'

'Yes and no. He's been in advertising all his adult life—successfully, until the latest recession.' I made a throat-cutting sign, and Jean's eyebrows bobbed in sympathy. 'But a shiny advertising executive—that wasn't how he truly saw himself. All Kit McNamara wants to do, all he's ever really wanted to do, is paint. His arty friends reckon he's the bee's knees.'

We'd strolled a couple of hundred yards when Jean halted. 'Ah,' he said, peering at a ramshackle structure half-hidden in foliage to the right of the path. 'The shearers' quarters.'

There were several decaying sheds on the land, and I hadn't yet been into all of them. This one looked like the cottage in a fairy story. It had two windows and a door—eyes and nose—and a chimney at one end.

Jean pushed at the door. 'Something is making this stick . . . one big shove . . . there! I have got it open. It was this dead bird, you see, jammed underneath.'

I looked at the lump of black feathers. 'Charming.'

Jean was edging it out of the doorway with his foot. 'Oh, long dead and dried up. Doesn't smell any more. It will have got trapped in here, poor creature. Nasty way to go.'

He held the door for me, and I stepped past him into gloom. The hut smelled of abandonment, of rotting wood and heated plastic. Jurassic cobwebs clung to the cracked glass of windows opaque with dust. There were tattered greyish curtains. Giant ferns pushed their way through the cracks between the timbers, robbing the place of light and tinting it with an ethereal green.

A bulb hung from the ceiling. I pressed the switch, and it glowed half-heartedly.

'Still connected up to the power,' I said, surprised.

'Of course. Shearers were quartered in here originally.' Jean turned a circle on his heel, looking around. 'More recently, forestry workers used it for their smoko hut.'

'Their what?'

'You don't know about smoko, Martha? But it's a national institution! Tea break, to you Poms.'

I explored the room. It was about twelve feet square, with an unlit lean-to at the back housing a toilet and basin. There was a pot-bellied wood burner, a table, wooden chairs and a rusty gas ring. There was also plenty of bird mess, especially on the windowsills. I guessed the creature had been imprisoned in here for a while before it died. At the far end I found sacks of fertiliser and sheep dip, which explained the plastic smell.

'Perhaps Sacha might like this as a bolt hole,' I wondered. 'She can bring her friends—if she makes any.' I held up two crossed fingers.

'Yes! I can already imagine a sofa and a stereo. And when your boys are older they will smuggle in their girlfriends.'

'Not until I've vetted them,' I said primly.

As we left I stooped to look at the dead bird beside the door. It was completely desiccated. I could see an empty eye socket.

Jean picked up the sad bundle between finger and thumb and tossed it deep into the undergrowth. 'A mynah, I think. Excellent mimics. Maybe flew in the chimney. See, the doors of the stove are open? And once he came down, there was no way out.'

'A mynah?'

'They're vermin, really. Not native birds.' Jean seemed to think this made the death less sad.

'I'm not a native bird either.' I pictured the frantic creature hurling itself against the mildewed windows. I wondered how long it had suffered. 'I'll put a net over that chimney,' I said firmly. 'No more death traps.'

Nine

It was no way to behave at a funeral.

I blame the gleefully grieving mourners, with their hand-clasping and platitudes. They packed the pews. They swamped the graveyard with black umbrellas, a flock of dour ravens. Sacha stood close beside me in a black dress I'd found in Oxfam, staring with fascinated eyes at the awful, polished shape of Grandma's coffin. She was six years old, and she'd scarcely known my mother.

Poor old Vincent Vale had put on a grand spread for the love of his life, and held the after-burial do—what is it, a party? a wake? Rabbit's Big Bash?—in the function room of his historic pub. It smelled of old velvet and canapés. Good venue for a wedding. I was wearing a funereal smile, peddling sandwiches from a tray. It was a shield, because if anyone else grabbed my hands, wrinkled their eyes and told me I shouldn't blame myself, I'd knee them where it hurt. In that particular context, the words 'don't blame yourself' translated very precisely as 'this is all your fault, you spawn of the devil'.

Mum's younger sister was holding court, her neat figure set off by a polka-dot dress, flour-white hair caught in a black ribbon. This was mildly unsettling, because Patricia was the spitting image of my mother—right down to the patent court shoes and tea-rose-scented skin. She looked indecently composed; no hint of a rent garment.

'I'm a murderer,' I sighed, sinking into a chair beside her.

Patricia took a sandwich from my tray. 'She wouldn't blame you, would she?'

'Oh, of course she would, Aunt Trish. She's always blamed me for everything! She wasn't at death's door. It wasn't cancer that did for her, it was my tonsillitis.'

'Hmm. Never big on forgiveness, my sister. She changed her will more times than she did her knickers.'

'It was supposed to be our big reconciliation,' I complained. 'I dropped everything to get to the hospital for her birthday. How was I to know it'd kill her?'

'Think she'll haunt you?'

'Well, she always has. I don't see why being dead should change anything.'

The words weren't out of my mouth before Mum took a pot shot. Her sarcasm blasted right through my head; she might have been hovering above the chair.

Trust you!

'Mum,' I argued silently. 'Be fair. You could have gone anytime.'

Stupid girl. You and your Judas kiss.

I was about to defend myself when Flora—garden centre—touched my shoulder.

'Your dad wants to go home now,' she said, and I nodded. Dad had never stopped adoring his ex-wife with a quiet passion. It was the one bit of irrationality he'd ever displayed. 'I'll go with him,' said Flora. 'Could Sacha stop at his house tonight? She's asked to, and she'll be a tonic. Smiley girl.'

I looked at Dad's old friend, with her wispy hair and the faintest suggestion of a widow's hump. She *was* a widow, in fact. 'Yes, please. She's got a toothbrush in his bathroom cupboard.'

As soon as Flora moved away, a pair of my parents' ex-neighbours accosted me. The wife clawed at my arm while her husband regarded me with drooping bloodhound eyes. Ex-neighbours, from before Mum and Dad became ex-spouses. I couldn't remember their name. Bromham? Brigham?

'So sorry. So sorry,' whispered Mrs Ex. 'Cynthia was one of the best. Such glamour. Such poise. Razor-sharp mind.'

'I'm glad you're here,' I lied. 'Sandwich?'

'You mustn't blame yourself,' murmured Mr Ex.

'Life goes on, Martha,' said Mrs Ex. And then she added four utterly chilling words. And I do mean chilling. 'She lives in you.'

The horrifying image of my mother living in me froze the blood in my veins. Abandoning politeness, I reeled past them and into the hall. The door swung shut behind me, deadening the hubbub. I stood for a moment, clutching my tray and breathing hard. There was a payphone in the narrow hall, and an old-fashioned smell of painted radiators and slightly mouldy telephone books. Hardly any natural light, just feeble, dusty stuff creeping through the stained glass of an outside door.

I wanted refuge from that sombre crowd, all looking sideways at me and idly wondering whether I'd killed her on purpose. They'd go back to their own lives, soon. They could watch telly, feed the cat, talk about the lovely funeral and how dignified Vincent had been. But I wasn't alone. A sprawling male figure slumped on a chair by the phone, invading the space, spoiling the sanctuary; I had a vague impression of dark, rampaging hair. He raised his head, and I found myself staring into a pair of uncannily vivid eyes—cobalt blue, under heavy brows. They weren't quite focused, but they were mesmeric.

'No,' he said loudly. The voice was unmistakeably slurred, but I didn't mind. Helpless inebriation was much more fitting than wordless hand clasping. 'I don't want a focking sandwich.'

And those were Kit's first words to me. Our eyes met over a focking sandwich.

I lowered my tray to the floor. 'Go on, take a couple. Mop up the alcohol.'

'Disgraceful behaviour. I'm drunk at a funeral, and it isn't even my own.' He looked thirty or so, just a little older than me. The striking eyes were spaced wide apart in a pale, shield-shaped face. An overcoat and scarf hung over one arm. 'Did you know her?' he asked.

'No. No, I'm just a waitress.' I closed my own eyes for a moment. Couldn't shut it out, though. Death isn't shut-outable.

He hiccupped. 'Waitress.' Dimly, I wondered about the engaging lilt of his accent. It wasn't strong, but I've an ear for these things. Ireland. West coast, maybe. 'Me neither. I've spoken to Mrs Cynthia Vale . . . actually, I could count the number of times on this hand. I don't think she liked me.'

'So are you one of these funeral junkies? Did you come for the free booze?'

'You're a funny kind of waitress,' he said mildly. 'No, not a funeral junkie. I'm flying the flag. My uncle is great mates with Vinnie, but he's in Madeira.'

'Well. You're the only one who's bothered to get drunk for her.'

He smiled. 'You know, I saw you and your little girl in church. You were following the coffin with your sister. The three of you look very alike, but none of you resemble Mrs Vale very much at all.' His eyes were alight with humour, and I found myself smiling back.

'Thank you,' I said fervently. 'That's the most comforting thing any-one's said to me all day. Where are you from?'

'Shepherd's Bush.'

'No you're not. Sorry, but you just aren't.'

'Okay, Sherlock. County Kerry.'

'Hmm.' I sat down on the floor beside my tray, stretching my legs across the corridor. 'So what brought you to Shepherd's Bush?'

'Long story.'

'Go on. I've got oodles of time. I'm *never* going back into that bar.'

He glanced at his watch, then slid off the chair and leaned his back against the opposite wall to mine. We pressed our four feet companionably together, like a pair of schoolkids at break time. He was wearing a dark suit and a sober silk tie, slightly loosened. His shoes were posh, black and polished; mine were cheap, grey and scuffed.

'Okay then,' he said. 'Since you've asked.' His family had existed on the west coast of Ireland forever, it seemed, farming in the ancient hills. He was eighteen when his father died of a heart attack during a bracing dip in the Atlantic. As he was the only son, his mother and five sisters—he called them 'the coven'—expected him to run the farm and save the family fortunes. But my new friend didn't want to be a farmer. He dreaded living and dying in that community, the latest in a perennial stream, known only as his father's son. So he ran away to art college in Dublin—where he picked up a wife—and then to London, where she promptly left him.

'And in London I stayed,' he finished. 'And here I am.'

'What happened to the farm?'

'Coven made a go of it. They keep goats. They make cheese.'

'Cheese?'

'Organic goats' cheese. Wins awards, you can buy it in Harrods. So there you go—diversify to survive. I've been gone nearly half my life, but whenever I visit they blather on at me. They can't believe I'll not come home in the end.'

I felt his shoes pressing against mine; I was intensely aware of the contact, as though my whole nervous system was centred in the soles of my feet.

'I'm off in five minutes,' he said, and I felt a tug of regret.

'Not driving, I hope?'

'No. I left my phone somewhere, so I called a taxi on this old-fashioned tellingbone. They'll be here at half past.'

'Oh.'

He didn't move. 'Coming with me?'

I felt my eyes prickling. 'I can't. I've got to stay here and do this . . . do this . . . all this funeral thing.'

With surprising swiftness, he was at my side. 'But will you be all right?'

There was more caring in those six words than all the tragic clawing and don't-know-what-to-say and your-mother-was-a-wonderful-woman-who-frigging-well-lives-in-you. I was so grateful. It tipped me over the edge.

'I've got no mother,' I sobbed in panic. 'She was a bitch. Or maybe she wasn't. Maybe I am. Not sure.'

'I expect you both were.'

I pressed my nose into a tissue, gulping, dimly aware that my cheeks must be traffic-light red. 'We started fighting when I was about . . . I dunno, a day old? She said she couldn't believe I was hers. I disappointed her every step of the way. Everything was a battlefield. Piano—I didn't practise; friends—she banned them; meals—I wouldn't eat them. But none of it was for *me*. It was all about her status as an icon of bloody womanhood.

I ditched my law degree and she didn't speak to me for a year. When I was twenty-one I got pregnant.'

'Did you marry the father?'

'What father?'

'Ah.'

'I went to the hospital on her birthday last week. Couldn't even get that right, could I? My daughter made a beautiful card, I baked a cake, thought she'd approve of that—kissed her and I had a strep throat. It finished her off.'

He drew my hair from my face, and I felt his fingers brush my ear. Vincent Vale chose that moment to appear in the doorway. He spent most of his life prowling around on soft-soled shoes, trying to catch people out. His gaze fell on me, the murdering baggage, sobbing all over a dark stranger.

'Not here,' he muttered, and disappeared the way he'd come.

'Ambiguous,' said Drunk Man. 'Ambiguous, I call that. What's not here? Who's not here? He's not, you're not, I'm not?' He lifted one of my curls and held it against his cheek. I could smell the starch in his shirt. A button had come adrift. I glimpsed pale skin beneath the cotton, and felt a strong urge to slide my fingers inside. I didn't think he'd mind.

Shameless hussy! Mum was enraged. *I'm not cold in my grave, and you're fantasising about—*

From the street outside, a car horn.

'Your taxi,' I said reluctantly.

He rolled easily to his feet and reached down a hand to pull me up. His grip felt more powerful than I expected. For a flickering moment, I was afraid of him.

'C'mon. They don't need you at this funeral thing, Martha Norris. Got the name right?'

'I can't possibly come with you,' I said, as we made our way outside and up to the waiting car. 'This is my mother's funeral. I've got to behave decently.'

He smiled confidently down at me, shrugging into his overcoat, and I felt my insides lurch. 'Come with me,' he said quietly.

The meter was ticking, the driver bored. 'Going to the station, mate?'

'Focus, will you?' I insisted. 'Where to?'

He dropped his forehead to touch mine. 'You tell me. I love a magical mystery tour.' Then he disappeared into the dark interior of the taxi.

Don't even think about it, howled Mum. *This is my funeral!*

I hesitated, turning back to Vincent's pub. People were leaving in little groups; they chatted and rummaged for keys, and cars were queuing to get out of the car park. I wasn't needed. If I let this man go, I might never see him again.

That's when I made the decision that changed my life. I gave the driver a local address. My own address. Then I ran around to the other side, threw myself onto the seat beside a perfect stranger, and slammed the door.

'Will you get drunk for me, at my funeral?' I asked, as the white car pulled away from the kerb.

I woke to the peaceful pitter-patter of rain on the window, and an odd relief that I'd buried my mother and could get on with my life. Ivory light was seeping around the curtains, and there was a wild-haired, unshaven stranger sprawled under my duvet. He lay on his front, one arm flung around my waist, a muscle twitching in the sandpaper cheek.

Carefully, I extricated myself and grabbed my kimono. Then I tiptoed across our scattered clothes—they were strewn all the way down the stairs—and into the kitchen. My visitor's jacket was lying by the door; I remembered tugging it off as soon as we crossed the threshold. Shameless hussy. Muffin hopped out of her bed, padded over to collect her quota of adoration and asked to be let into the garden. While the kettle boiled, I phoned Dad.

'Sacha's still in bed.' He sounded dazed. 'Fast asleep, like a little princess.'

'How are you doing, Dad?'

'Awful,' he said. 'I feel awful.'

It was his honesty that would save him, I thought. His willingness to admit weakness was his greatest strength. That was more than control or courage or stiff upper lips. 'How about you?' he asked.

'Um . . .' I recalled the lust and laughter of last night, and felt my cheeks flame. 'Not bad. Shall I come over?'

'No rush, love. Flora's here already. A kitten pitched up on my doorstep in the night; a black, bedraggled scrap of a thing.'

'Cute! You're keeping him, then?'

'Oh yes, I think so. Flora's named him Bernard. I'm going to plonk him on Sacha's pillow in a minute and see the look on her face!'

I hung up the phone, made a plunger of coffee and took it upstairs. As I sat near the man in my bed, he nuzzled his jaw into the pillow with a flutter of outrageous eyelashes. I trailed my fingertips across the muscles of his back. Last night he'd carried me up the last few stairs, both of us laughing, and his strength had come as a surprise because I'd had him down as the arty, elegant type—slightly dissolute, perhaps. I couldn't imagine him setting foot in a gym.

'You're still here,' I said. 'Why are you still here?'

The cobalt eyes opened. Then he smiled as though he'd known me forever, and I was bowled over by a wave of desire. It left me short of breath.

'Shouldn't I be here?' he asked, rolling onto an elbow and resting his cheek on one hand.

'Who are you, really?'

'Christopher McNamara,' he said, holding out his free hand. 'Nice to meet you.'

'Yes, I know your name. I may be a slapper, but I don't sleep with men whose names I don't know.'

'Non-smoker, thirty, good sense of humour.'

'Single?'

'Divorced. Told you that last night. Married two years—we were insanely young—divorced for seven. No kids. No baggage . . . and since then, just Lucinda and Zara and Bella and—'

'Shut up. Solvent?'

'Excessively.'

'Sane?'

'You tell me, Ms Bossy Occupational Therapist. Hey, d'you wear a uniform? Apron, cap, little stripy skirt?'

I leaned closer to slap his arm, and he caught my hand. 'Single, solvent and sane,' he murmured, pulling me closer. 'And stunning.'

'Hmm.' That was true enough. 'So what's the catch?'

He never told me. I found out for myself.

Ten

At first I think I'm becoming paranoid. There's a subtle shift in the way the nurses behave, a vagueness in the smiles of the orderlies. Suddenly, no one wants to know. They hurry past, terribly busy, heads turned the other way. Cups of tea stop arriving.

The night grinds on, and my mind is suspended in this scruffy-clean world with the blue lino floor and reek of cleaning fluids and sickness. Through the graveyard hours, patients limp in and others leave: a blond boy who's treated for asthma; an elderly man with palpitations. At about six someone, somewhere nearby, begins to make toast. The comforting warmth of it floats down the corridor, masking the disinfectant. It's a homely, happy smell. It's Sunday mornings, tea and marmalade, watching films under a duvet. *Aristocats* and *Ice Age*.

The night shift leave. Staff become ordinary people again, heading for home and families. The hospital shakes itself into the routines of daytime.

It's after seven when a surgeon appears—a Roman general, wearing scrubs instead of a metal skirt. I have an impression of corrugated-iron hair and battle weariness. He's flanked by two captains.

'Mrs McNamara?'

I am ushered dumbly into another little room. Terror sucks at my lungs. There is no air. No air in the world. They are the news breakers, this grim-faced posse. They've come to tell me I've lost my Finn.

They motion me to a chair and lean around the walls.

'Neil Sutherland, general surgeon.' The General has baggy eyes and powerful hands. He swiftly introduces his colleagues. There's a woman from the trauma team, and a paediatrician—a long thin giraffe, who says he has a special interest in child protection.

'Finn?' I ask faintly.

'He's been very sick,' says the General. 'We've done all we can for now, and he's stabilised. That's the important point.'

I look around at the three, trying to read their expressions. 'But what . . . he is going to . . . he *is* all right?'

'Well. We've established that there is no spinal injury, which is good news.' Neil Sutherland looks gloomy. 'The CT scan showed a ruptured spleen. It's been removed and we've stopped the bleeding there. He's fractured his right forearm—the orthopaedic team have dealt with that. The most pressing concern at the moment is a head injury.'

These are words I dread. I've seen enough of such injuries to loathe them. 'How severe?'

'Finn was extremely lucky.' Sutherland is avoiding the question. 'We don't actually have a resident neurosurgeon, but one was visiting Hawke's Bay this week to take a clinic. She's based at Starship Children's Hospital in Auckland, and she was right on the spot. She's done a superb job.'

I persist. 'How severe is this head injury? I'm an occupational therapist. I know what they mean.'

'All right.' Sutherland pinches the bridge of his nose. 'The scan showed some bleeding, and there were two unstable bone fragments which the neurosurgeon removed. She's inserted a small plate. We've induced a coma to reduce stress and swelling on Finn's brain.'

I shut my eyes.

'His condition is critical,' says the woman. 'He's in the intensive care unit.'

'He's in ICU? Can I see him?'

Sutherland sounds unhappy. 'Very soon. First, we need to ask you about something.' He hands me a sheet of thin paper. 'This is an image of Finn's upper arm.'

I feel bewildered by the irrelevance. It's grotesque to have taken a picture of Finn's tiny arm, while he lies in mortal danger. I won't even look at the flimsy thing. 'His arm? His *arm*? For God's sake! He's got a plate in his head and a ruptured spleen and you're telling me about his arm? Is this the one that's broken?'

'No.' Sutherland points with a blunt, well-manicured forefinger. 'See these marks around here?'

I look at the photograph, and then I understand. Completely. Until now, I didn't imagine things could get any worse.

'I don't know.' I sound drunk. My tongue seems to be swelling.

The neon light's too white. It isn't kind. It glowers and hums and accuses me of trying to kill my son. The image is a close-up of a child's arm. Around it are four small discs of a deep, livid blue.

Behind me, the giraffe moves in for the attack. He's an angrier man than Sutherland, overflowing with energy. 'It's bruising,' he says curtly. 'Finger marks, see? They're very obvious.'

'He fell,' I insist. 'He fell about fifteen feet. I imagine there is bruising all over his poor little body. Now, can I *please* see my son?'

I sense the three exchanging glances. Sutherland sighs. He wants to go home to bed but he can't, because there is this child. This injured child.

Giraffe jabs at the picture. 'There are four finger marks there, Mrs McNamara. See? And a fifth around the back of the arm, which we are agreed is consistent with a thumb. These suggest an adult hand, gripping the child's arm very forcibly.' He demonstrates a grabbing motion with his own long fingers. 'Like this, see? It's a classic presentation. Whose fingers, Mrs McNamara?'

'He's always squabbling with his twin brother,' I protest.

'An *adult* hand.'

'He goes to school. Maybe the teacher . . .'

They stare as I meander to a standstill. Then Giraffe says, 'From the colour, I'd suggest they could be contemporaneous with his fall. And they were made with considerable force. Whose fingers?'

I feel the heat spread up my neck, across my face. I try to swat it away like a fly, but I am pinned down by terror. For Finn. For all of us.

'Are you suggesting . . . what *are* you suggesting?' I stare at the image of Finn's vulnerability. 'He fell,' I repeat, stupidly. 'The flowerbed's edged with stones. That'll be what did it.'

'He was lying on his right side when the team arrived,' says Sutherland wearily. 'He's broken his right forearm. These marks are on the left, and they're the only visible injuries on that arm.'

'It's my fault,' I whisper.

'Why is it your fault?'

'Because I should have locked his door. Because I couldn't run fast enough. Because I brought him here in the first place.'

'Where's Finn's father?' asks the woman suddenly.

'Kit's on his way back from Dublin.'

'When do you expect him home?'

I only hesitate for an instant, but her gaze sharpens. 'I'm not sure exactly when. There was some complication. He changed his flight.'

'Have you been able to contact him?'

I shrug helplessly. 'No answer from his mobile, but then he'll have turned it off if he's on a plane. I've left messages.'

'Life must have been stressful for you recently,' she says.

'Stressful?'

'With your husband away, and two small boys, in that isolated area.'

'Well, fairly. But—'

'I gather you've only lived here a year. Perhaps you haven't any close friends yet? No one to call on when things get on top of you.'

'He fell,' I say dully.

They let the silence lengthen. Eventually Sutherland pushes himself upright. He doesn't look angry. He looks depressed. I really think he and I might have got on, if we'd met at a dinner party.

'I'm sorry, Mrs McNamara,' he says heavily. 'This issue has been raised now, and there are procedures that we have to follow. We must inform the paediatric social worker that there is a child injured and indications that it may be non-accidental. We'll liaise with her to decide whether there needs to be a formal referral to Child, Youth and Family. And possibly the police.'

'There's no need for that! The police have already been here. They were perfectly satisfied.'

Briefly, he lays a hand on my arm. 'That was routine,' he says. 'This, I'm afraid, is not.'

Eleven

That spring at Patupaiarehe, we were gypsies. The container with all our possessions was somewhere on the high seas, rocking and rusting, becalmed in the doldrums or tossed in the roaring forties. Through September and October we had no clutter. No *stuff*. It was liberating. We were settlers, blazing with pioneering spirit.

We fell madly in love with our house at the head of the valley. A couple of men came and rewired while others laid terracotta tiles on the kitchen floor. Within a day we'd stopped locking the front door when we went out; within two we'd given up bothering to shut it. The place felt so secure, so storybook, far up a pitted track and nestled into the motherly bosom of the forest. There *were* no evils, lurking. I was sure that if the twins ever wandered off, the only person to offer them a lift would be some taciturn farmer in enormous gumboots (Kiwi for wellingtons), sheepdogs tail-wagging on the flatbed of his truck. He'd haul them in and bring them home.

Sacha often stayed up until midnight to have Facebook conversations with English friends and complained—justifiably—about the slowness of our internet connection. She seemed to be coping, though; she thrashed us both at tennis, got her learner driver licence and quickly became adept on the quad bike. The one thing she wouldn't do was play her flute. It lay untouched in its case.

Once we'd repainted the shabbiest rooms, Kit asked Sacha if she'd help him with a mural for the boys. His thinking was that it would be good for her to have a project, and he was right. The pair of them were closeted for days, yelling convivially over the racket from Sacha's favourite radio station. They finally unveiled their masterpiece: an African savannah, teeming with animals. None looked hungry. Even the leopard contentedly dozed in a tree.

'These are mine.' Sacha closed the cupboard doors to reveal a flock of vivid flamingos standing in a lake. 'Aren't they cool?'

'They *are* cool.'

'Obviously Kit helped,' she admitted. 'Quite a lot, actually.'

Kit was cleaning brushes. 'No, the fabulous flamingos are down to you. What next, Sacha? Your room?'

She politely refused. 'I'm too old now,' she said, with a touch of sadness.

'Nobody's too old,' said Kit.

Instead, he whitewashed his conservatory-studio and hung yards of gauzy curtain to diffuse the brilliant Hawke's Bay light. Pamela showed him a wonderful art-supply shop and he threw himself into sketching, experimenting, practising. I guiltily searched the place more than once but found no hoard of bottles, full or empty. Finally he began a series of small landscapes in acrylic.

The studio was a sanctuary, with its mellow light and smell of tomato plants and paint. I used to spend my evenings peacefully lolling in a deckchair, intrigued by the confidence with which Kit mixed the subtlest colours and gave them life. I loved to watch his eyes, narrowed and intense, seeing things that I never could. It was as though those brushstrokes were a language; it was Kit's mother tongue, and at last he was allowed to speak it. I began to understand what Gerry Kerr had been talking about.

Now we had a base, Dad insisted on sending Muffin. We drove the five hours to Auckland to liberate our old friend from her crate—safe, well and crazy with joy at the sound of our voices—and brought her back in triumph to Patupaiarehe. She seemed to know she was home, taking a ladylike snuffle around the garden before plumping with a contented sigh into her basket in the kitchen. There she lay, groaning and wheezing with love, the treacle-black buttons of her nose and eyes half submerged in blanket and hair.

'I've even missed her smell,' said Sacha, brushing the shaggy coat. I knew what she meant. Now Muffin was in residence, the kitchen felt right.

Nostalgia is dangerous stuff, of course. Time blurs and distorts the past. When I look back on those first days I remember a holiday: sunshine and space, translucent air and silver-threaded sea; gangs of lambs playing King of the Castle on a rock. When real holidays end, you go home. You open your mail, phone your friends, maybe look through your photos and dream of owning a bar in Crete; but the next day you're back at work and showing off your tan. For us there was no going home. In October, the Christmas school term began.

On her first morning Sacha appeared downstairs in her hideous tartan uniform, fretting that she was having a bad hair day. She made brave, buoyant conversation in the car but her heart wasn't in it and her nails had been bitten. I was feeling slightly sick myself, as I'd arranged to meet my new manager after dropping her off. When we pulled up at the school gates the pavement was an ants' nest, swarming with adolescents—not one of whom we knew.

'Good luck, doll,' I said, with a tug of her ponytail. 'There's a best friend here, waiting for you.'

'Good luck to you too, Mum. Let's both kick ass.' She kissed Ivan's locket before sliding it under her shirt, and gave me a weak smile. Then she swung out of the car, wending her way through the crowd. I watched the lonely figure, remembering a self-assured celebrity who was mobbed as she left her school in England. We must have been mad, I thought. How can a lifestyle replace family and friends? Work is work, and school is school, however pretty the views. At that moment, if I could have turned back time and kept the whole family safe in Bedfordshire, I would.

Twenty minutes later I was grinding up a hill towards what had once been a tuberculosis hospital. The last set of buildings had an aquamarine sign: *CAPEVIEW LODGE, Residential and Community Rehabilitation.* Below, in smaller letters, I read NELSON HEALTH CARE SERVICES. I wasn't contracted to begin work until December, but my new manager had issued a summons. I was also keen to have a look at the place.

I parked, slapped on lipstick and presented myself to the bustling gorgon at the reception desk. It was ten minutes before a figure crept from behind a pot plant, proffering a lifeless hand.

'Lillian Thompson,' she murmured. My manager was getting on a bit, but cherry-red sugar cubes dangled from her ears and her hair was an implausible shade of ochre. I followed her into a worryingly tidy office, and we sat down.

'How are you finding New Zealand?' she asked, woodenly. It was a stock question; I'd answered it many times already. A trick question, too, I'd found. Ambivalence was not appreciated.

'Loving it,' I gushed, beaming. 'What a fantastic place to bring up kids.'

She nodded without pleasure or interest. I'd passed the first test. Had I failed to express unconditional love, I'd have been written off as a whingeing Pom who was never asked to come and could always go home if I didn't like it.

All I learned from Lillian Thompson is that there are managers with limp handshakes and chips on their shoulders in both hemispheres. I spent the next half hour trying to work out what, exactly, she disliked about me. After an awkward silence I realised she'd just asked something, but I hadn't caught it because I was mesmerised by those appalling earrings.

'Te Reo,' she repeated, with exaggerated clarity.

'Yep.' I'd expected this. 'Maori language. Fascinating! I've been mugging up.'

'This is not just a language thing; it's bicultural awareness. You need to do a paper that covers customary concepts, values and the Treaty of Waitangi.'

'Nobody mentioned this in the interview.'

'They certainly should have. You can do the paper largely by correspondence.'

'Okay. Sign me up.'

'Remind me.' Her pen ran across the pages of her desk diary. 'Your start date is . . .?'

'The fifth of December.'

'Can't you begin earlier?'

'No,' I said firmly, crossing my arms. 'Sorry, but I did make this clear in my interview. I start once my boys turn five and go to school.'

Her lips thinned. 'I shall be on leave. As you know, Nelson is a private health care provider. Capeview is our flagship facility . . .'

I glanced at the clock. Already ten fifteen. I imagined Sacha alone in the common room: snubbed, shunned, pretending to read the notices. I longed to be with her.

At last, Lillian rose and preceded me into the corridor. 'The other OT is out this morning, as are several of the team, because much of our input is in the clients' home or work environments. We'll have to create a space for you. Your position has been empty for so long that your office has become—'

'A rubbish dump,' growled a male voice, and a face appeared from a door to our left. It was smooth and folded, like melting cheese.

'Keith Emmerson. Clinical psychologist,' whispered Lillian, somehow making it sound as though she was introducing the local flasher, complete with dirty mackintosh.

Keith advanced with an extended hand. He'd be fifty or so, and there wasn't a lot of hair left. I counted at least three chins. In fact, it was impossible to say where chins ended and neck began. He sported a red tie with yellow teddy bears, and a stomach that cantilevered dangerously over his belt. It was all a joyous contrast to Lillian's insipid resentment.

'How are you finding New Zealand?'

'Loving it.' I took his hand.

'And how's your family settling in?'

'Um, absolutely. Never looked back. What a great place to bring up kids.'

He didn't let go of my hand. In fact, I felt the pressure increase. 'Crap,' he pronounced. 'You've airdropped—what, three children?—way out of their comfort zone. You've left everything and everyone that matters to you. You've suffered a massive bereavement—and you expect me to believe you've never looked back? Come *on*!'

With a grimace of relief, I capitulated. 'Okay. I've got homesickness like toothache, comes in waves. My daughter's really struggled. This morning when I dropped her at school I wished we'd never come. But we're still here.'

'Better.' He released my fingers.

Lillian was shifting restlessly. 'Well, Keith. I'll leave Martha in your capable hands.'

The facilities were impressive and my guide generous with his time. He was clearly popular. People stopped to chat, and I discovered that he himself had four daughters.

'Luckily we've got a male guinea pig,' he said, leading me past the swimming pool. 'I can always go and have some blokes' bonding time with him. I gather you've a special interest in head injury?'

'That's right.'

'Great. Just what we're needing.' He held a door open for me as we stepped outside. 'Our sensory garden! I'm proud of this, because it's my baby.'

The garden was an inspiration. Covering perhaps a quarter of an acre and criss-crossed with looping paths, it was a wonderland of scented plants, of texture and colour. Water bubbled calmly out of clay pots; bamboo tubes hung in trees, tolling and clicking gently. Keith and I paused for a moment on a wooden bench, inhaling the scent of rosemary. Far across a periwinkle bay stretched the pale cliffs of Cape Kidnappers.

'Quite a sight, isn't it? Kidnappers looks different every day,' said Keith, following my gaze. 'Sometimes you could almost reach out and touch it. You might know the story? No? It's named after an attempt by Maori to kidnap a servant from Captain Cook's ship, the *Endeavour.* Nowadays you can ride a tractor along the beach and visit the gannet colony at the end. Your kids'll have a ball.'

At lunchtime he walked me to my car. 'Your predecessor claimed to love it here,' he said seriously. 'She was English too. Came out with a husband and baby. Guess how long she lasted?'

'I don't think I'm going to like the answer to that question.'

'You're not.' He leaned hefty forearms on the open door. 'Six weeks, from landing to take-off.'

'Six weeks!'

'Turned their container around in Napier port. It never got off the dock.'

'Blimey. What did you do to her, Keith?'

He rubbed his chins. 'They were homesick. It was too big a change, and it wasn't necessary. They weren't running *from* anything, or *to* anything.'

'Neither are we,' I said, as he shut my door.

Perhaps I needn't have worried. Sacha's first week at school was a roaring success. She hit it off with a girl called Tabby, liked the teachers and found the bus journey useful for getting her homework done. Her class, Year Eleven, were in the run-up to their equivalent of GCSEs, and as Sacha had already passed hers she could take things easy. We spent the first weekend smartening up the smoko hut, ready for when our furniture arrived.

'A load of us are going to sleep in here after their exams are finished,' she said as we whitewashed the walls together.

'Both sexes?'

'Well, der.'

'Boys sleep in the house,' I said.

'Why?'

'Well, *der.*'

She laid an innocent hand on her heart. 'Mum! Don't you trust me?'

One afternoon after school, she went into Napier with Tabby and some sidekicks. They wanted to show her the shopping scene. It worked out well, because Kit and the Colberts were in town too, and brought her home. They'd been visiting a gallery in Napier; the manager had looked at Kit's small landscapes and promptly agreed to exhibit them.

Jean and Pamela stayed for a celebratory drink—'Here's to your glittering success, Kit'—and persuaded Sacha to parade her new outfits. They were bright, flimsy little slip-like dresses, and ballooning miniskirts.

'I hope the weather improves soon,' said Jean dryly. 'Or you will most certainly die of cold.'

Pamela asked about the new friends. When Sacha mentioned Tabby, she nodded calmly. 'Tabby Mills? Ah, yes. I know her grandmother. Very sporty family.'

'You see?' Jean's eyebrows had leaped up high. 'Everyone knows everyone around here. There's no escape.'

Kit topped up the Colberts' glasses, which were already half full. Then his own, which was empty. Then he caught my eye, and set the bottle down on the table with a dull thud.

It was a couple of days later that I found Sacha outside the school gates, surrounded by the St Trinians' lacrosse team: svelte, chattering creatures all carrying mobile phones and not a smidgen of flab.

Sacha introduced about five of them as I levered myself out of the car, feeling unfit and untrendy. I didn't get all the names—Tabby, Jade and, er, some others. The team chorused 'Hi' in cheery unison, showing orthodontist-perfect teeth. Tabby—clearly queen—was a real head-turner, with russet hair in an immaculate French plait and a waist you could have fitted through the eye of a needle. I'll wager she had on the same tartan skirt she'd worn in Year Nine. It was probably knee-length then, but it was scarcely worth wearing now and revealed the concave thighs of a catwalk model. Her courtiers were variations on the same glamorous theme.

Tarts, whispered Mum, and for once I agreed with her. *Gaggle of stick insects!*

They were confident, well-brought-up stick insects though, and made polite conversation until their buses arrived. Queen Tabby did big hugs with Sacha, and made her promise to be on Facebook that evening.

'So,' I began bouncily, as we headed out of town. 'You're settling in brilliantly.'

'Yep.'

'You're still alive.'

'Yep.'

'Nice girls?'

'Yep.' Sigh. 'Nice girls. Tabby does fashion modelling.'

'Hmm. Too thin.'

'You can't be too thin. They're having a sleepover this weekend. I don't really want to go.'

'Oh?' I was puzzled by her lack of enthusiasm. 'Sounds like fun. Did you find out about the orchestra?'

'Mm-hm. I can start anytime.'

'Flute lessons?'

'For God's sake! Yes, flute lessons.'

'C'mon, doll, talk to me. You look like you've swallowed a wasp. What's up?'

'I'm fine.' She didn't look fine.

'They all want to know you. That's good, right?'

'Only because I'm the new kid on the block.' She picked at her hem, mouth quavering. 'They know nothing about me. They've never been to England. They're not interested in where I've come from or who I really am. I've never watched any of their soap operas, nor do I want to, nor do I care how the New Zealand netball team is doing or which boy Tabby is dating this week. I don't play a sport and I'm never ever ever going to a gym. So where does that leave us?'

'I know what you mean.' The wind was gone from my sails. I thought of Lou, who'd shared my childhood. At that moment I missed her more than I could possibly have imagined.

'They're nice people, but they aren't *my* people,' said Sacha. 'They'll never be my people.'

'Give them time. Get a little common history.'

She'd curled up in her seat like a small child, and I wondered what had rattled her. We were weaving through the hills when she finally told me. 'Ivan's going out with somebody.'

I pulled into a gateway as the sad story came tumbling out. My poor girl. She'd checked her emails at lunchtime—it was against the rules, but everyone did it.

'He didn't want me to find out from anyone else,' she gulped. 'And he was just in time because straight after his, three other people had messaged me on Facebook. I was using a computer in the library and I was just staring at the screen, feeling sick, and everyone was going, "What's wrong, what's wrong?" I just couldn't face them all feeling sorry for me so I ran down the playing field and just about screamed. I mean, we agreed we should both move on, and I've been gone three months now, but . . .' She dissolved into sobs. 'I want to go home. I want to see Grandpa.'

I turned out of the driveway and drove on, wishing I could fix this for her. I felt stricken. A thought was fluttering in my mind, enticing and mischievous: I was wondering whether it was possible to turn our container around in the port and send it home. Perhaps I could get my job back and stick up two fingers at ghastly Lillian. All the way to Patupaiarehe I dreamed, picturing the joyful scene as Dad and Louisa met us at Heathrow.

Instead Kit met us by the car, almost dancing with suppressed delight. He had two pieces of news. The first was that the gallery had sold three of his paintings. Kit had to pay a hefty commission and the balance wouldn't make us rich, but it was a spectacular start and they were asking for more.

The second bulletin should also have been music to my ears. He'd had a call from the removal company. Our container had made it through customs at the Port of Napier. It had been held up by biosecurity but was in their warehouse now and would arrive at Patupaiarehe first thing on Saturday morning.

It was too late to turn it around.

Twelve

The twins were on watch straight after breakfast that Saturday, ploughing Dinky car roads in the dry mud at the top of the drive. As I hung up washing nearby, they discussed which of their long-lost toys they'd play with first. Charlie planned to tip Lego all over the floor and make the biggest plane in the world—big as a real one—*this* big! Finn was salivating at the prospect of riding his bike. Before we left England he'd already graduated from stabilisers, which was a source of much chest-puffing.

November had begun, and brought us a fine spring day. Muffin lay stretched on her side, snoring in the sun. Sacha came wandering across the gravel wearing a red halterneck top and denim shorts. Ivan's locket still hung around her neck. As she walked she was filming us with the pocket-sized video camera I'd been given as a leaving present.

'I'm making a DVD for everyone at home,' she explained. 'Uncle Philip's idea.'

'Swing me, Sash?' begged Finn, holding up his arms. Sacha took hold of his hands and spun, long hair flying, until Finn let go and staggered giddily. 'Whoa! Look, Charlie, I'm a shrunkened sailor.'

'You feeling a bit happier?' I asked quietly.

'A bit. Just got a text from a girl at school. She's invited me to a party.'

'Oh, that's great! Tabby?'

'Nah. Bianka. Spelled with a k. Says can I stay over at her place next Friday night.'

I'd never even heard of this girl. 'What's she like?'

Sacha was fiddling with the camera. 'Brainbox. Brightest pebble on the beach.'

'Except you. Careful! I love that camera, it's so cute.'

'Bianka's pretty offbeat. Talks about things like Sylvia Plath and Germaine Greer and how the nuclear family is obsolete.'

'How true,' I chuckled, hanging up Finn's trunks.

'She writes poetry.'

'Good poetry?'

''Course it's good poetry.'

'Is Friday anything special?' I grunted, reaching for another peg.

'Bonfire night on her cousins' farm. Can I go?'

'Well, of course. Maybe.'

Sacha crossed her eyes. 'Of course, maybe? Illogical, Captain.'

'I don't know Bianka's family. Are they . . . you know. Are they all right?'

'Hardly.' Jamming my camera into her pocket, Sacha reached into the washing basket. 'Her dad's a psychopathic mass murderer and her mum's a gangland hit-woman.'

'Well, they might be, for all I know.'

'It's fine, Mum. The dad works for the planning department. The only real and present danger is that he'll bore me to death.'

'Is there a mother, or is the nuclear family obsolete?'

'She's got cancer.'

I was immediately overwhelmed by that awkward mixture of compassion and relief that it was somebody else. 'Oh, poor lady.'

'Non-Hodgkin's lymphoma. She had it years ago, and it's back. She's had chemotherapy. Her hair all came out in clumps on her pillow. And her eyebrows.'

'Well then, obviously you can't go. The last thing they need is an extra child hanging about. And Bianka's mother might catch something from you. Like . . .'

'Like Grandma Norris did? It's okay. They want to live normally.' Sacha thrust her hands into her back pockets, swaying to some inaudible tune, her eyelashes long and tangled as she gazed down the drive. 'What d'you think these antipods wear for Guy Fawkes Night?'

Charlie touched her knee, wooing her with his most angelic smile. 'Sacha, help us make a daisy chain?'

'Daisy chains are sissy,' sneered Finn. 'But I'll help you pick 'em.'

I finished the washing, taking pleasure in the sight of the three smooth faces tilted close together. They were already a little tanned in the spring sun. A giddy fantail flitted around us, whisking in and out and piping cheerfully. Friendly little birds; they stay close to you, like robins, and their tails fan like a magician's pack of cards.

'Isn't this a beautiful place?' said Sacha.

Charlie tensed suddenly, standing rigid like a meerkat and gazing towards the road. 'I can see a lorry!' he screamed, and I heard the distant rattle of the cattle grid at the road gate.

'I'll get Dad. *Dad!*' Finn was pelting across to the house when Kit appeared at a run. 'The lorry's coming!'

'Here we are, old girl!' Kit put his arm around my shoulder when he reached me. 'A historic moment.'

Under a mushroom cloud of dust, a bright red lorry nosed its laborious way up the hill and into the garden. The driver, a heavyweight with an eccentric moustache, wound down his window. 'Bit steep, that bloody goat track,' he remarked as he backed competently under the walnut tree and cut his engine. It was the kind of understatement I'd come to expect of the Kiwi male.

Three men swung out of the cab. They had exactly the same body language as the trio of tea swillers who'd packed our house in Bedfordshire, only magically turned into New Zealanders and wearing shorts, socks and dusty lace-up boots. Almost every adult male—from school principal to farmer to bus driver—wore shorts, socks and dusty lace-up boots. You could spot a Jehovah's Witness a mile off in his pressed trousers and shiny shoes.

'McNamara?' asked the driver, removing a cap to mop his brow.

'McNamara!' roared the boys.

'Where to then, young fellas?' The man unlocked his container doors and threw them open with a grand gesture. 'Let's get you good people unpacked!' He was mobbed by Finn and Charlie, and I could have snogged him myself. It was like having Father Christmas pull up in a big red lorry.

It took the three men hours to carry everything inside. I thought the piano was going to give them all hernias but they refused Kit's offer of help. The twins were thoroughly unhelpful, officiously guiding furniture into the wrong rooms. Everyone dived headfirst into boxes with whoops of recognition as toys and clothes and the coffee machine emerged. Sacha and Kit carried a sofa bed and her portable telly straight into the smoko hut; she cranked up the volume on her stereo, and the poor old walls pulsated to the jungle beat of Ke$ha and Katy Perry. I dare say the sheep wished they had earplugs.

Halfway through the morning I brought out coffee for the men. The twins had found their bikes and were pedalling around the walnut tree, though Charlie's stabilisers kept getting stuck in the ruts. It was then that I noticed Sacha balanced on a fence, deep in conversation with the junior member of the team, a man mountain called Ira. Ira's complexion was a deep bronze; I assumed he was Maori and was partly right, though I later discovered there were Scottish and Samoan ancestors too. A heavy cluster of dreadlocks hung down his back and he had a calm, lopsided smile. I reckoned he'd be in his mid-twenties, and he looked as though he spent all his spare time lifting weights. Complicated tattoos with interlocking patterns rippled all the way up those impressive biceps. Perhaps most arresting was his voice, a gentle bass with an accent I couldn't identify. It was Kiwi, but different. The overall effect was quite startlingly luscious. If I'd been twenty years old, I'm sure I would have behaved very badly indeed. I delivered his coffee and loitered nearby, feigning interest in the washing.

'There was a mountain lake,' he was telling Sacha in his peaceful rumble. 'Up here, in the hills. A bottomless lake with rippling green waters. And three taniwha made their home there.'

'Ah! Taniwha.' Sacha had been reading our guidebook. 'Demons. Dragons. They live in water.'

'They do.' Ira's delivery was quite stylised. He was clearly an accomplished storyteller, yet I felt he was repeating the tale almost verbatim. Oral tradition, I supposed, at its very best. 'Well, as they grew bigger the lake became too small for them. It made them grumpy. So these three taniwha fell to fighting. They fought and fought, and their tails lashed and cut great gashes in the hillsides. You can see the battleground all around . . .' He turned in a circle, holding out his arms. 'Eventually they broke right through the side of the lake. So the water drained away into the sea, creating the river, here . . . this river that runs through your land.'

'What happened to them?'

'Two of them stormed away down the river. They fell into the sea and swam off joyfully, free at last. But the third one was stranded. He was too weak to push himself through the narrow gap. He lifted his great head and cried out in sorrow, but he couldn't follow. His brothers left him behind.'

'Aw! Sad.'

'He's still there—look, that long ridge, running along the edge of the valley.' Ira pointed, and Sacha moved closer to gaze along his muscled arm. 'You can see the bones all along his back . . . those rocks.'

'I can?' She squinted into the white light. 'I can! It *does* look like an enormous lizard.'

'The others were overjoyed to find themselves in the sea, and made themselves new lairs.'

'And perhaps they're still out there.'

'They're still out there, all right. Sometimes they fight. When the sea's rough, that's them rampaging around.'

'And maybe they visit their old home.'

'They do. They cloak themselves in water and move up the river. And that's how this whole area got its name. *Torutaniwha*.'

'It sounds like a different word when you say it.' Sacha was right. The name sprang to life as it rolled off Ira's tongue. It wasn't imitable.

'Toru means three,' he explained. 'Three taniwha, see?'

I moved a little further away, because Sacha had spotted me and given the bugger-off-you-interfering-old-bat glare.

'How come you know the story?' she asked.

'Because I was brought up in Torutaniwha. That's why the company sent me on this job, so Frank and John wouldn't get lost finding your place.'

'And what about this farm?' Sacha clasped her hands around her knees. 'Patu—no, can't say it. What does the name mean?'

'Patupaiarehe?' Ira shuddered in dramatic horror. 'Weird creatures. Fairies of the mist.'

'Wings and wands?'

'Ooh, no! These fellas are eerie.'

'Do they look like people?'

'Strange, supernatural people, with pale skin and red hair. They lived—live—deep in the forest among the clouds. You know how clouds cling to the mountaintops? Well, they lived in there, but they came creeping down in the mist or the darkness. They stole things. Sometimes they slipped into people's houses and put a spell on them so they seemed to be dead. And their cousins the ponaturi—sea fairies—tore humans apart and ate their flesh.'

'So they're bad news, these patu . . . fairies?'

'I wouldn't want to meet one on a dark night. And it's on dark nights that they made themselves heard. A lonely traveller would hear the ghostly music of their putorino—wooden pipes—and the hair would stand up on the back of his neck. The putorino can wail, but in the hands of the patupaiarehe it sang like a flute. The music hypnotised the listener, bewitched them, made them follow. Many were never seen again.'

'Like the Pied Piper,' suggested Sacha.

Ira clapped his hands. 'Maybe he was one of them! The patupaiarehe were known for luring beautiful girls into their clutches. Even if she was allowed to go home, the girl would be under a spell forever. The abductor had only to call and she would return to him.'

Ira's boss yelled from the lorry. 'Oi, Ira! Telling stories again? Smoko's over. Give us a hand with this washing machine.'

Sacha dropped down from the fence, took Ira's mug and walked alongside him. 'So how come this place has the creepy name?'

'You've got me there.' The young man hopped athletically into the back of the container. 'I'll ask my nana, she knows all the stories. Anyway, d'you think you can come?'

I whirled around, my ears flapping like Dumbo on take-off.

'Sure.' Sacha handed him her mobile and he added his number to her contacts. It was a done deal. A date, presumably. She could do worse, I thought, if she was after a springtime flirtation. Quite an antidote to Ivan Gnome. This one was altogether more eye-catching, and he knew how to tell a good story. On the other hand, he was far too old for her.

It was early afternoon before the container was empty. Ira strolled over to speak to me as his workmates climbed into their cab.

'Hi, Mrs McNamara,' he began quietly.

'Martha.'

A heart-lifting smile. 'Martha. Thanks. Look, Martha, your kids told me they'd like to go riding.'

I glanced at Finn and Charlie, hanging by their knees from the tyre swings like a brace of drunken bats. 'I'm sure they would.'

'My uncle breeds horses, and he does trekking. He'll take them down the beach. If you want to go tomorrow, I can come along.'

'That sounds wonderful,' I said doubtfully, 'but I'm sure your uncle's busy?'

Embarrassment flickered across Ira's handsome features. 'First time out is for free.'

So *that* was Sacha's date. I was the victim of a plot, and I'd fallen for it like a prize mug. Sacha was probably the mastermind—she was nuts about horses—but they were all three in it and they'd co-opted Ira, too. It was the oldest trick in the book: get the parent to agree in principle before mentioning the price tag; and rope in a visitor to do the dirty work.

'Tomorrow?' screeched Finn, dropping to the ground.

'That's between you and your parents.' Ira winked at Finn before hopping into the cab.

'See yer tomorrow!' Finn grabbed his bike and pedalled recklessly alongside as the lorry lurched away down the hill, gears grinding.

'It was Ira,' said Sacha. 'Riding along the beach that first day, remember? His uncle's our neighbour, and his farm stretches all the way to the sea.'

I felt Charlie's gentle hand in mine, and picked him up. We stood waving until the great red box disappeared behind a green gauze of willows.

Our move was complete. We were alone with our possessions.

All was well in the world, that evening. The twins tore into their dressing-up box and emerged as Postman Pat and a dragon. They scattered Lego across the floor, watched by the creatures of the Serengeti.

Kit had spent a happy afternoon organising his studio. You could get into it from the sitting room or the verandah. Windows on three sides looked out to the garden, the bush and the sea—obscured now by candy-floss cloud. Kit gave it Persian rugs, his leather armchair and the imp-faced portraits. Finally, with some ceremony, he placed his most prized possession in the centre of the longest wall.

'Now Sibella's here,' he declared, standing back and saluting the young woman in the portrait, 'we're truly home.'

Great-Aunt Sibella gave the painting to Kit on his eighteenth birthday, and it had graced the wall of every house he'd lived in since. It wasn't worth anything financially; the young artist never became famous before he joined up and was killed in France. He was Kit's grandfather. I'm sure he revered his sister; I know Kit did.

I stood beside Kit now, meeting the eyes of the girl in the painting. She seemed to see me through space and time; supremely poised, raven hair swept up and pinned under a little hat, eyes the same passionate blue as Kit's. It wasn't an entirely benevolent face: there was a knowing, cynical quality in her gaze. It was easy to see whose ancestor she was. Both Kit and Finn were carved out of the same rock.

Sibella murdered her husband. No, she really did. This is accepted family lore. She fell in love and married when she was too young. The bridegroom—so the story goes—was a local landowner, a sadistic and perverted man who showed his true colours on their wedding night. Within a month she had clobbered him with a fence post, fatally cracking his skull, and passed it off as a riding accident. His stablehand backed up her account and the entire district rallied around her. The young widow inherited her husband's estate near Tralee and ran it for the next seventy years. She never married again, although she and the stablehand were inseparable until the man's death half a century later.

Kit poured us both a glass of Jean's wine, and we happily squashed together in his armchair while I recounted Ira's stories of water dragons and strange fairies. Finally, as dusk crept across the hills, Kit got up and began to play with tints of lime and bronze. I left him to it, removing the bottle as I went. Better safe than sorry.

It was fully dark when Sacha opened the piano in the sitting room and tinkled a few notes. 'Out of tune,' she remarked, as Kit walked in from the studio.

'It's been in the tropics, all humid and salty, tossed in storms around Good Hope, frozen among the killer whales in the Southern Ocean.' Kit lifted the instrument's lid and peered in. 'I think you'd be a bit out of tune after all that. I know I would.'

I glanced at Sacha. She wasn't out of tune, really. She was going to a bonfire party next weekend, and she'd befriended a tattooed young hero who could ride like Genghis Khan. What more could I ask?

'Look,' said Kit. 'Some of the ivories have come loose. I'll have to stick them down.'

I watched—afraid to move, afraid to speak—as Sacha flicked open a black case, took her flute from its velvet bed and casually assembled it. Lounging over the piano, Kit caught my eye but remained studiously expressionless. I felt like a wildlife photographer, pretending not to focus on a grazing gazelle. I hadn't heard Sacha play since she left her old school. Not a note.

She rubbed her nose on her forearm, lifted the instrument to her lips and flung a silvery arpeggio around the room. The music was a bird, released from its cage and overjoyed to be free. Celebratory fireworks flared in my brain.

She broke off abruptly, grimacing; twisted the two halves of her flute, then tried again. A scale. A flurry of octaves. A snatch of Handel. Kit grabbed some sheet music from the piano stool and began to accompany her. He played a few wrong notes, and some of the keys sounded decidedly honky-tonk, but it was the most gloriously welcome sound I'd ever heard.

They were laughing. Sacha was throwing insults at Kit in between phrases and he was hamming up his incompetence, bending low over the keys with a lolling tongue like the village idiot.

I began to pile books onto shelves, feeling an absurd bubble of happiness. Sacha was playing her flute once more. Kit was painting. From the bathroom upstairs I could hear the twins, sloshing. They were probably flooding the place, but who cared? They were barefoot wildmen, Stigs of the Dump. It had all been worth it.

What is it about the early hours? I ended the day happy, but three o'clock found me fretting about my future, my family, my smugly slumbering husband. It was that time of night when the world is at its darkest. My mind seemed to be beating its wings against a dusty window in a room that smelled of hot plastic. At first I obsessed about Sacha's real father, and how I'd cheated them both. Then I thought about Dad and Lou and how I missed them. The more successful our emigration, the more certain it seemed that we wouldn't be going home. Suddenly, I ached for home. Homesickness is a rat that eats you from the inside. It has sharp teeth.

I had to be out of that room. I was suffocating. Easing my feet into slippers, I felt my way to the French doors and onto the balcony.

It was deathly quiet outside. The air felt damp and still, but at least I could breathe. I stood with my hands on the dry solidity of the wooden railing, and immediately my attention was caught by a bizarre sight. Just past the garden, where last night had been pasture and sheep, I could see the opaque gleam of a deep and unruffled lake. This large body of water filled the valley, ghostly white. Fascinated, I leaned over the rail, straining my eyes into the dark and thinking of the restless taniwha who cloaked themselves in water.

A silent whisper of wind stirred the surface of the lake, and tendrils of it broke away and began to creep up the side of the valley towards me. I watched with a sense of complete unreality until it dawned on me that the lake was not made of water at all, but mist. I leaned my arms on the rail, feeling wisps of cloud drift over and around me. It seemed to cling, to caress my face with clammy fingers. I stood dozing in a dream world of isolation and profound silence.

That was when I heard the sound. I imagine it was the first stirring of some bird deep in the trees, herald of the dawn chorus. A bellbird, or a tui. It was a hypnotically lovely melody, liquid and piercing. Just five notes. Five notes of almost supernatural clarity. After a hush, it came again.

It sounded exactly like a flute.

Thirteen

At last, they take me to Finn. But they're playing a cruel trick because this isn't him—not my beautiful, wilful son. Who is this disfigured doll, his face a death mask? They've shaved his shock of dark hair right off. His scalp looks obscene, plucked, and there's a dressing taped across it. His right arm is in plaster. A web of tubes and wires assaults his body, invades his mouth and nose, and there are monitors on his chest. Worst of all, his eyes are so swollen and bruised that I can't imagine them opening ever again. Finn looks scarcely human. He looks scarcely alive.

I hear someone sob, feel myself stagger. A youngish man—a nurse, I think—steers me gently into a chair. The cubicle is like the bridge of a spaceship, humming and flashing and beeping with technology.

'What's happened to his eyes?' I ask, horrified.

'It's the cranial bleeding,' says the nurse. 'People call it raccoon eyes. It's perfectly normal in head injuries, but I'm afraid it may get worse before it gets better.'

I touch the waxwork face. 'Can he hear me?'

'He quite possibly can, at some level.' The nurse is checking a drip. 'So talk to him, sing to him, whatever you want.'

I hold a limp hand. I feel self-conscious at first, but I begin to talk. I talk nonsense. I tell Finn about the exciting helicopter ride, and how

I'm here beside him, and how it's breakfast time and Charlie will be up, and how his dad's coming soon.

His dad. I tap out yet another text: *Kit please call me urgent!!!* Then I press *send* and imagine it flying through the ether, shaped like a little envelope, to land in Kit's phone. Wherever it is. Wherever *he* is.

In desperation I call my father's number in Bedford, cursing at the sound of his recorded message. I leave one for him: *Dad, it's Martha here. Um . . . please ring me on my mobile.* I read out the number. *We're in, um, a bit of trouble.*

Then I sit and watch Finn's breathing. In my state of panic and exhaustion, I honestly believe I can keep him alive as long as I count his every breath. In, out. Every breath is priceless. A watched kettle never boils. A watched child never dies.

In.

Out.

The sky is a black bowl, spangled with stars. My feet are pounding on the boards. And Finn plunges headlong, tiny hands clutching at nothing.

'Mrs McNamara?'

I jerk upright, eyes snapping open. A figure looms beside my chair, her face a respectful distance from mine. Not young; a stately grandmother with tea-coloured skin. Strong silver brows and white hair, real white old-lady hair, brushed from her forehead and caught into a high ponytail that cascades to her shoulder blades. A plastic ID hangs from a lanyard around her neck.

'I'm sorry,' she says. 'I woke you.'

'Just dozing.'

I'm rubbing the stupor from my face as she holds out a creased hand. 'I'm Kura Pohatu, the paediatric social worker.'

My insides jolt. 'Social worker?'

'They tell me Finn's doing pretty well.'

We both look at him. 'I don't know,' I say faintly. 'If he's doing well, why is he hooked up to ten machines?' I lean across to nuzzle Buccaneer Bob a little closer to Finn's cheek.

'A favourite toy?' asks Kura.

'Since the day he was born.' I almost smile at the memory. The twins were eight hours old, and Great-Aunt Sibella's arrival in the maternity ward seemed like a state visit from the Queen. She was ninety or so by then, swathed in a grey velvet coat and cameo earrings. She evoked adoration in Kit but a fair sprinkling of terror in everyone else, with her piercing eyes and merciless tongue. The nurses practically curtseyed. I sat on the edge of my bed trying not to look bloodstained and clutching a sapphire pendant Kit had given me.

Sibella halted by the babies' cribs, fishing in a Harrods bag. 'Be a pirate, nephew,' she ordered, dropping Buccaneer Bob on top of Finn, who was myopically blowing bubbles. '*Not* an accountant.' She'd brought Charlie a very snazzy remote-controlled car. He was asleep, and didn't stir when the toy landed right beside his bald head. 'Bit young, yet. But Kit will enjoy it. He's always liked fast cars. Fast women, too.'

I laughed, and she peered at me. 'How's my nephew coping with a double dose of fatherhood?'

'Kit? He's euphoric!'

'You need to watch him.'

I was bemused. 'Why, Sibella? Look at this beautiful thing. He gave it to me this morning, just to say thank you for his sons.' I held the pendant around my neck, and she moved behind me to do up the clasp.

'Moods,' she said dourly. 'He has a temper on him.'

'Oh, I can handle those. I've known him five years now. I've seen it all.'

'Black dog. When *that* visitor is with him, he's beyond help. Beyond help. You just have to wait it out.' She lifted my curls to free them from the gold chain. 'It takes one to know one, you see.'

Three weeks later, Sibella died in her sleep. I think she knew it was coming, and it wasn't long before I understood what it was she'd been trying to tell me. Her death triggered a terrifying darkness in Kit, like nothing I had ever seen. He tried to stave it off, poor man, but it was inexorable. He told me he'd been there before: after his father died, and again when his first marriage failed. He refused to see a doctor, said he'd been down that road, never again; nothing helped. When life became unbearable he tried to escape by drinking himself into insensibility. For six months, depression stole the joy from our family. Then, for no apparent reason, it began to lift. Kit's illness became a memory, a 'bad patch', something we rarely mentioned and hoped never to experience again.

I can see Kit stumbling, falling over the baby gym, and in the sleepless night pacing around Finn's cot as the baby wails with colic. Finn has been wailing for hours, and we're all at the end of our tether. Kit shouts. His fists smash against the bars. The baby screams still louder as I run to him.

Someone's touching my shoulder. It isn't Kit. I struggle to understand where I am, ebbing and flowing in waves of dream. Sorry, I say. Sorry. So tired.

Kura is watching me closely. 'Have you eaten today?'

'Not since . . . dunno when.' Not since I shared fish fingers and peas with the boys, and Finn used his fork as a trebuchet and I snapped at him, and his face fell. Oh, how I long to turn back the clock. I would let him flick all the peas on his plate. I'd give him the whole packet and draw him a target.

'I'd like us to talk,' says the social worker, 'and work out how best I can help.'

'I can't leave him.'

Her smile is too wide. 'The staff will page me in a flash if there's any change.'

'I could murder a . . .' I stop, think, and then guiltily ditch the metaphor. 'I'd love a strong cup of coffee.'

The hospital is shadowy. We pass an incredibly old man who touches the wall with trembling fingers as he navigates a mile of lino. He might have been inching down that corridor for weeks. We pass orderlies wheeling trolleys whose occupants look dead already. We pass the gift shop, skirting around its display of heart-shaped helium balloons on sticks.

The café isn't busy. We buy our coffee, and Kura insists that I eat a sandwich as well because my little boy doesn't need me fainting from hunger. She has natural authority. I picture her as Maori royalty, a queen in a cloak of feathers. She chooses a table to one side, far from eavesdroppers, and parks me closest to the wall. Perhaps she wants to block my escape.

'What we talk about here is in confidence,' she says. 'It's just between you and me, unless someone's safety is at risk. Do you understand that?'

Yes, I think. *I understand all too well.*

'Is there anything you need at this stage? Start with practicalities.'

'A toothbrush,' I tell her. 'I've just spent my last cent—you don't think to grab your handbag. Luckily my phone was in my pocket.'

'Okay . . .' I can see she's making a mental note. 'No problem. Now, who's at home at the moment?'

'My other children. Sacha and Charlie, seventeen and five.'

'Quite an age gap.'

'Sacha's my daughter from an earlier relationship.' I have no intention of discussing Sacha's paternity with a stranger.

'Do you need me to arrange care for them?'

'No. Sacha's very capable, but she's in bed with this winter bug that's going around. So my neighbour's looking after Charlie.'

'Who's the neighbour?'

'Just a neighbour.'

Bloody woman's like a terrier. 'I might know her. I've worked in Hawke's Bay for thirty years.'

I sigh. '*His* name is Tama Pardoe. The children know him well. And thank God, he answered his phone last night.'

She looks at me, assessing the information. 'So this neighbour, Mr Pardoe, came around after the accident?'

'Yes,' I agree firmly. '*After*. I called him once the helicopter was on its way.'

'What about Finn's father?'

'Kit's been in Dublin. He's an artist, and he's just had his first exhibition.'

'He must be rushing back?'

Fearful tears burn my eyes. 'That's the awful thing. He doesn't know yet . . . I'm still trying to get hold of him.' I don't want questions about when Kit's due to land, what flight he's on, so I deflect them. 'Oh! Those finger bruises. I've solved the mystery. Finn slipped in the bath last night. I grabbed his arm to try to stop him.' I reach out my hand, snatching at an imaginary child. 'He bruises very easily.'

The social worker looks non-committal. She's storing the explanation away, ready to write up her notes. No doubt she will talk to Sutherland and the giraffe, and ask if my story holds water. 'How long have you lived in New Zealand, Martha?'

'A year. We've got a lifestyle block out at Torutaniwha.'

The silver brows rise a fraction. 'Oh! Way out there? Unusual, for an English family.'

'It's beautiful.' I tell her about the little school, and the beach, and the river. She listens carefully, laughing when I describe Bleater Brown, our pet lamb. And even though I know she's merely doing her job, establishing rapport, I find myself giving her my life history. Well, some of it. The concise and abridged version.

'It sounds as though you haven't looked back,' she says.

'Not too much.'

'Got any family here?'

I shrug regretfully. 'Just the five of us. I'm very close to my sister and father in England, so we talk a lot on the phone.'

'You must miss them.'

'I do. Of course I do. It's been a massive upheaval.' Suddenly, I'm tired of this game. 'And yes, we're very homesick sometimes. Yes, we're isolated. And yes, sometimes it's bloody hard. But no, you're wrong if you think I harmed my own child.'

She watches me without comment.

'I'm sorry,' I say, rubbing my forehead. 'I'm very, very tired.'

'Could you take me through what happened on the balcony?'

'Um, do I have to? It's so . . . awful.' My hands shake at the memory, and coffee slops onto the table. I'm like the old man in the corridor, trembling. I imprison my hands between my knees.

Go on, go on! begs Mum. *Here's a nice, kind, sympathetic person.*

'Okay,' I whisper, and swallow. 'The balcony's very long, you see. It runs the whole length of the house. All the bedrooms on that side open onto it. Kit and I are at one end, then the twins, then Sacha. We've an old sofa out there, beside our bedroom door. Last night I couldn't sleep, so I went and sat out there. I was looking at the stars.'

For pity's sake, Martha! Throw yourself at her mercy.

Kura fishes in her handbag and hands me a tissue. 'Why couldn't you sleep?'

'I'm a bit of a night owl. I was enjoying the peace. I heard a door open and Finn came pottering out from his bedroom. I wasn't surprised because he often sleepwalks. I once found him curled up in the dog's bed. Muffin was most disgruntled.'

Kura smiles. 'So Finn came out . . .?'

'He walked down to the far end where there's a rail at right angles to the long one. It was so dark, I could hardly see him at all. I stood up. I was planning on taking him back to bed, but I wasn't rushing. It doesn't do to make sudden movements, you know? The next moment I realised he'd climbed onto the rail, right at the other end—maybe thirty, forty feet away from me. It all happened so quickly. I ran, I ran and I screamed at him. Then he was falling . . . oh my God, he was falling, he was falling, and I heard him hit the ground.'

I feel the thud. It knocks the breath out of me.

Kura waits as I curl in on myself. She doesn't try to touch me, doesn't invade my grieving with her own need to console. She gives me time before she speaks again. 'How high is the handrail?'

'Oh, I don't . . .' I hold up a hand. 'Waist height to an adult, even a bit less than that. It's old. I think they're made higher nowadays.'

'So Finn's about the same height?'

'Um. Bit taller, maybe.'

'And it's made of what? Metal?'

'No, no. It's all the original wood. Turned posts. Finn climbs anything, just like a monkey. He knows not to play on the balcony rail normally, of course he does, he's not *stupid*. He wasn't awake. Poor little guy . . . I should have locked his door.'

Kura has horizontal lines on her face, like a child's portrait of an old person. 'Martha.' She leans closer, searching my eyes. 'Are you safe?'

'Am I . . .? Of course I'm safe. It's Finn whose life is in danger.'

'I think you know what I mean. Are you safe at home?'

I stare her down, my mouth pressed into the tissue. 'You're barking up the wrong tree. There's no villain. This was an accident.'

'I'm here to walk alongside you.' Her hand rests briefly on my upper arm. 'I'm here to help you to help yourself. If you need to get your other children out of that home, I can help. Tell me: what do you need to go forward from here?'

'I need . . .'

Help! Mum's actually shrieking. It's out of character. *You need help!*

'I don't know how I got here,' I whisper. 'I don't know what I'm doing here. I need to wake up now, please.'

Later, I sit in the chair and watch Finn breathing. He's so tiny, in that adult bed. Kura has found me a toothbrush. She's also given me her phone number.

She wants to help. I wish she could help.

Fourteen

Following Ira's instructions, I drove halfway to Jane's café before turning off towards the sea. We bumped our way down a rutted track until we reached a set of sandy yards where horses milled around.

The three children and I climbed out, dazzled in the strong sunlight. There were two men working among the animals, wearing broad-brimmed hats and dusty leather boots under their jeans. You could have filmed a western, then and there. I tried to look confident, but I wasn't. Even the twins were subdued. This wasn't our world at all. I wished I'd taken Kit up on his offer to come with us, but those blank canvases were calling him, I could tell.

One of the men looked up. It took me a moment to recognise Ira under the leather hat, though those waist-length dreadlocks should have been a giveaway.

'Dudes!' he cried delightedly, vaulting the fence. 'Great to see you. Hi, Sacha. Hey, this is my Uncle Tama.' He gestured back at his companion, who lifted a hand. I saw the hawkish nose and walnut-tanned skin of the shepherd in the rain. 'Come and meet a little fella,' said Ira, beckoning the children away. 'Just a week old.'

I was left to sit on the fence, watching Tama Pardoe's tall, spare figure. Thinking he hadn't noticed me there, I was trying to guess his age. The charcoal hair curling around his neck was liberally streaked with silver, but his movements were those of a young man. Flies settled on the horses' ears and swarmed into their eyes, making them throw up their heads. A scuffle broke out with a squeal and a kick, but he calmly ignored it. Horses followed him almost like dogs, nuzzling against his back.

He was lifting a hefty saddle from the fence when I heard his voice for the first time. He didn't look at me. 'You coming?'

'Me? No!' I realised I'd injected a girlish giggle into the word, and cursed myself. 'Definitely not.'

'Any reason?'

'Well, because . . .' I was caught off-guard. 'This isn't for me, it's for the children.' I watched as he placed the saddle on a horse's back and reached underneath for the girth. 'It's their turn to have adventures like this. I've *had* my turn. I'm just the mother.'

He smiled quietly to himself, and deep furrows appeared around his mouth.

'My job is to sit on the fence and wave,' I said. 'My job is to take the photos. And I'm a bit, er . . .'

He straightened. 'A bit?'

I heard myself burbling. 'I had riding lessons when I was small. I loved horses—typical little girl—but I could never get past my fear. When I was fourteen, a horrible bully of a horse pretended it was terrified of a windsock and bolted. I screamed blue murder and my teacher yelled, "Show him who's bo-o-ss!" Then the horse slipped in the mud and we both went down.'

Tama nodded unemotionally. 'Happens.'

'I broke my leg in three places.'

He looked across at my leg, and I stretched it out to show him. 'Here, here and here. I spent six weeks in traction. Never enjoyed riding again.'

'C'mon, Ruru,' he murmured, tapping the leg of a magnificent piebald creature.

'I've seen this horse before,' I confessed. 'And you. In the rain.'

'I know.' The great horse lifted a heavy foot and Tama cradled it against his knees, examining the underside. Ruru stood quietly, swishing his tail at the flies.

'No shoe,' I noticed.

'No shoes on any of 'em.' Tama grasped another colossal saddle and swung it effortlessly from the fence. 'These horses aren't like anything you've ever ridden before.'

I looked sceptical.

'They don't bolt,' he said.

'They would if I was on 'em.'

'No. They wouldn't. They're working horses. Now, Martha McNamara—just the mother—would you like to hop down here and give me a hand, or are you going to sit up on that fence like a fantail, and chitter away while I do all the work?'

By the time Ira reappeared with the children, each self-consciously wearing a riding hat, I was doing my best to groom a honey-coloured mare called Kakama. Her foal, a leggy miniature of his mother, bounced around nearby.

'Kakama's for you to ride one day,' Tama had said, as he handed me the brush. 'So you'd better make friends.' Then he'd smiled his private smile, and left me alone.

Sacha stood beside me now, watching him lead two horses, a hand lightly resting on each. Dust danced around his boots. I felt her elbow jab my ribs. 'Eye candy, isn't he? As old guys go.'

'Sacha!' I felt myself blush, possibly because I agreed with her.

She patted my arm. 'I know, I know. You love Kit. But it's not a sin to do a little window shopping, is it?'

'Get away with you,' I said, smiling. 'Go on, go riding.'

One by one, Ira and Tama gave their pupils leg-ups. After a little girth-tightening and stirrup-adjusting the five began to wind their way out of the yard. Finn and Sacha looked elated; poor Charlie was terrified, clinging to the saddle and doing a fair imitation of a sack of potatoes.

'This probably isn't the kind of riding you're used to,' grunted Tama, flinging himself carelessly onto Ruru's back. He held the reins in one hand, and his stirrups were long. I noticed that Ira didn't even bother with a saddle. 'There's no bit in their mouths. How would you like to run around with a piece of metal on your tongue?'

'This saddle's like an armchair!' Sacha rocked back and forth.

Tama showed his little posse how to turn. 'These guys *want* to work with you. So you don't yank at the reins. You don't lean forward, you sit back.' He glanced at Charlie. 'That's it, my friend. Perfect.' Instantly Charlie's chin lifted and his back straightened.

I climbed onto the fence with my video camera, thinking of the film I'd send to Dad: Finn's ebony hair, blue sky, streaks of cirrus, two men who looked as though they'd been born on horseback. A flashing diamond of a sun, and dust in clouds around twenty hooves.

When the riders strolled away between the dunes, I resisted the temptation to follow on foot. I'd brought some work to do for the Maori culture paper, so I fetched it from the car and sat under a tree. The rest of the herd began grazing nearby. I could hear their strong teeth as they tore at the grass. I felt almost marinated in peace.

I think I'd dozed off when Finn's shrill chirrup heralded the return of the adventurers. He was telling Tama and Ira all about Muffin and how she had flown on a plane. They rode up bright-eyed, buzzing and wet.

'We swam in the sea,' piped Charlie. 'Our horses really swam! The waves came right over us. And Sacha and Ira galloped!'

The best sight of all was Sacha. Her cheeks were flushed, her tawny eyes glittering as she slid to the ground and kissed her horse's neck.

'How was it?' I asked, and she laughed breathlessly.

'That was the best hour of my life.'

I cornered Tama in the yard. 'They'll be back,' I said. 'Thank you.'

The following Friday morning Sacha lugged a backpack downstairs, clutching her flute in its case.

'Can you give me a lift to the bus?' she puffed. 'I'm late, and the driver's a complete jerk—won't wait ten seconds.'

'Sure.' I eyed the backpack. 'Got everything you need for the fireworks party?' I was about to ask for Bianka's address and telephone number when I checked myself. Sacha was sixteen, and she had her mobile.

Kit fished in his wallet. 'For a taxi,' he said, handing her two twenty-dollar notes. 'Just in case. If you don't feel right for any reason and you want to get out, you can always call a cab.'

'I won't need this,' she protested, trying to give the money back.

'Keep it for emergencies,' said Kit. 'And remember: you can call us any time of day or night. If you don't feel safe, we'll come and get you. We'll moan and complain like buggery but we'll come and get you.'

Dimpling, she kissed her stepfather's cheek. 'You're a big leprechaun softie.'

'And you play your parents like you play that flute,' retorted Kit. 'With scary skill. Be good.'

Sacha drove as far as the road. She had to slide the seat way back and shot down the track, spinning the wheel one-handed before slewing to a halt by the letterbox.

'We start study leave next week, because of the exams,' she said. 'This is turning out to be a pretty cruisy term for me. We get loads of time off.'

I tweaked her ear. 'You're still wearing Ivan's locket.'

'Whatever happens, he cares about me. As long as I'm wearing this I've got a friend with me.'

'How's orchestra?'

'Good. Oh—I've got a form for you to sign. I'm taking the performance diploma next year. My new flute teacher's inspiring! She's played all over the world.'

'Wonderful. You're lucky.'

The bus hove into view, and Sacha scrambled out. 'So you'll meet me tomorrow, eleven o'clock, by the cathedral fountain?'

'Sure will. Have fun.'

She blew me a kiss as she ran, ringlets streaming in a westerly wind. I watched her hop aboard the bus and disappear into its gloomy interior. Grinning faces were pressed mockingly to the rear window, smeared against the glass like Halloween masks. Why do the troublemakers always sit at the back of a school bus? It was the same when I was at school. I know, because I was one of them. We used to lob things at passing bicycles.

An apple core rocketed out, curving in an elegant parabola before exploding onto the bonnet of my car. It was followed by a yoghurt pot.

'Clean, green New Zealand,' I sighed, selecting reverse gear. 'One hundred per cent pure.'

*

Kit threw the balcony doors open early the next morning. It was still dark outside, though I could see a fiery gleam on the rim of the sea.

'What on *earth* are you doing?' I whispered.

'Sorry.' He padded closer, kneeling on the floor to kiss me. I felt his unshaven cheek. 'I didn't mean to wake you up.'

I grabbed him by the ears, trying to haul him back into bed. 'Get in, you silly man,' I ordered. 'It's freezing out there!'

I saw his smile, white in the half-dark. 'My plan is to get up at this time every day for a fortnight,' he said. 'That view from our balcony is astonishing. Have you ever wondered how it is that nature always whips the pants off anything man-made, in terms of sheer beauty? I'm going to paint it every morning, bang on sunrise. Hopefully I'll end up with fourteen very different studies.'

'Bloody Nora! Why the hell would you do that?'

'It's an exercise. I need to understand the way the light works.'

'That's it.' I pulled the duvet over my nose. 'You've gone bonkers. I knew this would happen.'

He looked hopeful. 'Um, d'you want some tea? It's going to be a lovely day.'

The rising sun glowed on Kit, humming to himself as his gaze shifted from horizon to canvas. It also found me, curled on the shabby sofa under a duvet, sipping tea and feeling supremely content.

At eleven o'clock, I spotted two girls sitting on a bench beside the cathedral fountain. They were facing one another, deep in animated conversation. When I tapped Sacha's shoulder, she jumped up.

'Hi, Mum! This is Bianka.'

Her companion might have walked straight off the set of a 1930s Hollywood extravaganza, with dark blonde waves in her hair and elegantly arched eyebrows. She got to her feet, smiling with sad, cupid's-bow lips. I noticed blackberry-coloured lipstick.

'We all love Sacha.' It was a low voice, oddly adult. 'Thank you for bringing her to us.'

Sacha nudged her in happy embarrassment. I was asking about the party when a woman approached from across the road; a redhead, wearing a rather chic linen sundress and straw hat.

'Hello!' she called, as she came closer. 'You'll be Martha? I'm Anita Varga.'

I took the proffered hand. Anita's arm was pale and freckled. She was probably in her forties, as tall and fragile as a champagne flute. Creases radiated from the outer corners of her eyes.

'Thank you for having Sacha to stay,' I murmured, as though my daughter was three years old.

'I hope we'll see lots more of her. The girls have had a ball—sorry, I'm afraid they didn't get much sleep.'

We chatted for several minutes. Pleasantries. Anita's hair had a nylon sheen, and I forbade myself to stare. In the end she mentioned that she was about to begin more chemotherapy.

'You're doing well,' I said, and meant it.

'I *am* well. Today.' Her smile never faltered. 'I'm still here. Which of us can ask for more?'

'Amazing woman,' I marvelled, as Sacha and I wandered along Napier's side streets.

'She totally crashed last night. Didn't even get to the party.'

'Oh, dear . . . How was it, then?'

'Awesome.'

Awesome? That sounded markedly antipodean. We found a pavement café where families of fat little sparrows hopped on and off the tables, stealing crumbs. I was desperate for espresso, Sacha chose a milkshake and carrot cake, and we sat under tall palms in the sunshine. A young busker was playing his recorder nearby, and Sacha gave him a dollar. She was wearing a silk scarf around her head, with the rich coffee and gold patterning of a giraffe. It echoed her warm colouring.

'C'mon,' I prompted. 'Tell me about last night.'

'Just awesome. Bianka's cousins have a farm by the Tukituki River. They'd made an *epic* bonfire! There were lanterns in the trees, and a whole pig on a spit. We danced all night, had leftover pork for breakfast. Never bothered going to bed.'

'You must be shattered.'

'Nah! I feel great.'

The youngest, fluffiest sparrow in the flock hopped onto her plate and made off with a crumb of carrot cake.

I rapped the table. 'Tell me more! Give me the low-down. Did you meet anyone new?'

'Loads of people.'

'Like who?'

'Mum, you could get a job with the Spanish Inquisition. What you're really asking is, were there any hot guys?'

'Hot . . .?' I let my jaw drop in innocent indignation. 'That's not what I meant at all.'

'Yes it was. And yes, there were actually. In fact, Bianka's brother is a total sizzler. *Whew!*' She fanned herself with a hand.

'What's he called?'

'Jani. He's a student down at Massey University, been coming up at weekends because of Anita being ill. Hang on, 'scuse me.'

A bizarre hum was sounding from the pocket of her jeans. She pulled the vibrating phone out of her pocket, scanned it, and smirked while pressing buttons at manic speed.

'Bianka? Tabby?' I asked, surreptitiously squinting at the screen.

'Nunya.'

'Nunya who?'

'None of yer business.'

She was still chirping like a budgerigar at the start of our drive—I couldn't get a word in edgeways—but a night's dancing took its toll and she suddenly fell asleep, her batteries flat. She opened bleary eyes once we'd pulled up.

Kit had taken the boys grass sledging that morning, but as soon as I returned he dashed off to his studio, rubbing his hands. I began to unpack the shopping, feeling sorry for myself. Sacha was slumped groggily across the kitchen table; Finn pinched Blue Blanket, which made Charlie caterwaul. I'd have loved to moan about parenthood with Lou, but she wouldn't appreciate a call at three in the morning.

I was at my lowest ebb when Ira rumbled up the drive on a motorbike. His uncle Tama had killed a sheep, he said, and sent over a roast for us. I felt my spirits lift at the sight of his easygoing smile, though Finn and Charlie immediately dragged their hero off for a game of soccer on the front lawn. Sacha draped herself down the verandah steps, looking about as energetic as a wet dishcloth, so Ira appointed her referee. Once the twins had scored three goals in a row I offered him a beer. He accepted gratefully, throwing himself into the swing seat with grass stains on his jeans and mud on one cheek.

'English lads,' he gasped. 'You'll be strikers for the All Whites, both of you.'

The boys grabbed a leg each and tried to haul him onto the floor, but they couldn't shift his massive frame a single inch. He gamely let them manhandle him for a few minutes, then leaned forward and held them both by their noses.

'Give me ten minutes to chat,' he suggested. 'We'll have another game before I go, eh?'

Once the boys had set off for their sandpit, I handed Ira his beer. 'So you're born and bred here in Torutaniwha?'

'Born, anyway.' He took a swig. 'My mum left Hawke's Bay when I was a kid. Took my brother and me up to Auckland. I've just come back.'

'Oh.' I had a feeling this might be a sore subject. 'So you went to the primary school down on the beach?'

'Yep. Until I was twelve. Then she took me away. But I've been coming down in the summer holidays to help Uncle Tama when the trekking gets busy.'

'And now you're back permanently?'

'Hope so. This is home for me. Mum's grandfather, old Duncan Pardoe, emigrated here from Scotland in 1910. Then he fought in the First World War and was helped to buy the land . . . there was this government scheme to resettle returned servicemen. Glengarry's a thousand-acre block, about four hundred hectares.'

'That's a big farm, isn't it?'

'Hmm . . . not really. Sounds like a lot, but it wasn't productive back then. There's some pretty steep hills and gullies and it was all covered in scrub. The Pardoe block was originally part of Patupaiarehe Station, but a lot of that got taken off the absentee landlords and broken up. My great-grandfather cleared Glengarry single-handedly. Took him the rest of his life.'

'So Tama is farming land that was cleared by his grandfather?'

'Yep, that's right.'

'Hey.' Sacha stirred. 'Did you find out about those fairies?'

'Fairies? . . . Oh, yes! I asked my nana.' Ira grinned. 'She's eighty-five, used to ride a horse to school when she was small. She told me the whole story. Ooh, yes. It seems the patupaiarehe were up to their tricks around here!'

Sacha perked up. 'Go on, then.'

'Well.' The young man leaned forward and slipped into storytelling mode; big hands up, speaking in his formal, florid way. It was mesmerising. 'There was an ancient pa near here—a fortified village. The forest came right down to the edge of it. A beautiful young woman lived there. Her name was Hinemoana, and she became the wife of a powerful man. They were very happy. One evening when the mist was swirling in the valley, Hinemoana went out to fetch water from the river. At the same time a group of patupaiarehe crept down from the hills to hunt for eels in the pools. Well, she didn't see them, but as she turned away from the river a gust of wind parted the mist. The moonlight shone full on her face, and they saw *her* all right. She was so young and lovely that one of their hunters decided he would have her for his own.'

'Typical man,' I muttered.

'The next night he snuck down and waited for her to come. When she stooped to fill her calabash, he played his putorino. My nana told me the music made the darkness tremble with its beauty. She said it was like clear water, and it cast a terrible spell. Hinemoana dropped her calabash, and her steps took her towards the sound. The patupaiarehe lured her deeper and deeper into the forest until he took hold of her. Then he carried her through the dripping leaves of the trees to his whare—his hut—wreathed in cloud on the mountain summit. My nana didn't go into the details of what happened there, but all night long Hinemoana lay shaking with fear while the eerie songs of his people drifted through the doorway. At dawn, the patupaiarehe returned her to her own village. When her husband asked where she had been, she told him the whole truth. He held her in his arms, and they wept together.'

'Nice of him,' remarked Sacha, looking dubious. 'Trusting.'

'They tried to be happy and forget, but Hinemoana was still under that spell. Every time the patupaiarehe played his putorino, she *had* to answer the call. This happened again, and again, until the girl found she was pregnant. She knew that this child was that of the nanakia—the cunning one—and she knew then that she would never be free. So she fell into despair. One night she looked out and saw that the mist was crawling along the ground, and she feared that soon she would hear the call of the putorino. So, while her husband slept, she made her way down to the sea. Some fishermen saw a young woman weeping bitterly in the starlight. As they watched, she walked into the water with her black hair flowing to her waist. Then she submerged herself and was never seen again.

'You know that long hill at the southern end of the beach—just a little way down from the school?'

'Yes, I know the one,' I said. 'It's got cliffs with hundreds of birds nesting in them.'

'Well, have a look next time. If you use your imagination, it looks like a woman lying on her side. You can see the shape of her body, and her face. The rocks are long hair, swirling into the sea. That's Hinemoana's hill. I knew the name, but I'd forgotten the story.'

After a brief silence, Sacha sniffed. 'I wonder if she fancied the fairy guy. You know, just a little bit.'

Ira burst into laughter. 'Only a woman could think of that! Well, perhaps she did. Anyway, I guess those European settlers heard the same story, and that's the name they gave their station.'

I was still pondering on his tale when the twins reappeared, bouncing their soccer ball. Finn yanked at Ira's arm. 'Time's up,' he announced, in a robot voice. 'You have five seconds to take your place. Five, four, um . . . three . . .'

'Playing, Sacha?' asked Charlie hopefully, laying adoring fingers on his sister's forearm.

Sacha hauled herself up. 'Nah. It's freezing. I'm going in. Sorry to be unsociable, Ira. I've been partying all night.'

'No stamina,' chuckled our visitor, with a good-natured click of the tongue. 'Right, bros. Who's in goal?'

By suppertime Sacha was monosyllabic, her cheek propped on one hand and her elbow on the table, listlessly prodding Tama's roast around her plate. The boys were squabbling merrily but she ignored them as though they were unsavoury strangers at the next table in a restaurant.

Elbows off the table, hissed Mum. *Manners maketh man.*

'Elbows off the table,' I parroted. Sacha regarded me expressionlessly, then slid her arm off the table and plonked her forehead down beside her plate.

'Sacha,' I warned. 'Manners maketh man.'

'Yeah!' Finn began to chant in a piercing soprano while drawing a face on his plate with tomato ketchup. 'Manners—maketh—man!'

'Oh, God,' moaned Sacha. 'Get a life.'

'I think *you'd* better get some sleep,' said Kit. 'And don't talk to your mum like that. She doesn't deserve it.'

I laid my hand on her cheek. 'Feeling ill? Have you got a fever?'

'No. I'm just totally shagged. Goodnight.' And without further discussion, she stumbled out of the room and up the stairs.

'Teenagers,' said Kit, contentedly shovelling her untouched meal onto his own plate. 'They're not right in the head.'

Fifteen

Kit was a man possessed, captivated by the shifting colours and moods of the land. He spent much of November tramping through the bush and along the coast. He visited farms and vineyards and saleyards then rushed to capture their blend of harshness and romance on canvas. Even when he went to watch the children riding he came home with pages of vibrant sketches. Once—and I'm not proud of this—I caught myself wondering whether I didn't prefer the drunk, glowering, depressed Kit to this sober workaholic. That other man needed me desperately. I wasn't sure the new one did.

'Why bother with all this reconnoitring?' I asked one evening, as we were washing up. 'You can see, right? You can paint what you see. Right? Well. Voilà!'

Kit tutted affably at my superficiality. He'd spent the day in a shearing shed and reeked of farmyard. 'It's the spirit of the thing you're after.'

'Really, though?' I wasn't impressed. 'Your little landscapes seem popular, and you can knock those up in a matter of days. Why not just get on with it?'

'Because that wouldn't be honest.'

'Don't you go all arty and pseudo-intellectual on me, Kit McNamara. *Honest?* What kind of bollocks is that? You made and lost a fortune in advertising—what the hell do you care about honesty? Does a picture, or does it not, look nice hanging on the wall?'

'Shame on you!' He swiped his tea towel at my behind. 'I spent six hours in that shearing shed. It was crazy in there! Bleating, barking, a radio on at full blast, whirring machinery and *bang* go the doors as they drag the sheep through. One of these guys cut a sheep, blood everywhere, and a woman stitched it up with baler twine.'

'Ouch!'

'The point is this: I will paint that scene completely differently now that I know what it smells and sounds and even *tastes* like.'

'Kit, seriously.' I put my arms round his waist, imprisoning him, looking up into his face. 'I start work on the fifth of December. That's only a fortnight away. I need you on board to take care of the boys.'

'I know that. I shall be a dedicated house-husband. Anyway, they'll have started at school.'

I pointed out that the school day is a short one, and was warming to my theme when the phone rang.

'Saved by the bell,' said Kit, swinging out a hand to answer it. 'Louisa! How the devil are you?' He chatted to my sister for a while then handed me the phone and disappeared upstairs.

'Kit's on good form.' Lou sounded cynical. She hadn't forgiven us for emigrating. Probably never would.

'He is. I've just had ten minutes of arty codswallop.'

'Well, that's what you wanted, isn't it? You should be happy.'

'Of course I'm happy!'

'Hm?' I heard Lou inhale and knew she was lighting up. 'Or a teensy bit jealous? He wasn't this fanatical about advertising. Seems you've got a rival for the first time.'

I denied it hotly, of course—I never admit weakness to Lou if I can help it—and changed the subject. The call lasted an hour, and as always we found plenty to gossip about. Lily had a new rabbit, Philip hated his job, Vincent Vale was engaged to a busty barmaid. Just froth, really, but I felt a lot better by the end.

I found Kit in the studio, showered and changed. 'Mind if I sit here?' I asked, settling into the armchair with my feet tucked under me.

'Funny thing,' he said without looking round. 'I like having you there.'

He was leaning on a tall stool, squinting thoughtfully at the canvas.

Shearers were already beginning to take shape; four men in a row, stretching back from the eye. Occasionally he'd simply paint out an entire figure, then swiftly outline another.

It was late when I stood up, stretching my arms. 'That man Gerry Kerr was right,' I said. 'You *are* a fucking genius.'

'I wish.'

I brushed my lips against his ear. 'Yes, you are. But d'you know it's after eleven?'

He put down his brush. I felt his hand in the small of my back, steering me towards the door. 'Let's go,' he said happily.

We were halfway upstairs when the phone began to ring.

'*Bugger*,' groaned Kit.

'It'll be your mother,' I said accusingly. 'She can't get her head around the time difference.'

We stood irresolute as the thing rang on, and on. We hadn't got around to putting in an answer machine.

'Let's leave it,' suggested Kit, trying to push me up the last few stairs.

'I'm sorry,' I said, laughing. 'It's a total passion killer, knowing your mother's on the other end of that line. You'd better answer it.'

It wasn't Mary McNamara at all. It was Gerry Kerr. Kit talked to him for a long time. When he finally appeared in our room, he was looking stunned. I was reading in bed.

'Jesus,' he breathed, rumpling his hair distractedly. 'He wants me to get a collection together for his festival.'

'Does he know the sort of thing you've been doing?'

Kit looked faintly embarrassed. 'He does, actually. I've been emailing photographs.'

'This is fantastic news!' I knelt up on the bed, throwing my arms around his neck. 'When's the festival?'

'Next August. What a stupendous opportunity. But bloody hell, just over eight months to get a collection together . . . better get my skates on. No time to waste.'

So much, I thought uncharitably, for the dedicated house-husband.

*

The following morning, though, I woke happy. Air billowed through the open French doors, clear and fresh as spring water. You could drink it. We *were* lucky, after all. We lived in a sort of heaven; we had our children and one another—and now this news from Dublin. I stretched my toes before turning over to smile at Kit.

He was gone, of course. His side of the bed was cold.

'I'm an art widow,' I grumbled out loud, pushing my feet into slippers. 'Addictive personality, that's his problem. If it's not booze, it's bloody creativity.'

It was a Saturday, and the children were due to go riding. I was making coffee, yawning, when Finn and Charlie screamed into the kitchen, impersonating a couple of jets as they careered into me. Finn was in his underpants; Charlie had no clothes on at all.

'I'm going to canper soon,' bragged Finn. 'Tama said.'

'Not canper!' Charlie scoffed at his brother's ignorance. 'Canker.'

I poured them each a bowl of cereal. 'Sounds pretty clever.'

'Please will you come with us today, Mummy?' asked Charlie, blinking up at me. His cheeks were still crimson with sleep. 'I want to show you all the things.'

I ruffled the soft tangle of his hair. 'We'll see.'

Finn joined in. 'You should see Tama riding. He goes like this—and this—and Ruru stands way up on his hind legs. Cool! He looks just like Zorro!'

We were almost ready to leave when Sacha announced that she was opting out. She'd managed to cadge a lift into town with a friend's aunt who lived out our way.

'Not coming?' I stopped in my tracks. 'I thought you loved riding more than anything in the world?'

Her eyes slid away from mine. 'I'm not eleven years old any more,' she declared flatly. 'I've done that girly horsey thing.'

'Oh.' I felt deflated. 'That was sudden.'

'Tabby wants to meet up.'

'Well that's fine, but why don't you bring your friends here, like you planned?'

She shrugged ruefully. 'Changed my mind. What would we actually *do*?'

'Well . . . I don't know. Hang out. Play tennis. Listen to music. Bonfire on the beach.'

'And count sheep.' Sacha yawned. 'Yeah, right. We don't even have broadband. You're a skeleton by the time you've downloaded a music video. I'm sorry, Mum, I'm not trying to hurt your feelings, but there's sod all for a bunch of teenagers to do out here.'

'Don't you like us anymore?'

'Silly sausage.' She smiled and touched my cheek. 'I just need my own space a little bit. Anyway, must get on—I've got half an hour to practise this new piece.'

She set off to the sitting room and after a moment I heard the flute. It was a dreamy, haunting melody, a little like birdsong. I stepped into the hall to listen, and the music broke off.

'Mum, stop loitering out there!'

I stuck my head around the door. 'What's that gorgeous thing you're playing? Sounds familiar.'

She had her flute in one hand, scowling at the music. 'Debussy's *Syrinx*. I've always wanted to learn this.'

'Ah, Syrinx. Now, this is one of those Greek myths where the girl gives her life to save her virtue, isn't it? Good, old-fashioned values.'

'Mm. Actually it's a really sad story. It's about Pan. He was chasing this red-hot chick, Syrinx. When she got to a river she had nowhere left to run, so she begged for help from the gods. Instead of doing something useful like giving her wings, they helpfully turned her into marsh reeds and that was the end of her. Pan was really upset about the whole thing, so he cut the reeds and made them into pipes.'

'Pan pipes.'

'Pan pipes. Then he played this lament for her on those same pipes. So it has to sound kind of ethereal, like those creepy patupaiarehe playing their wooden flutes. Brrr!' She pretended to shiver. 'Come to think of it, Syrinx and Ira's Hinemoana have a lot in common, don't they? They should set up an enchanted maidens' self-help group.'

As she spoke, her phone began to vibrate. She took a look at the screen, and frowned.

'Who?' I asked, leaning closer.

'Tabby.' The phone disappeared into her pocket.

'I see you've taken off your locket.'

'My—?' She touched her throat.

'Your locket that Ivan gave you. Does that mean you've moved on?'

'No.' A shadow of anxiety darkened her face, and I fervently wished I hadn't mentioned the wretched thing. 'I left it by my bed, and now I can't find it. Really worried. I just hope it's in the house somewhere.'

'It will be,' I said. 'Don't worry.'

'Okay.' Tama watched me climb out of the car. 'No Sacha, I see. That must mean it's your turn today?'

'Yes!' yelped Charlie. 'She promised!'

I raised both hands. 'No, no. Sorry. I'm chauffeur.'

'Suit yourself,' said Tama placidly, and I felt a twinge of disappointment.

Finn climbed up on the fence to practise his tight-rope walking, while Ira and Charlie went to see the newest foal. Tama soon had me picking out some spiny seeds that were caught in Ruru's piebald coat. It wasn't easy because the massive horse loved to wander around the yard, nudging his master's shoulder.

As he moved unhurriedly among his animals, it struck me that Tama Pardoe seemed entirely content precisely as he was. How many of us can claim to be unequivocally content? Everyone believes they would be happy *if*... if they had a different job, perhaps, or they hit a lottery jackpot; if they had better-behaved children, a bigger house, a happier marriage. Me, I'd always reckoned my cup would overflow if I had a bikini body.

'Ever thought of becoming a Buddhist monk?' I asked.

'I am a Buddhist monk.'

'*Really?*'

'No, not really.'

When it was time for the riders to go, Charlie made one last appeal to my better nature. '*Please* come,' he begged. 'You'll really, really love it.'

The wide eyes were too much. 'Okay,' I blurted. 'But if I break my leg, you're all *dead*.'

If he felt any triumph, Tama hid it well. There was just a twitch of the mouth and a brief, dark-eyed glance in my direction as he reached for another saddle. 'You've met Kakama,' he said, patting the mare's creamy neck. 'She's your hostess for today.'

I managed to get myself astride without nose-diving right over the top and off the other side, and the five of us headed sedately through the dunes. Kakama's foal cavorted alongside, whinnying. Finn and Charlie were already confident, singing as they rode and occasionally breaking into a bumpy trot as we crossed the beach and began to walk along the glittering sand below the high-tide mark. It was a glorious scene, but I couldn't admire it. I'd forgotten how insanely high you are when perched on a horse.

'I feel awfully . . .' Waves swirled around Kakama's legs. 'I haven't done this for . . . um, and these great big saddles are pretty wacky.'

Tama was riding beside me. He leaned down and disentangled a twig from Kakama's mane. 'You're looking good.'

Gradually, I was soothed by the leisurely sway of the horses' gait. I could hear the boys behind us, yakking, bending Ira's ear. I began to feel more secure. Actually, I felt great. Tama was right: Kakama wasn't about to bolt. She had no malice. If she'd been a human being, she would have been the kindly sort who makes tea and pats your hand.

Eventually, Tama glanced at me. 'Shall we take the brakes off?'

I gulped.

'You'll be fine,' he said, with infectious confidence. 'She will take care of you.'

'But the boys—'

'—Will be safe with Ira. They won't set off after us, I promise. Now, never mind rising in the trot; in fact, never mind trotting. None of that English riding school malarkey. And don't lean forward!'

'I'm not sure—'

'You'll be okay, Martha. Trust me. Watch this.'

And with no apparent effort, Ruru had broken into a gallop. It was instantaneous. Tama stayed upright, hat flying behind him on a cord while sand shot up around him. Kakama behaved like a lady, though, and made no attempt to race. When Tama pulled up and whirled around, I was stroking her muscled neck and trying to rally my courage. I admired this man, and childishly wanted his approval. I longed to be a daredevil but I was paralysed by the memory of a horse bolting, tumbling, a leg snapping. Ahead of us lay a long stretch of unbroken sand, but then the beach curved around a headland and was scattered with wicked boulders.

You've got children! Mum was apoplectic. *How can you consider such selfishness?*

'Go on, Mummy,' called Finn scornfully. 'Don't be a pussy-wussy.'

'Okay.' I shut my eyes. 'Okay. Here goes.'

No, no, no! You're hopeless. You'll break your neck this time.

'I won't. Tama says I'm safe.'

You've a long way to fall, Martha.

'Shush.'

Your irresponsibility knows no—

'Oh, piss *off*!' I yelled aloud, and kicked with both heels. Kakama's power was overwhelming: I felt as though I was driving a Porsche and had jammed my foot flat onto the accelerator. I could hear the boys cheering—*Go Mummeee*—as the foal threw up his tail, bucked gleefully, and dashed alongside. Tama fell in too as we tore along the sand.

I thought I was going to die. No, really. I leaned forward and clutched at the saddle and a handful of cream-coloured mane, sobbing in rigid terror at the wavelets flashing past. The rocks on the headland loomed ever closer, and I imagined the carnage when we hit them.

Then I heard Tama's voice. 'You're fine.' He sounded amused. 'Martha, settle down, girl! Sit back.'

Gritting my teeth, I forced myself to release my grip on the saddle and straighten up. Nothing bad happened. With a rush of joy, I relaxed into the rhythm. It was like being injected with exhilaration. Pounding along the foreshore, salt spray flying up around us, I felt as though I would never be frightened again. I wasn't a mother. I didn't have two little boys who needed me every moment; I didn't have a husband who waltzed with alcohol and depression; I didn't have a beloved daughter who was growing apart from me. I was Martha, and the gates of freedom were creaking open. I heard myself whooping.

Tama slowed as we neared the end of the beach. Kakama—behaving immaculately—did the same without my having to ask, settling through an easy rocking-horse canter into a dignified walk. My heart was smashing right out of my ribs as we sloshed through a couple of feet of waves and safely rounded the headland.

'See?' said Tama, replacing his hat. 'No problem.'

'Whew.' Shakily, I leaned forward to kiss Kakama's sweating neck.

Another beach stretched before us, rockier and edged by pine plantation. The air smelled of seaweed and resin. I felt a sense of something deep within myself, something I didn't quite recognise. After thinking for some minutes I realised that I was actually proud of myself. I'd done something I'd been afraid to do. For once I hadn't sat on the fence and watched my children; I hadn't been the photographer, the waver-off, the cheerer on the sidelines. It had been a long time since I'd had an achievement that wasn't vicarious.

Mum was appalled. She launched a major nagging offensive, but I shoved her bodily into a cupboard and locked the door. I could hear her muffled protests, hammering and demanding to be let out.

'What a buzz,' I said. 'I feel ten years younger.'

Tama smiled, and the grooves deepened beside his mouth. 'You're not just the mother. Or just the chauffeur. Or just the wife. I see too many parents sitting on that fence while the kids do all the living.'

We turned back, chatting easily about local history. Tama described how the early farms would have shipped their wool to Napier from the beach, and their supplies in. He talked about a Maori walking track that ran along the coast before any Europeans arrived. He also had a stash of tall tales about his Scottish grandfather. When Hinemoana's hill came into view, I remembered the enchanted maiden.

'Ira told us her story,' I said. 'How she was abducted by the patupaiarehe.'

'The people of the mist.' Tama looked thoughtful. 'Y'know, I was talking to a joker who reckons they still exist. Swears he saw a couple of 'em in the headlights of his car. Scared him so much, he was still shaking a week later.'

'Did you believe him?'

Tama considered the question for a moment, while a breeze stirred the silver-tinged charcoal of his hair. 'D'you believe in the Loch Ness monster?'

At the end of November, Kit and I took the boys across the hills to Taupo for the day. It was a birthday treat. On their actual birthday they'd be starting school, hurled onto the inexorable treadmill of education. Sacha politely elected not to come, and no amount of bribing or emotional blackmail would change her mind.

Even so, we had a marvellous time. Kit and I lolled in geothermal hot pools while our offspring screamed down a taniwha-mouthed water slide. We picnicked beside the roar of the Huka Falls and spent an hour entertained by the bizarre spectacle of adrenaline junkies hurling themselves off a cliff with bits of elastic strapped to their ankles.

Both boys were fast asleep as we drove up to Patupaiarehe. A brilliant moon was rising above the sea. Kit and I got out of the car and stood for a few minutes at the edge of the garden, wrapped around one another, entranced by the magical light.

'It's so still,' I whispered. 'We could be the only people in the whole world.'

His arms tightened around me. 'Now there's a happy thought.'

We heard Finn stir, and became parents again. 'Looks as though Sacha's got company,' said Kit. 'See the car down by the smoko hut?'

I walked a few steps closer and squinted along the track. I could just make out the pale shape of a vehicle. 'Who d'you think it is?'

'How should I know?'

I tiptoed closer still.

'You're a disgrace,' said Kit. 'Here, have a camera with a zoom.'

'Shush. I'm trying to listen. She might have a man in there.'

'Why don't you just wire the joint and be done with it?'

'She's my baby girl,' I protested.

'I'm not sure the young male population around here see her in quite that light. Leave 'em be, Martha! You don't want to catch her doing anything embarrassing, do you?'

'Nope. That's where you come in. I want you to get straight down there and make sure there's no shenanigans.'

In an open display of insurrection, Kit laughed and turned on his heel. 'Mummy's gone a bit bonkers,' he remarked, leaning into the car for Finn, who was drowsily humming with Bob tucked up his sweatshirt. 'For Pete's sake, Martha, stop acting like a KGB colonel. Come inside and froth up some of your famous coffee.'

I took his advice, and it wasn't long before Sacha appeared in the kitchen doorway at the vanguard of a small crowd. Close behind her was Bianka, who greeted Kit with her usual self-possession. I could tell he was struck by her old-fashioned glamour, or perhaps it was the blackberry-coloured lipstick. Sacha gestured at two more girls. 'Teresa and Taylah.'

Bianka was a hard act to follow, of course, but this duo was spectacularly unmemorable. They had too much eyeliner, straightened hair and a conspicuous lack of dress sense. Neither managed to raise their gazes from the ground, let alone greet me like human beings. I tried to engage them but they just looked gormless. They could have been any pair of production-line teens, anywhere in the western world.

'And Jani,' said Sacha.

A young man appeared from behind the group. You could tell whose brother he was, and whose son. He shared the same bloodless beauty as his sister and mother; green eyes, and a suggestion of freckles. He laid an arm around Sacha's shoulder, and said what a magnificent place we had here. We asked him about his university course. It turned out that he was studying architecture, and Kit's eyes lit up.

'Coffee, guys?' he ventured hopefully. But they were just off. Inevitably, the dull girls had to be home by eleven, so Sacha walked her friends to Jani's car.

'Well,' observed Kit, 'I think the politburo can agree unanimously that Jani Varga is a dish. If vampires are your thing.'

'An improvement on Ivan.'

'Maybe.'

'But I don't think I trust him,' I fretted. 'He's too old, and there's something just a little too smooth.'

Kit laughed as he opened a tub of Pamela's ginger crunch. 'No man will ever get past quality control. If you have your way, that girl will live and die an old maid.'

Sacha stood waving as the car crossed the cattle grid, then came skipping back to us. She looked tail-waggingly pleased with herself, like a gundog dropping a pheasant at the feet of its master. 'Lovely, isn't she?'

'*She?*' echoed Kit.

'Bianka. She has the sweetest smile.'

I had to agree. 'A stunner, in a retro way.'

'Spitting image of Greta Garbo,' said Kit.

'Did I tell you she's a lesbian?'

I gaped. '*Bianka?*'

'Openly gay. But nobody gives her any shit, because she is so totally okay with it herself. She's "take me or leave me, this is who I am".'

'Well. Um.' I forced my features into a look of blasé unconcern. 'So are you . . .?'

'If I was bi, I'd definitely fall for Bianka. I'm not, sadly.' Sacha hugged herself. 'They're amazing people. Anita, the mother . . . you met her, Mum. Just incredible. The doctors don't think they can beat the cancer, but she's having all this awful experimental treatment just to buy a little more time. She wants to see her children become adults, says that's all she asks. The dad's gone to pieces. Jani found him crying last night.'

'Poor bloke . . . Ginger crunch?'

'No thanks. I'm on a diet.' Sacha stood by the sink, pouting like a supermodel at her reflection in the window.

Kit helped himself. He loved Pamela's baking. 'Daft girl. You're perfect as you are.'

'Tabby makes me look like the Michelin Man.'

'Bet she's got no bust. I can't be doing with these flat-chested women.'

'Er, no,' Sacha retorted dryly, looking me up and down. 'So I gathered. You like to have something you can get hold of, don't you, Kit?'

I squealed in outrage, and she giggled. 'Well,' she announced, stretching her arms above her head, 'lovely night. I'm going to walk down to the road gate and back.'

'*Now?*' I protested.

'Oh, for goodness' sake. There's a full moon, bright as day. Look, there are even shadows.'

'Moon shadows,' said Kit.

'Take cover!' Sacha held her hands over her ears. 'Omigod, he's about to burst into song. Has anyone taken the poor dog out today? No, I thought not. C'mon, Muffin!'

With a wheezy woof of excitement, Muffin hauled herself out of the basket and padded adoringly after her mistress. The air was so clear that I could hear Sacha talking to her long after they'd disappeared over the brow of the hill.

I so wanted my family to be happy. It was all that mattered. Perhaps that's why I didn't notice the glittering snake as it uncoiled itself in our garden.

Sixteen

It isn't peaceful in an intensive care unit. It's the front line: commotion, alarms, crises. People are dying. People die.

Only last night, Finn was chasing our chickens and catapulting peas off his fork. Now his face has the mottled pallor of sour cream. His eyes are grotesquely puffed up, the whole area a deep, unnatural blue. They've put him on a ripple bed, a special mattress to ward off bedsores. He would like that idea. I hold his hand and murmur to him until sounds blur and the light becomes one vibrating sheet of grey. His nurse is watching my every move. Slowly, it dawns on me that the man's on tenterhooks. He thinks I might try to hurt my son.

All morning, Finn is visited by a stream of medics. I'm only now realising what a massive mobilisation took place when our helicopter landed in the night. Neil Sutherland drops by, still looking tired. The paediatric giraffe, too—his bedside manner hasn't improved much. There's an anaesthetist, who tries to explain how the coma works. They all do their best to keep me informed, but none of them can promise that my boy will be himself again.

At two o'clock, the Auckland neurologist appears.

'I'm an OT,' I tell her, trying not to sound hysterical. 'I'm all too familiar with traumatic brain injury. Please be honest. Will Finn be permanently affected?'

She is Chinese, about forty, slightly severe. She thinks carefully before she replies. 'The surgery went well, but I can't give you a firm prognosis at this early stage.'

'You must have an opinion?'

'Well, there are several positive factors. He's very young, and he had early intervention. The intracranial pressure is already considerably lower. I don't think we'll need to maintain this coma for very long, which is a real plus.'

'But can you give me an idea of the extent . . . What about blindness—deafness? What about his speech? His personality? His . . . well, you know, his intellect?'

She looks at Finn's little body. Her face is a blank mask. 'Recovery is not the same for any two people. We'll be in a better position to discuss prognosis once he's conscious. I'm sorry.'

I thank her. Once she's gone I try Kit's phone yet again. Voicemail. Needing Tama's unquestioning calm, I call home.

'All good on the western front,' he says. 'Don't you worry about anything here. Ira's coming in later. How is the little guy?'

'Stable.' I feel stronger for hearing his voice. 'Thank you, Tama. I don't know how I would have managed.'

'Cut that out.'

'How are Charlie and Sacha?'

He hesitates. 'Well, as you'd expect, pretty upset . . . Sacha just about fainted when I told her what's happened, poor kid. In a hell of a state. She's fast asleep right now, though. Flat out with this flu. Her friend's here.'

'Friend?' I was bemused. 'What friend?'

'Er . . . young lass called Bianka. She's upstairs in Sacha's bedroom. Been with her all day.' I'm digesting this information when he speaks again. 'Charlie came for a ride on Ruru this morning. Sat up in front of me like a little prince. We moved some stock, had a great time . . . didn't we, fella?'

I hear Charlie's voice piping in the background.

'He wants to speak to you,' says Tama. 'All right?'

'Um . . .' I clear my throat. 'Yep. Put him on.'

Muffled conversation, then the sound of small hands dropping the receiver. I wait with closed eyes, dreading the gentle optimism of Charlie's world because I know it may soon be destroyed.

'Mummy?'

I nearly let him down. Sorrow surges into my throat. I swallow it back but it sticks somewhere in my chest. 'Hello, Charlie! Have you . . .' My voice splinters. I take a long breath. 'Have you had a nice time with Tama?'

'He took me riding. We saw baby calves . . . Where's Finn?'

I look at the ruined figure on the bed. 'He's here, beside me.'

'Did he fall off the balcony?'

'He did, Charlie.'

A sniff. 'Silly old Finny. Is he coming home today?'

'Not today. But he will be all right, you'll see. He'll be all right. The doctors and nurses are looking after him.'

'Can I talk to him on the telephone?'

Tears force their way past my defences. They hurt. They bruise. 'No, he's asleep. But I'll give him your love.'

'He hasn't got his Game Boy.'

'True, but he does have Buccaneer Bob. And when he's a bit better, you can bring him his Game Boy.'

'Tama and me fed the lamb. Tell Finn.'

'I'll tell him.'

He must have dropped the phone again. I hear scrabbling, and Tama's voice. Then Charlie's. 'Where's Dad?'

Good question. 'He'll be home soon.'

'He *is* home. He was by my bed in the night.'

I'm silenced for a moment, appalled. I can hear Mum laughing. Then I whisper, 'No, sweetie. Dad's not back from Ireland yet.'

Charlie shouts in distress, 'He was *here*, though. I saw him.'

'You didn't.'

'I did! He kissed me. He picked Blue Blanket up from the floor and tucked it in with me.'

'You were dreaming. We all miss Dad.'

Heavy, stubborn breathing. 'Wasn't dreaming.'

'He'll be home before you know it.'

'*Wasn't dreaming!* He promised to take us to Jane's. He wanted to see the baby rabbits.'

'And he will. Everything's going to be all right.'

'Mm.' There is a long pause, with babyish snuffling. I see the thumb going in, the wide and wondering eyes. 'Where do people go, when they die?'

'Charlie, nobody's going to die.'

'If Finn dies, he will be lonely. He'll want to come home.'

What do you do when someone you love has made the world explode?

Seventeen

Charlie and Finn turned five on the first of December. In line with New Zealand tradition, we plotted to pack them off to primary school on that very day—midweek—thus committing the poor little buggers to thirteen years on a wheel of suffering. Some birthday present.

We'd visited the school already. It had taken the twins about two seconds to work out that Torutaniwha Primary was paradise, even if they couldn't pronounce its name. Mr Grant, the bearded principal, gave them lollipops, and the new entrants' teacher fussed over them like a broody hen. Mrs Martin was young, enthusiastic and heavily pregnant.

On their last night as preschoolers, we went for tea in Jane's café. There, I got chatting to a school mother, one of those chinless types who talk in little-girl voices. She had disturbing news. Michelle Martin had developed complications and was out of action for the rest of the pregnancy. Her replacement had hurriedly been shoehorned into the job.

'Mr Taulafo,' said the mother.

'Oh dear. What's he like?' I was in a froth of anxiety.

'The kids love him. He's brilliant with them.' She leaned forward with her hand covering her mouth. 'I want to *eat* him,' she whispered, and giggled.

Charlie, who'd been listening with a quivering lower lip, reached for his blanket. 'I like Mrs Martin.'

Brings out the worst in you, sending your children to school. One day you're wishing they'd grow up and sod off and leave you in peace; the next you're sniffling pathetically as you pack their spare underpants. Tiny Y-fronts, in case of accidents.

'It's at Hinemoana's hill. Hee-nay-mo-ah-na,' I coached them neurotically, as they bolted their breakfast on the first school day of their lives. They'd been up since six, opened all their presents and eaten the chocolate buttons off their birthday cake.

'Ringy Moaner,' said Charlie, his fair curls stuck out at zany angles.

'Thingy Mamma,' added Finn, ramming a Sugar Puff up his nose. He giggled, inhaled sharply and got a piece of processed wheat stuck two inches up his nasal passage. I had to fish it out with tweezers.

Now that school was finally upon them, they seemed not the slightest bit awed by the solemnity of the occasion; not even Charlie. They ducked my hairbrush as though it was a cat-o'-nine-tails and strutted importantly out of the house in their blue school shirts and grey shorts. While Kit and I searched for shoes they hopped merrily into their booster seats, backpacks bulging with Superman lunchboxes.

'So this is it,' said Kit, strolling out to the car with me. 'Our babies are schoolboys, Martha.'

'Where did the last five years go?' I asked sadly.

'Passed in a flash.' He looked into the car, where the boys were serenading themselves with a tuneless chorus of 'Happy Birthday to Us'. 'But they've not been wasted, that's for sure.'

As I parked behind the dunes, the entire school—about thirty children—seemed to be playing rugby. Not one of them wore shoes. A couple of vagabonds were hoisting the New Zealand flag up a pole. The next time I looked, my sons were gone. They'd joined a blue-shirted mob of desperate characters, all trying to tackle one spindly little fellow who was making a run for it. He went down hard under the swarm, and mine were somewhere deep in the dog pile. Then the ball came shooting out from beneath a mound of wriggling bodies, and the game was off again.

Feeling abandoned, I made my way to the new entrants' classroom, a technicolour haven with miniature chairs and tables. I hoped to meet the new teacher. A powerful male form dwarfed the furniture, balancing on a chair as he hung paintings along a string.

I stared. 'Ira?'

He looked round, his face lighting up. 'G'day, Martha!' His hair was tied back and he was wearing a shirt with rolled-up sleeves that more or less covered the artwork on his biceps.

'Nice to see you,' I said. 'What brings you here? I was looking for Mr Taulafo.'

'Yup.' He jumped down from the chair. 'That's me.'

It took a good five seconds for this information to sink in. 'You . . .? But you never said!'

He shrugged. 'Conversation never got around to it.'

Thinking back, I realised I'd never tried to find out much about Ira. I had been happy to like him as the brawny removal man who rode like a cowboy, was a magnet to small boys and told magical, mystical stories. I felt ashamed.

'You might have mentioned it to the twins, though,' I scolded. 'They would have been *so* excited.'

'Didn't know myself. I've been doing casual work like the house moving and relief teaching around the district while I looked for something permanent. Only had the interview for this job two weeks ago. I was waiting to hear if I'd got it. Then last week Michelle Martin went to the doctor for a pre-natal and he took one look at her blood pressure and slapped her on bed rest. So I got a call: "You've got the job, bro, can you start tomorrow?" I've been chasing my tail ever since, no lesson plans organised or anything. And with all the chaos it was only this morning I got told I had two new entrants coming—I was pretty happy when I found out who they were!'

'So you've finished your training?' I asked.

He nodded. 'Did a couple of years' teaching in Auckland, but I always wanted to end up back in the Bay. Can't believe I landed this job! I sat in this same classroom when I was a kid, used to daydream and look out at old Hinemoana.'

He strode across to the whiteboard and began to print in clear, slightly sloped handwriting: *Morena, tamariki. Good morning, children. Today is Thursday—Taite.*

'So,' he said, deftly outlining a sketch of SpongeBob SquarePants. 'Boys all ready for the big day?'

'They are! I'm not.'

He gave SpongeBob a speech bubble, writing inside it: *KIA ORA TO FINN AND CHARLIE McNAMARA!*

'They're going to have a riot,' he declared cheerfully, and I didn't doubt him for a second.

It was awfully quiet in the people carrier on the way home. No story tape was playing. No one was squabbling, or singing, or asking random questions. There were two empty booster seats where my merry men ought to have been. Buccaneer Bob sat in one, looking forlorn. Blue Blanket lay crumpled in the other. I leaned into the back, reached for Bob and snuggled him under my chin. I was still cradling that pirate as I wandered into the childless house.

Soon it was my turn: my first day at Capeview. I was determined to arrive early, to be calm and collected. Which, presumably, is why I was running late.

Kit had crept down to his studio at an unseemly hour. Actually, he hadn't crept. He'd crashed around on what he clearly thought were his tiptoes, banging things and sneezing in that annoyingly noisy way men do. At eight o'clock, though, Finn was still curled under his duvet, doing an imitation of a sloth on Mogadon; Charlie was eating Rice Crispies one grain at a time, picking them up between thumb and forefinger with infuriating delicacy. I made a half-hearted attack on the washing-up from last night, in a futile bid to leave things looking as though I was a real mother.

'Get a move on, Charlie,' I begged, as I struggled to find lids for their lunchboxes. 'I've still got to have a shower. What d'you want in your sandwich? Peanut butter?'

He looked as though I'd offered him road kill. 'Peanut butter is 'scusting.'

'Oh. I thought you liked it. Um . . . ham?'

'Yeuch.'

'Tuna?'

He was making gagging noises when Kit appeared in the kitchen carrying a bug-eyed, bed-haired Finn. 'You'll have peanut butter, young Mr McNamara, and like it,' he growled in his pirate voice, and Charlie giggled.

I glanced at the clock, cursed, and raced upstairs. Where does the time go to when you're late? I was in and out of the shower in five minutes and pulling on some clothes—after a brief moment of despair, I found one last pair of clean knickers under the wardrobe. My tights got stuck on my legs and then I smudged mascara down one cheekbone. Still, it felt novel to walk downstairs in proper grown-up work clothes. Kit had taken charge of the boys and was shoving minuscule pairs of swimming trunks into their bags.

'I need a memory stick for the school computer,' said Sacha. She'd chosen to go in to do an ICT course, though Year Eleven had finished formal school for the year. 'Can I have twenty-five dollars? They sell them in the office.'

'Okay.' I began to riffle through the nest of old receipts in my wallet. 'Bugger. I've run out of cash . . . no, I can't have. I got two hundred out of a machine the other day.' I tipped everything onto the table. 'Bloody hell, where did I spend it all? I think I'm going mad!'

'You'll have bought lattes in every café in Hawke's Bay,' said Kit soothingly. He fished in his wallet and gave Sacha thirty. 'I'm Stay-at-Home Sid so I never spend any dosh. You can blow the change in the canteen.'

'Thanks, Kit.' Sacha folded the notes and stashed them in her pocket.

'Mr Taulafo took us onto the beach,' said Finn. 'We played ball tag.'

I was searching distractedly under a pile of school newsletters. I was sure I hadn't spent all that money. We needed to watch our budget.

'That's Ira,' explained Finn. 'But at school we call him Mr Taulafo. He tells stories after lunch.'

'He's got a gorgeous girlfriend,' said Sacha. 'She coaches the Kapa Haka group at school. Seriously cool—she can sit on her hair. I spotted her and Ira at the cinema.'

I gave up on my search. 'You're not jealous?'

She gaped at me in contemptuous incredulity; it's a look teenagers reserve for their parents' most ill-informed remarks. 'Euw! Mum, I don't hit on teachers. Can I drive to the bus stop?'

'Car key, car keys,' I chanted anxiously.

'They're in the ignition,' said Kit. 'Chill, old girl.' Humming a waltz, he slid his hand onto my back and danced me to the door. 'Remember in England we used to lock the doors and set an alarm whenever we went out? Like rats in a cage, we were.'

He was right, I thought, as we spun our way across the yard. We were wrapped in a cocoon of peace and isolation. Kit kissed me, wished me luck and stood saluting as my chauffeur drove me away.

Once on our way, Sacha glanced at me. 'How're you feeling, Mum?'

'Very glad to be earning some money at last.'

'Butterflies?'

'Millions of 'em . . . Did you have breakfast?'

'An apple,' she said happily. 'My self-control is legendary.'

'Sacha, you don't need to diet so much.'

'OMG! There's the bus.' She wrenched at the handbrake, and was gone.

Five minutes later my phone sang its text song. Those butterflies were going crazy. I could almost see my stomach rippling.

I pulled over. Sacha's name was on the screen.

Luv ya mum. Gd lk. Knk m ded :) xxxxx

Mercifully, Lillian Thompson was on leave. Keith was expecting me though, and showed me into my cell. Someone had scribbled appointments in the diary.

'Where's all the junk?' I asked, looking around.

His chins wobbled. 'In Lillian's cupboard. She's going to have a fit when she opens the door and it all falls out. How are your children getting on?'

'The boys have started school.'

'Happy so far?'

'Happy as prehistoric man on a woolly mammoth hunt. Their teacher's a friend of ours. He's got dreadlocks down to his waist, and he's the best storyteller I've ever heard. It seems at this school they have pet days, rock pool days, wacky hair days . . .'

'Any actual learning days?'

'Nah, don't think they have those. But the boys don't care, and neither do I.'

The next eight hours were a kaleidoscope of images and personalities. I was straight into the deep end with a thirty-year-old airline pilot. Gareth's life had been a roaring success until the moment when his motorbike met a power pole. The broken limbs had healed; the brain injury shattered his life forever. He needed us to teach him how to brush his hair, how to tie his laces, how to get through his day. One side of his face drooped. He had lousy short-term memory, poor concentration, no patience. He roamed the corridors of Capeview like an angry wolf, and he wished he'd died. He wished it bitterly, openly and justifiably. His wife was thin and twitching. She didn't bring their children to visit him.

From there on I didn't stop. I had two visits to assess work environments in Napier and a staff meeting at which I finally got to meet Jenna, the other OT. She was about my age with micro hair and little oblong glasses. She'd emigrated from Zimbabwe five years earlier with her husband, her mother and two children.

'How are you finding New Zealand?' she asked.

I glanced at Keith, who was listening with amusement. 'It's . . . well, what a dream lifestyle. But I can't pretend we're never homesick. Everyone is so very far away. How about you? Do you ever wish you'd stayed home?'

'No, I don't.'

'But you must miss your country?'

'We don't allow ourselves to look back.'

'How sensible,' I said half-heartedly.

'Back in Zimbabwe, three men broke into our home. They held us up at gunpoint while they robbed us. As they were on their way out, one of them put his gun to my head'—she pressed two fingers to her temple—'and pulled the trigger. I actually heard the click. I thought my children were going to watch me die.'

I stared at her, aghast. 'What happened?'

'I was so, so lucky. The gun misfired. He hit me with the barrel of it instead. Knocked me out. We left a month later. New Zealand took us in—thank God—and this is where we have made our lives. For us, there *is* no going back.'

Eighteen

The temperature rose as Christmas approached. Pesky mosquitoes droned through the night, pausing only to suck our blood. I soon invested in nets. We watched our hills fade from lush emerald to a parched expanse of dust, leached of colour. It was hard to believe that the sheep got any nutrition at all.

'Drought,' remarked Pamela, who'd dropped by to warn me about the voltage on a boundary fence; she was putting through a massive charge because she had bulls in the next field. On the back of her truck there was a dead sheep rolling around like a rug with ears, and three dogs chained to the cab.

'Is it a problem?' I asked, following her gaze across the desiccated landscape.

'Well, it's either drought or it's floods. That's farming for you; always something to gripe about.'

It was ten o'clock on a Saturday morning, and I'd had a frantic week. There was such a lot to learn: new faces, new hang-ups and a massive geographical area. At the same time, I was trying to get my head around the cultural nuances and keep up with assignments on my Maori paper. I'd been on autopilot in Bedfordshire, and suddenly I was back at the controls. It was exhilarating, but exhausting.

I'd thrown off my kimono and dived into a sundress when I heard Pamela's truck. My hair looked like a bird's nest, a frizz of wet straw.

Pamela, by contrast, had the air of someone for whom the day is half over. She seemed quite human this morning: almost smiley in an efficient, no-frills kind of way. She was wearing a peaked cap and smelled of lanolin and sheep.

'Been crutching,' she said, as we strolled around to the verandah.

'Been what?'

'Cutting the dags off the sheep's backsides.'

'Dags?'

'Sheepshit.'

'Oh.'

'We'd get flystrike, otherwise. Maggots. They eat the stock alive.' And with this delicate observation she handed me an ice-cream punnet full of ginger crunch.

'You know the way to my heart!' I enthused. 'Coffee?'

'Lovely.' She followed me into the kitchen. Christmas carols were playing on the radio. 'It's pretty quiet around here.'

'The boys have a schoolfriend over. They're all glued to the telly, I'm afraid. Sacha's staying in town.'

'Again? She was there last weekend, wasn't she?'

'She has orchestra on a Friday—extra late at the moment, because of the Christmas concert—so it's tempting to stop with one of her friends.'

'You must be pleased! She's settled in very well.'

'You've got four boys, haven't you?' I was looking for our milk jug, because a plastic bottle was good enough for us but not for minor royalty like Pamela Colbert. I eventually found it at the back of the fridge, harbouring congealed gravy.

'I have a seven-year-old grandson, too,' she said, puffing out her chest. I hadn't expected Pamela to be an adoring grandmother. It seemed too mushy a role for one so no-nonsense.

'Where are they all?'

'The eldest, Jules, is in Perth.'

'Scotland?'

'Western Australia. He's a geologist in the mines. He's single—it's not a life for a family. But we live in hope.'

I was searching for another jug. Kit had inherited a silver one in the shape of a cow. 'And the younger three?'

'Michel is in Wellington. He does something in graphic design, and I have no idea what that is but I'm sure it's very clever. He's got a girlfriend called April.'

'D'you like her?'

'No.'

'Oh dear.'

'April's imagination is as limited as her chest is copious. But she's got her feet firmly under the table, so I'd better get used to her.'

Wretched jug wasn't in the cupboard where it belonged. I stood on tiptoe in the pantry, checking the top shelf among the jam jars. 'That's two.'

'Ah, yes. Philippe was our afterthought. He's only seventeen.'

'Really? I thought you and Jean were empty nesters. Let's sit on the verandah,' I added, coming out of the pantry and lifting the tray. 'Sorry about the uncouth plastic bottle. Couldn't find a jug. Chaos in this house.'

I was startled when she laid a hand on my arm. 'Martha, cut that out. You never, *ever* have to stand on ceremony for me. I think you imagine I'm some kind of domestic superwoman with polished dustbin lids. I'm not, believe me. I'm very flawed.'

Touched, I led her outside and poured our coffee. 'Your youngest, Philippe . . . he must still be at boarding school?'

'Philippe chose to leave school. He's working on a farm in Canterbury.' Pamela's mouth twisted. 'That boy's drifted. He isn't happy in his own skin. His latest ambition is to cycle from the Caribbean coast to Tierra del Fuego.'

'Good Lord! Through . . . my geography's shocking, but that's through places like Brazil. The Amazon. What do *you* think about it?'

'I think I can't stop him.' Pamela held her mug to her cheek. Perhaps the warmth was comforting.

'So you've mentioned three,' I persisted. 'The fourth must be the father of your grandson.'

'Yes, that's right. Daniel.'

'And what's Daniel up to?'

'I don't know.'

'Oh.' I hesitated, sensing a raw nerve. 'But isn't he—'

'He died.'

I blinked, fighting that unforgiveable, inevitable urge to giggle in horror and embarrassment. 'Pamela. I am so sorry.'

She chewed on the side of her mouth, looking down the valley. 'It happened very . . . suddenly.'

'When?'

'Ooh . . . over seven years ago now.'

'That's no time at all.'

'No time at all,' she agreed. 'Sometimes I feel as though it happened yesterday.'

'How are you both coping?'

She made a small moue, bless her, and tried to wave the subject away. 'That's life. You just have to get on with it.'

'No. No, Pamela. Don't pretend it's just a slight inconvenience.'

'There's never a day goes by when we don't think of him. He was twenty-three . . . he was my third son. My precious third son.'

'What happened?'

She sipped absent-mindedly at her coffee. 'He'd just become a father. The mother's a lovely girl. Hannah. They met at university in Otago.'

'Are you still in touch with her?'

'Hannah is like a daughter to me, so I lost a son and gained . . .' Pamela took a long breath. 'Visiting hours came to an end at the hospital, so Daniel went out with a couple of friends to celebrate his new baby.'

She broke off as Kit made a noisy entrance from around the corner of the verandah, brogues drumming cheerfully on the wooden boards. His hands were in his pockets, and he was whistling.

'Pamela Colbert,' he declared, throwing himself into the swing seat. His hair was an ebony thatch, blue eyes amused and vital. I wondered for an anxious moment whether he'd been drinking. 'You are a vision of loveliness.'

She wagged a forefinger at him, as unruffled as though we'd still been discussing the weather. It was an impressive performance, and it put her up several hundred points in my estimation. 'You're a shameless Irish flirt,

Kit,' she scolded severely. 'I may be a vision of something, but it isn't loveliness. I'm a beanpole in shapeless slacks.'

Kit poured himself some coffee, and Pamela looked out at the hills.

'Your dam's getting low.' She shielded her eyes, skin taut across her cheekbones.

'Our . . . oh, the pond.' I squinted down at the patch of water with its sentinel of cabbage trees. The air carried a faint smell of drying mud.

Kit sprawled in the seat, rocking himself with one foot on the ground. He always enjoyed Pamela's company. 'Ask me what I'm working on,' he begged. 'Go on, ask me.'

Pamela rolled her eyes indulgently. 'What are you working on?'

'Glad you asked me that! It's a trompe l'oeil.'

'Ah!' She grasped her hands around one knee. 'Tell me more.'

'Well, I got the idea from Sacha—she said she was too old to have a mural on her wall and I thought, what about murals for grown-ups? Imagine a window framed by shutters. Through your window there is a view. Can be any view. *This* paradise could keep me going for a lifetime. But for example,' he extended both arms towards the valley, '*that* view. Those bare hills, drawing the eye down to the sea. In the foreground, purplish light reflects from this glorious bougainvillea.'

'And emphatically three dimensional, isn't that the idea? It tricks the eye.'

'That's it! But I didn't want to lose spontaneity; it isn't photographic. I've spent the last ten days working with native bush.' Kit began to sketch in the air like a conductor with hyperactivity disorder. 'A vine curls across the sill. You can almost touch it. Tree ferns, vines, trunks of magnificent kauri. Arrows of sunlight—'

'Enough!' Pamela smacked her hands onto her knees before standing up. 'This, I have to see. Lead the way.'

I followed them into the studio. Work had been so all-consuming that I hadn't found time to sit and watch Kit painting. I missed those companionable evenings.

Pamela glanced up at Sibella's portrait. 'Morning, ma'am,' she said. 'Now, you *are* a vision of loveliness. Though I wouldn't like to find myself on the wrong side of you, I think. There's flint in those eyes.'

No wine bottles in sight, full or empty. I'd seen Kit making a frame for a vast canvas, and there it was against one wall. His work in progress stretched towards the ceiling and was perhaps four feet wide. The three of us walked around to stand in front of it.

We were looking out of an open window—with a sill and a frame—and straight into the dense understorey of a rainforest so real that I could almost smell the lichen; yet the effect was produced by light and colour. I was spellbound. It was somehow more real than reality.

'How long have you spent on this?' asked Pamela, examining a mirrored water droplet that glittered on a fern.

'Eighty, ninety hours so far. Martha and I have been two ships passing in the night.'

The pair of them began to discuss technicalities: working with such a large canvas, getting it safely to Dublin, sourcing wooden shutters to complete the window effect.

'Might try vineyards next,' said Kit, pulling out a sketch. 'Think what you could do with those mathematical patterns!' He was about to expand on the thought when Finn shot through the doorway, hands gripped around an imaginary steering wheel and Formula 1 noises bubbling through pursed lips.

'Wanted on the phone, wanted on the phone, Kit McNamara. Will a Mr Kit McNamara please come to the phone? It's Granny from Ireland.' Then he made a handbrake turn and accelerated out again. I heard him changing gear on the verandah. Kit waved an apology to Pamela, and trotted off.

'Kit's mother,' I explained, as Pamela and I followed at a more dignified pace. 'She can't sleep, and then she's bored. So she phones Kit.'

'Your man is exceptionally talented,' said Pamela. 'Did you realise that? If I had a fraction of his ability I'd be singing from the rooftops.'

'New Zealand inspires him.'

'Just wait until the autumn. Oh, such colours!'

We strolled onto the lawn, and I asked Pamela's advice about some shrivelling of the leaves on our citrus bush. But there was an elephant in the garden. I couldn't ignore it.

'I'm so sorry about your son,' I said.

She patted my arm. 'I'll tell you the rest of the story, but another time. People don't usually want to hear. It spoils their day.'

When we reached the glossy shade of the walnut tree, she leaned across the back of the truck and let her dogs off their chains. 'You don't get over it, you know. You never do. But if you're very lucky, you get through it.'

I watched my neighbour drive down the track in a confident whirlwind of dust. The dead sheep slid around on the flatbed of the truck, and dogs raced alongside with maniacal joie de vivre. She looked the archetypal competent woman. Everything in her world obeyed Pamela Colbert: the husband, the dogs, the sheep, the garden.

Well, no. Not everything. Even she couldn't control Death.

Sacha arrived home soon after Pamela had left. She'd made her own way up from the road gate, a bottle of Coca-Cola in one hand, and burst in as I was wrestling with a pile of ironing.

'Don't panic!' she crowed, as the door hit the wall with a plaster-shattering crack. 'I'm back!'

'I'd have collected you from the road,' I said, crossing the kitchen to hug her.

'Mmwah!' She gave me a noisy kiss on the cheek, dropping her back-pack onto the floor. 'Where is everyone?'

'Have you been dragged through a hedge backwards? That's the wildest hairdo I've ever seen. It'll take hours to get the tangles out.'

She touched her head vaguely, then did that intensely annoying teen-age thing—wrenched at the fridge door and stood looking at the shelves. I once read a statistic about how many weeks of our lives we spend looking into fridges. It was horrifying.

'Why are you drinking Coke?' I asked. 'You don't even like it.'

'Shows what you know about me.'

'We've got leftover lasagne there, on the top shelf.'

'I haven't eaten a thing today,' she said, putting the bowl into the micro-wave. 'D'you think the diet's working yet?' She turned side-on to me and inhaled sharply. 'Tabby's given me some of her clothes.'

'I think it's time to forget the diet. You're overdoing it. Tabby was born a different shape from you.'

'Oh my God, I forgot to set the microwave going.' She pressed the start button and stood watching the plate doing its wobbly dance on the turntable. 'I wonder what it's like to be in a microwave?'

'Fatal, unless you're a plate of lasagne. So you've had a good time?'

'Yep. Ting! That was quick.'

Giving up on the ironing—surely a metaphor for all that is fruitless and sterile in the modern world—I joined her at the table and asked about her evening at Bianka's house, which seemed to consist of listening to music and talking all night.

'Any reason why you're so jolly?' I wondered whether I really wanted to know. I had a nasty feeling it might be to do with Jani. No parent of a sixteen-year-old girl likes to imagine . . . well, you know.

She shrugged. A burnished strand of her hair fell into the cheese sauce.

I tried again. 'I hope you didn't, er, didn't go too far.'

'You mean did I screw Jani?'

'No!' I was tight-lipped. 'Um, well . . . I mean, I hope you're making good choices.'

'Oh I am,' she said, laughing uproariously. 'I *am*. I'm fantastic at making good choices! I'm a legend in my own lifetime. No, Mum, I didn't sleep with Jani. Chill. Now if you'll excuse me, I've gotta go and see who's on Facebook.'

'You haven't got to do anything of the kind. You've got to finish that lasagne—you've hardly eaten any.'

She bent over the table, held her hair back with one hand, and piled the whole lot into her mouth. 'Happy?'

'Go on, then,' I sighed, and the next moment she and her backpack had gone. I strode into the hall, calling after her, 'Have a shower! You look like a tramp.'

Her head appeared over the banisters. 'Now, Mum, that's not PC, as you ought to know. We don't call them tramps, we call them homeless persons.'

'Get away with you,' I said, laughing. 'Don't forget to scrub behind your ears.'

The bathroom door slammed shut.

Why d'you think she's locked herself in there? I hadn't heard from my mother in a while; I'd almost missed the old boot.

'To have a shower, of course.'

Really? Not to throw up all that lasagne you've just made her eat?

'You're paranoid,' I snapped. 'Silly woman.'

At some appalling hour the next morning, Finn and Charlie tottered into our room with tea in bed—well, tepid water with tea leaves floating in it. They were buttering us up, they said, so we'd take them to explore the rock pools for intergalactic starfish.

'We're going to the beach,' I announced, throwing open Sacha's window. The sky was airforce blue. 'Coming?' Her head dipped below the duvet, and I huffed. 'I'll take that as a no, then.'

Kit chortled when I complained. 'What teenager have you ever met that leaps out of bed at seven o'clock on a Sunday morning? You don't know how lucky you are. Our girl's an angel.'

The seashore was deserted except for an elderly strolling couple, holding hands, picking their way around the foot of Hinemoana's hill.

'That'll be us one day,' said Kit. He sounded happy about the idea.

It was low tide. Charlie and Finn waded into rock pools, leaning on one another for support while keeping up an almost superhuman babble of nonsense about intergalactic life forms. We'd been on the beach half an hour when, feeling a sudden gust, I glanced behind us. Hinemoana's hill had disappeared.

'Don't look now,' I said, squeezing Kit's arm. 'But I think we're about to get very wet.'

Murky shadow slanted out of the clouds and spread far across the sea. It was alarmingly beautiful. The water had become an unearthly mass, a weird, luminous crème de menthe flecked with whitecaps, and a fretful wind tugged at our clothes.

'Better run for it.' Kit cupped his hands to his mouth. 'Guys!'

By the time the twins were on dry land the squall was upon us, driving horizontally from the south. The day grew thin and spectral as the sky dissolved. Sand whipped up and stung our legs. In the end Kit and I turned around and walked backwards, leaning against the wind, cradling a boy each in our arms. I've never been so pleased to see a big white people carrier.

'That was wicked,' yelped Finn, somersaulting onto the back seat.

'Does this mean the drought's over?' I gasped.

Kit started the engine just as a rainbow appeared in the sky, arching from one horizon to another. It seemed to have been illuminated with the flick of a switch, like a neon sign. Behind and beneath it, the horizon merged into gloom.

'Hot chocolate?' suggested Charlie hopefully.

'And pancakes?' added Finn.

'And coffee,' said Kit, as he flicked on the wipers.

That first squall was swiftly followed by another. I made pancakes with Finn's help while Charlie spun plastic plates across the table like frisbees, howling the theme tune to *Dam Busters*. Sacha was up, dressed and trying to work the espresso machine. Meanwhile Kit hunted through the dresser drawers.

'Where's my camera? I want a photo of that massive cloud with the rainbow.'

'Um . . . is it plugged into the computer?'

'Hang on, I'll check . . . Nope. Guys, anyone seen my camera?'

The rest of us looked blank. The twins had begun squirting syrup over their pancakes, over the table, over the floor.

'Coffee, Kit?' asked Sacha, handing him a cup. 'I think I got it right.'

'Looks perfect!' Kit took an appreciative sip, then went to fetch his older camera from our bedroom. He spent the next half hour striding around in the garden, taking photographs of the strange storm light.

'So weird,' said Sacha, looking out of the window. 'It's not our garden any more. It's kind of alien.'

I stood at her shoulder. 'Spooky, isn't it? Like a solar eclipse.'

'Do you ever feel a bit . . . you know, funny about this house?'

I pantomimed quivering horror, but she didn't smile. 'Do you?' I asked.

She nodded. She looked quite strained, with bluish shadows along her eye sockets. 'Sometimes I feel as though we're being watched.'

'You mean by people?'

'It freaks me out the way it's so totally *dark* at night. It sort of presses on your eyeballs. Don't you feel as though the bush is . . . I don't know, alive? Like there's something out there?'

'You've been listening to Ira's scary stories,' I said lightly. 'Now—to more pressing matters. Where's my coffee?'

The weather moved on during the evening, leaving a sulky night. At nine o'clock I poured myself a glass of merlot and sat on the porch steps. Sacha had turned in early, complaining of a headache. Kit was working. The light from his window spread a ghostly eiderdown on the dark lawn.

There were no stars. No moon. No other dwellings. Just the blackness. I was wondering uneasily about the silver cow jug and Kit's camera, Sacha's precious locket and my missing cash. I remembered the patupaiarehe who crept down from the hills in the night, their sharp fingers reaching through the windows. They stole things, even people. I imagined a pale being tiptoeing up behind me with a leer of cunning. The hair rose on the back of my neck.

Suddenly, I stopped breathing.

There was something in the magnolia, right above my head. Something quite big, and very furtive. Rustle, rustle. I stared wildly up into the shadows.

A long silence. The calm deepened, and slowly I relaxed. Must have been a bird. I heard a lamb bleat, and its mother answered. I picked up my glass.

Then my heart burst right through my chest as an unearthly din tore the silence: a rasping, demonic hiss. It was like nothing I'd ever heard in my life before. I was on my feet and halfway across the porch before I'd had time to make a conscious decision.

Yelling for Kit, I grabbed a torch from the table and swung the beam into the upper branches of the tree. A pair of eyes gleamed, and that terrible hiss broke off as a lithe shadow ran along the branch and onto our roof. I heard footsteps skittering on the tiles.

'Possum,' said Kit's voice. 'Cute.'

'Possum?' My heart was still beating wildly. I was covered in spilled wine. The glass lay on the lawn where I'd dropped it. 'How d'you know it was a frigging possum? It sounded like the devil himself.'

Kit walked down the verandah. 'Jean showed me one the other night. The bush is overrun with them, and they're death to the native trees. They're vermin—that's what all those plastic bait stations are about. The Colbert boys used to earn pocket money by shooting possums. They'd head out at night with torches, shine light into their eyes and—*bang!* They skinned 'em. Got paid ten bucks for every pelt.'

'For God's sake. This country is barbaric.' Tonight, I agreed with Sacha. I wished we could see other lights, hear some man-made sound. A road, a pub, a party: anything but this endless blinding blackness. There was nothing; just an alien canopy of sky and the gloomy mass of the bush. Waiting. Watching.

I shone my torch along the roof. 'If that thing can climb the tree and get onto the house, then so can any other creature.'

'Yes, indeed. And New Zealand is swarming with man-eating sheep.'

'*People*, Kit. People can be man-eaters.'

He put his arm around my shoulders. 'Martha, when did we last even lock the front door? There are no villains here.'

'I miss Milton Keynes,' I whispered. 'I miss the M1 and that twenty-four-hour Tesco and the horrid orange streetlights that shone right into our bedroom. I miss the juggernauts rattling our house.'

'Careful,' warned Kit. 'No sane woman would talk like that.'

'I keep thinking about things . . . the silver jug, your camera. Sacha's locket.'

'They'll all turn up. We're not even unpacked yet.'

'I'm starting to think we have a poltergeist.'

He waved his arms. 'Woooh!' Then he leaned against me, resting his chin on top of my head, and I could feel him shaking with laughter.

I looked up onto the roof. I swear those eyes were glinting, in the dark.

Nineteen

Christmas. Barbecues and cold beer, mosquitoes in the airless nights. It wasn't right; it was cock-eyed. The Colberts threw a party and we met more neighbours. We cut down a small cypress from beside our track and stuck it in a pot as a gawky Christmas tree. Cards poured in from England—snowy scenes and red-breasted robins perched on the handles of spades. My father sent an e-card with a bunch of fabulously camp reindeer, all singing an inane but cheery little song. I watched it about a thousand times, but I only cried twice.

Sacha's solid-gold school report arrived in the post and my chest stuck out for a week. *Exemplary student... talented musician... delight to teach... asset to the school.* I never once had a report like that. Perhaps if I had, my mother would have liked me.

The primary school put on a nativity play set in Rarotonga, followed by their end-of-year barbecue, a laid-back shindig on the beach. Kit drank a little too much, along with half the other parents. People were friendly but they weren't my own. I'd have given up ten such events for a single hour with Lou and Dad.

By Christmas Eve, Kit and I were sickened by the way we'd been seduced—yet again—by the glittering insanity of the season. We vowed to have a present-free Christmas the following year. We promised this every year and never even got close, although as a sop to my middle-class conscience I always put a goat or duck for Somalia in each stocking. The twins were overexcited and I had a splitting headache. Sacha took pity on me, offering to do bedtime and bribing the boys with extra stories.

'Sit down,' ordered Kit, pulling out a chair at the kitchen table. 'Take five minutes.'

He opened a bottle of sauvignon and poured us both a glass. I was watching from under my eyelashes—despising my mistrust—and leafing through *Hawke's Bay Today*. There was news about a fatal shooting in Auckland. *Gang-related killing*, said the report, as though that explained everything. Kit draped himself around my neck, reading over my shoulder.

'Do you mind?' I asked, nuzzling my cheek sideways onto his.

'Not at all.'

I turned the page. 'Well, I do. It's really annoying having you breathing all over me like that.'

'Just pretend you're on the Tube. People always read your paper on the Tube. Hey, look!' Kit pointed at a photograph on the third page. 'There's Jean.'

'It is?' I leaned closer. It wasn't a very clear photo, but I could see two men shaking hands. 'Good Lord, you're right. *Jean Colbert presents his petition to the MP for Napier, Robin Smythe.*'

'Presents his what?'

I looked again. 'Petition. I didn't know Jean was an activist. Can't imagine him having the motivation to do anything except bumble bow-legged around the vineyard with his trousers rolled up.'

'Unless he's lobbying for the wine trade?'

'Just a sec . . .' I was reading. 'No. No, it's political. Blow me down, how eccentric! He's one of these hangers and floggers on sentencing.'

Kit laughed incredulously. 'You're kidding.'

'Strange, but true. His petition's demanding longer sentences for drug dealers.'

'Nah. Can't be the same guy. He doesn't strike me as a bigot. Must be the wrong caption.'

'Hang on. I'm trying to read.'

'Vengeful diatribe is not his style,' insisted Kit. 'Lovely fella.'

'Shush . . . Gawd, that's random. Jean collared the poor MP as he was doing some Christmas appearance down at the hospital. *"Life should mean life for those who commit violent offences while under the influence of pure methamphetamine, or P."'*

'Pee? I didn't know urine was a narcotic.'

'Shut *up*, Kit! *"The government of New Zealand must introduce a policy of zero tolerance," said Mr Colbert, as he presented his petition. "This is an evil of epidemic proportions, a poison which is destroying our society. Those who are involved in its supply, and those who offend while under its influence, must be brought to justice and irrevocably removed from our streets."'*

'Strong stuff,' said Kit, who'd begun rootling in the larder. 'Who'd have thought it? Old Jean turns out to be a redneck. Have we got any crisps?'

I was still bent over the paper, trying to reconcile the Jean I knew—the Gallic charmer who shambled dotingly after his wife and kissed me on both cheeks—with this obsessive who'd made the effort to track down an MP on a Christmas baby-kissing visit.

'Oh no,' I said suddenly. 'I get it. Oh my God.'

'Well? Don't keep me in suspense.'

'This is horrible.' I smacked my head into my hands. 'I told you Jean and Pamela lost their son?'

'Yep. I remember that.'

'He was murdered.'

Kit stopped smiling. He stepped closer, squinting at the newspaper. 'What's the story?'

'*Mr Colbert has been a staunch campaigner since the death of his son Daniel seven years ago. Daniel died after an unprovoked attack in Wellington city centre. "My son had become a father that day," said Mr Colbert. "He was a sincere and brilliant young man, a committed conservationist who was working to make a better world. And he died because someone did not like the colour of his hair."'*

'Did they catch the bloke?'

'Er . . . hang on. Two blokes. Pleaded guilty to murder and got life with a minimum non-parole period of ten years.'

'Jesus.' Kit sank down opposite me, running a hand down his face. 'Is that all they'll do?'

'Ten years is a lifetime to a young man. Any longer and there would be no chance of rehabilitation.'

'Martha, my darling, don't give me that liberal hug-a-hoodie bunkum. They might still be in their prime when they come out. How would you feel if it was one of your boys murdered?'

From upstairs, elephants' feet shook the floorboards. Finn and Charlie were serenading Sacha with their favourite naughty song. It was set to the tune—well, to call it a 'tune' might be disingenuous, as both boys appeared to be almost tone deaf—of 'John Brown's Body'.

'*We've tortured all the teachers, we've broken all the rules,*

We've fried the headmaster, we've set fire to the school . . .'

'Some parents forgive their children's killers,' I said. 'There was one on *Oprah* a few years back.'

'*Oh glory, glory allelu-iah, Teacher hit me with a ru-ler . . .*'

Kit's eyes had darkened. Every trace of laughter had gone. 'Forgive them? I'd kill 'em,' he said. 'If someone hurt one of our three, they wouldn't be doing a life sentence, they'd be dead. I would hunt them down and kill them.'

'Not that you're a redneck.'

'No. I'm a father.'

'*So I shot her in the butt,*

With a cannonball coco-nu-u-ut.'

The boys began Christmas Day at an ungodly hour. I could hear them jumping on Sacha before the three of them burst into our room, dragging their hauls. Kit groaned. We'd been up half the night, ramming water pistols and Mr Men pyjamas into stockings.

'Cool,' enthused Charlie. 'Jarmies, with Mr Men on them. Have you got some too, Finny? *Finn!* Did you get some too?'

'Look at this,' snarled Finn, tearing at a package. 'Electric toothbrush! Santa's a cheeky old thing.'

'Thanks, Santa.' Sacha waved a Lily Allen CD. 'He's a clever girl. C'mon, boys! Who's up for a water pistol fight?'

Once they'd gone, Kit and I stepped out onto the balcony, inhaling the tang of sea and pasture as we gazed down the valley. There were no exhaust fumes, no lawnmowers, no motorway hum, just the endless hissing and clicking of cicadas in the pristine blueness of our world. I saw that view ten times a day, but it still made me stop and stare.

'Most people have to die to get to heaven,' said Kit quietly. 'How come we get to live there when we're still alive?'

Finn's blood-freezing war cry shattered the peace, and I caught a glimpse of dark mane and thin bare legs as he scaled the magnolia tree. Sacha tiptoed around the corner of the house with her weapon loaded and Charlie pressed close behind her. My curly-headed boy was, frankly, a bit of a drip. In any physical confrontation with Finn he would be the loser, but today he had a mighty protector.

At nine thirty, Kit hared off to the nearest Catholic church, whose doors he had scarcely darkened since we'd arrived. His faith was rather like his relationship with his mother: much neglected, but a vague source of comfort. Fleetingly I pondered whether we should all go, but Sacha had made a chocolate log and the boys were busy mutilating it with Christmas angel figures. Anyway, none of us was dressed.

Lily Allen began to sing a very rude song at full volume, her glorious profanity soaring across the valley. On a whim, I phoned Louisa.

'Happy Christmas!' I said brightly.

Lou sounded world-weary. 'I still haven't finished the stockings, then I've got to eat the carrot and the mince pie and leave soot all over the place. The great Father Christmas myth denies one fundamental truth—Santa is female.'

We had the usual conversation about what time it was, and what the weather was doing. Hot here, cold there. Light here, dark there. Lou's voice became increasingly feeble until I asked her what was wrong. Big mistake.

'Our first Christmas without you,' she whispered shakily.

'For God's sake!' I could have nutted her.

'The kids think you'll be here for lunch as usual. They can't understand why you aren't coming. And poor Dad misses his grandchildren terribly.'

'Rubbish. Dad's fine.'

'He's *not* fine. We try to see him more often, but there's only so much we can do.'

I ground my teeth. 'He isn't complaining. *You* are. Get over it, Lou. I'm the one who's supposed to be homesick, remember?'

'You chose to leave. Nobody made you. You're all right, Jack.'

'Fine,' I snapped, and hung up. Then the five-year-old in me burst into tears and had to run upstairs. I took a shower and washed my blotchy face. By the time I tottered down again, Kit was home.

'Lou called,' he said matter-of-factly. 'Says she's sorry. Why's she sorry? No, don't answer that—I can guess. Says you caught her at a bad moment. She's going to bed now, so don't call her back.'

'I've no intention of calling her back! She's been a complete bitch.'

'Can we open our presents?' asked Finn, who'd been digging around in the pile.

'One each, and the rest after lunch.' Kit picked out two parcels. 'How about these ones from Grandpa?'

The boys attacked the booty, dragging off a kilo of bubble wrap to reveal a pair of porcelain piggybanks: blue porkers with long eyelashes and drunken leers. Finn shook his pig, and it chinked. When he prised out the stopper, a pile of notes and coins spilled onto the floor.

'Treasure!' he breathed. 'Look, Buc'neer Bob. This 'ere be pirate's gold.'

'UK money,' said Kit. ''Fraid the exchange rate's against you.'

Finn wasn't interested in the vagaries of the international money market. His tongue stuck out the side of his mouth as he sorted his loot into piles. Charlie did the same, and the two small capitalists gloated over their hoard. They had no idea what any of the coins were worth—I don't think they cared—and in the end Kit lay down on the floor and helped them. The whole process took half an hour, while Sacha and I lobbed a picnic into bags.

'Fifty quid each.' Kit began to shovel the coins away. 'You tycoons can take it down to the bank when you want to cash up.'

We were ready to leave when the telephone rang. I got to it first.

'Martha,' rumbled Dad's voice. 'Happy Christmas to you, Kit and all the little piglets.'

'Dad! Must be midnight there?'

'I'm waiting up. Going to catch old Santa in the act. There's a few things I'd like to discuss with him.'

'Are you by yourself?' I felt sad. Dad always used to stay with us on Christmas Eve.

'Don't fret. I'm off to Louisa's in the morning.'

I had a vision of my family around Lou's overloaded tree, raising glasses of mulled wine. 'Oh, lucky you. Um . . . I hung up on her just before.'

'So she told me. She's a little fragile at the moment, Martha. Don't think less of her.'

'Give her my love . . . give them all our love.' I had a lump in my throat. 'I wish I was there.'

'I wish you were, too,' he said briskly. 'But I bet you're going to have an exotic day. Barbecue?'

'Picnic at the river, actually. Swimming and bubbly, chilled in the shallows.' Finn and Charlie were prancing as though they had a swarm of bees down their shorts, trying to wrestle the receiver out of my hand. 'I'd better throw you to the wolves now, Dad. You've got to speak to all the children . . . and Kit sends his love.'

'And I send mine to you all, dearest Martha. Have a wonderful day.'

Sacha looked deflated once the call ended. 'I miss him,' she said. 'I miss them all.'

'Me too.' Charlie reached for his blanket, round-eyed. 'Will we be going home soon?'

I wished we could board a plane right away and just go home. Then I thought of Jenna, who had heard the click of a gun at her temple. She didn't have the luxury of wallowing in homesickness. I clapped my hands. 'Hats and sunscreen on, please! Got your swimming trunks?'

'Togs!' shouted Charlie. 'They're not trunks, they're togs.'

I realised with a jolt that my boys were beginning to sound like New Zealanders. It was just a hint: a flattening of the vowels, a slight rise at the end of the sentence and the odd word—'chippies' instead of crisps, 'lollies' instead of sweets—but nevertheless it was undeniable. I didn't like it. It felt like a loss of my own identity.

With Muffin panting beside us, we ambled in the gathering heat across shrivelled pasture and down a steep hillside to our favourite bend of the river. There was nobody there, of course. No sign that there ever had or ever would be. That was the extraordinary thing, that's what you couldn't get your head around if you were brought up in suburban Britain.

Our stretch of river was a beauty spot on a world-class scale. Cool water flowed across its shingle bed with the clarity of a glacier mint, pooling under little limestone cliffs where swallows flickered with impossible speed in and out of their burrows. There were swirling eddies and waterfalls and trout pools so pure that their depths looked like blue glass, all beneath a flawless mauve sky. The Colberts' vineyard swathed the far bank, adding a touch of the Mediterranean. I wished Lou could see it. I was sure she'd forgive me then.

The grey river stones scorched our feet. Muffin plodded straight in, grunting with pleasure as the exquisite chill streamed through her coat. The boys were next: sleek wet otters in orange water wings. Muffin circled happily around them, her ears flat on the water. Sacha plunged, grabbing Charlie's ankle and making him shriek with nervous delight. Weeks of sunshine had bleached his corkscrew curls.

Cooled by the massage of the current, Kit and I sipped New Zealand bubbly out of plastic glasses while the riverbed rang with laughter. 'Good decision?' asked Kit, prodding my cheek with his toe.

I didn't answer. I was looking at Sacha in her bikini top and board shorts, a fountain of diamonds spraying around her shoulders. It was some time since I'd seen her in a bikini. A worm of anxiety stirred in my gut.

Kit's foot again, nudging insistently against my cheekbone. Sometimes he could be as demanding as his sons. 'Hey. Calling all Marthas, come in please!'

'Don't you think she's getting much too thin?' I asked.

'Who? Sacha? No.'

'I can see her ribs.'

'She doesn't have an eating disorder—really, Martha, she doesn't, she's just trying to stay in shape like every other teenage girl. You've yo-yo dieted yourself for most of your life.'

I grimaced. 'I've never been as thin as that.'

'Martha. Relax. Everything's good.' He raised his glass. 'Happy Christmas, Ms Pioneer.'

Twenty

I think I've been in this hospital all my life, but it is still the first day.

I fall asleep after talking to Charlie, kneeling on the floor with my face near Finn. I don't know how long it is before I feel a hand on my upper arm. Kura Pohatu is crouched beside me.

'Hello, Kura.' We try to be polite and controlled, even when everything is imploding. Will the human race exercise self-restraint when Armageddon comes? Will we make small talk as the lights go out? Yes, I think we might.

'You all right, Martha?' she asks.

'Mm?' I struggle upright, pummelling my face. 'Yes, yes.'

Her gaze takes in my bleary eyes and the marks of the sheet etched into my cheeks. 'Come to a family room,' she says, and steers me out of the ward, down a corridor and into a small room with a couple of armchairs. A television is jammed into one corner, and there's a pile of old magazines on a round table.

'The sun's still up,' I say in dull surprise, standing at the window. A blue and grey sky stretches above the city of Hastings. Light blasts off the windscreens of cars and the clouds have pale undersides, like sharks. Until now I couldn't have told you whether it was day or night. I could scarcely have told you who I was.

'It's only four o'clock,' says Kura. 'Like some tea?'

My phone rings. I pull it out of my pocket.

'Mum?' Sacha's words tumble and tangle. 'What's going on? What's happening? Oh my God, Finn.'

'Finn's all right.'

'Just woken up . . . I've got to come to the hospital. Bianka's here, she says she'll drive me.'

Quietly, Kura lays a mug and two biscuits beside me. I raise my eyebrows in thanks. 'No, don't come today.'

'I've *got* to!'

'Sacha, they don't need fluey girls in ICU! They've enough illness in there as it is—your virus could kill people. Anyway, there's no point. They're keeping him unconscious.'

She's skidding into hysteria. 'Why didn't you wake me?'

'There was nothing you could have done.'

'I can't believe I didn't hear anything. He must have been right outside my door! Why did he have to climb on that stupid rail?'

A tide of rage smashes into me. I almost tell her, here and now. If Kura Pohatu wasn't sitting nearby, nonchalantly pretending to turn the pages of a magazine, I swear I would spew out the whole story.

'Sacha,' I say firmly. 'I'm really sorry, doll, but I have to go now. I'll call again soon. Finn's doing well, just hold onto that.'

She's sobbing. 'Give him a million, trillion kisses. Tell him I love him.'

'Finn's sister,' I explain, as I end the call.

The social worker smiles and closes her magazine. 'I thought we should talk again, because I'm not sure we really covered everything last time.'

'So you've come back for round two?'

'This isn't a boxing match. I'm here to work *with* you. If you need help, you only have to ask.'

'Thank you. I appreciate your offer, but all I need is for Finn to come back to us.'

'There are other children in your family,' she says, with heavy meaning.

'And they're quite safe. Scared, upset, but safe. My neighbour is taking good care of them.'

'Your neighbour . . .' She inhales, and I see her nose tighten as though something doesn't smell right. 'Why did you come to New Zealand? What made you take that final plunge?'

'It isn't unusual. Immigrants are pouring into this country every day.'

'And each has their reason. What was yours? You had a job, a family, friends. You had a lot to lose.'

I'm tired, suddenly; tired to the very core of my being. I am tired of watching and of being watched. I'm tired of covering things up. 'Kit's business folded.'

She doesn't react, but she's listening.

'The downturn,' I say. 'Work dried up, clients stopped paying and he went under. He tried to go freelance but that was hopeless in the recession. Eventually it wore him down.'

'Tell me about how it wore him down.'

'Kit's such a vibrant person, always the life and soul. He . . .' I run out of words, but Kura waits for me to find more. 'Every morning he watched me get up and dressed and off to work. Every night we worried about money. He couldn't see a future.'

'I expect he was angry?'

'I didn't say that.'

'Well, anyone would be angry.'

'He was *low*. It was . . . destructive.' I clamp my mouth shut, determined not to say another word, but the patience of the woman is unsettling. 'He was only forty, far too young to retire. So it was a good time for an adventure.'

'And how is he now? Did your gamble pay off?'

'He's happier than he's ever been in his life before. He's painting. It's a dream come true.'

'Whose dream?'

'Mine, too.'

Outside, a harassed mother—or is she harassed? Actually, she looks rather cheerful—is loading her children into a car. The toddler cavorts around the pavement as though chasing an invisible butterfly. They're a happy, hopeful family, like ours used to be. Nobody has fallen.

'Martha?' Kura is peaceful yet persistent. 'When did things begin to go wrong for you?'

Someone is knocking at the door. Kura looks irritated, but she stands up and opens it. There's an urgent, whispered conversation. I think I hear my own name.

'I'll just be a moment, Martha,' she says, and steps outside.

I watch the mother drive away, with her children. Lucky things. They're going home to supper, and stories, and cuddles.

A series of choices, I think. *A right turn, a left turn; inching through the maze. A left turn, a right turn, and a wrong turn.*

Twenty-one

Kit and I huddled on our verandah steps as a quavering disc of fire emerged over the edge of the world. The first dawn of the year.

The boys were fast asleep. Sacha had gone with Jani and Bianka to the midnight fireworks display in Napier. When I'd dropped her at the cinema the previous evening, Jani came over to wish me a happy New Year. He was wearing a collarless shirt with a green cloth knotted around his neck. The effect was very nearly camp, but not quite. As I drove off, I adjusted my rear-view mirror just in time to see Sacha's hand twining with his.

I told Kit about those twining hands, as the sun inched higher.

'You *happened* to adjust your rear-view mirror,' Kit chortled.

'He was definitely holding her hand.'

'Of course he was,' he murmured, then gathered my own fingers in his.

'She's sixteen. He's twenty-one.'

He kissed my knuckles, one after the other. I felt his breath on my palm.

'At twenty-one,' I fretted, 'he'll be wanting things that at sixteen she shouldn't be giving.' Kit's mouth ran up the inside of my arm while he adeptly untied the bow on my kimono. 'She's still my baby,' I said, but I was rapidly losing interest in the conversation. I began to undo the buttons on his shirt, and had slipped it off one tanned shoulder when an unpleasant thought struck me. 'Finn and Charlie could appear at any minute, you know.'

'Too true.' He got to his feet and pulled me to mine. Giggling, half-dressed, we ran along the verandah in our bare feet and locked ourselves into the studio. Standing on the rug in the calico light, Kit bent to kiss my collarbone. 'I am a lucky man,' he said quietly.

An hour later, our house was calm. Kit and I dozed, tangled on the rug, my hand touching his face as the warmth of the sun found its way through the old windows and onto Sibella's portrait. For once, the twins slept in. But the snake was wide awake now, and beginning to throw its coils.

Sacha phoned after lunch.

'Where are you?' I had one eye on Finn, who was struggling manfully to load the dishwasher. He'd been bribed, of course.

She sounded slightly out of breath, as though she was walking fast. 'Marine Parade. You know that play park?'

'Aren't you a bit old for swings?' No reply. I had the impression she was having two conversations at once. 'Sacha?'

'Sorry. Just buying ice creams. They're amazing flavours. Mine's boysenberry and it's a taste sensation.'

'Have you had fun?'

'A blast. The fireworks were so cool.'

'Any sleep?'

'Sleep's for losers.'

'Aren't you tired?'

'Hell, no. Only *old* people need to laze around like cats, getting hours and hours of sleep. I've never felt more awake in my—whew!'

I heard muffled thuds, and a squeal of laughter. 'Sacha? You still there?'

'Sorry. Someone pushed me really fast on the roundabout and my phone went flying off into orbit.'

'Who else is with you?'

'Sorry, Mum, I gotta go. Speak to you later. Um . . . I'll be back tomorrow, okay?'

'Tomorrow? I thought today—'

She'd gone.

Finn was carrying a tall stack of glasses. It was doing a fair imitation of the Leaning Tower of Pisa. 'Aw,' he moaned, as I took them out of his hands, 'I was doin' it!'

'Just a bit wobbly.'

He stood glowering as I loaded the top rack. I could tell he had something on his mind. 'I still get a chocolate though, don't I? I was doin' it until you butted in.'

'Sure do, Batman.' I lifted a box of Quality Street from the top of the fridge, and he grabbed one. 'Take another for Charlie,' I said.

His jaw dropped in outrage. '*What?* No! Did Charlie help with the dishes?'

'Well, no, but—'

'No dishes, no chocolate.' Finn folded his arms. I could see the family murderess appraising me with livid blue eyes.

'Remember the workers in the vineyard,' said Kit, appearing from the hall. 'Jolly useful parable, that one.'

'The who?' Finn blinked uncertainly at the dishwasher. 'I never worked in a . . . thing yard. I helped with the dishes.'

Kit laughed, and made for the kettle.

'Midnight in the UK,' I said, looking at the clock. 'Big Ben is striking. I wonder what Dad's doing?'

'Probably dancing naked in the garden with all his hippy friends. They'll re-enact a druidical solstice ceremony.'

'Ooh!' Finn looked scandalised. 'Who's naked? Grandpa? Grandpa's in the nuddy!'

It wasn't an image I wanted to dwell on. 'I'll phone him,' I decided. 'Off you go, Finn. Charlie's riding his bike round the walnut tree.'

'Okay,' said Finn, rummaging in the chocolate box and surreptitiously shoving a handful down his shorts.

As it happened, Dad was seeing in the New Year with Flora. We were chatting happily when I was distracted by a resounding metallic smash, followed swiftly by screams. They weren't angry yells; they were high and panicked. Seconds later, Kit pounded through the kitchen and out of the back door.

'Gotta go, Dad,' I said, and dashed after Kit. Under the walnut, Finn was sobbing in his father's arms.

'Finn's bike did a roly-poly,' said Charlie, making his arm swing in an arc. 'Like this—*bam!*'

'The wheel got stuck,' wailed Finn.

I knelt beside him. 'Did you hit your head?'

'Not my head, my arm. Ow!'

'Naughty bike,' commiserated Charlie, laying a sympathetic hand on his brother's leg. 'I'll get Buccaneer Bob for a cuddle.'

Kit carried Finn into the sitting room where I took a closer look at him. There was no sign of concussion. He clutched Bob, stroking his own ear.

'Where does it hurt?' I asked.

With a tragic pout he held out his right wrist. It looked normal save for a small lump on the thumb side, and he could move all his fingers.

'Probably a sprain.' I gave him some Pamol while Kit filled a sock with ice and bandaged it onto the wrist. By the time we'd finished, Finn was calm and asking for *Mary Poppins.* She was always wheeled out at times of stress. Whenever things went wrong, the boys would want the magic nanny with the sweet smile and indefatigable confidence.

Kit followed me out of the room. 'What's the verdict?'

'Gave us all a fright, but no harm done.'

'Concussion?'

'Nah. He's sure he didn't fall on his head.'

'I could take him to a doctor. Get him checked out.'

'On New Year's Day?' I flapped a hand. 'Nearest medical centre's in Napier. I don't know about you, but I don't feel like driving all that way just to be told he's sprained his wrist. He's much better tucked up at home.'

After the film Finn rallied, eating toasted sandwiches and playing Ludo. He fell asleep before bedtime, though. We found him lying on the sitting-room floor with his rear stuck up in the air.

'Big day for a little chap,' I said.

Kit picked him up. 'You sure I shouldn't drive him down to the hospital?'

I shook my head, yawning. Our early start was catching up on me. 'Nope. It's too far, and the emergency department will still be heaving with drunken revellers. Just put him to bed.'

'You're the expert.' Kit gathered his son closer, and carried him upstairs.

At about three in the morning, Finn wandered whimpering into our room. I could barely drag my eyes open, but gave him some more Pamol and settled him down between us. He was happy enough for the rest of the night; his parents, on the other hand, were kneed and jabbed and elbowed by a pocket-sized tyrant. As the sun came up I heard a creak and saw Kit by the chest of drawers, pulling on his trousers.

'Where are you off to?' I asked, turning the clock around to face me. 'Bloody Nora, man. Ten to six! Have you finally lost your marbles?'

Kit jerked his head at Finn, who was sprawled horizontally across the bed. 'McNamara has murdered sleep,' he said softly. 'I'll get down to the studio and make the most of the peace.'

Stretching, I stole his pillow. 'Any chance of a lovely cup of tea, while you're on your feet?'

A sleepy voice piped from beside me, 'Dad . . . Dad?'

Kit instantly sat and gathered the small figure onto his lap. 'Finn . . . Finn?'

Watching father and son smiling at one another, I was struck by how very alike they were. Physically it was obvious—you couldn't miss the wayward dark hair and wide-set blue eyes. It was more than looks, though; it was their restless passion. Both were selfish yet generous, quick-tempered yet funny, mocking yet vulnerable. Brooding storms one day, sunshine the next. There was a deep, exclusive understanding between them.

Finn reached out a small hand, patting his father's cheek. 'Will you take us to the beach today?'

Kit pretended to bite the hand. 'For you, Finn McNamara, anything.'

Sacha sent a text later, asking to be collected from town. I had some grocery shopping to do, so I said I'd be there in an hour.

As I pulled up at the kerb, she got in without a word.

'Happy New Year!' I cried. 'Had a good time?'

'Yep.'

I felt deflated. 'Anything wrong?'

'Nope.' She closed her eyes.

'Shall we go for lunch in a café?'

'No thanks.'

'How's Jani?'

'Fine.'

I couldn't stop prodding. 'Have you two had a fight?'

'Nope. Everything's fine.'

'How's—'

'I'm tired, Mum. I feel sick, and I'm aching all over. Going down with a stinking cold. I caught it off Bianka—she was in bed all over Christmas. And no, I didn't drink too much.'

'Thought never crossed my mind,' I protested, which was a bare-faced lie. I'd never seen anyone more clearly hung-over. Except Kit, of course.

Shopping was always fun with Sacha around; she had a gift for transforming commonplace into comedy. But this time, while I was backing into a parking space, she jerked her seat down flat and put her feet on the dashboard. When I tottered back half an hour later with a week's worth of groceries and a traumatised credit card, she hadn't moved at all.

'Look, you've obviously had a fight with Jani,' I said loudly, as I slammed my door. 'But that's no excuse for being downright rude. I'm here to listen, if you want to talk.' I started the engine. 'No? Well. Fine.' She was dead to the world, and I drove out of town with the radio for company.

I'd begun meandering through a narrow valley and was listening to a rather dreamy radio play when my eardrums seemed to explode. I glimpsed a tattooed arm as a motorbike shot past, inches from my door.

'*Shit*,' I gasped. My pulse was throbbing. The bike seemed to have come from nowhere.

Sacha rolled her head. 'Mm?'

Another bike screamed by, so aggressively close that I almost ran into the ditch. Then the world shook with thunderous revving, and a glance in my mirror revealed a gang of God knows how many—twenty? thirty?—massed right up my exhaust pipe. It was impossible for me to pull in safely. If their intention was to intimidate and harass, they succeeded, because I felt like a deer among a pack of baying wolves. Some wore German soldier helmets and were lying almost prone on their bikes. Many had their faces covered with scarves. Gang patches—insignia—dominated leather jackets. I'd seen such bikers before; they were a common enough sight in Hawke's Bay, but never so close nor in such numbers.

'And a happy New Year to you too, effing wankers,' I yelled shakily, as the last of them roared into the distance. Maybe they were just nice men out for a joyride—perhaps to spend a merry afternoon knifing someone in the Torutaniwha pub—but I felt horribly vulnerable. As I turned into our drive, it struck me that the police could be a long time arriving if ever we needed help.

As soon as I pulled up, Sacha rolled out of her seat and headed for the house.

'It's okay! No problem! I can carry all the shopping,' I shouted at her retreating back. She didn't look round.

The rest of my family bowled in from the beach while I was attacking a pile of washing up. The boys, wrapped in sandy towels, were unusually mellow. They clung like bushbabies to my legs, giggling quietly, hiding their faces in my skirt.

'Coffee!' gasped Kit. 'Leave my girlfriend alone, lads. Bugger off and break your Christmas presents.'

Finn sneaked into the pantry, emerging on tiptoe. The biscuit tin bulged under his towel as the pair of them sidled away. Kit and I smiled, and turned a blind eye.

'How's the arm?' I asked, scrubbing at a baking tray.

'Arm? Oh, Finn's arm. A bit stiff. Can't be much wrong with him though, the way he was rocketing around. He's like a flea in a jar, that kid.' Kit switched on the coffee machine. 'Sacha home?'

'She certainly is.'

'How was her New Year?'

I snorted. 'Claims to have a cold. She's blatantly hung-over and I think she and Jani have had a tiff. Anita seems a lovely woman, but they're obviously pretty relaxed in that household.'

'Oh well. It takes all sorts. They've got their own problems.'

'Jani is a *very* bad influence. Hung-over, at her age!'

Kit laid a hand each side of me on the sink, nuzzling his nose through the curls at the nape of my neck. 'You have to stop expecting that poor child to be immaculate and superlative in every way. She loves her brothers, helps around the house and gets the best school reports I've ever seen—bloody swot. Jesus, what more do you want?'

I leaned back against him, swaying slightly. 'So I leave her to go off the rails?'

'You leave her to make her own mistakes.'

'You think I'm behaving like my own mother, don't you?'

He pressed his mouth onto the side of my throat. 'If the cap fits . . .'

'It doesn't. Mine was impossibly controlling.'

'Sacha's a fantastic girl,' he murmured, 'and you're a fantastic mum. Maybe sometimes just a teeny bit of a fusspot.'

'I resent that remark!'

'I'd tread lightly, if I were you,' he said as he headed for the studio. 'You may have influence, but you no longer have power.'

Twenty-two

January was breathless. We spent the nights spread-eagled like intergalactic starfish under our mosquito nets, longing for the cool of the morning. Sometimes we'd trudge down to the river and sit gasping as the cold water rushed around us.

Under that burning sky, Kit was truly at peace for the first time since I'd known him; perhaps for the first time in his life. I had to work flat out during the long school holidays, but he threw himself into his role as house-husband with galling competence. To my delight, Sacha gave up most of her summer holidays to help. With their father and sister—and sometimes even Bianka—at their beck and call, my lucky sons had the best summer of their lives.

In early February, Pamela Colbert invited us for Sunday lunch. Her grandson was visiting and she wanted some playmates for him.

It was a shimmering day. Sacha drove her brothers on the quad bike through our fields and across the river, Kit and I following on foot. Singing warlike songs, the three children rushed downhill through parched summer grass and across the vineyards, accompanied by a zinging orchestra of cicadas. The Colberts' place was a 1970s bungalow with picture windows, deep eaves and a garden straight out of a magazine. Finn and Charlie tore off their clothes and began to cavort in the sprinkler, coloured light arching over their heads.

'There have been small boys playing under that sprinkler for over thirty years,' said Pamela, who'd come out to meet us. 'Ah, William!'

A boy emerged from the house; perhaps seven or eight, he stared at the twins, arms held stiffly by his sides. He had delicious auburn hair in a short back and sides, like a grown man, and dark eyes. When Pamela beckoned he marched solemnly up to us and held out a hand.

'My grandson, William. This is Martha, Kit, Sacha, and these are . . .' Still talking, she steered him towards Finn and Charlie, who were ballooning up their shorts with water.

Finn was the first of the boys to speak. 'Wanna havva go?' he asked courteously, offering the sprinkler. 'It's great. You fill your shorts, see? It looks like your bottom's a 'normous melon.'

Pamela chuckled. 'William won't be shy for long. Come on in, the rest of you. Glass of wine?' She led us into the taupe gloom of the kitchen, where she had a bottle of white chilling in the fridge. 'William is home-schooled—poor Hannah's very protective, understandably—so I'm keen for him to have a bit of rough and tumble. Lemonade, Sacha?'

'Please!' Sacha looked around. 'Anything I can do to help?'

Pamela made a face that said *bless*. 'Well—could you take this out to the boys?' She watched as Sacha left, carrying lemonade. Home-made, inevitably. 'Credit to you, that girl. Is she still seeing a lot of Tabby Mills?'

'Not so much, actually,' said Kit. 'She's not, is she, Martha? That friendship seems to have fizzled out a bit.'

It was true. Sacha had talked about Tabby constantly for the first school term, but we'd not heard of her since Christmas. Bianka had the top spot nowadays.

'I'm glad, really,' I said. 'Lovely girl, but maybe a bit—I don't know—a bit too *cool* for Sacha.'

'Too skinny, she means.' Kit put an arm around my shoulders, smiling at Pamela with a suggestion of eye-rolling. 'Martha thinks Sacha's got anorexia, or maybe bulimia.'

I shrugged him off, feeling patronised. A minute or two later I left the two of them in the kitchen, heads bent over a book of sculptures by a very trendy Australian artist who left me stone cold, and followed delicious cooking smells out to a paved terrace where Jean greeted me with an exuberant wave of his barbecue fork. I was relieved to see he wasn't wearing a novelty apron or silly chef's hat.

'Brought you a present,' I said, handing him a glass. 'Your best year, apparently.'

The terrace was a pleasant spot, shaded and bathed in the scents of barbecue and wine, lavender and dry grass. Beneath us, vines ran down the hillside in parallel lines with rose bushes at the ends. I'd always thought these were to encourage bees, but Jean explained that they were a bit like the canary in a miner's cage—if there was disease around, the poor old roses would cop it first. Across the lawn I could see the three boys jumping together on the trampoline, talking urgently. They were best mates already.

Sacha came to join us, kissing Jean's cheek. 'William is *so* cute,' she said.

Jean glanced over at the boys. 'It would have been his father's birthday today.'

'Oh no!' Sacha—dear, warm-hearted Sacha—seemed ready to cry. 'Jean, I'm so sorry.'

'We like having William to stay with us at this time each year, and it gives his mother a few days to herself.'

'How are you?' I asked. 'How's Pamela?'

'So-so.' Jean lifted a shoulder. He couldn't meet my eye. 'Daniel would have been thirty-one today. He was just starting out . . . a brand-new father.' He smiled weakly, and patted Sacha's cheek. 'You would have liked him, Sacha. You know, I really think he might have saved the world . . . But I mustn't talk like that. Pamela says it isn't productive.'

'I read about your petition,' I said.

'Do you know what happened to Daniel?'

I felt terribly ignorant. 'Just what it said in the paper.'

He glanced at Sacha. 'I'll tell you another time. I think perhaps this isn't a subject . . .'

'It's okay, I won't be upset,' insisted Sacha.

'You will.'

'Really, Jean,' I said. 'We've never sheltered her from life.' Privately, I wasn't sure I wanted to hear this story.

'Well.' My neighbour breathed deeply for a moment, frowning fiercely, steadying his voice. 'Daniel was out in Wellington, celebrating the happiest day of his life. He had a baby son! Was it a crime, to have a few drinks? I don't think so. He left his friends in a bar for a moment, nipped over to a cashpoint machine. And that's when his luck ran out.

'Two men were walking up the street. They'd been bingeing on pure meth—P—and they'd fried their tiny brains. They hadn't slept for a fortnight and they were in a state they call tweaking. These people were already a waste of space, but this night they were psychopaths. One of them pretended to make a grab for Daniel's money, just to distract him. The other one struck a massive blow to the back of his head. Daniel fell to the ground. Then they began to kick him as he tried to crawl away. It was a feeding frenzy . . . they were laughing out loud as they booted my son. They screamed like karate fighters, exhorting one another to greater savagery. They took run-ups and kicked his head as though it was a football. This carried on long after he'd stopped moving. Finally they walked away, laughing fit to burst. How do I know all this? Because it was caught on the CCTV cameras.'

'Oh my God.' Sacha's hand was pressed across her mouth, her eyes bright with horror. 'Oh, Jean.'

'I've watched every second of it many times. I've even seen it in slow motion. I know every blow by heart.'

'Didn't anyone try to stop them?' I asked.

'A group of girls ran up, shouting—not much older than you, Sacha—and pulled out their cell phones to call the police. That was when the morons finally walked off. They didn't even run! They just swaggered away, jeering and pulling fingers at Daniel's body. I admire those girls. I don't believe they were the only people who saw, but they were the only ones to take action. A crowd began to gather, and Daniel's friends came to find out what the commotion was about. But he was already beyond help. The doctors kept him artificially alive on a machine until Pamela and I could get there to be with him. Hannah had come from the maternity ward with the baby, and spent some hours with him. We were holding Daniel's hands when they switched him off.'

Sacha stared into the vineyard, blinking desperately, a tear spilling down her cheek. I sat silent. These parents had witnessed the end of their son's life. I couldn't imagine it.

Eventually, I found my voice. 'They caught the attackers?'

'Of course.' Jean shrugged contemptuously. 'Easily. The whole thing was on film. And you know what one of these scum said when they arrested him? He said it was "hug a ginga" day. It was, too. That's an idea invented by some genius at a radio station.'

'Ginga?'

'Redhead. Daniel had auburn hair. So this monster said he and his mate decided it was "pulp a ginga" day. They went out looking for a redhead. He was still giggling about it when they put him in the back of the police van.'

'I don't believe I'm hearing this.'

'One pleaded guilty to murder. The other said he didn't intend to injure Daniel.'

Sacha's mouth fell open. '*What?*'

'He'd been playing a violent computer game for seventy hours straight. Claimed he had some temporary psychosis and believed Daniel would "respawn" somewhere, get up and walk away. Pamela and I were there for every single second of the trial. We watched that video again and again. You can imagine how we felt. That was our son on the ground.'

'But surely the guy didn't get off?' I asked.

'No, he didn't get off. There were hours of legal argument, three psychiatrists gave evidence, and on the third day he pleaded guilty. So the pair of them got life imprisonment, which doesn't mean life at all. They'll be out quite soon. Those worthless imbeciles took Daniel's future, yet *they* still have a future. They can even become fathers. One of their mothers dared to appear on the television and complain that her son was a victim!'

'How could she possibly say that?'

Jean folded his hands and mimicked the whine of a spoiled child: '"It was the P that did it, the P changed her son, he was such a lovely gentle boy, always helping old ladies across roads. Poor me!"' Jean snorted. 'I felt sick to hear her.'

'Stupid woman!' Sacha looked disgusted. 'Her son wasn't good enough to tie Daniel's shoelaces.'

'She never said sorry?' I asked.

'Sorry?' Jean held up despairing hands. 'Not in her vocabulary! It was all about how she'd lost a son, too. Well, boohoo. I hope he hangs himself in jail. The world would be a better place.' He shook himself. 'You must excuse me. I shouldn't say these things. Pamela says it's my obsession.'

Sacha put her arm around his shoulders. 'Those monsters ruined your life.'

Jean closed his eyes for a moment. 'The worst thing is that my grandson will never know his father. William's birthday is the anniversary of Daniel's death. Every year his mother tries to make it a happy day, and every year she fails.' He turned a knob on the barbecue and lifted a tray of steak from underneath. 'One of our own beasts.' He sounded choked. 'You won't find a cut like this in the supermarket.'

'What was Daniel like, Jean?' asked Sacha. I was surprised by her courage; at her age, I think I would have wanted to change the subject.

Jean thought for a second. 'Look through the French doors, there—you'll see him above the fireplace.'

We leaned to peer into the Colberts' sitting room. Family photographs lined the mantelpiece, and above them hung a painting of four boys. The scene was redolent of Hawke's Bay in the summer, blue and brown and ochre. Three were freckled, rangy lads—teenagers, I'd guess—sitting on a hillside with their arms around one another's shoulders. One had striking auburn hair. A much smaller boy sat on his lap, laughing. The four looked like a team, like comrades. You could sense the brotherliness.

'Our boys,' said Jean warmly. 'See, Daniel is holding Philippe? Poor little fellow, he thought the world of Daniel. Pamela's mother commissioned that painting for a Christmas present when they were all quite young. It's a local artist.'

'What a wonderful idea,' I said.

'But you ask what was Daniel like?' Jean rocked back on his heels. 'There's a big question! Our third child, the peacemaker of the family. Where Michel and Jules fought like cat and dog, Daniel would defuse the situation with his wit. He was very funny. Wit was his skeleton key, opening all doors . . . And what else? A dedicated scientist, a conservationist. As a schoolboy he gave his holidays to the kiwi breeding project up here. Just before he died he'd begun a doctorate, working to save a little bird called the fairy tern from extinction.'

'The fairy tern?' I said blankly. 'Sorry, I haven't come across it.'

'Most people haven't. To Maori, it's the tara-iti. A truly delightful creature, but mankind has destroyed its habitat and it has the doubtful distinction of being New Zealand's rarest breeding bird—there are just a few pairs left. Daniel was passionate about its conservation. He felt that focusing on the exquisite details of nature was as vital as big, sweeping projects. He and his team were relocating four breeding pairs from Northland to an estuary on the East Cape. Not easy.'

Jean turned the meat competently, with a flick of his wrist. 'What else? Well . . . he was the light of our life. It's true. The world changed forever at the moment when we heard the news. It became a darker place, not only for Pamela and myself but for everyone who knew Daniel. It is still a darker place.'

'His young brother?' I asked.

Jean nodded sadly. 'Philippe was just ten. He's constantly striving to find meaning in his life and Daniel's death. So you see, when those two imbeciles butchered my boy for fun, they destroyed more than one life.'

'But you have William,' whispered Sacha. Her eyes were still glimmering.

Jean managed a smile. 'Will! He is hilarious.'

'That kid's a dag,' said Pamela, who'd arrived with Kit in tow. She was holding a beeswax candle. 'They're up to something, Martha. William swiped a roll of cling wrap off my kitchen bench, and now they're all three giggling in the bathroom.'

'Oh no,' I groaned. 'That's the twins' new prank. They'll be stretching it across the loo.'

A minute later the boys sidled out of the house and up to Jean, smirking. Finn and William nudged Charlie. *Go on, go on.*

'Excuse me, Jean,' wheedled Charlie, opening his eyes wide. 'Would you like to go to the toilet?'

'Definitely,' replied the Frenchman genially, with a wink at Sacha. She smothered a smile and wiped her eyes on her sleeve.

'Now?'

'After lunch, I shall be busting. I assure you of that. First, let's eat.'

It took a minute to get the boys around the table. Once they'd stopped giggling, Pamela raised her glass. 'Here's to our new friends, the McNamara family, who have joined us from across the world!'

'It's an honour to be here with you,' said Kit, and we did that absurd clinking thing with our glasses. Finn and Charlie stood on their chairs to reach.

'And happy birthday to Daniel,' added Pamela, striking a match and lighting her candle. 'Wherever you are, my darling.'

Twenty-three

March. The first breath of autumn.

The air held a new crispness. Willows and beech began to flame along the river bank, and the sky was high and delicate as blue porcelain. We needed our duvets at night, and to our joy the mosquitoes began to disappear. On Saturday morning walks the boys and I would stop to marvel at umbrella-sized spider webs hanging in the bushes, spangled with billions of dewy pearls. The new school year was well underway, with Kit umpiring cricket matches and running sausage sizzle fundraisers like an old hand. He was also putting in inhumanly long hours in the studio, muttering cheerfully about Dublin.

Sacha passed her restricted test and was allowed to drive on her own. We bought her a cheap little diesel. I felt as though a last cord had been cut, but it made life a lot easier because she could get herself into and out of town. She was in Year Twelve now, and the pressure had come on with a vengeance. Every week there seemed to be some test or assignment; her flute teacher wanted a pound of flesh, too.

'I can't concentrate with these little nutcases in the house,' she complained one Sunday morning, pretending to bang the boys' heads together. 'Can I light that stove out in the hut? So much work this weekend, it's a nightmare.' There were mauve crescents under her eyes, and she had a couple of spots around her mouth. She looked taut as a rubber band.

'Got a face like death warmed up,' remarked Kit. 'Those bastards are pushing you too hard.'

Sacha blinked at him. 'Put it this way, Kit. I worked all day yesterday, but I've still got an essay, five pages of physics *and* a debate to prepare. I'm totally screwed.'

'By when?' I asked, feeling sorry for her.

'By tomorrow! It's frickin' ridiculous.'

'There's no need to jump down my throat.'

She picked peevishly at a mosquito bite on her arm. 'Dammit Janet, I *need* to do well in that essay. It's an assessment.'

'I'll help you take some wood across,' said Kit. 'C'mon, let's get the wheelbarrow. And if you're very very nice to me, I'll cut you some kindling.'

Sacha slaved all day. I ferried sandwiches and biscuits across to the hut and hung around to make sure she actually ate them. When she came in for supper that evening she seemed much happier.

'I'm on track,' she announced. 'The essay is going to be awesome. I reckon I'll ace an Excellence.' She lifted a fist, miming a superhero's biceps. 'Brainygirl is rising to the challenge!'

That night, Finn walked in his sleep. I heard a bedroom door in the dark. It was enough to jerk me into consciousness. Hunched under the covers beside me, Kit's voice was slurred, his tongue paralysed by sleep. 'Yoo goan, Marfa, or me?'

'My turn.' I sat up, patted his shoulder and padded out onto the dimly lit landing. Finn was in his pyjamas, just standing, looking steadily at a fixed point in midair.

'D'you wanna come?' he asked some phantom companion. 'Be fun.'

'I'll come, Finny,' I said amicably, and took his hand. He let me lead him to the toilet—his aim was disastrous—and back to the delightful warmth of his bed where he snuggled down, stroking his ear. I was kissing his cheek when I heard a muffled crash from downstairs. My heart leaped into my throat as I ran to the banister, straining my eyes and ears through the dark. There was a thin vertical gleam at the kitchen door, and a voice—a female voice. I listened for a full minute, until I was sure it was Sacha's. Then

I trotted down the stairs and pushed at the door. A shriek of terror greeted me.

Sacha was fully dressed, whirling around with her hand to her chest. 'Oh my *God*, Mum! Just about wet myself.'

'Sacha!' I cried, with an incredulous glance at the kitchen clock. 'It's two fifteen! What the hell are you doing?'

She was standing with one hand on the kettle, and she'd turned white. Muffin stirred in her basket, eyeing us dozily. 'Whew, that was freaky,' gasped Sacha. 'The way that door kind of swung open . . . I expected one of those spooky fairies to poke his head around.'

'Yes, but what's going on?'

'I've finished my work! Thought I'd have a Milo to help me sleep.' She held up a mug. 'Want one?'

'No thanks. Look—this isn't on, you can't work all night.' I watched her pour boiling water into the mug. 'I heard a crash.'

'Yeah, sorry. Knocked a saucepan off the draining board.'

'And talking. Who were you talking to?'

She looked sheepish. 'Sorry again. Been practising my speech for the debate tomorrow. Going to whip their arses! Want to hear it?'

'No, I . . .' I blinked. The situation felt surreal. 'I mean yes, of course I want to hear it but not at two o'clock in the morning! Look, doll, I think you're going to have to give something up. You need your beauty sleep.'

She stirred her Milo. 'All the teachers set work at once. They all think their own subject is the only one that matters. I'm off to bed now.'

We whispered as we climbed the stairs. 'Did that saucepan wake you?' she asked.

'No. Finn was sleepwalking again.'

She kissed my cheek. 'I love you,' she said. 'You're the best mum in the history of the universe.'

A few days later, Sacha turned seventeen. Kit and I gave her an iPod Touch with all the bells and whistles. This soulless piece of technology was what she wanted most in the world; apparently her older, cheaper machine was totally *yesterday.* Dad sent cash, Lou a silver filigree bracelet. Finn and Charlie made clay models which they swore were Homer and Marge Simpson, but looked more like daleks. Bless her, Sacha managed to be ecstatic about them.

We threw a party the following weekend: a birthday-cum-belated-housewarming bash. After three days of rain, the sky cleared just in time. Sacha had invited an amorphous mass of young people, of both genders. Tabby couldn't, or wouldn't, come. The two dull girls fetched up with their monosyllables and slumped shoulders. Bianka arrived early to help us get ready, but—mysteriously—not Jani. In fact, I hadn't heard his name mentioned since New Year.

The district turned out in force: Jean and Pamela, Ira with his graceful girlfriend, Jane and Destiny, and several local families. Keith Emmerson from Capeview brought his wife but not the four daughters. They all hopped out of their cars carrying boxes of cold beer and plates of goodies—venison burgers, paua fritters and a meringue delight called pavlova. They described this largesse as 'bringing a plate' and seemed to think it perfectly normal. I was mildly offended at first—what, did they think I couldn't manage?—but later discovered that Hawke's Bay people never turn up at a party empty-handed.

Tama came too, climbing the boundary fence. I saw him strolling across the valley with the inevitable box of beer in his arms, and went to meet him.

'You're looking harassed,' he said, as we drew near enough to speak.

'Not harassed. Busy. Work work, children children, party party.'

'You should come out riding with us again. Therapeutic.'

I laughed. 'You know, I might just do that.'

As we wandered across the pasture I told him about Gareth, the pilot with a head injury. After a year of hellish struggle, his young wife had finally cut and run.

Tama opened the gate into our garden, standing back to let me through. 'Do you bring these sad things home with you?'

'Usually I can leave work behind. Just occasionally one of them gets into my head. Gareth's one of those. He's lost himself.'

It was a good evening. I began to feel as though these people could be my friends. I have an impression of Tama and assorted farmers in shorts, staunchly glued to the barbecue in a legs-splayed, beer-drinking stance. They held bottles in fists in front of their chests; a story, a joke, an explosion of laughter. Meanwhile, women gathered in the kitchen to swap defamatory tales about their husbands. Finn and Charlie patrolled the garden with a band of merry men, swinging in the trees and terrorising parents with water pistols. Finally Sacha and her mob emerged from the smoko hut, requisitioned the pistols and sprayed each other, their yells reverberating across the valley. Even Tama's horses lifted their heads to stare.

We had speakers out on the verandah. I put on something Greek and atmospheric, and Sacha and Bianka were the first to dance as the sun went down. Sacha was wearing a leopardprint sundress, decidedly skimpy, and the filigree bracelet Lou had sent. As I watched, it struck me with unpleasant force that dieting had changed her shape completely. She wasn't my bouncing, busty-and-proud-of-it daughter any more. She looked fragile, the once rounded young cheeks showing the bones of a *Vogue* model. Her complexion was suffering, too. After a zit-free adolescence, she'd developed some acne on her face and was using foundation to cover it up.

All the same, the two girls were a picture as they jived in the lemon light under swathes of bougainvillea. Bianka seemed hypnotised by Sacha. She smiled whenever she looked at her, which was often.

As the alcohol went down, noise levels went up. The teenagers retreated to the smoko hut. I turned on our fairy lights, and more people began to dance in the fragrant dusk. Kit was pacing himself with the booze, I noticed. He was in his element, everywhere at once, making sure no one had an empty glass. Everybody seemed to know and like him. I even heard him pick up an invitation to go deep-sea fishing; this high-tech hunter-gathering was evidently a traditional male bonding ritual.

I was sashaying exuberantly with Jean when Bianka sought me out to say goodbye. My neighbour was teaching me to salsa, which was shambolic but hilarious.

'Thank you.' Bianka embraced me. 'Your daughter is so beautiful.'

Surprised, I looked into the pale face. 'You're not staying?'

'No.' She hesitated. 'No.'

'But—no, Bianka, you must stay. I thought you were all bringing duvets?'

'Martha . . .' She stood looking at me, her mouth turning up and down at the same time as though she was about to howl.

I laid a hand on her arm. 'What's the matter? Has something happened?'

'I have to get home. Mum's not well.'

'I'm so sorry.' I walked her around the house. 'Please tell your mum I'm thinking about her. Come and see us again soon.'

She thanked me again and got into a car, taking three other girls with her. Haunted by a sense of deep unease, I watched them drive away. I was still standing under the gloomy canopy of the walnut tree when I felt Kit's arm around my waist.

'Never saw a girl so sad,' he said quietly.

'Her mother's dying.' There was a wobble in my throat; for Bianka's sake, and because I was tired and a little drunk. And maybe because I didn't quite know who I was, just at that moment. 'All those years,' I said. 'All those friends, the special places we used to go, the things that made us happy . . . they're just history, now, aren't they?'

'They're *our* history, though.' Kit smoothed my hair.

'And we're just history to them, too. We've deleted ourselves. We've been cut from there and pasted here.'

'C'mon,' he said, taking my hand. 'Let's dance.'

The last of Sacha's mates had gone by lunchtime the next day. She slumped into the kitchen, complaining of nausea and denying that she'd had a drop of alcohol.

'You're in a state,' I nagged, putting a hand to her forehead. I found a vitamin C tablet and lobbed it into a glass of water. 'And you're ruining your complexion with this silly dieting. What time did you turn in last night?'

She was roaming up and down the room, staring into the fridge, banging drawers. She opened one cupboard three times. 'About two.'

'Five, more like. You'd better go back to bed.'

'I might do that.' She rubbed her face. 'Aching all over. I've got another filthy cold coming on. It's this freakin' country, there's all these new viruses I've got no immunity to.'

'I hope you didn't give it to Bianka. They don't need it in their household.'

'Bianka.' Sacha hissed a filthy word under her breath—just audibly enough for me to be shocked—then scratched herself on the upper arm. 'Dog's got fleas.'

'I was surprised she left so early last night.'

'Yeah. Well. Whatever.' She walked into the larder, lifted down a packet of dried noodles and tore them open. Half the contents fell out.

There was a brief ceasefire, sulky on both sides.

'I still think those two girls are incredibly boring.' I knew I was needling, but I couldn't help it. 'Those skinny ones, Taylah and . . .'

'Teresa.'

'That's the ones. I really don't know what you see in them.'

'Better boring than narrow-minded and judgemental.' Sacha was picking up every packet in the pantry, looking at the labels.

'Don't be cheeky. What are you after? Dustpan and brush, I hope. Noodles all over the floor.'

She found a bag of mini chocolate bars and unwrapped one, jamming it into her mouth. 'Anita's not responding to radiotherapy,' she mumbled. 'I don't think she's going to make it. D'you think she's going to make it? The dad's in denial. Can you believe that?'

'Yes, I can. Are you—'

'He won't let anyone say the word cancer, wants to pretend it isn't happening.' Sacha poured boiling water over her noodles, talking loudly. 'I think narrow-minded people are the real villains, trying to repress free speech and free thinkers . . . I mean, why should we live by the rules of people who know and understand nothing about us? It's my age group who understand the technology, your generation haven't a clue, can't keep up with all the changes. You're just totally out of date. You're—'

'I am *not* out of date.'

'—dinosaurs, and you know what happened to them? We actually rule the world because we have the knowledge. Knowledge is power!'

'You're spouting rubbish. Go and have a shower and get changed.'

She looked sidelong at me. It was quite sinister. 'Why?'

'And bring down your washing. There are piles of it in your room.'

'How do you know what's in my room? Christ, will you back off? I'm not a frigging two-year-old!'

'Well, you're behaving like one!' I sounded like one of the hens. No, it was worse than that: both in words and tone, I was my own mother. I'd never thought that day would come.

'You can't handle it, can you?' snarled Sacha. 'Everyone has to be totally reliant on you, or you fall apart. You've got to be everyone's little saviour.'

'Look—'

Her anger filled the room. 'You're pretty pleased with yourself. You think you're a legend as a human being. You always have to be the life and soul of the party. It was *my* birthday but *you* had to be the centre of attention, dancing on the verandah. I could hear your fake laugh from the smoko hut.' She tossed her head, imitating brassy, pretentious laughter. 'Other women fancy your husband—that's a real plus for you! You've got something they want.'

'Why d'you have to get all hormonal and hellish now, Sacha? You used to be a dream teen.'

She lifted the corner of her lip. 'Trophy husband, complete with sexy Irish accent. What a devilish charmer! Nobody would believe Kit had a little *problem*, would they?'

'He hasn't. Not any more.'

'Well, he was a honey pot last night. You'd better watch out, Mum. Mind you, perhaps you've got your own distractions. I saw you rushing across the paddock to meet Tama Pardoe.'

'Don't you dare!'

Behind me, the door to the hall creaked. The boys tiptoed in. 'What's the matter?' Charlie almost mouthed the words. 'Why are people shouting?'

To my amazement, Sacha threw herself to the floor and pulled her brothers onto her lap. Gone like a puff of smoke was the horrible hormone monster.

'I love you guys,' she whispered, and held them to her chest.

Then she went to bed and slept and slept, like a princess in a tower.

Twenty-four

I'm woken by a door shutting. Kura Pohatu is back, and there's a new purpose in her gait. It's as though she's rolled up her sleeves.

Day and night have merged; sleep and waking, nightmare and reality are one and the same. I am in a strange room, with a television and a pile of magazines. I struggle to remember how I got here.

Kura folds herself into the same chair as before. 'Sorry,' she says. 'One of the paediatricians wanted a word with me.'

'That's all right.' I try to shake the fog from my head. 'I think I should be getting back to Finn now, though.'

She watches me shrewdly for a final moment. She's taking aim. Then she fires. 'Has Finn ever broken a bone?'

'Um . . . yes. A toe.'

'Nothing more than a toe?'

'No. Why?'

'The team took another look at his X-rays this morning.'

'What for?'

'Until now they've been working to save his life. They concentrated on vital organs. Now he's stabilised they've been able to look for signs of . . . Well, Martha, what if I just tell you that Finn has a fracture to his right wrist.'

'I know he has. We all know that. He's got a bloody great plaster cast on it.'

She shakes her head impatiently. 'I haven't made myself clear. This break is older, though close to the site of the new injury. The orthopaedic surgeon thinks it was a greenstick fracture and estimates it occurred several months ago, maybe six months or more.'

'That's impossible.'

'There is calcification where it's healed, but we have no record of Finn's being presented to a doctor or emergency department. Why is that?'

I struggle to understand. Perhaps I'm still dreaming. 'Six months?'

'Or possibly earlier. Certainly since you arrived in New Zealand. That was a year ago, wasn't it? All right. Well, since then.'

'No, no. Finn has never broken his arm.'

'I'm afraid he has.'

I stare at her as the implications sink in. 'I honestly and truly know nothing about this.'

'I can get someone to come and show you the X-ray if you like. They know what they're talking about.' The regal grandmother seems a little menacing, suddenly. I want to run away. 'Martha, I can't help if you won't be open with me. I'm not suggesting you did anything yourself.'

I feel a guilty blush spreading up my throat. They think we've been hurting Finn for months. They think we broke his arm. Well, of course they do. He has a fracture, and I didn't even know. How could I not know? Bad mother. Bad mother.

'There has to be a mistake,' I insist desperately.

'I don't think there's a mistake.'

Kura lets the silence lengthen. She's not afraid of silence. That's what gives her power. The minutes tick by, and she waits like a cat at a mouse hole.

'Six months.' I try to remember every fall, every fight since we arrived here. In the life of a small boy there are many falls, and many fights. My memory is suddenly opaque, a sludge of panic.

Then it comes to me. Something so small, so silly. A bicycle wheel, stuck in a rut under a walnut tree. 'Hang on . . . Oh my God. I think I know. Maybe.'

Kura pulls out a notebook as I tell the story of Finn's tumble on New Year's Day. She scribbles as she listens. I don't think she believes a word. I don't blame her. 'So you never got him to a doctor?' she asks dubiously.

'Sorry . . . I know it sounds pretty slack, but honestly he seemed fine. In a few days he was back to normal.'

'Did he need a lot of analgesic? He must have been in pain.'

'Er . . .' I think back. 'I remember giving him Pamol a few times.'

She looks unconvinced.

'I can't believe we're the first parents to miss a fracture,' I argue helplessly. 'In fact I've heard of GPs making the same mistake.'

She closes her notebook. 'I'll discuss this with the team. It sets alarm bells ringing when an injured child isn't presented to a doctor.'

'Oh, marvellous. So in your book we're either abusive or we're negligent.'

'The two aren't mutually exclusive.'

'Look,' I say, 'I feel really awful about not spotting this fracture, but Finn's an adventurous five-year-old. If we carted him off to hospital every time he fell off his bike or out of a tree, we'd spend our lives in a queue!'

She just looks at me. I fear her; she is too perceptive.

'I'd like to go back to him now,' I say, standing up. I'm afraid I'm going to cry.

Kura doesn't move. 'Martha. I really am not the enemy, you know. Why won't you tell me who is?'

The hospital gift shop is closing for the evening, which doesn't matter much as I have no need of a helium balloon in the shape of a heart. There are armchairs nearby. Hiding in one, I call home.

Ira answers. No, Kit hasn't been in touch. Everything there is fine.

Beyond the empty café I find a door marked *Chapel.* The lights are on but the room's empty. There is a small altar in front of a stained-glass window, and a book in which people have scribbled messages or prayers. I suppose it was cathartic for them. A note promises that the chaplain will pray for those in the book.

I leaf through it. Each line tells its own tale. Everyone in the world has their story.

Please walk with Cynthia as she makes her lonely journey.

Dear Lord, comfort Ruth and family at their sad loss.

Thank you!!! Bryan going home today. You answered our prayers!

Don't take my little boy away from me.

Actually, I wrote that last one. Sorry. Hard not to be banal when life has fallen apart.

Twenty-five

April. A blue-sky morning with a distinct nip in the air. As Pamela promised, autumn had brought yet another glorious palette of colours to our world.

The Easter holidays had come and gone. Kit was making school lunches while harrying the boys to get dressed. Sacha was still in her nightshirt. It had coffee spilled down the front, and she was riffling through her schoolbag. She walked to the laundry and looked in, then back to her bag. She seemed distracted.

'Lost something?' asked Kit.

'Just need a shirt.' She picked her barefoot way out to the washing line.

'Peaky,' remarked Kit, watching her tug a shirt from the line.

'She's run-down. You don't think it might be glandular fever?' I fretted. 'Or some kind of post-viral thing?'

'No, I don't. I think it's too much hard work, too many late nights and maybe too much dieting.'

Sacha reappeared and I dropped the subject. It wasn't the moment for serious discussion, anyway. Kit and the boys were going on a school outing for the day to the National Aquarium in Napier, followed by a pantomime. They'd be home after supper at McDonald's. Kit was condemned to spend all day with a posse of women and thirty small children before eating a Big Mac and fries. He looked astonishingly cheerful about it.

Sacha scratched her arm with furious fingers. 'This is driving me crazy. Frigging chickens have lice.'

'Maybe we should spray the smoko hut?' I suggested. 'It might be infested with something.' I glanced at my watch—the waterproof one I wore for work—and realised it had stopped. Cursing, I nipped upstairs and spent too long searching for the one Dad gave me. I looked in my jewellery box, which was where I'd last seen it; then I checked in my drawers.

Perhaps the patupaiarehe had been at it again. One day, I thought as I hurried back downstairs, I'd stumble upon the lair of that mischievous spirit. I'd find the precious watch, and Sacha's locket, and Kit's camera, and all those other things it had spirited away with wicked little fingers.

'Maybe we should have this house exorcised.' I wasn't quite joking. 'My gold watch has disappeared now.'

'Dad's coming on the bus,' chanted the boys, dancing around their sister like a Sioux war party circling a totem pole. 'Dad's a parent helper, Dad's a parent helper.'

'Stop it.' Sacha pressed her hands to her ears.

But they didn't stop. They cavorted and shrieked until Finn careered into the kitchen table.

'Frick's sake, will you ever shut *up*?' screamed Sacha. Shouldering her schoolbag, she pushed Charlie so hard that he sprawled on the floor. Then she banged out of the house.

The little boy lay where he'd fallen. 'Sacha was mean,' he whimpered.

'Women, eh?' Kit held out his arms. 'Come and have a cuddle, buddy.'

'Dad's going to sit next to me,' said Finn, unruffled by his sister's outburst.

'Me,' insisted Charlie through his tears.

'We'll go on the back seat, all three of us, and do moonies out of the big window,' said Kit.

'What's a moony?' asked Charlie. Finn, with an air of sophistication, cupped his hand and whispered in his brother's ear. I caught the giggled word *bums*. Charlie's tear-filled eyes grew large, and he covered his mouth with his fingers. 'We *can't*!'

I watched Sacha get into my car. I could have cried. 'What are we going to do about her?' I asked.

'Hard to believe these two cherubs will ever end up like that, don't you think?'

I smiled weakly. 'They'll be worse. And two at once.'

'Great gangly gargoyles, breaking out in acne,' groaned Kit, clapping a hand to his brow. 'Wearing their baseball caps back to front and their jeans halfway down their arses.'

I kissed the three of them goodbye. Kit was looking romantic in a pale blue shirt and khaki shorts, and I felt a twinge of jealousy. 'The other mothers are going to have a *lovely* time,' I sighed.

I was giving Sacha a lift to school that day. We travelled in silence until we were on the main road.

'What was that about?' I asked. No reply. I turned the radio off. 'I'd appreciate an answer, Sacha.'

'They do my head in. Why do they always have to be such maniacs?'

'No, but you—'

'*Leave* it, will you?' Her voice was high and strained. 'I'm fine.'

'Sorry, I just—'

'I hate the way you always have to know everything that's going on in everybody's lives, all the time. Just keep out for once, for fuck's sake!'

She might as well have slapped my face. I drove mechanically for the next fifteen minutes, feeling utterly miserable. 'Sorry,' I said eventually. 'Whatever it was I did, or said, I'm sorry.'

'I'll tell you what you did. You cheated me of my real father. You made me come out here. You put Kit and the boys first. You always have, and you always will.'

She's got a point! crowed Mum.

'It was for all of us, Sacha, because we're a family! If we'd stayed in England we'd be living in a concrete box right now, and you'd have changed schools, and Kit would be . . . God knows. We'd probably be divorced.'

The anger seemed to have gone from her. 'I just want to go home.'

'Have you heard from Lydia lately?'

'It's hard with people in the opposite time zone—especially with no broadband. Anyway, we've nothing much to say any more.'

'You've got your new friends.'

'They're just . . . I just miss everyone so much.' She rubbed her eyes on her sleeve.

'Sorry, doll.'

I parked a little distance from the school gates and stroked her head. She sat, winding her hands around one another.

'Orchestra tonight?' I asked.

'Yes. I'll get the later bus. Mum . . .'

I was watching her hands. There was something disturbing about the way she was wringing them. It was as though she was compulsively washing, trying to erase some dirty spot, like Lady Macbeth. 'I'm all ears,' I said. The hand rubbing grew more frenzied. 'Sacha? Are you in some kind of trouble?'

'No.' She reached down for her bag. 'Just leave it. See you.'

Once she'd disappeared through the gates, I checked my work diary. I had a hectic schedule that day, starting with a staff meeting. Soon my car was headed towards Capeview, but my mind wasn't.

Just before the meeting began, Sacha sent a text. She must have been hiding her phone under her desk, because lessons started at eight thirty.

Soz mum luv you sooooo much xxx grumpy teen

The sun burst through the clouds.

No probs doll love you too XXXXX

Keith plumped himself down beside me as I was pressing *send*. 'Soppy text to Sacha,' I explained sheepishly. 'Actually, I'm in a state of panic.' I described the morning's events.

He looked sympathetic. 'That all sounds familiar. Parenthood's terrifying, isn't it?'

'You don't think she could be bulimic? Or . . .'

He waited, eyebrows raised. 'Or?'

'Or, well, bipolar or something?'

'Sacha?' Keith looked amused at the suggestion. 'I had a long chat with her at your party—a confident young woman, having a ball. She's doing nothing mine didn't do. What makes you think yours should be perfect? Many teenage girls—and boys too—have irrational tantrums. You know that! It's what they do, even if they haven't just emigrated. I suspect you're letting Sacha's mood swings rule your life.'

'Of course I am. My happiness is dependent upon hers. She's been my constant companion since I was twenty-one. In a way, we've grown up together.'

He patted the back of my hand. '*He that hath a wife and children hath given hostages to fortune.* Francis Bacon, I think. Makes you wonder why so many of us do it, really.'

As I turned up our drive that evening, I had a kaleidoscope of half-formed thoughts in my head. I considered spraying the smoko hut for fleas, and decided to Google *bedbugs* when I had a moment. I worried about a client I'd just left, a teenage boy with spinal injuries. Finally I imagined Kit at McDonald's with thirty screaming five-year-olds. The image had me chuckling as I crunched into first gear for the steepest part of our hill.

I was still smiling crookedly as I parked under the walnut. It was fruiting now, and I gathered a couple of nuts from the ground. Muffin was lying in a patch of sunlight, but she came plodding over to greet me, crooning a hello. When I squatted down to give her a pat, her coat felt dusty and warm. The kitchen door wasn't shut; Kit must have left it open for the dog. I hoped the chickens hadn't got in and made a mess.

They hadn't. The room seemed just as I'd left it. Muffin turned round and round in her basket while I dropped my jacket over a chair. I'd picked up the post from our letterbox at the road gate. Junk mail, two bills and a postcard from Dad, who was on a walking holiday in the Lakes. I was engrossed in his handwriting as I reached for the kettle.

Windermere in winter is wondrously winsome, wantonly windy and wistfully wet.

My searching fingers didn't touch anything. Reluctantly, I lifted my gaze from the postcard and looked to see where the kettle had got to. It wasn't in its usual place by the bread bin. With my mind still on Dad's holiday, I searched the other surfaces.

I saw Mrs Tiggywinkle today. Jeremy Fisher, too. He was out fishing in the rain again. You'd think he would learn.

I wondered vaguely why Kit had moved the kettle. Perhaps he'd had a last-minute tidy-up before he left. Come to think of it, the room might be slightly neater than usual. I stopped reading and looked around.

No, not neater. Emptier. Finally, I focused.

No radio.

No microwave.

No bottles in the wine rack, and the tin where we kept spare cash was upside down on the floor.

With a feeling of sick certainty I ran across the hall and into the sitting room. Television and DVD player, both gone. They'd left the dinosaur desktop, though—presumably there was no market for them. It was an efficient violation, and chillingly tidy. These intruders hadn't pulled out drawers or smashed windows. They'd taken their time, as though they knew they had all day.

A nasty thought struck me: perhaps I had disturbed them. Perhaps they were still here. I stepped out through the kitchen door and into the low autumn sunlight, looking around. There was no sign of a vehicle, but my skin was crawling as I shaded my eyes and peered into the gloom of the bush.

A small violence in the branches of the walnut made me jump half out of my skin, but it was only a tui launching itself with a whirr of wings. I considered driving off somewhere, maybe to ask for help from Tama, but I wanted to be here when the rest of the family came home. Anyway, I could no more leave my house alone and undefended than I could have abandoned one of my children.

In the end I used my mobile to call the Napier police station. The woman on duty took my details and said they'd see who was in my area. I had the impression they might make it by Christmas if they really hurried, and made a mental note to call a twenty-four-hour plumber if there was ever a real emergency—a crazed axe murderer, for example. The nice man in his van would probably be the first to arrive by several hours.

I tried Kit's phone, which went straight to his messages. He'd have turned it off in the theatre. I sent him a text. Then I forced myself to walk back inside and creep up the stairs. I felt sure someone—or something—was inches behind, leering at the back of my head. Once I felt a touch on the shoulder and swung around in abject terror, eyes popping, heart going like the clapper of a church bell. But it was only my hair.

Something was moving on the landing. I froze, then realised it was a curtain, flapping lazily in the breeze.

In our bedroom the drawers had been left open. I had a pervading image of dirty, thieving hands digging through our clothes, and sure enough the snazzy little video camera was gone from my socks drawer. My jewellery box had moved slightly, though its lid was closed. There wasn't much of great financial value in it: a string of pearls Dad bought for my eighteenth, a brooch that had been Mum's, and the sapphire pendant Kit gave me when the twins were born. I reached out with shaking hands—I could actually see the tremor—and lifted the lid.

Empty. I sat on the bed with it in my hands, feeling sick. Then, struck by a new thought, I hurried down the landing to the boys' bedroom. A shaft of afternoon sunlight spilled an oval pool onto their worn carpet. The cupboard doors were wide open: lake-coloured doors, with Sacha's careful flamingos spread across them. The shelves were bare, the boys' clothes and books strewn across the floor. In a daze I began to pick everything up, wanting to have it all tidy and normal before the twins came home. They were too young to be confronted by such callousness.

It wasn't until I had everything back in place that I realised what was missing. It was painfully obvious, because there was a blank space on the shelf: the blue piggybanks with their Christmas money. I searched the room, frothing with rage, but there was no sign of the two tipsy pigs. By the time I closed the cupboard doors I was ready to kill. Jewellery, DVD players—bad enough. But what kind of a perverted monster steals a child's piggybank?

I began to roam through the house, teeth gritted, looking for clues. I wasn't afraid any more. If I had found a man lurking in the pantry with a stripy jersey, a mask and a bag marked *swag*, I swear I would have kneed him where it hurt. *String 'em up*, I muttered to myself, *every last one of 'em.* That was pretty hypocritical, as I have been a member of Amnesty International all my adult life and abhor the death penalty. But dammit, *piggybanks!*

A racing engine. Some vehicle was heading up the drive, and fast. My bravado faltered. I caught myself squinting out from behind a curtain while calculating how long the bathroom door would hold if I locked myself in there. The car swirled into the yard and Kit leaped out, hair standing straight up.

'How bad?' he yelled, as Finn and Charlie spilled out of their doors in a thrilled little flood.

'Did we really have a buggerer?' asked Charlie.

'Burgerer,' corrected Finn. 'We've been burgered.'

'Did they take Blue Blanket?'

'No, no!' I hoped I sounded cheerful. 'Blanket and Buccaneer Bob are still here. Nice, tidy little buggerers.'

Then I broke the news about their piggybanks.

'Gone?' repeated Charlie pathetically, his eyes pooling as he looked up at me.

'My money!' Finn's fists became balls.

Kit and I began a systematic search of the house, trying to work out exactly what had gone.

'Oh no. Bastards have taken my laptop,' he moaned when we got to the sitting room. 'That's going to be a real pain.'

Charlie had crouched down on all fours and was staring into the denuded DVD cupboard. 'Did they really need *Mary Poppins*?'

When Sacha arrived home from orchestra, the twins rushed to tell her the news.

'A feef came to the house and took our things,' screeched Charlie.

Sacha's hand flew to her mouth. She turned slightly green, as though she was about to be sick.

'Your room looks okay,' I said quickly. 'Helluva mess, but I don't think that's the burglar's fault.'

She swung around the kitchen, staring at the blank spaces. Then she spun on her heels, crashed through the door and pelted towards the smoko hut. There was a short silence before an anguished yell tore the air. Kit and I met at the kitchen door, both running, and sprinted down the track. The boys trotted after us.

Sacha was kneeling on the floor of her hut, smashing her fist against the wooden wall. 'The bastards!' she screamed. 'The fucking idiots!'

'Hey, calm down,' I said, taking hold of her shoulder. 'You're scaring the little ones.'

'Those sodding bastards, I'll kill them! They took my stuff.'

We looked at her, baffled. She wasn't Sacha at all. This was a different being altogether: a furious, maddened creature.

'What stuff?' I asked.

'My stuff! My new iPod. My speakers. My money. Even my little telly.' She drove her fist right through a rotten piece of wall. 'This is bullshit!'

'Mine too,' said Finn. 'I told you. They took our piggybanks. Our *special* piggybanks, that Grandpa gave us.'

'All gone,' added Charlie sadly.

For some reason, those words seemed to pop Sacha's rage like a pin in a balloon. 'This is awful,' she whispered. 'This is hell. I want to go home.'

'It's only a burglary,' I said firmly. 'It's not a disaster. In England I know people who've been burgled lots of times—the Caldwell family, remember? Three times in three years. We've got good insurance. At least you've still got your laptop—you took that to school today, didn't you? And look, there's your old iPod in your pocket.'

'We're all fine, that's the important thing,' said Kit, pulling a boy onto each knee. 'Nobody's hurt.'

'Hurt?' wailed Sacha. 'We are! Of *course* we are. We're all hurt.'

A police car pulled up an hour later, and the local bobby heaved himself out. I recognised him as one of the school parents: Robert Andrews. He had two rugby-playing children, a boy and a girl. I'd seen them on the field, menacingly shoving their mouthguards in and out of their mouths like hunting chimpanzees then passing and tackling with a deadly blend of skill and psychopathy. Robert was one of those slow-moving middle-aged men who have developed a permanent shelf sticking out in front, upon which to rest their beer bottles. He made me feel positively lithe and fit. There was something reassuring about his sheer solidity; he was like one of those toys that wobble but don't fall down.

He gave me a laconic nod. It's a special Kiwi rural male nod. It means 'hello,' and 'please don't display any emotion,' and sometimes, 'I can't remember your name.'

'Hello,' I said, advancing on him. 'Martha McNamara.'

He shook my hand with his hairy paw, glancing over my shoulder with a twitch of the facial muscles that I thought was probably his version of a smile. 'G'day, mate,' he said. 'Been having a bit of drama, I hear.'

Kit had stepped out of the kitchen doorway. 'Thanks for dropping by, Robbie.'

I was surprised by all this first-name matiness. Then I remembered that Kit did school trips and sausage sizzles and umpired cricket matches. He did McDonald's. He was one of the in crowd, down at Torutaniwha Primary School.

'You've been unlucky,' said Robbie the bobby. 'We don't have many house burglaries around here. Once in a blue moon.'

He and Kit strolled off for a session of knowledgeable squinting at windows and checking of flowerbeds for footprints. Eventually they arrived in the kitchen. Robert was gloomily certain of the method. 'Tidy job. In through the *unlocked* kitchen door, clean the place out, off in a vehicle.' I had the impression his crime report would read pretty much like that. Economical.

'More than one?' I asked.

'Hard to tell.'

'They can get away by continuing along the track,' said Kit. 'It runs on through the bush, meets up with a forestry road and comes out three miles north of here.'

The policeman nodded. 'I know that,' he said. 'And so do all the other locals.'

'How come?' I asked.

'The trail ride comes through this bit of land most years.'

'Trail ride?' I pictured romantic horsemen, men of Rohan, re-enacting some venture of yesteryear—perhaps with teams of packhorses and wagons, sleeping under the stars, eating around campfires and communing with the spirits of the land.

Robert stirred half a pound of sugar into his coffee. 'The school holds a ninety-kilometre trail ride as a fundraiser.'

'Lovely. Horses?'

He chortled into his mug. 'Motorbikes. Trail bikes, off road. We ride along the beach, up the riverbed, through the bush here and then into the forestry. You want to come next year, Kit? You've got a four wheeler, haven't you? Bring your lads.'

'I might,' said Kit. 'Thanks.'

'Well, me too,' I huffed, as the feminist in me buzzed militantly to the surface. How dare the man assume that it would be Kit who would want to take part in this festival of daredevil, petrol-headed machismo? On the other hand, it sounded very long, boring and environmentally deeply dodgy. And after all, what was the point?

'My kids go every year,' said Robert, with fatherly pride. 'They've had their own bikes since they were five.'

I was impressed. The Andrews children weren't much bigger than mine—seven and nine, maybe—yet they happily rode their trail bikes for ninety kilometres on riverbeds and steep hills. Try doing *that* in Bedfordshire. You'd be deafened by the storm of tut-tutting. Child protection agencies would go into hyperdrive.

'Anyway,' I persisted. 'This burglar. Or burglars. D'you think they knew the other way out, then?'

'Quite possibly,' said Robert. 'They like an escape route in case someone comes home and they have to leg it. They don't want to be trapped—that's their nightmare. I'll go out and look for vehicle tracks in a minute.'

'But doesn't that imply they were locals?'

'Or forestry workers. As I say, we don't get many burglaries.'

'I don't understand why they picked on us,' said Kit. 'This house isn't visible from the road. And how did they know we were all out? It was only by chance that I was on a school trip.'

'Maybe they've been watching us,' I said uneasily, glancing out of the window. 'From the trees. Sacha sometimes feels we're being watched.'

'I have the impression they knew what they were looking for,' added Kit.

Robert raised his eyebrows. 'Who was your removal firm?' I told him, and he looked interested. 'D'you remember which lads?'

'Frank, er . . . a man called John, wasn't it, Kit? And Ira Taulafo—well, you know Ira from school. He was just casual, in between jobs.'

The policeman downed the last of his coffee and stood up. 'Better go. Wife's expecting me half an hour ago. There'll be trouble in the camp.'

'Do you know something about those men?' I asked, opening the door for him.

'Can't comment at this stage, but working for a removal company is a pretty neat way to check out who's got what.'

We walked him outside. Robert took a swift look along the track that ran on past the smoko hut, but found no sign of recent vehicles. When he ambled across to his car the twins were loitering, awed and whispering.

'I'll turn the lights on, shall I?' asked the policeman. When his weight hit the seat, the whole vehicle sagged. Blue lights began to flash as he stuck his head out of the window. 'D'you two lads want a ride? Hop in, then.'

They tumbled into the back seat. Robert circled the yard three times, throwing up dust, and dropped them a hundred yards along the drive. I heard a burst of farewell sirens before the twins came pelting back across the cattle stop, their upset at the burglary momentarily forgotten.

'That was cool!' yelled Finn, high-fiving with Kit.

I watched as the police car disappeared behind the willows. 'You don't think it was anything to do with those removal men, do you?'

Kit didn't answer. He was peering into the bush. 'You could hide an army of burglars in there.'

'Or worse things,' said Sacha, from behind us.

Robert hadn't seemed interested in fingerprints, and it didn't look as though he was going to send a forensic team in white bunny suits, so we cleaned the house with obsessive care and a lot of disinfectant, trying to remove the grubby feeling left by the burglary. The place needed a spring clean, to be honest.

'They're still there,' said Sacha. It was Sunday morning and we were tired of scrubbing. 'I can feel their eyes.'

'No you can't,' I retorted, mopping a squashed mosquito off the wall. 'Look. We are not the first people in the world to be burgled, and we sure as hell won't be the last. No way is it going to spoil our lives.'

'It is,' said Sacha, scrabbling at her wrist. 'It's not just the burglary. It's something evil that creeps out of the bush.' Her phone made a noise like a bleating goat. She glanced at the screen. 'Bianka. Wants to go to a film this afternoon. Her dad got some free vouchers. Can I stay with her? I'm completely spooked here.'

As she spoke I was absently looking at her phone. She held it to her chest. 'Hey! Don't read my texts.'

'Keep your hair on.' I dug in a plastic shopping bag. 'I've got this spray for your hut, look . . . in case it's infested with something that's biting you. What film?'

She named some romantic comedy, unmemorable but harmless enough.

'What about school tomorrow?'

'I'll take my uniform.'

'Have a lovely time, doll.' I sighed. 'A night away, and you'll be right as rain. Thanks for all your help.'

That evening, Kit and I sat in low deckchairs beneath Hinemoana's hill, sipping Jean's wine. Kit was sketching. Despite the chilly evening air we'd all taken a dip, washing off defilement in the freezing salt water. Now the twins were building an ambitious ball run.

Liquid gold rolled down the hills and flowed in long fingers across the beach to meet the water. The boys circled their mound with a natural, artless grace. Kit's sketchpad was soon covered in images so vivid that they seemed to dance on the page. As the sun sank lower, he got up to collect driftwood.

Finn came to stand beside me. He was stroking his left ear with one hand but the other arm he laid gently around my neck. His woolly pullover felt warm and sandy.

'What's up, bud? I asked, kissing his cheek.

'Who d'you think they were, the men who came to our house?'

'Oh, Finn. I don't know. Sad, silly people, I expect. Not scary men.'

'Will their children be watching our DVDs?'

Charlie had stopped building, too. He sat up on his heels and looked across at us. 'Will they come back?'

Two anxious faces were turned to mine. 'I don't think they'll be back. We don't need to be scared of them.'

'I'd hide in the attic,' said Charlie.

Finn marched to our pile of firewood and picked up what was—in his hands—a hefty stick. 'I would *wallop* them with this!'

I thought about my little boy trying to tackle a marauding adult; a thug, tearing the puny stick from his hands. A sense of mourning draped itself over me. Meanness had intruded on their world, and spoiled it. I dropped down in the sand beside their run. 'This ready? Where's the ball?'

'Let it rip!' they screamed, as Kit returned with more firewood.

Later we sat around the fire, digging our teeth into blackened marshmallows.

'Poor Sacha,' said Charlie. 'She's missing this fun time.'

Finn lay on his back, turning his face up to the moon. 'One day please can we sleep here, on the beach?'

Kit sloshed more wine into his plastic glass, emptying the bottle, and a dark goblin of anxiety came sneaking into my mind. ''Course we can,' he promised. 'In the holidays. Just you and me, boys. Okay? We'll leave these bally women behind, and we'll come down here and sit around the fire and tell swashbuckling tales.'

Finn made angel shapes in the sand. 'Better not leave any bally women alone in the house,' he said. 'Those bloody burgerers might come back.'

Beneath the prone body of Hinemoana's hill a clump of seaweed lay half-submerged in the surf. The waves tugged and pushed, making the dark fronds sway fretfully, like long hair. My eyes were drawn to it, though I tried to look away. It looked so terribly like the corpse of a young woman.

Twenty-six

At first, I thought the call was benign.

I was in my pokey office at Capeview and had spent lunchtime talking to a patronising idiot at the insurance company who wanted valuations of everything stolen. A migraine was mustering forces behind my eyes, and I wondered about taking a couple of ibuprofen. Which was when my phone rang.

'Martha McNamara?' It was a pleasant voice. Female. 'Lyndsay Carpenter, Sacha's dean. Is this a good moment?'

'Yes! Hello,' I said brightly. 'Is it about the Performance Diploma?'

'Not directly.' The dean sounded taken aback. 'I'm calling about Sacha's attendance record.'

'Her what?'

'Her name came up at today's staff meeting. It's a problem. She has missed a number of internal assessments.'

'She's missed *what*?'

'Internal assessments. They are essential if she's to gain enough credits to pass—'

'Yes, I know what internal assessments are. But isn't this an overreaction? She's had a week off with a cold, maybe a couple of other days. I don't think she's missed anything important.'

'Sacha's attendance was less than sixty per cent last term, and the pattern is continuing.'

I was flabbergasted. 'Are you sure we're talking about the same girl?'

'Well, take today as an example, Martha.' New Zealanders rarely do the surname thing. 'You are aware that she's absent from school?'

'No, she . . . Are you sure?'

Lyndsay was inexorable. 'A message was left on our absence line at . . . let me check . . . nine fifteen this morning, ostensibly from you. It said that Sacha was unable to attend school today due to a dental appointment.'

'No. I think there must be a mistake.'

'There's no mistake. I checked the records myself after the staff meeting. The head of music raised the issue. She's suspended Sacha from the orchestra for non-attendance.'

The little room spun. It wasn't possible.

'She's one of our most talented musicians, but she appears to have given up,' said Lyndsay. 'Her flute teacher hasn't seen her for weeks.'

'Is Bianka at school? Her friend, Bianka?'

'Bianka Varga . . .' there was a pause, just long enough for the teacher to check her computer files, '. . . is at school today. Yes. And her attendance record is excellent.'

'Oh.' I was deflated. 'So Sacha isn't with her?'

'I'm afraid not.'

I was thinking frantically. There had to be an explanation. My daughter was not a truant; she was good and honest and biddable. Then I remembered how jealously Sacha guarded her texts from prying eyes. Modern tormentors used technology to harass and torture their victims, even after the school bell had rung. 'Perhaps she's being bullied,' I suggested. 'I think she might be getting abusive texts. She never lets me see them.'

'Okay. Well, that's a thought. We have a zero tolerance policy on bullying, and text messaging is a live issue . . . I think the best thing is for us all to meet as soon as possible.'

'But where is she now?' I asked helplessly. 'Do I call the police?'

'That's up to you, but I'd expect her to turn up,' Lyndsay predicted briskly. 'She'll come home in the usual way, which is presumably what she's done on all those other occasions. We have a lot of truants, Martha. You're not alone.'

As soon as the teacher rang off, I called Sacha's mobile.

Hi, this is Sacha. Don't bother to leave a message.

I felt so powerless. She'd been attacked, abducted, raped in the cellar of some sordid house, waiting to be skinned like the girl in *The Silence of the Lambs*.

Redial. Same result.

And again.

And again.

And—

'That you, bro?' It was a breathless, garbled voice. Male.

'S-sorry, I think I've got the wrong number,' I stuttered. 'Is this Sacha's phone?' Muffled voices. Howls of laughter. 'Is that you, Jani?' I asked sharply. 'Jani?'

Then Sacha's voice, spiky and long-suffering. 'Yeah?'

'Where the hell are you?'

'At a friend's.'

'Why aren't you at school?'

'I felt really, *really* ill.' Another burst of hilarity from the background.

'I'm coming to get you.'

'You're not,' she said flatly. 'I'll be home on the school bus, and there's fuck all you can do about it.'

The line went dead. I stared at the phone in my hand. There was indeed fuck all I could do.

Kit was painting at an orchard near Hastings, and greeted the news with maddening calm. 'She hasn't really gone *missing*, has she?' he reasoned. 'I'd call it AWOL.'

'Kit, a man answered her phone! Bet it was Jani. I'm going to have him arrested.'

'Sacha's a young adult.'

'She's not,' I protested. 'She's a child.'

'She can leave school any time she likes, legally. This is going to get blown out of all proportion if you make a ginormous fuss.'

I could have throttled him. 'What a stupid thing to say. I'm *fussing*, Kit, because she's left fake messages on the absence line and I've absolutely no idea where she is right now, and actually it's time you fucking grew up.'

Slamming down the phone, I reached for the ibuprofen.

Adolescents surged out of the school gates like a flood from a washing machine. Some of the boys needed to be shaving, and a few of the girls wouldn't have looked out of place in a singles bar. You could smell the hormones. I'd parked the car and was leaning against it.

My phone rang. I grabbed it, but it wasn't Sacha. It was Kit.

'Have you heard anything?'

'No,' I said tersely. I was still smarting. 'I'm waiting outside the school.'

'Sorry,' he said. I huffed. 'Really, Martha. I'm sorry. It's time I fucking grew up.'

I couldn't help but smile. The best thing about Kit McNamara is his voice; it melts me still.

He seemed to sense a thawing. 'I've got the boys,' he said. 'I'll wait for you at home. Stay in touch.'

A school bus started its engine and pulled away, followed by a second. There were only two left when someone spoke behind me, and I spun around. It was Bianka: a Hollywood waif in a gingham miniskirt.

'Sacha sick today, Martha?'

I folded my arms. 'Don't play games with me. Sacha isn't at school and she isn't at home, as I'm sure you know. So where is she? And where's Jani?'

'Oh my God.' I caught the fear in her voice. 'Martha . . .' She took a step closer to me, glancing over her shoulder. 'I'm so scared.'

At that moment a figure hurtled up the street, a crumpled slapper with grubby hair. She looked terrifyingly like a girl who'd just climbed out of somebody's bed.

I grabbed her arm. 'Where the bloody hell have you been?'

Heads turned; a long row of parents, bored in their cars, all entertained by the family drama. Bianka slipped away. Sacha pulled free of my hand, dragged the passenger door almost off its hinges and threw herself in.

'*Where?*' I screamed.

She shrugged, jamming headphones into her ears. 'I'm here now, aren't I?'

'Take those frigging things out of your ears!' I was shrieking. 'I thought you might be dead in a ditch! Were you with Jani? You answer me, or I'll—'

I was furious. So furious, that now I had her sitting beside me—alive, not skinned—I burst into tears.

'She won't tell me anything.' I was unburdening myself on the phone to Dad the same evening, sitting on the verandah steps in the dark. 'She was scruffy. She *smells*, Dad! She's avoiding school, but she won't say why. If someone's bullying her, she won't say who. I drove straight into the staff car park and marched her up to the dean's office. Sacha had to admit she's missed loads of school—a week with flu, admittedly, and two other Mondays she was genuinely ill.'

'Always Mondays? Mondayitis?'

'Mm. I hadn't thought of that . . . And all those times she said she was going to orchestra, and wasn't.'

'Fibbing on the absence line,' murmured Dad. His voice was immensely calm. 'Devious. Not like our Sacha at all.'

'Kit spent an hour talking to her this evening. He's been really good, but he got nowhere. She'll get herself suspended if she carries on like this.'

'Has she promised to stop truanting?'

'Oh yes. Solemnly. But since none of us know what's going on, how can we protect her?'

'What about the other girl? The friend?'

'Bianka knows something, for sure; but nobody's prepared to pile on the pressure because her mother's in hospital again. She may or may not pull through the latest crisis.'

'Could Bianka herself be the bully?'

'Family of beautiful vampires,' I mused. 'No. I don't think she's the problem, but she knows who is. And then there's her brother . . . everything started to go wrong when he arrived on the scene.'

'Hm.' Dad paused for thought; I imagined him stroking Bernard's black fur. 'Have you looked at Sacha's phone?'

'She's wiped all her messages.'

'Laptop?'

'She gave Kit her password, but there's nothing. She's got hundreds of Facebook friends. Even Lou's on the list.'

'Any nastiness at all?'

'No, just complete drivel. Can't believe they waste their lives writing that stuff. Lol and rofl and wtf, streams of consciousness. Oh, and an absolutely priceless four-second clip of Belinda Rothman falling off the stage after the Christmas show, kitten heels and all. You've *got* to see it.'

Dad was silent.

'I've been so busy,' I said. 'I haven't been on the ball. She's been off key since . . . I dunno. Off and on for months. So edgy, so volatile. There's no fun in her any more.'

The possum chose that moment to run along the bough above me. I jumped, but I was growing used to its midnight dancing. I took a breath. 'It's as though she's . . . well. Never mind.'

'Go on,' prompted Dad. 'I *do* mind.'

'As though she's possessed. Some devil has taken my Sacha.'

After talking to Dad, I walked along to the studio. 'What a day,' I groaned, collapsing into a chair.

Kit regarded me bleakly. It made me think of the day the squall caught us, and sea and sky became one bruised shadow.

'Kit?' I sat bolt upright.

'They've been back.'

'Who's been . . .?' My hands flew to my cheeks. 'God, no. Not the thieves? In here?'

'Yep.' He turned a full circle, looking around the studio.

'But there's nothing worth taking . . . There can't be an illicit trade in art materials, surely?'

The light was gone from Kit's eyes. His face looked heavy. 'Visa card,' he said. 'A new one came in the post. It was still in the envelope.'

'Bollocks. We'll have to put a stop on it.'

'I don't care about the fucking visa card.'

Following his gaze, I looked up at the wall. Great-Aunt Sibella was gone. Her absence left a square, dusty ghost.

'Jesus Christ, Martha,' breathed Kit. 'Is nothing sacred?'

Twenty-seven

Kit was drinking. I could no longer ignore the signs. When I caught him heading for the studio with a bottle in his hand, I lost my rag.

'We had a deal,' I said. '*We* come out here. *You* control the booze.'

He swung around to face me, his movements grandiose, holding out his arms. 'Martha, we've been burgled. Sibella's been stolen. My step-daughter's behaving like a little bitch. Can you blame me if I want to relax on a Saturday afternoon?'

'We've nowhere left to run,' I pleaded. 'Don't do it. Just don't.'

I saw his point, though; our New Zealand honeymoon was certainly over. Sacha had been grounded for the first time in her life. Every day for a week I had escorted her to Lyndsay Carpenter's office, and collected her in the afternoons. It was like having a cloud in the car. She spent her evenings barricaded in her bedroom, complaining bitterly because all her teachers were demanding she catch up on missed assessments. She'd only herself to blame, of course.

'You've got a visitor,' snapped Kit, nodding towards the driveway as a vehicle rolled across the cattle stop. Then he barged past me into the studio and locked the door.

It was Ira, returning our quad bike. He'd borrowed it for a fishing expedition further down the coast. The young teacher looked steadfast and sane as he climbed out of Tama's truck. 'Hi, Martha,' he called cheerfully. 'Thanks for this.'

'Ira! Stay for coffee. Please. I need your advice.'

He looked surprised; but he sat on the verandah steps, cradling his mug and listening gravely while I told him about Sacha. The boys were closeted upstairs with a story tape and a bag of chocolate fish, which would probably make them sick.

'Were you bullied at school?' I asked.

'Well . . .' A rueful smile. 'I got into a lot of fights.'

'Do you think Jani's manipulating her? It's as though she's had a personality transplant. She's all over the place.'

He thought for a moment. 'How long's this been going on?'

'I'm not sure. It crept up on us.'

'I don't know much about girls, Martha, but I don't reckon you should worry too much. I've got a cousin who was a horror as a kid—used to scream the place down! She even ended up in the police cells for a night. Now she's twenty-five and a solid citizen. Takes some people a bit longer to grow up.'

We heard another car, and voices. Pamela and Jean appeared around the side of the house, carrying several small pumpkins. I was getting used to the Kiwi habit of arriving unannounced.

'Hello, my friend!' Jean shook Ira's hand. 'These are from our garden, Martha. Marvellous for soup. Are we interrupting?'

'Not at all. I've got coffee here with your name on it.'

'And I've got ginger crunch with yours,' said Pamela, holding up a tin. 'Kit's favourite.'

'He's in his studio. Er . . . working. I daren't disturb him.'

'I'm not afraid of your husband,' she retorted, and stalked off down the verandah.

'We wondered if we could borrow your boys tomorrow?' asked Jean, rubbing his hands. 'William's coming to stay.'

'Wonderful! Wait here—I'll refill the coffee.'

You had to hand it to Pamela: she had force of personality. I'd just emerged with a refilled plunger when she arrived on the verandah with Kit in tow. He pulled out a chair for her before sprawling in one himself.

'I wonder what it's like out there,' pondered Jean, who was watching the white sails of a yacht inching along the horizon. 'How does it feel to be those sailors on that great ocean, looking back at us landlubbers?'

'Lonely?' suggested Pamela.

'Safe,' said Kit, with a little too much emphasis. He was in control, but he wasn't sober. I'm sure our visitors knew it, too. They'd smell the alcohol. 'No bastards can nick your stuff when your back's turned.'

Pamela slapped her hands onto her knees. 'Time for a post-mortem. Is the insurance company going to replace everything?'

'They've finally agreed,' I said, putting up two thumbs. 'So no harm done, really. Not financially. But some of the things aren't replaceable.'

'Ah! Wait a minute.' Jean looked pleased with himself. He bumbled off in the direction of their pick-up, reappearing a minute later with something in his hand. 'For the boys.'

I took the proffered gift. It was a DVD—*Mary Poppins*. 'They love this!' I exclaimed.

'Pamela bought it on the internet,' said Jean, smiling at his wife. 'Poor little Charlie said losing that video was the worst thing about the burglary. Or buggery, as he called it.'

Pamela waved my thanks away. 'You're more than welcome. Now, have the police made any progress?'

'Well . . .' I looked from her to Kit. 'You know, if I were the superstitious type I'd think we have little thieving beings living in our forest.'

'Oh sweet Jesus,' muttered Kit.

'No, really, Kit. You know very well what I'm talking about.' I smiled apologetically at our visitors, all three of whom were looking politely embarrassed. 'Things have been going missing for . . . well, for months. Long before the burglary.'

Jean looked curious. 'What sort of things?'

'Er . . . jewellery, silver. A camera. A very special watch. It's as though there's a team of goblins who sneak in at night.'

'Never mind goblins. There was a team of filthy bastards snuck in during the day,' growled Kit. There was no mistaking the slur in his voice. 'And those same thieving scum came back to my studio last week and took a portrait that won't have fetched more than fifty bucks.'

'Not Great-Aunt Sibella?' gasped Pamela.

'Yep. A twentieth-century Irish painter nobody's ever heard of.'

'Oh, *no*.'

'What do the police think?' asked Jean.

Kit shrugged. 'Someone with local knowledge. Someone who can watch the house . . . For God's sake, we're a mile up a bloody track, how can anyone watch our house?'

'Bob Andrews asked about our removal firm.' I put a hand to my mouth. 'Sorry, Ira. Not you, obviously! We told them they were barking up the wrong tree . . . Ira?'

The young man was looking stunned, his dense brows lowered until they almost touched his nose. He fingered his mug, full lips pursed in thought.

'That's all right,' he said, recovering himself. 'They told me the boss had a visit from the cops, but he got it all straightened out. Um, I'd better get going. Thanks for the coffee.'

I walked him to the truck. I could tell he had something on his mind. 'I've never thought it was your workmates,' I said. 'Honestly.'

Ira swung into the driver's seat. He couldn't get away quick enough. 'No worries. They've got broad shoulders. It goes with the job, being accused of breaking stuff or taking stuff. Occupational hazard.'

'You're not offended?'

He looked at me with kind brown eyes, and turned the key. 'Got no reason to be offended. You take care of yourself, Martha, all right?'

I watched Ira Taulafo race down the hill in a tornado of dust. And I wondered.

At ten o'clock that night, the phone rang.

I'd last seen Kit sitting on a stool, staring at his latest work in progress and looking saturnine. He was nine-tenths of the way to a drunken stupor. There was no reasoning with him in such a state; he would only become more belligerent. I'd prescribed myself a bit of therapy, chopping pumpkins to make soup using—I'm embarrassed to admit this—a recipe Pamela had given me.

I turned down the radio and held the receiver under my chin, still chopping. I was thinking, *if this is telesales, you are dead.*

'Martha?'

I winced as the knife bit. 'Tama!' I searched for a tissue and pressed it against my lacerated finger. 'Er . . . how are you?'

He ignored the small talk. 'At Sacha's party, you said you'd like to try riding again. How about tomorrow afternoon?'

Ooh, watch it! counselled Mum. *Something fishy here. His intentions cannot be honourable.*

'Did I?' My mind was racing. 'I don't know if tomorrow . . .'

'There's no strings attached, Martha. You'll be quite safe.'

'Well, no. I never thought—'

Tama was quiet, but unrelenting. 'I need to talk to you.'

'You *are* talking to me.'

'Face to face. And alone.'

The answer is no. Do you hear me, Martha? No!

I watched my blood as it blossomed like a red rose across the tissue. 'What time?'

'So you're going for a jaunt with Clint Eastwood?' Kit hadn't moved from his stool, though no progress had been made with the painting.

'Mm-hm. We're going to make passionate love before galloping into the sunset. You'll never see us again.'

He sloshed more wine into his glass and caught me watching. 'For Christ's sake, get the scowl off your face.'

'You're going on a bender, Kit. You're breaking your promise.'

His mouth was an inverted U, almost ugly. 'What if I object to you gallivanting around with that fucking horse whisperer?'

'Your problem.'

He lurched to his feet, face darkening. 'I don't like being made a fool of.'

'I'm going to bed,' I said coldly, ignoring the threat. I'd had enough of Kit for one day. 'Don't forget to lock up. I've checked the windows already.'

'Fort Knox. This is our sanctuary, Martha. We shouldn't be locking ourselves into our sanctuary.' Suddenly he looked forlorn, swaying in his baggy sweater and polished brogues, a glass in one hand.

'Come up with me,' I said.

'Soon.'

Sighing, I made my way through the house, turning off lights. I was halfway up the stairs before I looked up. And then I almost died.

A figure was standing on the top step, its face turned towards me. I grabbed the banisters and staggered back, though it took only a split second to realise that this apparition was Finn, gazing glassily with blank eyes.

'Finn!' I breathed.

His eyes widened in speechless terror, and I took the rest of the stairs two at a time. I knew that rabbit-in-the-headlights stare. He didn't know who I was, or where he was, and he was scared.

'Come on, baby,' I whispered, taking him by the hand. 'Don't be all spooky, you gave me a fright.'

Leading him to the boys' bedroom, I crossed my fingers. If I was lucky, he would return to deeper sleep. He snatched up Buccaneer Bob and lay down, mumbling. His eyes were closed by the time I covered him up. I waited for a couple of minutes, stroking his hair as his breathing deepened, then slid out.

I looked in on Sacha. Her room smelled like a locker room; she needed to sort out her washing. My girl was curled up under her duvet, one hand resting on her cheek. She was snuffling a little, and her face felt cushiony soft when I kissed it. She looked barely older than her brothers.

All was well.

All seemed well.

Kit passed out in the studio that night, surfacing with the mother of all hangovers the following afternoon. By then the boys had gone to play with William Colbert. Kit drooped by the kitchen stove, guzzling Alka-Seltzer and apologising twice a minute. He was wretched, but I was too furious to be appeased. I gave him the silent treatment.

'Can't believe myself,' he said. 'It won't happen again.'

I shrugged. I was pulling on lace-up boots for riding.

Kit hunched, dropping his forehead onto his fists. 'I'm going teetotal until I leave for Dublin. How's that?'

I managed a hollow laugh.

'C'mon, Martha. I'm pulling out the stops! Teetotal. Cold turkey. Not another drop.'

'I'll believe it when I see it.'

'Where are you off to?' he asked as I picked up the car keys. I think he'd really forgotten.

'Galloping into the sunset with Clint Eastwood,' I snapped. 'Got a problem with that? Deal with it.'

Kit capitulated like a lamb. Mum didn't. In fact, she yelled all the way down the drive. *Are you mad?*

'Tama said he just needed to talk to me. He's an honourable guy. I trust him.'

Yes, but do you trust yourself when you're so angry with Kit?

'Chill. I'm much too fat to have a fling. I couldn't possibly take my clothes off for a new man! I'd need to spend six months in the gym first.'

Remember Sacha's father!

Ouch. She had a point there.

Tama was waiting as I parked next to his ute. We were away within minutes.

'What are those boys up to this afternoon?' he asked, as we crossed the dunes.

When I explained about William Colbert, he nodded. 'I've known Pamela since we were both small.'

'Really? Isn't she much older than you?'

'She was at Torutaniwha Primary School with my cousins. Most of 'em fancied old Pam. She had the boys pawing the ground in her younger days, but that Frenchie got in first.'

We rode steadily, side by side, casting blue shadows. The autumn light was soft and diffused; it was hard to tell where the air ended and the water began. Tama didn't seem anxious to talk for a time, and I didn't prompt him.

As we reached the headland, he scratched his nose. 'This isn't easy,' he said. And indeed, he looked less at ease than I'd ever seen him. For one deliriously skin-tingling but deeply embarrassing moment I thought he was going to make a move then and there, dragging me off Kakama and onto the sea-washed sand. Mum was going ballistic. If she hadn't already been dead, I really think she might have had a heart attack.

'Go ahead,' I prompted, feeling my cheeks burn. 'I'm listening.'

He tilted his hat lower over his eyes. 'I've heard things.'

'Heard things?'

'You've been losing things.'

I was bemused. 'Well, we were burgled and—'

'I'm not talking about the burglary.'

This wasn't at all the conversation I'd expected. 'We're chaotic. We've still got stuff in cardboard boxes. I expect it'll all turn up.'

'An antique painting? You really think it's lying around somewhere?'

'Well, no.'

'How's that lovely daughter?' he asked, in what seemed an abrupt change of subject.

'Sacha? She's . . . well, she's fine.'

'Fine?'

'She's a teenager—all tantrums and tiaras at the moment.'

Then he seemed to change the subject yet again. 'My sister used to live in Torutaniwha. Her husband was a top bloke. Samoan guy. He worked in the forestry. Got crushed by a log and killed. She had two little kids, and they gave her a payout.'

'Ira and . . .?'

'Jonah was the older one. Anyway, she started sleeping with some idiot and he talked her into running off to Auckland with the boys. I didn't like it but it was her life, not mine. The new boyfriend spent all her money then ditched her but she wouldn't come home, she stayed in Auckland and brought up those kids pretty well on her own. Ira was top student at teacher college.'

'He's a credit to her,' I said, with feeling. 'What about the other son?'

'Jonah's an electrician. He had a girlfriend, flash car, widescreen TV. All the things people seem to think they need. Even managed to buy a house. He's no angel; always pushed the boundaries, partied hard.'

'But he's doing okay?'

'He tried a few drugs. Weed, ketamine, all kinds of shit he put into his body. He could still hold down his job, never took a day off sick no matter how rough the night had been. But in the end he began to dance with the devil itself.'

'What does that mean?'

'It means he went too far. It's called P over here. You know what that is?'

'Of course. Well, sort of. Not really.'

'Ice, or whiz—lots of names. Crystal meth. Pure methamphetamine.'

'Amphetamine. That's speed?'

'It's nothing like the speed people used when I was young. They call it P because it's *pure.* It can be almost a hundred per cent pure. If you read in the paper about some really nasty murder, chances are this stuff was involved. Sometimes it's gang wars, because this is a multi-million-dollar business. Sometimes it's some poor punter who hasn't paid his dealer. Sometimes it's just plain evil.'

The penny was dropping. 'Oh . . . like Jean and Pamela's son.'

'Daniel.' Tama looked bleak. 'Lovely kid. He was in Jonah's class at Torutaniwha. They were mates.'

'We're surrounded by ocean. Can't we stop this stuff at the border?'

'It still gets smuggled in. Anyway, you can make it in your kitchen! If you look on the internet you've got a choice of recipes. So it's being cooked up all over the place—in kitchens and cupboards and cars, what the papers call clan labs. You know how resourceful we New Zealanders are. Kiwi ingenuity, Martha! We have a can-do attitude. We can fix anything with number-eight wire, so you bet we can cook our own fries.'

'Fries?'

'Jonah called it that. I asked him why, he said because it fries your brain.'

I felt something very nasty in the pit of my stomach, a squeezing hand so cold that it ached. 'So . . . what happened to Jonah?'

'He's safe, for now.'

'That's good.'

'No. Not good.'

'Is he—'

'In prison.'

I looked at the shadowed profile. Did this uncle—this self-possessed, profoundly dignified man—queue up at the prison gates on visiting days? Did he stand quietly with arms and legs akimbo while guards searched his pockets and sniffer dogs circled?

'People using this stuff need money,' he continued unhurriedly. 'They need a truckload of money. If they're a lawyer or dentist or something, they can afford it. Plenty of users are professional people. It's everywhere, I'm telling you. Everywhere. I couldn't believe the things Jonah told me. Your accountant, your lawyer, your doctor could easily be using it. But if they've got no income they have to find other ways of paying.'

'Burglary, you mean?' I was wondering whether this jailbird nephew could somehow have burgled our house. Perhaps that was what Tama was trying to tell me. I was ready to be nice about it.

'They start by selling everything they have. They'll sell the shirt off their back if they have to, the food from their shelves, they'll sell their bodies. Nothing matters except getting the next hit. It's all they think about. They'll steal from their families.'

'Is that what Jonah did?'

'Martha! Listen to what I'm saying, will you?'

'I *am* listening.' But I wasn't, not really. I didn't want to. We rode on, while the ice fingers twisted my gut.

'Is Sacha still playing her flute?' asked Tama.

'What's that got to do with anything?'

'*Is* she?'

I leaned forward to lay my cheek on Kakama's neck, breathing in the warm horse smell and taking comfort from her strength. I felt chilled all over now.

'Jonah became a different human being,' continued Tama. 'It began small, the thing. The terrible devil thing. Just a cute little demon. But he made a pet of it, and it grew. He began to miss days at work—one time he was so wired, he phoned his boss at two in the morning to tell him he wouldn't be coming the next day! So he was out on his ear. A qualified electrician, but nobody would employ him. He'd lost control—talking big, acting wild. He'd be up for a week and then he'd sleep for days.'

You know how it can be when someone is trying to point out a curiosity to you? A rare hawk, say. They point excitedly and they shriek, 'Look there, beyond the tree . . . between the pylon and the windsock . . . *there*, see it?' And you strain your eyes but you still can't see the bloody thing. And then they whisper patiently, 'No, look again. It's next to the red chimneypot. Got the red chimney? Right, well just to the left of that . . . hovering . . . see?'

Tama was still talking. 'He lost interest in everything, even in life. He lost his home. Car got repossessed, so did the TV but he'd already sold that. He sold everything. He stole stuff from his girlfriend and her parents. So she dumped him, and he didn't even care. He thieved from his mother and aunties and nana.'

I didn't want to hear any more. I wanted to go home.

'He got scared, reckoned people were out to kill him,' said Tama. 'Well, perhaps they were. It's a dark world he'd got into. The trade's big business—*big* business. It's mostly controlled by gangs, and life is cheap to those people. You don't want to piss them off.'

I remembered the motorbike gang on the road, and shuddered.

'Maybe he owed someone money,' said Tama. 'By this time he was on the streets. I went and got him and brought him home, thinking maybe I could straighten him out. The poor kid . . . you know, he tried to get clean. He said it was like crawling in the desert, dying of thirst, but there's cool water gushing from a spring. You *have* to have it, nothing else matters. And then . . . well, we lost him. Things began to disappear. You know what I'm saying? Little things, at first. Cash. Then other things.'

And suddenly there it is, that bird. It balances and wheels and dominates the landscape. You can't miss it. You wonder how you could have been so blind.

My hands began to shake. I could barely hold the reins. 'I don't . . . Look, Tama, I understand what you're suggesting, and I know you're only trying to help. But you're just plain wrong. You don't know me very well, and clearly you don't know Sacha at all.'

'You've taken offence. Can't blame you.'

'I haven't taken offence, but this is a laughable idea.'

'Is it?' He looked into my face. 'I don't see you laughing.'

'For a start, I know for a fact that Sacha had nothing to do with our burglary. I drove her to school myself that day.'

'I'm sure she didn't burgle your house herself.'

'Well, then!'

Tama sighed. 'One of Jonah's user mates was a younger guy, an accountant's son. The kid could get his hands on cash . . . Dealers target people like Sacha. Do you understand, Martha? It's their method. They need punters whose families have some money. When they couldn't siphon any more from the dad's bank account, Jonah and his mate got desperate. So they borrowed the family car—a flash convertible. Parked it up in town, then phoned their dealer to come and get it. Told the parents it'd been stolen.'

'Look . . . we just aren't that kind of family.'

'A family like mine, you mean?'

'No, I don't mean that. Sacha wouldn't steal from us. She'd never experiment with hard drugs, either.'

'Who would have known when you'd all be out, both the day of the burglary and the day the painting was taken?'

I couldn't stand any more. 'Can we turn back now, please?'

At some silent signal from Tama, both horses immediately wheeled around, making ripples and eddies as they splashed along the tideline.

'What happened to Jonah?' I asked.

'He disappeared. A year later, he turned up in court in Auckland. Burgling, shoplifting, mugging. Thousands of dollars. I went to support my sister. That kid wasn't Jonah any more. He didn't talk like Jonah, didn't think like Jonah, didn't even *look* like him. He'd rotted away.'

'He admitted everything?'

'The police drove him around and he pointed out all the places he'd burgled. He was a wreck by then. Never saw anyone change so much in a couple of years. He'd been a fit, handsome guy. Big fella, like Ira. Truckloads of confidence. He ended up looking like an orc from *Lord of the Rings*, you know? Even his teeth went rotten. He thought there were bugs living under his skin.'

'Bugs? D'you mean insects?'

'Running around under his skin. They drove him crazy. He scratched and scraped until he was bleeding, then right into his flesh. I heard the probation officer call it "meth mites". It's the P flooding their system. The poisons get forced out of their pores.'

Dog's got fleas. Frigging chickens have lice.

'How's your poor sister coping?'

Tama shrugged. 'She says this thing will kill him in the end.' He twisted sideways in the saddle and looked me in the eye. 'Look, I hope I'm wrong. Maybe I'm just a fussy old coot. But I've seen Sacha change since you arrived here, and it's bothered me. Then yesterday Ira paid me a visit. He was pretty upset, wanted to tell me what's been going on at your place. It seemed like the last piece of the jigsaw.'

'All right. I'll ask her.'

'She'll lie,' Tama said sadly, running his hand down Ruru's twitching ears. 'They always lie. They get bloody good at it.'

'So what do I do?'

'Search her room. Search all possible hiding places.'

'And if you're right?'

He didn't hesitate. 'Pick her up and run for her life. Take her away, just as fast and as far as you can. Before it's too late.'

Twenty-eight

I never even went into the house. If Sacha was hiding something, I knew where it would be.

The smoko hut crouched in its thicket of foliage, perhaps four minutes' walk from the kitchen door. It was Sacha's place. Her den. Her lair. If she was hiding something, it would be here. I hesitated with my hand on the door. Then I pushed it open.

There was no unusual smell; nothing but dust and warm plastic. The room was very dark though, and I soon saw why. Someone had not only drawn the curtains but also pinned fertiliser sacks across the windows. I fumbled to press the light switch. Nothing happened, because there was no bulb. Irritated now, I walked to the nearest window, grabbed hold of a sack and ripped it down. Then I did the same with the other and pulled back the curtains.

I faced the little room. School books lay scattered on the sofa. Photographs smiled from the walls: Ivan, Lydia, Dad, Lou and my all-time favourite poster of Captain Jack Sparrow, his gold tooth glinting. On the chimney breast leaned a saccharine poem entitled 'Best Friends'; I remembered Lydia giving it to Sacha when they were ten.

The coffee table was actually a pile of suitcases. I opened each one. CDs, make-up, farewell cards. A teenager's detritus. By the sofa were two candle stubs in wine bottles and several lighters. I forced my hand down behind the cushions but found only a ten-cent coin and a lot of fluff. In the sink was a half-empty mug, with—I sniffed it—mouldy Milo. There were jam jars with coffee, Milo powder and sugar. Salt too, for some reason. The kettle was half filled and I lifted the lid. Water.

With increasing relief I began to tug at the drawers in the shabby table. They kept getting stuck. Teaspoons. Candle ends. A pair of scissors. Biros, most of which looked broken. A roll of electrical tape. Pliers. None of these were a surprise to me; things like pliers and electrical tape might have been there for years.

In another drawer I found a plastic pot of rat poison which I clearly remembered had been there when we arrived. Under the table sat the empty paint tin that Sacha used as a bin. Sensible girl, she'd lined it with a plastic shopping bag. Going through my daughter's rubbish had to be a low point; I hoped never, ever to do it again. A cursory glance was enough to assure me that the contents were innocent. Crisp packets. A couple of broken light bulbs. They must have been in the hut when we arrived because they were the old-fashioned kind, not those eco-friendly corkscrews of glass that take ten minutes to light up. Squeezed-out teabags. Empty plastic drink bottles, which should have gone into the recycling. Anyway, I wasn't going to demean myself or Sacha by ferreting any deeper. Enough was enough.

Nothing, I exulted as I slid the bin back into place. There was nothing. Not so much as an empty fag packet. I gave one last glance around the hut, nodded smugly to myself and walked out. *Up yours, Tama bloody Pardoe*, I thought as I slammed the door behind me. Your nephew may be off the rails. My daughter is not.

I'd almost reached the house when I stopped dead, turning my face up to the spreading branches of the walnut. A fantail swooped and dived around my feet. Seconds later I'd spun around and was running. The wooden door crashed into the wall as I threw myself on the floor. Gripping the paint tin, I scrabbled under teabags and crisp packets.

Light bulbs. Not broken, but tampered with. Their screw parts had been pulled out, leaving only the bowls. The white frosting had somehow been removed so that the glass was very clear. Too clear. And someone had wrapped duct tape around the tops, as though they'd been attached to something else.

I paced around the hut, looking now with different eyes. In the drawers—nothing. In the suitcases, in the toilet's cistern—nothing. I turned around and around, trying to imagine where I would hide a secret treasure. I was kneeling by the stove, my hand shoved up the metal flue like a deranged midwife, when my fingers brushed something snagged on a rivet. Closing the stove behind me—ludicrous, the need we have for order—I carried my find outside into the light.

The fantail whirled around my head, spreading his tail, wittering his merry tune. I shall always be grateful to that little fellow. He was my only companion at one of the most shattering moments of my life.

Just a silly little bit of plastic; a tiny snap-lock bag perhaps an inch square. When I held it to the light, its contents ran to one corner. White crystals, like ground glass. Pretty, really.

Suddenly the world seemed almost psychedelically miscoloured. Giant pungas moved in a weird slow motion, vast spider webs against the glazed emptiness of the sky. Even the sunlight felt pitiless. What had been good and pure was sordid now. My beautiful daughter had another life: a foul, degenerate life. She had betrayed us.

I sank onto the ground a few steps away from the hut. Sheep grazed nearby as though the world was still intact, and my fantail flew off home. Images swirled, twisted and fell together into an unbearable whole: cameras, watch, milk jug. Money, gone from tins and wallets and beloved piggybanks. A burglary. Great-Aunt Sibella. Sacha, lifting a broken bulb to her face and inhaling the poison.

I was still sitting there as the horizon deepened to a rich seam of orange. A blackbird trilled in the trees, and I longed for Dad's garden in the English summer rain. That was when Sacha came trudging up the track and walked straight past without seeing me.

She stopped dead at the sight of the open door, her face ghostly in the half-light. There was complete stillness for several heartbeats. Then she strode into the hut. With a sense of immense sadness I heard the stove's door creak. I pushed myself to my feet and stood in the doorway. She was on her knees, her head inside the stove, peering in.

'It's not there,' I said.

She swung round, her voice childish with fright. 'Mum?'

'How long did you think you could go on?'

She got up and stood facing me. Ash spangled her hair, and there was a smear of soot down one cheek. 'I don't know what you're talking about.'

I held up the bag. She looked at it, then at me. 'You don't think that's mine, do you?' And then I was baffled, because she laughed aloud. She picked up a lighter and lit the candles, glancing in disgust at my hand. 'Frick's sake. That isn't *mine*! Whadya think I am? Mental?'

'I don't know what you are, Sacha. I wish I did.'

'Jeez!' She sounded genuinely indignant, and my resolve faltered. She jerked her chin towards the bag. 'Tip that out. Be my guest. It belongs to a guy who crashed my party, a total penis head called Ed. We didn't even invite him, he just tagged along with one of the girls. What a creep.'

'You knew it was in the stove.'

'Sit down.' She was patting the sofa as though I was the child and she the parent. 'Yes, I did. Someone sent me a text. Said Ed had left his stash. I was about to chuck it down the pan.'

I so wanted to believe her. 'Sacha, please. No more lies.'

'For God's sake! You know I'd never touch anything like that. I've seen what hard drugs can do to people, they showed us a video at school and I totally despise it. Shit like this is for losers. Ed's completely fucked up.'

I began to feel a little hope. I was trying to think, trying to fit her explanation into the jigsaw puzzle. I held up the bag. 'So what *is* this?'

'How would I know? It's something that should be flushed down the U-bend.'

'Let's take it to the police. What's this Ed's surname?'

'Very bad idea.'

'Very good idea. I'll phone Robert Andrews right now.'

There was a flash, deep in the tawny eyes. 'Are you *nuts*? They might nick me—for being in possession of . . . well, of whatever it is. And what happens if you or I or any of us is convicted of an offence?'

'What?'

'Game over.' She drew her finger across her throat. 'Bang go our visas. We're not citizens, remember? We're here on sufferance. One false move and the McNamara family will be on the first plane home.' I sat stunned as she pressed her advantage. 'I've a feeling Kit might have a word or two to say on the subject.'

'But this stuff isn't ours.'

'Ed will say it is.' Sacha sighed. 'Mud sticks. You want to get deported? Well, go ahead. Be my guest.'

Her story made sense, if you were desperate enough. And besides, I knew Sacha wouldn't let thieves into our house. She just wouldn't. 'So you swear you haven't touched this?'

She crossed herself. 'Guide's honour. Cross my heart and hope to die.'

'And you never, ever will?'

'I swear on my little brothers' lives. I'm really sorry we let that dildo crash the party.'

Snuffing the candles, we left the hut and began to make our way up the track.

'Stupid jerk,' Sacha was saying as we stepped into the light from the kitchen windows. 'I'd have thrown him out if I'd known he was using P.'

'Using . . .' I stopped short. 'So you *do* know what it is.'

Her eyes flickered towards the bag in my hand. 'Well, someone told me . . .' She put up two forefingers in a cross, to ward off evil. 'You won't tell Kit, will you?'

I wasn't listening. I was thinking. 'Light bulbs,' I muttered. She didn't seem to hear, just kept walking. I caught up in three fast strides, put a hand on her arm and spun her around. 'Just a minute. Why is there no light bulb in the smoko hut?'

'Stupid things kept blowing. And I like candlelight. It's romantic.'

'Where are the bulbs, then?'

She looked at me as though I'd gone mad. 'How the hell would I know? In the landfill, I should think.'

'Oh Sacha,' I whispered. 'You're a good liar. I've seen them.'

'You went through my *bin*? How sick is that?' She whirled away and slammed into the kitchen.

Kit was reading the paper at the table, and looked up in almost comic surprise at the hurricane that had blown in. 'Girls, girls,' he said, looking faintly amused. His gaze travelled from my face to Sacha's, and then to the tiny bag I was holding up.

'What's that?' he asked quietly. It was slightly sinister, because the smile was still on his lips.

Sacha's eyes met mine. In the electric light I saw that her pupils were enlarged, taking up most of the iris; it had a demonic effect. For one last moment, I wondered whether I should cover up for her. She would never be so stupid as to dabble in drugs again. End of story, and nobody the wiser. Kit wouldn't even *want* to know.

'It's rat poison,' she lied, smoothly but implausibly. 'Would you believe it, Kit? Mum's making a fuss because the smoko hut's got rats.'

Kit reached for the bag, and there was another nasty silence while he held it under the light. 'Right. Who's going to do the talking?'

'Why should I bother?' raged Sacha, making for the door. 'Nobody believes me.'

I took her wrist. 'Where's your flute?'

'At school.'

'Shall I phone your dean and ask her to check?'

My daughter looked as though she'd like to strangle me. Her face was a mask of fury, the pupils still eerily dilated. I was afraid of her. This demon wasn't my Sacha. '*Fuck* you,' she hissed, thrusting me into the dresser. I heard her footsteps pounding up the stairs, and the house shivered as her bedroom door smashed shut.

I nodded at the miniature bag in Kit's hand. 'I think that's this stuff they call P.'

'Jesus. I do hope you're wrong.'

I told him about Tama's warning and my search. Once I'd described the light bulbs, he stood up. 'C'mon. Know your enemy.'

The sitting room was warm and bright. Kit had lit the fire, tidied up and turned on all the lamps—poor man, I realised dimly that he'd been trying to make amends for the previous evening's binge. He was drinking ginger beer. He'd even made a casserole. I flung myself into a chair while he bent down to the desktop, his face reflecting the blue screen.

'Times like this I long for broadband,' he said. 'What shall we try? Pure meth . . . P.' He typed, clicked, waited, then whistled incredulously. 'Will you look at that? There's a whole industry.'

Indeed there was. I was aboard my magic hearthrug again, but this time it was flying me somewhere I didn't want to go. Over the next hour we gave ourselves a crash course. To its many friends around the world the drug is known by fluffy nicknames—Tina, crystal, ice, glass. And, only in New Zealand, P.

Per capita, New Zealand has the highest addiction rates to Methamphetamine in the world. The crystal form is the most pure.

'One hundred per cent pure New Zealand,' breathed Kit.

Methamphetamine is a Class A drug. It is a very powerful psychostimulant, uniquely addictive and destructive. About ninety per cent of people who try methamphetamine just once continue to use it.

Facts leaped off the page and clouted me between the eyes. I found myself mesmerised, in a ghastly way. This was relevant to me, to my family.

'Sacha can't be using this,' I said, reading a list of side-effects—including stroke and death—that made my breath stick in my throat. 'She just can't be.'

Kit was clicking and typing. 'Bingo,' he said quietly. 'We'll have to give it a few minutes to download.'

Highly educational, is YouTube: a grainy, sordid little home video, showing us exactly how to make a meth pipe out of a light bulb, then heat crystals over a flame and inhale the vapours. Things I'd seen in the smoko hut—apparently innocent—became horribly significant. The bulb was the star of the show, but also in the cast were the pliers, the duct tape, the empty biro tube, the lighter and the top part of a plastic drink bottle like the ones in the bin. There was even salt, to sandblast the frosting off the bulb. It was all done in a lonely, godforsaken silence. You never saw more than the addict's mouth, but you could hear his heavy breathing. It was an intensely sleazy experience. I felt dirty just watching. It was repulsive, yet at the same time almost erotic, like a peepshow in the back streets of Amsterdam.

'For crying out loud.' Kit sounded shaken. 'Let's go to the police. Right now. Tonight.'

'We can't.'

'This is poison, Martha! They'll give Sacha a warning and put the fear of God into her.'

I reached for his hand, lifted it off the mouse and traced my finger down the familiar lines on his palm. 'If Sacha's in trouble, we're all in trouble. We have to be of *good character.* Remember all those police checks before we got our visas? I don't know, but using a Class A drug doesn't sound like good character to me.'

Kit understood immediately, and banged his other hand onto the desk. 'Hell.'

The video started itself up again. We watched the process with fascinated revulsion. The bulb filled with white vapour, swirling and thickening. It was all obscenely matter-of-fact, as though this degradation was normal and everyday; a *Blue Peter* presenter showing how to make a pencil case out of a shoebox and sticky-backed plastic . . . *And here's one I've made already!* The anonymous lips closed caressingly around the tube, and the addict inhaled deeply. Then he murmured something. His tone was that of a lover, whispering in his beloved's ear.

'I've seen enough,' said Kit abruptly.

We climbed the stairs together. Sacha's door was locked.

'Sacha.' Kit gave the panels a hefty kick. 'Let us in or—so help me—I'll walk down these stairs and phone the police. You can take your chances.'

The door swung open and she stood with her hand on the handle, mocking. 'You wouldn't dare.'

It struck me—with sickening force—how my dazzling girl had changed. How could such horrors have slipped beneath my radar? This creature was thin, sallow, sad, with sores on her face and arms. Her hair was dirty, her eyes deadened. The signs had been there to see.

She was in trouble, sneered Mum. *But you were too busy with your work and your twins and your lovely new life.*

The room was a bombsite, with the rancid smell I'd noticed the night before. Sacha used to be organised, tidy, fussy about hygiene. She threw herself full-length on the bed. 'Okay, okay. I tried it. I'll never touch it again. Happy?'

'For Christ's sake.' Kit rammed his fist into his palm.

'What did you expect? You pack me up and drag me halfway around the world as though I was a piano. What did you *expect*?'

'Not this,' I said.

When she saw that Kit was prowling, opening drawers and cupboards, she jumped to her feet. 'Get out! You're not my father. How dare you invade my privacy?'

Kit stood looking around, brows drawn. 'What am I going to find, Sacha Norris?'

'You bastard, Kit. There's nothing in here. I've just had some filthy burglar going through my stuff, and now you . . . Put that down!'

Kit had hold of her backpack. He took one last look at his stepdaughter—who was making a wild lunge towards him—and shook the pack upside down. Clothes fell out: a t-shirt; a manky towel, wrapped around Sacha's bikini; and finally a pair of socks rolled into a ball, which hit the floor with a hideous clunk.

We all looked down at those socks. Kit picked them up. As he unrolled them, something fell into the palm of his hand. It was the video camera I'd been given as a leaving present. My decadent toy, stolen in the burglary.

'Jesus Christ.' Kit stared in sickened fascination at the thing in his hand. His voice was ominously gentle. 'It's true. You had us burgled.'

Sacha crumpled onto the bed, her arms wrapped around her head. I felt as though she was a stranger.

'No choice.' Her breath was coming in fractured gasps. 'I didn't have any choice.'

Kit crossed the floor in one stride, took hold of an arm and pulled her half off the bed. It was as though he'd attacked a rag doll.

'No choice?' he spat, his face distorted with rage. 'No *choice*? You little bitch. You told them when to come. Told them where to look. Maybe you even drew a helpful map. Did you have a good laugh about *Mary* bloody *Poppins*? What have Finn and Charlie ever done to you?'

I stepped closer. 'Kit . . .'

'They love you.' Kit's whole body seemed electrified with fury. He lifted a fist. 'Those poor little bastards! They worship you. Was that their crime? Worshipping you?'

'I needed to pay someone,' she wailed. 'I owed someone.'

'Who did you owe?' I asked.

'Can't tell you.'

'Oh yes, you can.' Kit pushed her away. 'Who is this person you love so much that you will betray your family for them? Is it that slimeball Jani?'

'We have to call the police,' I said.

'No!' Sacha began to rock back and forth on the bed, her arms locked behind her head. 'I'm so scared . . . They'll come after me.'

Kit sighed. 'Where's Sibella's portrait? I want it back.'

'Shh! Did you hear that?' Sacha looked terrified. 'There's someone on the balcony.'

I opened her door and looked out. The night was still. Not a sound, not a movement; not even the lights of a ship out in the bay. 'Must have been a possum,' I said, stepping back inside.

'Oh, I wish it was.' Sacha's mouth stretched wide. 'I'm sorry, Mum. I'm sorry. I'm so sorry. I'm in so much trouble.' Her bare feet were stuck out in front of her, the toes splayed. I thought of a film I once saw about cholera victims, their dead feet laid out in rows.

'You've got to talk to us,' I said tiredly. 'No more lies, Sacha. Please. I can't take any more lies.'

Kit glanced at his watch. 'Shit. We were supposed to collect the boys an hour ago.'

'You go,' I said.

He hesitated. 'Will you be okay?'

'Yes. I'll talk to her. Don't hurry back—we don't want the boys upset.'

As he was leaving, a horrible thought struck me. 'The Colberts! This is what killed their son. They mustn't know, Kit. Nobody must know.'

Twenty-nine

What do you do when your daughter smuggles a snake into Eden? It isn't in the manual.

I hoped I was dreaming, because this was a terrifying nightmare. I wasn't reading a book about some naive and witless mother whose child had gone off the rails. This wasn't Hollywood. This was me. Perhaps human beings need—for their very survival—a fundamental belief in their own invulnerability. It won't be my family killed on the roads. It won't be my husband in love with another woman. It will be someone else, and I'll feel very sorry for them while secretly suspecting that they brought it on themselves. It *definitely* won't be my child who takes drugs. That's for other, more careless families.

Parking Sacha in front of the sitting-room fire, I staggered into the kitchen and grabbed the hot chocolate. It seemed an absurdly homely and jolly thing to be doing, but it gave me time to think. As I slid a saucepan of milk across the hob, my eye fell on the phone.

Just dialling his number made me feel closer to my father. It was early morning in Bedfordshire, but he'd be up. The telephone would be calling out to him now, in that softly coloured kitchen. I saw him with the cat on his knee, stretching out his hand to answer me. I had never needed him more than I did at that moment.

Click. Dad's resonant greeting. 'Hello there. This is Hereward Norris.'

Dad, please be in. I don't know what to do.

'I'm sorry. You've missed me this time, but leave me a message and I promise to call you back.'

I stood mute as the seconds passed. Milk rose mutinously in a white froth, seething over the edge of the saucepan. Then I quietly replaced the receiver. How could I confess catastrophe to a tape recorder?

Tama answered at the second ring. I think he was waiting.

'You were right,' I said. 'Thank you.'

'I'm sorry.'

'Kit's furious.'

'Yes.' A moment's quiet. 'If I can ever help, Martha . . . you know where to find me.'

Sacha sat hunched on the end of the sofa, a blanket over her shoulders like a pantomime crone, worrying at her arm.

'Feeling better?' I asked, setting down our mugs. 'Start at the beginning.'

Scrabble, scratch. 'You won't listen you won't listen.' She spoke too fast, no pauses at all, blinking rapidly. 'You'll shout at me.'

'I promise I won't shout. Are you on something right now?'

'What? Oh . . . yes. Coming down actually, crashing, I really needed another burn when you found me in the hut and right now I'm starting to feel pretty shit. It's going to get worse, oh God oh God a *lot* worse, it's really going to hurt.' She stared into her mug, shivering. A minute passed.

I shook her by the shoulder. 'Sacha!'

'Sorry.' Tears slid from the corners of her eyes. 'I was so lonely.'

Guilt was banging on my door, leading a lynch mob complete with pitchforks and flaming torches. Guilt is female, and she always has the moral high ground in a peculiarly irritating way. Like my mother, come to think of it. The best way to fight her off is by a volley of defensive mortar, which is what I fired now. 'Don't try to shift the blame. This is all your own doing.'

The next moment she'd slowed down, right down, like a train with the brakes on. 'We got here, nice place and all that, tennis court, river, all lovely for the twins and you and Kit. But so far away . . . I got this ache inside me and it wouldn't stop.'

'I had that ache, too. You were homesick.'

'I kept thinking how if I found my real father he'd send for me. I imagined flying back to England and this tall, kind man called Simon waiting at the airport, and both of us crying with joy. I just kept obsessing. I couldn't sleep sometimes because this picture was going around in my head.' Sacha looked as though she'd lived a thousand years and hated every second of it.

See? Mum's voice was accusing. *You sow the wind, you reap the whirlwind.*

'I tried to be jolly, tried to fit in. I made friends with Tabby and the cool crowd.'

'I know you tried.'

'The Ivan thing, it was just too much. Somebody else was making him happy. He didn't need me, Lydia didn't, even you didn't. I was kind of . . . unnecessary. I ran out of the library and I was having a meltdown at the bottom of the playing field. Bianka found me there. She looked after me.'

'You mean *Bianka* got you onto this stuff?'

'No! I mean she listened, understood, made me feel I wasn't an alien. Mind you, she did . . .'

'Did what?'

'She gave me a spliff.'

I was about to explode when I remembered two things: first, that I had promised not to shout; and second, that it was at precisely Sacha's age that I first tried the same thing.

'Didn't do a lot for me though,' continued Sacha. 'Just made me feel shit. We met up with a crowd at that fireworks party—remember? Jani, some cousins and—dunno who. We were all on top of the woodpile. Bianka and these other guys were passing their spliff and having this weird conversation, laughing about the most random things.' Sacha looked bewildered at the memory. 'I didn't see what was funny but they were just about wetting themselves. I was an outsider again. I just wanted to crawl away and hide in a hole. Which was when these people started talking to me.'

'Who?'

The shutters came down. 'Just people.'

'Jani?'

'We went and sat in a car.'

So. While I'd thought she was sipping fruit punch at a wholesome party in the country, my daughter was huddled in a shadowy car with complete strangers.

'That was stupid,' I said. 'Anything could have happened.'

'Anything *did* happen. There was this glass pipe. They were passing it around. I hadn't a clue what it was, probably just some kind of cannabis, but they said I'd love it. I thought I'd give it a go. What did I have to lose? So I—'

'I've warned you a zillion times,' I moaned.

'And where were you while I was sitting in that freakin' car? You knew nothing about my life. You were too busy being everyone's ray of sunshine. I thought, what the hell. And when the pipe came to me, I tried it.' Incongruously, her mouth curled up into a glorious smile: the old Sacha smile, wide and brilliant. 'My life turned to gold . . . like my head was full of fireworks and music. A brand-new world was just beginning. I could do anything I wanted. Anything.'

'The elixir of happiness,' I said quietly, and she nodded, twitching and blinking. Just talking about the stuff seemed to disturb her.

'Oh, yes! Spot on. The elixir of happiness. Maybe it was all worth it, just for that moment. I don't think most people ever in their lives get to feel such fantastic . . . what's the word?'

'Euphoria.'

'*Euphoria.* It was a million times better than anything I'd ever felt before. Think of something that gives you a buzz . . . driving fast with the music on, or . . . I dunno, riding a horse. Anyway, imagine that and then times it by a million, all tinged with sunlight. I had so much energy and power . . . I was a fantastic dancer, I was beautiful and popular . . . I felt like a film star and a superhero all rolled into one.'

She'd danced all night under the lanterns, on a farm by the Tukituki River. I'd been so happy for her. Now I saw a different scene: Sacha in a shadowy car, her lovely face wreathed in a noxious vapour, like the addict on the video; Sacha's mind, clouded and distorted; and Sacha's body . . . I couldn't bear it.

'Did you . . .' I hesitated. 'In the car. With this unnamed person. Or people. Did, um, anything else happen?'

'D'you really want to know?'

'In the old days, there were no secrets between us.'

'Old days.' She looked away. 'I tried it again next time I was offered. And the next. And the next. It was wonderful! One time this guy picked up my mobile and put his number in my contacts. He said I only had to send a text and he'd fix me up with some. I didn't have to wait for a party or whatever. I said, "That's too much, I'll never do that," and he said, "Oh yes, you will." And he was right, I did. He meets me outside school.'

'I'd like to strangle him with piano wire,' I said fiercely.

'Why? He's just like me.'

'Of course he isn't!'

'You don't get it.' Words began pouring out of her again. 'He needs the money, same as I do. It's a bit like pyramid selling. He's not Mr Big, he's way down the pyramid. D'you see? You know, I thought I was in control of it for a while. I could stay up all night and do my homework. It made me so brainy, it was like a miracle. I could lose masses of weight, didn't even *want* to eat, and get the body I'd always wanted—just freaking awesome! I could stay awake—and I mean *wide* awake. I was like . . . *ping!*' She opened her eyes too wide. 'Remember all those nights I said I was going to stay over at Tabby's, or Bianka's? Well, most of the time I never even saw them. Actually, I dumped Tabby ages ago. She's so frigging perfect, she'd have told her parents.'

I clutched at my forehead. 'So where *were* you? This is awful, Sacha.'

'Different places. Flats in town.'

'But who were you with?' Sacha in a dingy room, among the dregs of humanity. Sacha's mouth around a glass tube.

'Random people. Other users. 'Cos they're the only people I want to see, 'cos nothing else matters. You wouldn't believe how many people are doing it, you really wouldn't. It's not just drop-outs, it's all sorts, all ages. At New Year . . . oh my God.' Scratch, scratch. 'We didn't sleep the whole time, just kept having another little smoke, then another little smoke. Coming down was like . . . this dark place, like a torture chamber, like a dentist's drill in your brain. I thought I was going to die. And I wanted to die, I really did.'

'New Year.' I thought back. 'You stayed out two nights. I collected you from town, and you wouldn't come into the supermarket with me?'

'Wouldn't? *Couldn't.* If you'd put a gun to my head I'd have said "fire".'

Sacha shied as a log fell out of the flames and rolled across the hearth. I picked it up with a pair of tongs. A wispy spider shot out from under the bark, zigzagging, trying to escape its fiery hell.

'Was it Jani, Sacha? Is he behind all this?'

'Jani? Jani?' She was angry and agitated at the flick of a switch. 'I haven't seen *Jani* since I stormed out of the cinema on New Year's Eve.'

'But . . . yes, you went to the Napier fireworks with him and Bianka.'

'Never went near those frigging fireworks, never saw him or Bianka after I left the cinema. Jani hated the meth. He said I had to choose—him or it. I told him to run away and find himself a nice clean girl.' She gave a contemptuous shrug. 'Never seen him since.'

'But his sister stood by you.'

'Ah well, Bianka, that's a different story. She even talked me into giving it up for a while. She absolutely begged me. I did pretty well, stayed clean for most of the summer holidays. Remember when we went for lunch at the Colberts'?'

'Of course. Jean told us about Daniel.'

'I hadn't had any for three weeks, and I was thinking it wasn't so hard to give up after all. When I heard about Daniel, I swore I'd never use again. Then school began, and all that work, and he was waiting by the gate—this guy—and I thought just one more go . . .' Her speech was accelerating, a runaway train. 'And *bam*! I started using by myself, I didn't need company any more, you know what company means to me? All it means is I have to share and I don't want to share because every little crystal is so precious. It's funny. I'll have a burn in the hut—the smoko hut, great name—I can do it in there because there's no smell or anything, not really, remember the time I had to write an essay and a speech and . . . God knows what . . . and Kit helped me light the stove?'

Yes, I remembered.

'I was coming down that morning, felt like shit. But with a little help from my *friend* . . . no problem! I was buzzing all night, met you in the kitchen and we had a nice chat, I thought that was hilarious! The times I've come in and I'll be having lunch with you all, and I'm totally fried but you don't seem to get it, you've just got no idea.'

The spider was running up and down the log. It wouldn't climb onto my finger. I blew, hoping to dislodge it onto a piece of newspaper, but the poor creature shrank from my breath and disappeared back under the bark. Sap bubbled from the sawn end of the log, and smoke was billowing into the room.

'I bet most people never feel that great in their whole lives.' Sacha's voice was high-speed now. She peered intently at the back of her hand, then began to tug at a scab. 'I mean, just like—*pow*! Superwoman!'

'Most people don't steal from their families, either.' Giving up on my spider—which would surely be incinerated by now—I reluctantly tossed the log back onto the fire. Sparks shot up the chimney.

'A while ago I started to get freaked,' said Sacha. 'I'm still freaked, oh my God I'm freaked. I never feel okay any more, just totally shit . . . I can't get that great feeling back, no matter how much . . . I just need more and more.'

'So how much did all this cost?'

'Hundreds. Thousands. I used everything in my bank account. You started saving in there when I was a baby, didn't you? Well, it's all gone. I raided your and Kit's wallets, I got hold of your plastic card and got cash out, I sold Kit's camera, I filched that ginormous stack of pounds sterling you kept in a shoebox in the loft—you haven't even noticed yet, have you? Five hundred pounds, I changed it for over a thousand dollars—stuff from the silver cupboard I thought you wouldn't miss. I took your watch, your special watch that Grandpa gave you.'

'Oh, no.'

She mumbled to herself, picking, picking, tearing at that scab. 'Nothing else matters, nothing else matters, it's just like—whatever, whatever. I pawned my flute. I pawned, um,' she swallowed, 'Ivan's locket. But I still needed more. I ended up owing money, I was really scared they'd do something to me, but the people up the pyramid said no problem, no problem at all, they were sure my family had a lot of nice things, I just had to tell them where and how and let them know when there was nobody in.'

Suddenly, it was too much. I picked up our mugs and stumbled into the kitchen where I stood leaning on my hands against the table. My head was pounding. After a minute I heard her footstep behind me.

I didn't turn around. 'Who broke into this house?'

'Don't ask, don't ask! I can't tell you.'

'Oh yes, you can. I want names. I'm going to have them locked up. Somebody's got to stand up to these bastards.'

'You *can't*! They'll kill me.' She sounded panicked. 'They might hurt the twins, or set fire to the house. They're totally psycho, Mum. They're off their heads.'

At the mention of Charlie and Finn, adrenaline raced through me. *Life is cheap to those people.*

Sacha gasped and hurried to the kitchen door. I watched as she cupped her hands to the glass, peering out. 'Did you hear an engine?' she whispered. 'Oh my God, there's a car!'

'It's just Kit,' I said, looking past her.

'I think they're after me,' said Sacha.

I tucked my only daughter up in bed. She'd bathed in the twins' bubbles, and I washed her hair—something I hadn't done for years. I made a hot water bottle and dabbed tea-tree oil on the ghastly sores she'd excavated in herself. She smelled clean and loved.

At the weekend I got stung by a be. My Mum cuddled me and put speshal creem on from her hambag. It made me beta.

'I hate it.' Her eyes were flicking rapidly from side to side as though some enemy was about to leap out. 'It gets into my head.'

'We'll beat it together,' I said, rocking us both.

'Help me!' Scratch, scratch.

'Shh.'

'When I look in the mirror . . . Mum, I don't know who I am.'

I took a little while to tidy the mess in her room. The next time I looked at Sacha, she seemed comatose. Her skin was translucent, wet hair smeared across the pillow. My heart ached. She was just a little girl, really, and she was in such trouble.

Just before we left England, she was soloist in the school concert. She stood on the stage with the orchestra around her, playing Telemann. She was wearing a borrowed white evening dress, her hair up, stray ringlets framing her face; a Greek maiden. Ivan's locket glittered on her collarbone. The sound my daughter made that evening was too much for me. I thought I might burst. It was like watching a bird with the sun on its wings, weightlessly soaring and spinning in the blue, and knowing that your own clumsy feet will be mired to the ground forever. Lydia's mother, sitting in the row behind me, leaned forward. 'Bet you're proud,' she said.

Proud, yes. Of course, proud; but jealous too. By what witchcraft could Sacha touch our souls? Love and loss poured from her flute and scattered itself in the air. Instead of the dutiful clapping that generally ended the concert, this audience were on their feet and so was the orchestra. The music teacher took Sacha's hand and held up her arm. A first year presented her with flowers, which made her cry. So much success. So much adoration. And I the traitor who took her away.

I was tiptoeing out when I heard a frightened whisper. 'Are you leaving?'

'I'll be just in my room,' I said. 'I'll listen out for you.'

'Promise?'

'Promise.'

I heard her crying, as I turned out the light.

'So what's the plan?' asked Kit. We were lying in the darkness, wide awake and bewildered.

'She says she's through with it.'

'D'you believe her?'

I thought carefully. 'I do . . . yes, I do.'

'I can't get over the way she's treated us.' I could tell Kit's teeth were gritted. 'Stealing, and lying, and living a sick, grimy kind of double life. When I think about Sibella's portrait . . . I don't know, Martha. It's hard to forgive.'

I agreed with him. Hard to forgive. Impossible not to. 'She's terrified,' I said. 'Absolutely terrified. It's got way, way out of her control. I think she's secretly glad to have been busted. We need some really strict rules, though.

I've confiscated her car keys and her phone. She's got to come home every day—I hate to imagine the disgusting places she's been staying.'

'No money,' said Kit. 'We've somehow got to cut off her supply; change our PIN numbers and hide our wallets. If she's got no money, she can't buy the stuff.'

I hesitated, then came out with it. 'Tama thinks we should go home.'

Kit seemed to stop breathing. He turned onto his back, staring up at the pale ceiling. 'What's his logic?'

'Get her away from all the influences.'

'We're so happy here,' said Kit, sadly.

'Sacha isn't.'

'Something like this might have happened anyway, if we'd stayed in Bedfordshire. She was bound to run into boyfriend trouble and get a broken heart. She was bound to have bust-ups with her friends and her parents—it was all on the cards.'

'But dabbling in drugs?' I asked doubtfully.

'There's plenty of that back home. Maybe this particular stuff is less common, but there's others. You think she'd never have tried anything at one of those nightclubs in Bedford?'

'I don't know.'

'If we were still living in the most populated part of the dear old UK, she'd be offered little coloured pills sooner or later; or something to smoke, or something to snort. Emigrating was just a catalyst, wasn't it? Take her away, and she might be shaken up all over again.'

'We'd all be shaken up.'

From next door, Finn shouted. His words were nonsensical, his tone urgent. We waited, ears pricked, but he must have settled into sleep again.

'You don't think we should go home, do you?' asked Kit.

Ah, there was a question. I thought for a long while.

Home. Part of me longed for it. Back to Dad; back to Lou and Philip. Back to my old job, perhaps, or one very similar. Maybe Sacha would be safe there, whole and well again.

Home. We had no home in England. We'd changed. We'd moved on, and we'd never be able to put things back as they were. The boys would be torn away from all the things they loved here; and Kit . . . well, Kit would probably slip back into his darkness. I'd lose him.

'It won't be like we remember it,' I said. 'We'd be screwed financially, with the costs of moving here and back again. Sacha couldn't go back to her old school, so it would mean yet another change for her. Nothing would be the same as it used to be. Not the house, not the school, not the lifestyle. Might do more harm than good.' I moved closer, and rested my head against his shoulder. 'No, I don't think we can run from this one.'

I felt Kit's arm tighten around me. I felt drained, beyond tears.

'I thought I knew her,' I said.

Thirty

Dusk blankets the hospital. I'm just leaving the chapel when I encounter Kura.

'Martha.' She falls into step. 'Mind if I walk along with you?'

Of course I mind. 'Go ahead.'

'Have you heard from Finn's father yet?'

'Er, no.'

'Nothing at all? That's a pity. I have to tell you that I've liaised with the rest of the team. We've just had a multi-disciplinary meeting involving the police child-abuse team, medical staff and Child, Youth and Family.'

My stride falters. 'Oh. And?'

'There are indicators.'

'Indicators of what, for God's sake?'

She looks sideways at me. 'Now. There's a lot more ground to be covered. I'm not saying we're sure anyone hurt Finn. But the accident raises concerns in itself.'

'Children fall off things all the time.'

'Yes, falls are extremely common—probably the single most common type of accident we see here. But not at midnight; not in these circumstances. We've got bruising on Finn's arm, consistent with rough handling. We've got a historical fracture that was not presented to medical services. I've also spoken to Finn's school principal, who tells me he can be a live wire.'

'Mr Grant said that? Well. Finn *is* a live wire. I'm proud of it.'

'*Challenging*, was the word he used.'

'Okay, okay, challenging. Along with every other five-year-old in the universe. It doesn't mean anyone would want to kill him.' And Mr Grant is a two-faced beardie freak, I add silently.

Kura stops walking. 'Then there's your husband, who seems to be avoiding contact with you, Finn or us.'

'Kit's overseas, for God's sake!'

'Martha.' She fixes me with a look of tragic disapproval. 'I don't think you've been straight with me. We've done some checks. A Christopher McNamara flew into Auckland from London late yesterday afternoon.'

The corridor turns into a swing boat. I find a low windowsill and sit down, breathing hard. Kura watches me.

'All right,' I say faintly. 'He drove home last night. He arrived at about ten, but we had a stupid row and he stormed off again. He was gone by half past.'

The social worker waits for a long time. When she speaks, her voice is too soft. 'What did you argue about?'

'That's absolutely none of your business.'

'Do you often have arguments?'

'No comment.'

She sighs.

'Just a minute.' She's only doing her job, and doing it well. I know this, but fear makes me belligerent. 'Excuse me, Kura. I have described exactly how Finn toppled off the balcony while he was sleepwalking. Are you calling me a liar?'

'No, Martha. I'm saying some of the indicators are there. So there are issues around child protection—'

'So you *are* calling me a liar.'

'—and we feel there should be a more detailed risk assessment.'

'I can't believe you people. Talk about shutting the stable door. Finn's life hangs in the balance, and you're doing *risk* assessments?'

'You have other children. Charlie and Sacha. Are they at risk? I've still got this feeling there are things you'd like to talk about.'

I think about Charlie and Sacha, left at Patupaiarehe, at risk. Kura is right: a part of me longs to tell her everything and beg for help. But I can't.

'Leave me alone.' I'm shouting now. People in the corridor look around. 'Leave my family alone!'

Kura is unmoved. 'I'm sorry. I can't do that.'

I get to my feet, giddy with terror. They'll take them all away, not only Finn. I'll lose my children. I turn my back and stagger away from her, faster and faster up the corridor.

'My door's open,' she calls after me. 'When you're ready.'

Back at Finn's side, I take out my phone. The battery's getting low. Soon it will be dead.

I call Kit's number. There's no answer, and a part of me is relieved. I've no idea what to say to him. I cannot envisage a future for us.

Thirty-one

Expectations change; goalposts lower. I dream of my daughter becoming a concert flautist, a brilliant surgeon, a mother herself. I dream of my daughter conquering addiction. I dream of her living a normal life.

Sacha didn't even raise her head from the pillow when I looked in the next morning, though I chirruped like a fantail about what a lovely day it was. 'Beautiful,' I declared, drawing the curtains. 'Clear and blue from one horizon to the other. I'm just off to work.'

She lay without blinking. I sat down on the bed.

'How're you feeling?'

'Can't see the point.'

'Point of what?'

Long silence. 'Didn't my real father want me?'

For a wild moment, I thought about telling her who she was. Maybe she'd be healed and made whole by the knowledge; or maybe she'd be destroyed.

'He would be very proud of you, Sacha.'

'I think . . . maybe that's why you won't let me contact him. Did he want to get rid of me? Did he want me aborted?'

'No!' I was appalled. 'Truly, that isn't right at all.' I patted her knee where it stuck out from beneath the covers. 'Look, doll. The sky's blue. The grass is green. You're young and pretty and talented. You're going to have a wonderful life and bring happiness to lots of people.'

'I don't bring happiness.'

'Bianka phoned just now, worrying about you.'

This seemed to make matters even worse. A tear snaked down the side of Sacha's lifeless face and into lank hair. 'I don't deserve her.'

'C'mon, give yourself a shake. You've got so much; you're so lucky.'

'I know. I'm ungrateful.'

'There will be rules, of course, but we'll talk about those tonight. So— let's all move on! Shall we go away for a weekend? I thought we might drive up to Auckland to see the Russian Ice Dancers? We could even fly . . . I've got all those air points.'

Another tear roamed across her cheek.

'Jump up,' I said, giving her knee a final pat. 'Have some breakfast. Kit's in the studio.'

She shut her eyes, and I left her lying alone with the sky ablaze at her window.

She didn't get up. She fell into a bottomless well. For the next three days she slept like the dead. We had to force her to wash, to eat, to take care of herself at all. I began to fear she might try to take her own life, and had Kit checking her every hour. I used the fast internet at work to scroll through hundreds of websites, falling on any crumb of advice, learning about this venomous enemy.

There was a telephone helpline. I wrote the number down, but I never rang it. Sounds easy, doesn't it, just to dial a number? But believe me, it isn't easy. I seized up at the thought of discussing my Sacha with a stranger. I had this overwhelming terror that they would trace my number and turn up with flashing lights and handcuffs. For the same reasons, Kit and I decided not to seek professional help. Secret keeping becomes a habit.

The only bright point was that I managed to buy Sacha's flute back from the pawnbroker. It had sat unwanted on their shelf and they were happy to see the back of it. They made a hundred-dollar profit. 'Not much demand for flutes,' said the man, lugubriously. He reminded me of our one-armed petrol attendant. Perhaps everyone has a doppelganger in the opposite hemisphere.

Sibella was never seen again. Sacha said she'd given the painting to someone who paid her with a few crystals. We emailed a photo of the portrait to pawnbrokers and antiques shops, with no joy. Perhaps Sibella was lying among the rubbish in a sleazy flat; some junkie might have drawn a moustache and spectacles on her exquisite face.

Lou telephoned during this time. She sounded warm on the surface, but still—after almost a year—there was that chilly undercurrent of hurt.

I forced a smile into my voice. 'Big sis! How's life up top?'

So-so, apparently. Phil was applying for new jobs. 'And how's my darling Sacha?' she asked. 'Put her on!'

Her darling Sacha was curled foetally upstairs.

'Thriving,' I said firmly. 'But she's at orchestra practice.'

I didn't tell Dad either. Didn't even call him. I felt so horribly ashamed. In the end, he rang us.

'Everything all right?' he asked, in the first thirty seconds.

'Fine! Fine.'

He must have caught the brassy brightness because his voice sharpened suspiciously. 'Finn and Charlie?'

'Mad as hatters.'

'Kit?'

'Hard at work. Dublin exhibition coming up in August—three and a half months to go. He must be serious, because he's sworn off the booze until then.'

'Good Lord. Congratulate him from me! Sacha?'

'Well, she's been better. Just endless colds, you know. It's nearly winter here. And . . . well, maybe the first friends she picked turned out to be the wrong kind. She wasn't being bullied after all.'

'I'm pleased.' There was concern in his voice, but he didn't press for more detail. He's good like that. 'She hasn't replied to my last email. Tell her to write to old Pop.'

'Will do,' I promised, and changed the subject. We talked for ten minutes, and I suppose I made it all sound extra good.

'Lolling around the vineyards.' Dad chuckled. 'Life of Riley. You lot certainly have fallen on your feet.'

Mum popped up. *Ha! You've fallen all right, but it isn't on your feet.*

*

They say time is a great healer. Sacha's mood gradually lightened; after a fortnight she was back in school and keeping all our rules. She had pock-marks on her arms and hands, and I was sad to see that two sores around her mouth were slow to heal. I thought they might never quite disappear, but they could be covered with make-up. If they were the worst scars left by this evil, I told myself, she'd got off lightly.

Kit made a valiant effort to forgive his stepdaughter ('If I'm honest, I was a total knob myself at her age') and focused on the exhibition. I loved him for that. He was getting through a lot of ginger beer. Bianka stuck by her friend, staying with us when she could. Life returned to normal. Almost normal.

In May, it began to rain. The duck hunting season was in full swing and volleys of gunfire echoed across the hills. This didn't go down well in our family.

'Those guys are either downright sadistic, or they're total tossing morons! Don't they know paradise ducks mate for life?' stormed Sacha. She and the boys painted a sign in red letters—*NO SHOOTING!!!*—and leaned it up at the road gate. Within hours, the word was out in the duck world. Skeins of them circled like jets waiting for permission to land, calling to their lifelong mates, swooping to the sanctuary of our dam.

Sacha seemed anxious to be a good sister again. One weekend when it rained so hard and so long that the paddock turned to mush, she taught the boys to play Monopoly; on a sunnier day, she and Bianka took them to the river where they made a miniature slipway. With the ceremonial cutting of a ribbon they launched boats made of ice-cream punnets and paper sails. I knew she was trying to make amends for the damage she'd caused, but I didn't mention it. There are some things better left unsaid, some memories that should be buried six feet under.

During June, the last copper leaves fell from the trees beside the drive and a gale blew them into swirls along the river bank. The boys rushed bright-faced through crackling drifts in their bare feet, screaming into the clean wind, throwing themselves on their backs with their arms flung out like gospel preachers. A shadow was lifting. We had a sense of darkness moving away.

July was mid-winter. We took the family skiing at Mount Ruapehu in the school holidays. It was a reward for us all, and a celebration. The twins, whose centre of gravity was about a foot off the ground, graduated from the nursery slope after two lessons. Finn was a fearless speed freak who spent half his time upended; Charlie had more sense. Like me, he meandered messily down the mountain, doing the side splits and getting in the way of hooded Neanderthal snowboarders. Sacha had once been on a school ski trip to Austria. She and Kit explored the mountain together, and I gave her back her phone so we could stay in touch. By the third day, her face was burnished and her eyes glowed with their old life. One time when she and Kit were in the chair ahead of the rest of us, the lift stopped. I saw her rolling around, making their chair rock; I heard Kit pretending to squeal in fear, and Sacha's laughter glittering in the icy air. The malevolent spirit had lost, and we had won. His spell was broken. Sacha had escaped.

On the last afternoon I left Kit in charge of the boys. The lifts would soon close, and I was determined to ski right down the mountain without falling over. Reaching the crest of the last tow, I slid shambolically off my bar and almost collided with Sacha. 'Help,' I gasped, managing to stop beside her.

She'd pushed up her goggles and was gazing across at the perfect volcanic cone of Ngauruhoe, blinding white. Merry ringlets, each covered in a light frost, corkscrewed from under her cap. The peace was profound: just the clicking of the lift and a light wind blowing down our collars.

'Is this heaven?' she asked quietly.

'If heaven is half as heavenly as this, I might start going to church.'

'I don't think I'm going to heaven when I die.'

'Better not die, then.'

After a minute, she stirred. 'I stole from Bianka. I took her iPod and her phone. I emptied her father's wallet. She is the most loyal friend I've ever had, her mother is terribly ill, and I did that to her. I'm *so* going to hell.'

'Is she more loyal than—say—Lydia?'

'Bianka's so deep. When she says she's your friend . . . well, it's a different kind of friendship. It's for life.'

'I'm sure she's forgiven you.'

'That's the awful thing. She has.'

Our breath clouded in the thin mountain air. People came up the lift and swept past us, but we didn't move.

'She left our party early,' I remembered.

'I was roaring that night, Mum. Absolutely roaring. Didn't you notice at all? Some of the guys were users, and we had our own party out in the hut.'

'Ed?'

'Yes, Ed does exist, and he did bring some with him—a birthday present for me. Bianka went mental and tried to take it off me. I screamed in her face and pushed her out of the door. I called her a cunt. I told her to get out of my life.'

'But those dull girls,' I said thoughtfully. 'They stayed.'

'Taylah and Teresa. Yes, Mum. The dull girls—has the penny finally dropped? It was them who gave me my first pipe, in a car at a fireworks party. Boring enough for you?'

I was shaken. 'They didn't look like drug pushers! Shouldn't we tell their parents?'

'Too late. Taylah's family threw her out. The last I heard she was selling sex to gang members in return for drugs. Teresa got caught when the police raided a clan lab, so God knows where she is now. There was an anti-P campaigner came to our school. He said it's a five-year drug. In five years you'll be one of three things: locked up, covered up—that means dead—or sobered up. Not many people get sobered up. I'm lucky: I've been given a second chance, and there's no way I'm going to throw that chance away.'

A couple of snowboarders were dragged over the brow of the hill; boys, kitted out in bandannas and mirrored goggles. As the tow sprang away they shot classily to one side and promptly tumbled, tangling legs and boards. Sacha smiled. One of them—a young thug with sun-bleached locks—cursed, made a snowball and threw it full in the face of the other.

Then they spotted us and instantly became serious sportsmen, scrambling upright and banging ice off their boards with gloved hands.

'Hey,' said one, nodding in Sacha's general direction.

'Hi,' replied Sacha.

'How yer doin'?' grunted the other.

Having exhausted their store of erudite conversation, they began to zig-zag down the run.

'Cute,' I crooned fondly, as the blond one tried to do a very small jump and ended up face-down in a snowdrift.

'He's cute all right,' said Sacha. 'Nice bum.'

I giggled, ecstatic at the normality of it all. Turning my face up to the immaculate summit of Ngauruhoe, gilded now, I muttered a fervent prayer of thanks to . . . well, I don't know. The spirits of the land, maybe. God, even. The mountains were watching us, and they were kind.

'No one else is coming up,' Sacha said reluctantly. 'Must have closed the lifts.'

She was right; it was later than I thought. A blue gauze of shadow lay across the white undulations. I turned around, laborious and duck-footed on my skies. 'We'd better call it a day, or Kit will have them sending out the Saint Bernards for us.'

She didn't move. 'I don't want to go. I feel clean up here.'

'Last one to the café's a sissy!' I yelped, frantically paddling with my poles. Seconds later, a red-suited figure was flying past me and down the slope, snow and ice spraying up around her.

'Pitiful!' She was crowing with laughter. 'It's like racing a dying snail!'

We've made it, I told myself exultantly.

Ha! We'll see about that. It was my mother, with her inimitable flair for piddling on my fireworks.

'No, Mum. Really. We had a problem, but we dealt with it.'

The hubris! Pride comes—

'Yeah, yeah. I know where pride comes. Now shush and let me concentrate. This bit's icy.'

By the time I'd crawled my way to the bottom, the rest of the family had handed in their skis and were drinking hot chocolate outside the café. The boys sat on either side of Kit in their dungarees, swinging tired legs and exaggerating their prowess as future Olympians. They cheered sarcastically as I limped up, doing the ski-boot moonwalk.

'It's the dying snail!' cried Sacha. 'Saved you some of my Twix bar.'

'I may not be speedy, but I'm stylish.' I sank down at the table, pulling the instruments of torture off my feet with a sigh of relief. 'Got any hot chocolate for a dying snail?' Kit handed me his own cup.

'I like going skiing, Dad,' said Charlie. He rested his head on his father's arm. 'When will we come back again?'

Kit grinned at me. 'Ask your mother. She wears the trousers around here.'

'I wish it wasn't over,' said Sacha.

That Hawke's Bay winter had no bite. Misty mornings were followed by shining days. Late in July the earliest lambs arrived, rickety legs and tails like helicopter rotors. Daphne flowers bloomed once more, filling the garden with lemony sweetness. Their scent took me straight back to that dreamlike day—nearly a year ago—when we first saw Patupaiarehe.

With only weeks to go until the Dublin exhibition, Kit was practically living in the studio. Call me fickle, but his sobriety was almost becoming a drag; I missed sharing a glass or two. Sacha, too, was working under pressure. She was back in the orchestra and always preparing some esoteric subject for the debating team—*This house believes that God is dispensable*, and *This house believes that chivalry is dead*—or it may have been the other way around, I forget. She asked to wheelbarrow across a stack of timber for the smoko hut and work in there at weekends, and we agreed because the twins were irrepressibly noisy. She was never to lock the door or draw the curtains, though. I often burst in unannounced but there were no signs of anything but coffee, music and hard work.

One day, Charlie lost his Game Boy. We searched everywhere.

'Keep looking,' I said cheerfully, while my heart sank. 'It must be somewhere. It's just gone AWOL.'

And there it was, under his bed.

'You were scared I'd taken it, weren't you, Mum?' teased Sacha, who'd helped in the search. 'Oh ye of little faith.'

'No!'

'You're a terrible liar.' She skipped up, put her arms around my neck and kissed my cheek. 'I'm sorry I went off the rails.'

Kit and I renegotiated the ban on her car, and she began to drive into town to do the family shop. She always brought home a receipt and change, solemnly laying them on the kitchen table. I'd pretend to throw the receipt away, but once she was gone I checked that everything balanced.

The third trip went very wrong. Sacha seemed to be gone a long time. Finally she ran into the kitchen without any shopping, gabbling incoherently, her face flushed and tear-streaked. I caught the words *car* and *totalled*.

'Whoa.' I held up my hands. 'Stop, doll, stop. Have you had an accident?'

'No! It's the car, I was in a shop and when I came out . . . Some frigging *arseholes . . .*'

I was already heading across the yard. 'Hell,' I breathed, staring. 'What on earth?'

Sacha's poor little Toyota had been ambushed. There was a scar right across the bonnet, the paintwork bubbled and faded. The rear windscreen had been smashed and there was glass all over the interior. It looked like a person who's been savagely beaten, their nose bleeding, their face a pulp.

'They've thrown something on it,' said Sacha, her eyes wide with horror. 'Acid or something . . . you can smell it.'

'Did you see who did this?'

'Imagine if that was someone's face.'

I shivered. 'I'd rather not. This happened where? The Countdown car park?'

'No. I stopped at a dairy on the way out of town because I remembered you wanted a paper. When I came out . . .' She gestured at the carnage.

'Have you been to the police?'

'I came straight home. I was so scared . . .' She pressed both hands to her mouth. 'There was a load of really freaky guys hanging around outside the shop—you know, leather and gang patches.'

'Could you describe any of them?'

'No way! I didn't even look at them, I just got in and drove straight home.'

'It will have been kids with nothing better to do,' I assured her. 'We should feel sorry for them, really.'

'I don't feel sorry for them.'

'So you never actually saw who did it?' The policewoman squinted glumly at Sacha's rather sparse statement. 'Not much to go on.'

'Sorry.' Sacha was twirling a plastic bangle.

'What d'you think it is?' I asked. 'Some kind of acid?'

'Brake fluid probably,' said the officer. 'Makes a mess of old paint. It's cheap and easy to get hold of.'

'CCTV cameras?'

She looked pained. 'If there were any, and if they were on, and if they were facing the right way.'

'Mindless vandalism,' I suggested, and she gave a world-weary sigh.

'There's some idiots about. Sign here.' Then she filed Sacha's statement, presumably under H for Hopeless.

On the way home I kept glancing at Sacha's plastic bangle. She saw me looking, and smiled resignedly. 'You're wondering where my silver bracelet's gone, that Lou gave me.'

'Not really.'

'You think I'm back on the meth.'

'No! It's just . . .'

'We're not allowed to wear jewellery at school. It's against the rules apparently, but nobody bothered to tell me. Got confiscated.'

'Oh, for heaven's sake. How petty. When do you get it back?'

She made that teenage 'I dunno' noise, and I wondered how long it would be before I stopped looking over her shoulder.

We had the broken window replaced. Later, Sacha spray-painted the bonnet, disguising the ravaged paintwork with swirly flowers. But she didn't go shopping again.

The first of August was the anniversary of the day our plane touched down at Auckland airport. On cue, the weather finally turned wintry.

There was ice in the air, and dripping cloud clung to the hills. I had the fire blazing all day in the sitting room as well as the kitchen, but I still felt shivery.

I'd invited the Colberts, Tama and Ira to dinner on the Saturday, to help us celebrate the day. I phoned them all in the morning, though, and cancelled. According to the local paper, a quarter of all children in Hawke's Bay had been off school with the latest strain of flu—which in practice seemed to mean anything from a life-threatening virus to a cold—and our house was no exception. Kit had been in bed with a fever, which was stressful because he was leaving for Dublin in ten days and didn't have time to be ill. The boys were whiney and flushed, though happy enough as long as I let them take their duvets downstairs to watch *Ice Age*. Sacha was in a miserable state.

'You've given her your virus,' I told Kit, coming downstairs after taking her temperature. 'She can hardly move.'

Kit had his feet up on the kitchen stove, drinking Lemsip with a hot water bottle stuffed up his jumper. He turned a page of his newspaper. Then another. I didn't think he was reading. 'Sure it's flu?'

I wagged a finger. 'Hark at you, Mr Death's-door! You've been moaning for days, and the boys aren't too bright either. Half the country's off sick. So *yes*, I'm sure it's flu. What happened to the poor teapot—did someone drop it?'

He looked around his paper at the remains of the china pot, stacked neatly on the bench in three pieces. 'Finn used it for target practice. His new sling is very effective.'

'So I see. I'm going to confiscate that thing . . . Of course it's flu. Shame on you for asking.'

'We're both thinking it. Why shouldn't I say it?'

'Swine flu, bird flu, man flu. Who knows? We've got to stop suspecting Sacha all the time. We have to move on.' All the time I was talking, I was looking for our Wedgwood pot, a wedding present that we never used. It wasn't in the cupboard, or the laundry, or the wooden chest where we kept vases. 'We have to trust her,' I muttered.

'What are you looking for?'

'This,' I said quickly, lifting out a glass vase. 'I'm going to pick some daphne flowers. I love the smell. It makes me happy.'

He looked at the vase, and then at me. We stared silently at one another for a moment. Then he lifted the paper in front of his face, and I hurried outside.

Thirty-two

Kit was on his way to Dublin.

Our place was chaos in the week before he left. We'd never have managed without Pamela. She telephoned the airline and found out exactly how to transport the canvases he was taking with him. With her help they were meticulously wrapped, covered in *Fragile* stickers and stowed in the car for their journey to Auckland airport. Kit had booked the cheapest flights possible because our budget didn't run to luxury; of course, this meant multiple stopovers. There were a thousand technical problems to solve in transporting the paintings, but he thrived on every one. He was alight, alert, incandescent with excitement. It was like living with a sparkler.

On his last evening, I'd shut the office door at Capeview with a sigh of pleasure. I'd booked a stretch of leave and was feeling demob happy. It was dark when I arrived home. The Colberts' blue pick-up was parked under the tree. I heard quiet voices from beyond the woolshed, then a plaintive, feeble snickering.

Rounding the corner I came upon a scene straight out of a children's storybook: in a makeshift pen a paraffin lamp rested on the ground, casting a yellow pool of light. Finn was kneeling in the straw, his back very straight. Charlie was jammed up against his brother while Kit and Jean leaned on a fence nearby. Resting on tiny knees and sucking on a bottle in Finn's hands was the smallest lamb I have ever seen. I made an amazed face at Kit as I tiptoed closer. The tiny creature sucked, bleated, butted Finn and sucked again. I could hear slurping and bubbling as the milk left the bottle.

Jean's eyebrows arched in comical kindness. 'I hope you don't mind, Martha. A baby girl for your menagerie.'

I looked at the lamb, whose tail was wagging ecstatically. 'No mother?'

'Died,' declared Finn knowledgeably, as though he'd lived seventy years on a farm. 'They do sometimes, y'know. It happens.'

'She's Bleater,' said Charlie. 'Bleater Brown. Is it my turn yet, Jean?'

Jean gave a theatrical start. 'Oh yes, I forgot. Master Charlie's turn.'

Finn handed the bottle to Charlie, but the milk was almost gone and Bleater was soon enthusiastically sucking at an empty bottle.

'Here,' murmured Jean. 'You sit like this, young fellow. Stick your legs out in front. That's it.' He gathered the animal in his arms and laid her in Charlie's lap where she lay still, eyes drooping.

'She's a day old,' whispered Charlie. 'Come and touch her, Mummy.'

I crouched beside him and fingered the warm, springy topknot. The lamb smelled of milk and lanolin. 'She's falling asleep,' I said. 'Little motherless baby. Can we eat her with mint sauce?'

'Not funny,' scolded Finn, kicking me quite angrily. It hurt, but I didn't complain. I probably deserved it.

'We have to feed her every four hours,' said Kit.

'*We?* I suppose you mean the royal we, Kit McNamara, since you're on a nice restful plane to Dublin tomorrow.'

'No need to feed her at night.' Jean picked up the empty bottle. 'One at your bedtime and another first thing is fine. When she's much older, she will have lambs of her own and the boys will sell them and be very rich.'

'Sell them where?' I asked, which was a silly question.

'Well, let's cross that bridge when we come to it, shall we?' suggested Jean. The adults began to wander inside, leaving two boys and their baby in a huddle. 'Farming is red in tooth and claw, Martha. Lambs are generally bound for the meatworks. Perhaps the male offspring could rejoin my flock and then . . . well, quietly disappear.'

As we rounded the corner of the shed, a wind came galloping to meet us. Jean glanced up at the sky. 'Blowing up there, see?' he said, pointing at clouds spread thin like butter on toast. 'Better get your washing off the line tonight, or it will fly to Auckland with Kit.'

'You'll stay for a beer, to wish him bon voyage?'

'I should be honoured.' Our neighbour stepped out of his gumboots, and we followed him into the kitchen.

'I'm ready for Dublin,' said Kit. 'So I can have a drink, at last.'

Jean looked around hopefully. 'Sacha not home yet?'

I was looking in the fridge for three bottles of beer—it seemed an agricultural sort of occasion, calling for something a trifle earthier than sauvignon. 'In her room, I should think,' I replied absently. 'She generally works up there after school. Tui or Steinlager?'

'Oh—I forgot to tell you. Sacha phoned,' said Kit. 'She's got an audition for *High School Musical*. Said she'd catch a lift and be home by seven.'

I stared at him. 'She phoned? When?'

'It's fine.' Kit took a step closer, eyes covertly swivelling in Jean's direction. 'It's *fine*, Martha. She'll be almost home by now. She's going to text you when she gets near, and I'll meet her at the road gate.'

Jean was busily opening beer bottles, but he'd caught the tension. There was a bird-bright glance from under those clown's eyebrows.

Kit began to explain that he'd been on the wagon. 'I promised Martha,' he said, smiling at me. 'But I'm looking forward to this one! Cheers.'

I found my gaze straying to the clock. Six fifty. It was all right. Sacha would be home soon. Perhaps she'd got a part in the school play—now, that would be fantastic. I imagined her face at the window of a car: smooth, soft cheeks and long lashes. She'd be holding her phone in one hand, waiting for a signal so that she could text us: *5 mins away.*

The boys burst in, screaming with laughter, and shot upstairs. I followed, ran the bath and bribed them into it with snorkels and masks. As I trotted back to the kitchen I could hear splashing and squeaking as they slid around on the porcelain.

No sign of Sacha. I sent a text: *where are you?*

Jean was talking about the South Island. He and Pamela were about to take William for a skiing holiday in Queenstown. 'Just hope I don't break my neck! It's been a few years and now—well, there is more of me to fall.' He patted his paunch.

Five past seven. I sent another text: *?????* Then I called her.

Hi, this is Sacha, don't bother to leave a message.

'They've had a ton of snow down there, haven't they?' Kit opened a packet of crisps and poured them into a bowl. 'All the newborn lambs are dying.'

They were off, then—the weather, the high dollar, commodity prices. And all the while a stone of dread sank down, down, out of my chest and into my bowels. I couldn't concentrate, couldn't think. I could only dread.

'Isn't it, Martha?' said Kit.

'Mm?' I forced a weak smile. 'Sorry, blonde moment. Didn't catch that.'

'Too expensive for us all to go back to the UK for a holiday,' Kit enunciated the words with exaggerated slowness, as though I was a deaf centenarian. 'Maybe a hearing aid would help, old girl.'

Pulling myself together, I flicked him on the ear. 'Don't be bloody cheeky. You're the one with the grey hair.'

'One!' Kit held up a single finger. 'One grey hair doth not a dodderer make!'

This inspired Jean to embark on a story about how his grandfather, a watchmaker in Rouen, had his head shaved after a drunken bet. In his animation, Jean's eyebrows virtually climbed on top of his head, as though he'd pushed them up like a pair of sunglasses. It was a good story, but the clock was ticking.

'His wife's eyes flew open—my grandmother Agnes was a terrifying female, like a charging rhinoceros—and she looked across at him on the pillow.' Jean made a wrathful rhino face. '"*Henri!* What has happened to your head?"'

'You think *your* grandmother was a holy terror,' chuckled Kit, opening another couple of beers. 'It was my Great-Aunt Sibella taught me to play the piano. If I made a mistake she'd drop the lid on my fingers.'

The laughter and companionship seemed far away. Kit and Jean had receded into the background, like a telly with the sound turned down. The only reality was that Sacha had gone off the radar. Mum was banging a saucepan lid, chanting, *Late. She's late. She's late . . . Wedgwood teapot, bracelet, flu . . .*

'Kit,' I said loudly, breaking into their revelry. 'Look at the time.'

He took a glance at the clock—seven thirty—and stiffened. 'Have you tried her mobile?'

I was calling her phone for the tenth time when Sacha flung herself into the house, breathing hard.

'Whew,' she panted cheerfully, sliding her schoolbag off her back. 'Helluva wind! I've run all the way from the road gate. Oh hello, Jean! *Salut! Ça va*?'

Jean was replying with a cordial bow when I interrupted. 'You were going to text us,' I said. 'It doesn't take a moment to—'

'Well I didn't need to text you, did I, because I didn't want collecting from the gate.' Sacha spoke over me in a high, sarcastic voice, waggling her head like a puppet. 'I thought I'd very kindly save you the trouble. And anyway there's no signal and anyway I forgot and anyway I don't really think it's reasonable for you to keep tabs on me every minute of my frigging life. Do you?'

Before I could respond, before I'd even understood the question, she was off again. 'I mean, why not put a trace on me, and you and Kit can sit in an operations room and watch a screen and I'll go beep beep beep and you'll see this little coloured dot moving around.' She dug her hand into the crisps, talking at the speed of a bullet train. 'Look, there's Sacha heading for the science block, ooh dear, she's a minute late . . . there's Sacha going into the toilets . . . she can wipe her own bottom, thank heavens for that . . . she's getting a tampon out of the machine . . . oh, look! There's Sacha—'

'Stop! *Please*,' I begged, with a meaningful glance at Jean, who'd been watching this exchange, his forehead corrugated in concern and embarrassment. I leaned close and breathed in her ear, '*Have you taken something?*'

She slipped her arm around Jean's shoulders. The gesture was overly familiar. 'Jean doesn't mind. He's seen family fallouts before, haven't you, Jean?'

'I'd better go,' mumbled our poor neighbour, extricating himself from under her elbow.

'You've just ruined half an hour of your mother's life,' said Kit softly. 'It's time to apologise.'

She shrugged and stuffed a handful of crisps messily into her mouth. 'That's her problem,' she said, spitting bits. 'Nosey bitch. I never asked her to—'

Kit was on his feet, his jaw tight. 'I think you'd better go to your room.'

'Oh, Kit.' Sacha smiled widely, pressed both hands onto the table and thrust her face inches away from his. 'I think *you'd* better fuck off.'

I saw it coming, tried to shout. I heard the echoing crack of his palm on her face at the same moment as her whole body jerked sideways. She staggered, pressing one hand to her cheekbone.

Horrified silence. Then Sacha laughed. 'True colours,' she gasped, doubling up as though Kit had told her a hilarious joke. 'What a lovely, lovely guy.'

'I'd really better go.' Jean was wringing his hands.

'No, *I'd* really better go.' Sacha grabbed her bag and headed towards the hall. '*You* stay there and carouse with my stepfather. Watch him, though! He's got a shocking temper, as you can see, especially after a dram or three. Sometimes he just can't control it. Tut, tut, tut.' And she marched out of the room.

'She asked for that,' said Kit. Already there was uncertainty, a dropping of his shoulders.

'That's not the Sacha we all love.' Jean shook his head in distress. 'Boyfriend trouble, I wonder?'

'I'd better go and talk to her,' said Kit, but he didn't.

Our neighbour was a man of impeccable tact, and he knew an approaching storm when he saw one. 'I must be off,' he insisted, beetling towards the door. Outside, he laid a hand on my arm. 'Don't worry. She will come down in half an hour and pretend nothing has happened. My sons were crazy too, at this age. Forever exploding like fireworks. It's a growing-up thing.'

'But he *hit* her, Jean!'

'And you think I never laid a finger on my boys?' He hopped into his truck. 'Parents aren't saints, Martha. If they were, their children would never be conceived.'

Once Jean had gone, I stormed back into the kitchen. 'What were you thinking?' I hissed. 'You could be prosecuted!'

'She's back on that crap.' Kit was leaning against the dresser. 'It's all starting again. It's *all starting again*! Can I not be forgiven if it seems too much?'

I stood by the door, feeling the sky fall in. 'She can't be, though. She's got no money and she's not allowed out at night.'

He threw both arms up and behind his head, as though convulsed by a bolt of pain. 'Oh, come on! We've both had our heads shoved in the sand.'

'I just don't see how she'd get hold of any.'

'Noticed the odd bit of Wedgwood disappearing? Ever seen her silver bracelet again? Bianka hasn't been here for a while, has she? Not since . . . ooh, since we went skiing.'

'Anita needs her.'

'No phone calls, nothing. That girl's been ejected from Sacha's life, same as last time. We've seen the signs—oh yes, we have—but we've done fuck all about it because we hoped to God this wasn't starting again.'

He was right, of course. I sank into a chair. 'We've messed up.'

'No! *She's* messed up!' Kit was energised, striding around the table. A vein stood out on his neck.

'It's a disease.' I was arguing with myself as much as with him. 'It's not her fault.'

'Don't give me that crap, Martha. She's had choices all along the line. Ten years, I've treated that girl as my own daughter. I've doted on her, cared for her. Ten years, for Christ's sake! And how does she repay me?'

I knew what he meant. I was tempted to storm upstairs and scream at Sacha, and the truth was I'd felt like clouting her myself, just before. But I was stung by the intensity of his rage, and perhaps by the reminder that she was my daughter, not his.

'So you're happy to be her father while she's charming and delightful and you belt seven bells out of her when the going gets tough? Marvellous. What a bloody hero.'

His fist crashed onto the dresser. Plates fell, rolling and shattering on the quarry tiles. 'Fuck's sake, Martha! I didn't belt *any* bells out of her, though God knows I should've done. I slapped her because I'm only human, okay? The girl's a sad, depraved junkie who fouls everything around her.'

I lost my temper completely then. I suppose I was overwrought. 'Ha! Says Mr Sobriety McNamara, who had to be collected from the copshop like a dog from the pound.'

He stepped closer, his jaw thrust forward. 'Shut up.'

'Is that a threat?' I slid out of my chair, warily moving away from him. 'We came out here because of you, Kit. It's time you accepted that. Ironic, really—we ran from one addiction and straight into the arms of another!'

I regretted these words almost instantly; but the damage was done. We were a furious pair, facing one another like fighting dogs across the kitchen table. For the first time ever, Kit seemed ugly. I saw the face of a spoiled child: pinched, livid, self-absorbed. Muffin didn't like the loud voices. She crawled out of her basket and limped across to droop uncertainly beside me.

'I'm not going to stand by while you hit my daughter,' I said coldly. 'If you ever touch her again, I will leave you.'

'And I'm not going to stand by while she destroys Finn and Charlie's childhood. I'm not—they're not—' He broke off, gasping, and with a jolt I realised that he was battling tears. In all the years I'd known him, even in the months of darkness and self-doubt, I'd never seen Kit cry.

Love surged through me. Shocked, hushing him, I put my arms around him. He bent to press his face onto my shoulder, and I felt his fight for breath.

'This is never going to end,' he whispered.

I stroked his hair. 'Just a setback. We can cope.'

'I don't know if we can.'

Charlie wandered in, wearing nothing but a pair of underpants on his head. He seemed unsurprised to find his parents draped around one another. He pottered out, then came back again a minute later.

'Seen my Game Boy? Bloody thing's gone AWOL again.'

*

Later, when the boys were asleep and Kit had taken refuge in the studio, I called Bianka. I didn't know where else to turn.

'Sacha!' She sounded relieved. I suppose our number had flashed up on her phone.

'No,' I said. 'Martha here.'

'Sorry. I hoped . . .' Instantly, concern. 'Everything all right?'

'No. No, it's not all right. I think you know that, don't you?'

Her voice was faint. 'I've picked up my phone about fifty times, but I couldn't . . . I didn't know how to tell you.'

'Tell me what?'

'I love her.'

I smiled, despite everything. 'I know you do. And I also know she's back on the meth.'

A long pause. 'It's worse than that.'

Worse? How could it be worse?

'She isn't just using it, Martha. She's in trouble. Real trouble.'

'What do you mean, not just using it? For God's sake, what else can she do with the stuff?'

'You cut off her money supply,' said Bianka. 'Of course you did. Well, they didn't mind, they gave her credit . . . that's one of their tricks. They got her trapped, and then they turned the thumbscrews. She never had enough cash. She needed more and more, and she owed more and more, and these guys are freaky, I mean *really* freaky. She was petrified. So she had to get a . . . um, a job.'

A job?

And we're not talking a paper round here, said Mum.

'Is she . . . she isn't a . . .?' I coughed. I couldn't say it. The words *Sacha* and *prostitute* should never be uttered in the same sentence.

'She's a courier.'

'A what?'

The story came crashing down the line. It was as though poor Bianka had been carrying an immensely heavy load and was dumping it on my doorstep. 'Picks it up from the cook and delivers it to the dealers. She's perfect because she's in her school uniform, looks clean and white and respectable so the police aren't going to glance twice, are they? She actually carries it in her flute case. I mean, how innocent does that look? She does her runs at lunchtime when there are lots of Year Twelves out and about. She transports it and they pay her in . . . they give her enough for her own use and then she—' The words disintegrated into incoherence.

I stared at a calendar hanging on the wall: two emerald taniwha with swirling tails. The world had turned upside down and inside out. I despised the courier, the dealer, the cook, everyone involved in supplying those monstrous crystals to my beautiful girl. I loathed them. They were vermin, hiding under hoods and behind gang insignia. They were creatures with no self-respect, no future, scrabbling for rotting scraps on their filthy heap. I agreed entirely with Jean Colbert: put down poison, lay traps. They had to be eradicated.

Not Sacha.

Bianka's words were tangling. 'It doesn't matter what I do or say, she won't listen, just nuts off at me. I told her to go ahead and screw up her life—but I didn't mean it!'

Not Sacha. Sacha was a goddess in a white dress, weaving magic with her flute; a beloved sister who splashed her brothers in the river. She was a chatterbox with a high forehead and apple cheeks who never stopped smiling, and loved hot chocolate and marshmallows. When a bee stung her, I put on special cream. On my wedding day I told her I loved her most in the world, and she said she loved me more.

No, not Sacha. She wasn't vermin.

'Rival gangs,' Bianka ran on breathlessly, 'do anything to shut each other down. You don't mess with them . . . She told me someone attacked her car when she was doing a delivery. It was a warning. The deeper you get into this, the freakier the people.'

'Doing a delivery? No, no. She was grocery shopping. She can't have been . . . I mean, that was weeks ago.'

'She started using again the day after you got back from skiing.'

I saw Sacha on the mountainside, gazing at the pristine cone of Ngauruhoe. *I'm lucky: I've been given a second chance, and there's no way I'm going to throw that chance away.*

'That isn't possible.'

'Yes.' Bianka sounded heartbroken. 'Coming home brought everything back. She got hit by this craving and it was driving her crazy, she was afraid she was going to kill herself if it didn't stop. So she sent a text from your phone. Someone drove out and left the stuff under your letterbox. She took the dog for a walk and collected it. She thought she could handle it, she'd just have a little bit to perk her up and everything would be okay.'

The ground was opening. There was nowhere safe.

Bianka was still talking. 'Look—I'm sorry, but you've got to know—she sells it, too.'

'Sells it? You mean she's a dealer?'

'Well, sort of. She breaks it up and sells it to her mates.'

My legs were shaking. I pulled out a chair and fell onto it.

'Please take her away, Martha,' begged Bianka. 'She's screwing up her life, big time. Take her back to England while you still can.'

I couldn't move, after that call. I sat irresolute and stunned as the wind rose outside. So far, every decision I'd made had ended in disaster. I jumped in terror as a violent gust tore the lid off our dustbin, rolling it across the yard.

Pick up that phone and call the police! wailed Mum.

'Shut up, shut up. I'm trying to think.'

For heaven's sake, blow the whistle! This is too big for you now.

Dazedly, I lifted the phone. Once I'd shopped Sacha to the authorities, I could let go. They would take it irrevocably out of my hands. No more choices. Listening to the dial tone, I mouthed my first words: *Hello, good evening, hi, um, I'm calling to betray my daughter.* Perhaps they'd send a posse and arrest her tonight. She'd be so frightened, and what would I tell the boys? There would be police interviews and court appearances. She'd be a criminal, her life in tatters; and all because I'd made this call.

I dropped the receiver. I couldn't do that to her, to all of us. Surely we could sort this out behind closed doors? First, Kit must be told that his stepdaughter was a criminal, tied up with maniacs who attacked cars. I forced my steps across the sitting room and stood in front of the studio door. The handle shifted under my palm.

That's right, urged Mum. *Put him in the picture.*

But he'd never forgive her. Anyway, I reasoned, why burden the man with such terrifying knowledge on the eve of realising his dream? In a few hours he was off to Dublin for an exhibition that could change all our lives. If he knew what I knew, he might even cancel his trip.

I lifted my hand off the door handle, and crept away. I had another, perhaps even more difficult, conversation ahead of me.

Sacha was pacing in her room, half-dressed, her cheeks leached of blood.

'I'm sorry,' she sobbed. 'I'm sorry I'm sorry I'm sorry. I love you, I love Kit, I love the twins.' Her contrition seemed absolutely genuine, but the change in her was bewildering. It was as though there were several Sachas, all living within the same body. She took hold of my face and turned it towards her. 'They're out there.'

'Who?'

'Can't you hear them whispering?'

I listened. Yes . . . there was something. The possum was dancing on the tin roof, scrabble scrabble of little feet; or perhaps it was a family of rats gnawing on the rafters.

'They're coming.' Sacha's eyes were wild and staring. 'I've seen them, hiding behind the trees.'

'But *who's* coming?'

'I wish I was dead.'

Five minutes later she was limp, her eyelids thin as gauze. I covered her up and made her warm, because she was my special girl. My lost girl. When I kissed her, my own tears ran onto her face.

I lay in the dark, rigid as a board, listening to the wind trying to tear off our roof. Kit came up at midnight. He moved quietly around the room, and I heard his suitcase being zipped before he slid in beside me. To my intense relief, he was sober.

'I know you're awake,' he said softly.

'Wish I wasn't.' I turned over to face him, but I didn't move closer and neither did he. We lay two feet apart. Sacha's addiction was a physical presence, malevolent and ugly. It had lodged between us.

'She's paranoid,' I said. 'Thinks there are people prowling around outside.'

'People prowling . . .? Hang on.' Kit swung out of bed and strode to the balcony door, peering into the night. 'Maybe there *are*, though. Some of her burglar mates, d'you think?'

'She says she hears voices, people whispering. It's a bit like . . .'

He was still at the window. 'Spit it out.'

'Well, I don't know. Schizophrenia or something.'

'God help us.' Kit rolled back under the covers. 'Should we take her to hospital?'

'I don't think we can, without blowing the whistle. How are we going to explain the state she's in? Anyway, if she starts babbling on about hearing voices she could end up in the psychiatric unit! No way.'

'For Christ's sake.' His frustration was rising again. 'Stupid, *stupid* girl! Why is she doing this to us? Is she punishing us for something? Is this all about emigrating, or not knowing her father?'

'I don't know why she's relapsed. People do. Look at smokers.'

'Nicotine isn't quite in the same league.' Kit was silent for a minute. 'Look, I think I should cancel the trip.'

'Cancel the—?' I moved across to him, resting my forearms on his chest. 'After all your work? Don't you dare! In the world outside our troubled family, there is an art festival waiting for a collection of Kit McNamaras.'

His arms wound around me. He was alert; I sensed the watchfulness in his body, the rapid breathing. 'If she's using again, those lowlifes may come back. You're going to be alone here with the kids. What if someone breaks in at night?'

'She's not going to use any more,' I said confidently.

The deeper you get into this, the freakier the people.

Five hours later, Kit's alarm sounded. The storm had blown itself out, leaving frozen stillness. I don't think either of us had slept.

We huddled close together under the walnut tree, our breath misting. Kit had the engine running to defrost the windows. He turned my face up to his. 'If you hear anyone out here, get the children into the car and leave. Okay? No heroic stuff.'

'Okay. I promise.' I wondered how he'd react if he knew why Sacha's car had been trashed.

He looked strained. 'Keep your phone and car keys by the bed at night. Call the horse whisperer before you call the police—I'll bet he's a useful man with a shotgun.'

'You've an overactive imagination,' I said, letting my mouth brush the coarse skin of his cheek. He smelled of soap. I desperately, madly didn't want him to go. 'You are about to be the toast of Dublin. Your paintings will be festooned with *Sold* stickers. And when our famous—and disgustingly rich—artist comes home, we'll put up all the flags and bunting. We'll be happy as five pigs in clover.'

He ducked into the car. I stood in the icy dark, feeling bereft and trying to look upbeat. Suddenly he was beside me again, slamming the door behind him, squeezing me to his chest as though he'd never let go. 'I love you,' he muttered fiercely. 'You're my life, Martha. You know that, don't you? My whole life.'

Soon I stood alone on the drive, watching with cold misgiving as a set of tail-lights faded into the pearly pre-dawn.

Thirty-three

It was the worst crash yet. Sacha shivered in bed, sleeping and whimpering. As the days passed she became stronger physically, but she seemed to be living in a nightmare of her own. She'd get up at night and walk around the house, shying wide-eyed at shadows, but be comatose the next day. I contacted the school and collected work, though she never touched it. On the third day I persuaded her to have a shower. She could hardly sit still long enough for me to dry her hair. She ducked and twisted, tearing at her face and arms.

'Stop that,' I begged. 'Look, you've scratched a great hole.'

'They're crawling,' she raved, eyes flickering. Before I could stop her, she'd grabbed a pair of tweezers from the dressing-table and was trying to dig something non-existent from the back of her hand. 'Gotta get 'em out.'

The insurance money arrived, and I invested in a pile of DVDs to entertain the boys. I also sent them to play with friends when I could, determined to steer them out of Sacha's path. 'She's got a yucky snotty cold,' I told them. 'You don't want to catch it.'

So they drew pictures of Bleater Brown, and made them into get-well cards which I propped up on her bedside table. In a display of pure adoration, Finn showed up at her door with his greatest ever treasure—excluding Buccaneer Bob—held behind his back. 'It's for Sacha to play with,' he announced, holding out his Game Boy. 'Pretty good when you're stuck in bed. But tell her to keep it under her pillow, because the polty guy got Charlie's.'

'The what?'

'The polty guy. The guy who keeps sneaking in and taking things. He took Charlie's Game Boy. I heard you and Dad talking about the polty guy. If he comes into our room again I'm going to do a karate kick, *ha*!'—Finn demonstrated his skill, throwing his foot in the direction of an imaginary groin—'right on his meat and two veg. That'll send him packing.'

For a fortnight we froze. The wind turned to the south, and although I kept the fires blazing I suspect our house was colder inside than out. Stepping out of the kitchen into the hall was like walking into a crypt; the cold seemed to suck the breath from our bodies. It smelled like a crypt too, damp and deathly, as though we living people had no right to be there. The dark panelling of Patupaiarehe harboured shadows.

After a week the Colberts headed off for their skiing, leaving Tama to manage their stock. Kit phoned every couple of days, on a high. He'd had some glowing reviews and picked up two commissions. And—wonderfully—his paintings were selling. One of the vast trompe l'oeil had fetched over three thousand pounds.

'Oh, that's great,' I enthused. It wasn't just the money, though I was very relieved to see it coming in. If Kit was happy, everything else would fall into place.

'Sacha okay?' he always asked.

'Fine,' I always replied. 'More herself this morning.'

I think we were both buying into the same fiction because we so needed it to be true: Sacha had been through a little setback, but it was nothing we couldn't handle and the future looked rosy.

Towards the end of his trip, Kit phoned from his mother's house with the news that one of the New Zealand national papers wanted to do a piece on him. He planned to stay the night in Auckland on his way home, and fit in the interview then.

'You'll be jetlagged,' I said doubtfully.

'I'll have had a night's sleep first. It'll be no problem.'

I felt an absurd lift of happiness. 'It's all happening! The dream's coming true. I'm married to a famous artist.'

He chuckled; it was a beautiful sound. 'Maybe one day.'

'When do you leave?'

'Tomorrow morning. The coven are driving me to Dublin. Then it's London, Hong Kong, Sydney . . . Jesus, I wish I'd paid for a direct flight . . . a night in Auckland, do this interview, drive home to Napier on Tuesday afternoon. You'll have to iron me flat because I'll be stuck in a sitting position.'

'Next time you can travel first class.'

'I'd like to sleep flat on a plane, it's my new ambition. What are you clowns up to?'

'Well, it's been freezing down here in Godzone but today the sun's come out. The boys and I are just off to Jane's for Saturday morning pancakes. I need several shots of her coffee.'

'Sacha okay?'

'Fine. Fine. On the mend, I think.'

Actually, that was true. Sacha did seem chirpier that morning, although she didn't feel up to coming with us to Jane's. She said thanks, but she was looking forward to a long bath with lots of Body Shop bubbles and a darn good book.

The twins and I had a lovely time at the café. Destiny's lop-eared rabbit had new babies and they were improbably cute. Tama Pardoe dropped in for coffee when he saw my car parked outside. He was relaxed and mellow, and we sat in the winter sun at a cotton-reel table.

'I'm glad you're here,' I said, lowering my voice. 'We've had a relapse.'

Tama looked grave. 'How bad?'

'She's been a mess. You know, I really thought she'd beaten this bloody thing.'

'It puts up a fight.'

'Do you think I should get help? A counsellor?'

'You could.' He looked across at the boys, who were prattling to a floppy-eared ball. 'But it's not a magic wand. Jonah went to scores of counsellors and talking shops but he never really wanted to be there, you see? And the shrink isn't sitting beside them the next time they get offered the pipe or the needle.'

'What do we do, then?'

'The people who escape are the ones who make up their own minds. They somehow see what they're doing to themselves, and it wakes them up. But Sacha's friends, her haunts, the dealer she can contact with a single text—those things make it hard for her.'

'Oh God,' I sighed. 'You really think we should go back to England?'

'Only you and Kit can decide what's best for your family.'

The house looked peaceful when we arrived home. Bleater Brown heard us, staggered from her bed of straw and screamed as though she was dying of starvation.

'Now Sacha's better, we're going to show her how to feed Bleater,' said Charlie happily.

I trotted towards the kitchen door, intending to make up a bottle. Then I stopped in my tracks, and slowly turned around.

Sacha's car was gone.

I called Bianka.

'What kind of state was she in?' The poor girl sounded ready to keel over.

'Not well enough to come out to a café,' I said bitterly, 'but she's miraculously found the strength to clean us out and disappear. She's taken every bottle of alcohol in the house, and the new DVD player. Any idea where she might have bolted to?'

'None,' said Bianka sadly. 'You'll be going to look for her. Please—let me come too.'

Next, I rang the Napier police and fed them an anodyne pack of lies. The man who took my details was polite, reassuring and supremely unimpressed. A teenager stormed off? How old—seventeen? Well—hem-hem—they'd keep an eye out for her car, but it would be hard to spot her among all the other yoofs who didn't fancy hanging out with their families over the weekend.

I gnawed my knuckles. Sacha might overdose. She might be murdered. A 'drug-related killing', the papers would say, making it sound as though she'd deserved it. She might—yes, she really might—have decided to drown herself, like Hinemoana, in her desperation to escape the call of her enchanter. It was on the cards. Anything was possible in her world of wonky mirrors.

Finally, I called Destiny and persuaded her to babysit. I told her I'd been hauled in unexpectedly at work and might be busy all weekend, and I'd pay her well. She and Harvey arrived within half an hour, and I was gone three minutes later.

First, I checked the beach. No drowned girl. Not today. Then Bianka and I combed both Napier and Hastings. We set out with a map and patrolled the streets, sneaking down driveways and into back gardens in the hope of spotting a little Toyota with flowers painted on the bonnet. We stole a few hours' sleep on Saturday night but were off again by seven on Sunday morning, exploring the rougher suburbs where pig dogs snarled behind flimsy gates; we even dared to peer through a gap in the high fence of a gang headquarters. We searched parks and beaches, public toilets and churches. We checked ditches and dustbins, fearing to find a naked and mutilated body.

'I can't believe she's done this,' I said, as we parked on top of Napier's Bluff Hill. Sacha's car wasn't there, but we paused for a while. From our eyrie we could see Dinky-sized cranes unloading a ship in the port.

Bianka rubbed tired eyes. 'P messes with an addict's brain. They don't just want it, they *need* it. We need air to breathe or we know we'll die. An addict feels like that about P.'

'How d'you know all this?'

She seemed surprised that I should ask. 'When Mum was diagnosed, I learned everything I could about her disease. I go to all her appointments with her and ask questions. When Sacha got sick, I did the same—found out as much as I could.'

'You're a wonderful friend.'

'Sacha's the most amazing person I've ever met. She's got this charisma. It's like having a star drop into your tutor class.'

We leaned over the rail, dizzied by the murderous drop.

'Does Anita know what's been going on?' I asked.

'She does. She wanted me to help you. In fact, she's planning to go for a drive herself today, and look for Sacha. Don't worry, we haven't told Dad.'

'How is she?'

Bianka hesitated. 'The oncologist says they're running out of options.'

'I'm so sorry.'

'Don't be sorry,' she said quietly. 'Mum's lived with death for a long time. She says we all do, it's just that most people don't face the fact. She first became ill when I was a baby, and she thought she mightn't see me grow up.' Bianka smiled. 'She reckons she's almost won.'

'How's that?'

'She's determined to stay alive long enough to celebrate my eighteenth birthday. That's her ambition. Once I'm eighteen, she says her job is done and I'll be okay. She turns forty-five a couple of weeks later. It's a bit over a year away, so she's in with a chance.'

This didn't sound like much of an ambition to me. 'You know you're always welcome in our family,' I said, laying an arm around her shoulders.

I felt demoralised as we drove away. Sacha could be anywhere. She could be in Auckland, for all we knew.

'Where's our star, Bianka?' I asked.

By Sunday night the twins were rebelling. Charlie phoned three times, whining for me to come home. Bianka had school the next day, and I was starting to feel sick with exhaustion. I dropped my young friend home.

The Vargas' front door opened as we approached and a figure hurried out, closing it gently behind her. I hadn't seen Anita since that day by the cathedral fountain. She was wearing trousers and a rollneck sweater; the clothes were beautifully cut, but they couldn't disguise the painful fragility of her body.

'You haven't found her?' she asked.

Miserably, we shook our heads. Anita stepped closer and I felt her arms slide around me. The last woman to hug me was Louisa. Perhaps that's why it made me cry.

'You'll find her,' she whispered. I felt the strength of her will. 'Don't worry. She'll come home.'

It seemed a long drive back through the dark hills. Near Torutaniwha I saw a motorcycle gang parked in a layby. Some of the men watched as I passed, their heads turning.

Destiny was off like a shot when I arrived. I fed the boys cheese toasties then let them pile into my bed with me. Among so much separation, so much anxiety, we needed to be close together. They were asleep within minutes. I was not.

Sunday night. Kit would be well on his way by now. My brain spun like a fruit machine, trying to calculate. Perhaps he'd landed in Hong Kong? He would drive home on Tuesday after his interview with the paper, and then I'd have to tell him that Sacha had gone.

Sacha. Sacha. Once upon a time, I used to lie awake fretting about whether my daughter would be made a prefect, or get a distinction in her flute exam, or whether her boyfriend was good enough. Now my ambitions were more modest. I merely hoped she was still alive. Lord, what a silly cow I'd been back then. Perhaps this torture was my just deserts.

I wouldn't wish it on any parent.

The next morning—Monday—I dropped the twins in Ira's classroom before heading back into Napier. Forcing myself to think logically, I reasoned that Sacha would probably still be there, near her contacts and her dealer. I searched all day. I rang the hospital to ask if she was there, but she wasn't. In the end I walked into the police station, desperate for some kind of action. I had to queue. The officer at the desk was having a busy afternoon and the more hysterical I became the less seriously he took me. She was seventeen, right? And she'd set off in her own car? He put down his pen. Yes, they'd circulate her details again. Yes, they'd let me know if they heard anything. He was sure she'd be in touch.

I was late collecting the twins from school, and sprawled with them on the sofa while they watched *Ice Age*. I was finished. The computer of my brain had performed an illegal operation and would be shut down. The boys, sensing that I wasn't capable of putting up any resistance, filched packets of contraband and gorged themselves as the images on the screen faded into a buzzing oblivion. I drowned in it.

The phone was ringing. The film was over, the boys gone. It was dark outside. Sleep clawed at me as I struggled to my feet and staggered to lift the receiver. It dragged at my consciousness and numbed my tongue.

''Lo?'

'Mum.'

She was alive. It was the best news I'd had, ever. I was awake, alert, babbling with joy. 'Thank God. Thank God. Where are you?' I heard a strangled sound. 'Where are you?' I repeated urgently. 'I can't hear you.'

'Outside the cathedral.' Coughing. 'Can you come and get me?'

Thirty-four

It wasn't Sacha I brought home. Not my little laughing girl, not the confident bombshell people adored at first sight. It wasn't her body, and it wasn't her soul.

This was a sallow corpse with disgusting clothes and few words. There was nobody home inside this head. The flesh had fallen off her face with terrifying speed, her eyes had sunk into their sockets. Open sores defaced a drooping mouth. I don't believe she'd slept for three days. She had been fuelled by meth, not by food or sleep. She looked and smelled repulsive—putrid, like something I might have dug up in a graveyard.

I once had a cat who was a magnificent hunter. He was bitten by a rat and developed an abscess at the base of his tail. The poor creature was driven half mad before I got him to the vet. He licked furiously, walked a few yards, stopped, licked furiously. That was Sacha, slumped beside me in the car. Scratch scratch. Pick pick.

'Stop,' I implored, reaching to pull her hand away. 'You're tearing right into the muscle. Where's your car?'

'I owed a shitload of money.' She spoke in a low monotone.

'You sold it? How *could* you?' I heard myself raging on and on in an uncanny imitation of my own mother, forgetting that Finn and Charlie were sitting subdued in the back seat. I was wasting my breath. Sacha wasn't beside me at all; she was in some hell of her own.

Once we were home, the boys hovered around their silent sister with worry drawn across their foreheads. 'Bleater's calling, Sacha,' said Charlie. He pointed over at the woolshed. 'D'you wanna cuddle her?'

'You can feed her if you want,' wheedled Finn.

Sacha ignored them. She limped inside, to be greeted by a tail-waggingly rapturous Muffin. Dog and boys followed us like a funeral procession across the hall and up the stairs.

'She's just tired,' I told them. 'She stayed up all weekend, silly old girl.'

'She smells,' said Finn, holding his nose. 'It's yuck.'

'Can we watch *Mary Poppins*?' asked Charlie. It was a sure sign of anxiety. After all, Mary Poppins was unfailingly fragrant.

'Yes, while I make the supper.'

They loitered, casting worried glances at their sister's departing back. 'Has she got the yucky snotty cold again?' asked Finn.

''Fraid so.' I gave him a little push towards the sitting room. 'Off you go.'

Sacha was contorted on her bed, shaking and sweating. 'They're coming,' she said, very loudly.

'Nobody's coming,' I soothed, trying to cover her with the duvet. 'You're safe at home.'

'Can't you hear them?'

I listened intently, afraid I would hear the shattering roar of motorbikes on the drive. I imagined men with balaclavas and baseball bats and cruel, crazed eyes, coming to collect a debt or exact revenge. *Rival gangs . . . life is cheap to these people.* But there was only the chickens, clucking and squawking at some menace.

'It's those chooks. Something's upset them.' I reached out my hand to lay it on her forehead.

She shrank away, staring wildly around the room. 'We have to run.'

'This is all in your mind.'

'I wish it was.' She began to sob with fear.

I walked downstairs in a daze. I knew, now. There were no choices left. I had to save Sacha, even if it meant the end of my marriage, our adventure, the end of everything. We had to go back to England. The boys would not grow up in this extraordinary landscape, with space to breathe and play and live. Kit and I would never again sit on the verandah steps and watch the sun rise. It was over. I felt a desperate sense of loss, worse than when we left our home in Bedfordshire.

Finn was chasing our poor chickens. 'Fly!' he screamed, harrying them in a raucous mob around the yard. 'Fly, my hordes of darkness!' His hordes of darkness fled under the house, just as I bisected their tormentor's path and frogmarched him inside.

He was rattled; up and off, ferreting in the toy box, scattering chaos. During supper he used his fork as a trebuchet—inspired by a computer game, I suspect—and Charlie's face as a target. Then he refused to get into the bath.

'Daddy's coming home tomorrow,' exulted Charlie, rolling around under the tap.

'That's right. Tomorrow. Finn, will you please get in?'

'Jussa *minute*!'

'No, now.'

'Mind out!' he screeched, vaulting into the bath fully clothed. Charlie called his brother a no-good nincompoop. Finn grabbed Charlie by the hair and pushed his face under the water where he held it with fratricidal determination until I came to the rescue.

'That's *it*!' I growled. 'Straight to bed with no story for you, Finn McNamara.'

Eyes blazing, he stood up and grabbed the plastic jug we used for washing the boys' hair. It was full to the brim, and he emptied it over my head. The next moment he'd slipped on the soap, fallen face first, and had blood spurting out of his nose.

Pandemonium. Blood and water everywhere. I was still cleaning up when the phone rang. I ran down to the kitchen to find Finn holding the receiver close to his mouth, squinting censoriously up at me with a bloodied towel pressed to his face.

'Yes, she did,' he was insisting self-righteously, head bobbing up and down like a nodding dog. 'Yes. Would you believe that? She *did*! And now my nose is bleeding . . . Daddy wants a word with you, Mummy.'

I snatched at the phone.

Kit's laughter. 'Witch! Have you been battering my son?'

'Whatever he's accusing me of, it's all true. Are you in Auckland?'

'Better than Auckland. The interview was postponed.'

'No!'

'The reporter broke her femur. Snowboarding. I'm driving home.'

'Is that safe?'

'I'm already halfway. If I start to nod off, I'll find a motel. Otherwise I'll see you about ten.'

'I can't wait,' I said, and meant it.

'How's Sacha?'

'Sacha?' Now was certainly not the time. 'Fine.'

I read my boys a story. It's one thing to impose penalties; quite another to stick to them when your five-year-old has fallen and bumped his nose. I slid under Charlie's duvet and Finn climbed in too, with his hot water bottle. They lay curled close to me, just their beady eyes showing like a couple of cartoon clams.

We were reading *The Secret Garden*. The boys seemed captivated by the description of young Dickon and his pet lamb. When I closed the book, I felt Charlie stir.

'We've got a lamb,' he mumbled, his pride muffled by blanket and thumb.

'You have.'

He snuggled a little closer, gossamer hair tickling my neck. Once they'd dropped off, I eased myself out and transferred Finn to his own bed. He muttered something as I covered him up, and flung out a small arm.

Sacha too seemed to be asleep, swaddled in her duvet; but as I was turning off the bedside lamp, I heard her voice. 'Shut up.'

I looked round. She was sitting up. 'What? I never said anything.'

'Shut *up*. You're doing my head in.' She was staring fixedly over my shoulder. Spooked, I glanced behind me. A draught stirred the open curtains. The next moment she was screaming in terror, backing away up the bed.

'What is it?' I gasped. Her mouth was wide open, like a skull's. 'Sacha—what's happened?'

'D'you see it? D'you *see* it?' She pointed at the window. 'Oh my God, there's something looking in! Oh my God, see the face?'

I looked, but could see only our two reflections in the black glass. It took all my courage to walk across and open the door. I searched up and down the balcony. There was no sign of life, though leaves rustled in the magnolia tree.

'Nothing there,' I said shakily, shutting and bolting the door behind me.

The next moment she was beside me, digging her fingers into my arm. 'We've got to get out,' she hissed. 'They're here.'

I'll admit it: I sank half a bottle of pinot while I waited for Kit.

I phoned the Vargas. They were my staunch allies, a teenage girl and a dying woman. I needed allies. The father answered. Anita and Bianka were out for a walk, he said chattily. Seemed a funny thing to do on a winter's night, but they'd rugged up warm. Was I Sacha's mum? What a lovely girl. Shame they hadn't seen much of her lately.

Then I wandered around the house, closing curtains and feeling lost. I decided to put off telling Kit about Sacha's relapse. I wouldn't talk about going back to England, either. Not tonight, when he was coming home so happy.

At five past ten, a car crossed the cattle grid.

Now, here's a tip: reunions never live up to one's expectations; it's just a sad fact of life. This one was disastrous. I blame jetlag. I blame the awful secrets I was keeping. I blame stress and lack of sleep. I blame my half bottle of wine, and Kit's temper. Whatever the culprit, the effect was catastrophic.

Kit was climbing stiffly out of the car when I hurled myself across the yard. He held out his arms and I pressed my face to his, luxuriating in his closeness.

'Hey hey,' he said, nudging my ear. 'You're not blubbing, are you?'

Bleater Brown spotted us, and began to bawl as we walked inside, arms around one another.

'Tea, coffee, food?' I asked. 'Or just sleep?'

Kit was spaced out. His eyes looked bloodshot, his hair tousled. He dropped his car keys by the phone, yawning. 'Um . . . how about one of your special frothy coffees? I'll just nip upstairs, take a pee and kiss the children. Promise I won't wake them.'

'I wouldn't go into Sacha's room. She's . . . best not to disturb her.'

While he padded upstairs I switched on the espresso machine. Bleater was still making her feelings plain, so I made up a bottle. I heard the phone as I was climbing into her pen, but it was cut off after four rings so I knew Kit had answered it. Probably his mother. Bleater gulped down her milk in record time, but I lingered to put more straw in her bed.

Kit's call was over by the time I returned. He'd changed into a clean sweater.

'I'll froth your milk,' I chirruped. 'This is going to be the best Martha frothy-coffee special in the universe. Who was on the phone?'

'Bianka.'

'Oh?'

'Oh.' Kit looked immensely sad, his eyes turned down at the corners. 'Bianka. Wanting news. She and Anita have been out looking all evening. They were wondering whether we'd heard from Sacha yet.'

'Kit . . .'

'She was very relieved when I told her I'd just seen Sacha upstairs, asleep. Says she and her mum were really scared. I asked why scared? She said well, you hear of people being murdered for supplying P on some other dealer's patch. Those were her actual words, Martha. *Supplying P on some other dealer's patch.* What the fuck's going on?'

'It's a long story.'

'I'll bet it is. You thought I didn't need to know my stepdaughter's a drug dealer?'

'Courier.'

He exploded, kicking a chair across the room. 'Jesus Christ! Are you going to quibble about the job title?'

'No, but—'

'A dealer under my roof, living with *my* sons! Finn and Charlie could find that shit lying around and wonder what it tastes like.'

'Shh, Kit! Keep your voice down. The children—'

He didn't keep his voice down. 'Drug squad might smash the doors in any moment. A gang could come out here and torch our house. And you didn't feel like telling me?'

'You weren't here to tell.'

He turned away, shaking his head. 'This can't go on, Martha.'

I felt cold. 'What do you mean?'

'I mean it can't go on. I'll never trust Sacha again. Now I find I can't trust you either. One way or another, this must stop.'

One way or another . . . It was fear inside me, undulating sinuously like an eel. But I hid it with a good old-fashioned cavalry charge. 'You can piss off, if you're going to be so sodding sanctimonious.'

'Maybe I should piss off then.'

I poked my knuckles into his chest. 'You've been home five minutes and already you're throwing your weight around. I've carried this family single-handed through a horrific crisis. I think I deserve a medal, but no, apparently I deserve to be yelled at. You've had your head so far up your own backside this past year—you know nothing about how this whole immigration thing has been for the rest of us.'

'This whole immigration thing was dandy until that girl—'

I screamed over him, 'We came out here for you! We lost our home and our family and our country, for you! All because *your* career blew up and *you* couldn't handle it.' I punched him in the shoulder. 'How dare you come in here and start preaching to me?'

'I dare, because Finn and Charlie are my sons. I dare, because you haven't kept them safe. And if I have to leave you and take them with me, then—so help me—I will.'

I grabbed his car keys and threw them at him. I could barely speak. 'Get out.'

The next moment, he was reversing in a wild arc. He'd crossed the cattle grid and torn down the drive before I could draw a breath.

'He'll be back,' I said to Muffin, who was looking very worried. 'He always comes back.'

Thirty-five

My phone has finally died.

It's seven o'clock on Tuesday evening. Finn fell at midnight, less than a day ago. One day. One lifetime.

It must be completely dark outside by now. There are people on the ward, visiting other patients. They avoid my eye as they slide past, though their gaze flickers over Finn. They have their own horrors. A bewildered father and three very scared teenagers sit tearfully, trying to field telephone calls. Their mum went to bed with a headache last night, and when she wouldn't wake this morning they called an ambulance. The doctors say it is meningitis.

Hurried footsteps in the corridor. A familiar voice, fast and fearful, asking for his son. I'm on my feet and calling to Kit as he strides down the unit. He grabs my hand, his eyes fixed upon the little figure on the bed beside me.

'Jesus,' he whispers. 'Finn.' He drops onto one knee beside his son.

I begin to tell him what the doctors have said: how Finn's in an induced coma, and they hope to wake him when the time is right. Out of the corner of my eye I see the nurse, watching. I slide to the ground next to Kit.

'What have we done to deserve this?' he asks.

'I don't know.'

'I came home.' Shock is distorting Kit's voice. 'I came home. I brought you flowers.'

'Where did you go last night? Where on earth *were* you?'

'Driving around Napier in a hell of a stew. I was so tired, couldn't think straight at all, finally spotted a motel with its lights still on. I don't even remember getting into bed . . . slept fourteen, fifteen hours, God knows how long. Once I woke up and had a meal and a shower, I realised what a total arse I'd been. So I jumped in the car and drove home at ninety miles an hour . . . Ira came out to meet me.' Kit looks bleak. 'I was holding your flowers, like a total idiot. I clapped him on the back, asked if he was stealing my wife. He didn't smile at all, he said there's been an accident. I said what kind of accident? Then Charlie ran out in floods of tears, and he told me . . .' Kit's voice gives way. He pulls me close. 'My poor girl, you've been alone.'

'I called you a million times!'

'I don't have my phone.'

'Yes, you do. You took it to Ireland.'

'I did,' he agrees helplessly. 'But I dumped my jacket in our room last night. Remember, I got changed? Bloody thing was in the pocket.'

'All those calls, all those texts.' I imagine the phone bleating away in our room, forlorn and unheeded. 'It's almost funny.'

Kit doesn't answer. His eyes are tightly shut, his forehead resting on clasped hands. I think he's praying. It's a long, long time before he asks the question. I knew it had to come, but still I am not ready.

'What happened?' he breathes, his eyes still closed.

There is only one person in the world who knows how Finn came to fall. That person is me.

Thirty-six

A starry winter's night, and the hills were gentle swells against a singing sky.

I sat in the kitchen and waited for Kit to come back. I waited for an hour, ears pricked hopefully for the sound of an engine. From time to time I checked my phone for messages. I was darned if I was going to text him a cringing apology. I fed Muffin, stoked up the fire and thought of all the things I'd say when he came back. Oh, I had plenty to say.

But he didn't come back.

Finally, I ditched my pride and sent a text. *For godsake come home you prick the twins missed you and so did I. Just come home now.*

Before heading upstairs, I let Muffin out for a final pee. Bleater Brown fussed when she heard us. Switching off my torch, I lingered by the woolshed and peered into the billowing depths of the bush. The darkness in there was like a solid mass; it seemed to press into my eyeballs. In the inky shadows, something was on the move. A tree fern shivered from root to tip as though it had been shaken by the trunk. I stood still, watching, listening. Muffin got bored and shuffled back inside, and eventually I followed her.

I checked my phone, but there was no reply from Kit. I sent one more, while making a mug of tea. *Please come home.*

Our bedroom was a chiller, the empty bed supremely uninviting. Grabbing the duvet, I stepped out onto the balcony. The wooden boards shuddered under my feet. I paused at the handrail, feeling the moulded wood under my fingers and wishing we didn't have to leave. The night was a giant black-and-white photograph, growing sharper and more distinct as my eyes adjusted. I could smell sheep and forest and salt air, and I loved it; I loved it all. We'd lived in Patupaiarehe a year, and we'd made it our home. This life, this house, these people were a part of us. I wanted it to be our future. I longed for the twins to grow up in this magical valley, and be free. I longed for Kit to be an artist in his studio, happy and fulfilled.

I can't say how long I stood there, grieving. From across the fields tore the screech of a plover; the mother-in-law bird, bossy and reassuring. My own mother-in-law was twelve thousand miles away. Poor lady, she missed her only son.

Finally I sat down on the old sofa and pulled the duvet up to my chin. Still no engine on the drive, not even a distant whine from the road. The magnolia stretched its fingers onto the balcony. There was nothing to set its branches shivering; not a possum, not a stirring bird. The silence was a presence in itself.

Time passed.

And then a small movement. A handle twisting, further down the balcony. A door swinging open. Furtive and cunning, like the creeping patupaiarehe.

They're here.

'Who's that?' My voice was high with fright.

A slow shadow appeared, silent and indistinct. I could feel my heartbeat, fast and shallow, ticktickticking like an overwound carriage clock. Then a small creature was standing in the gloom, facing me.

'Finn?' I touched my chest with a rush of pent-up breath. 'Good Lord! I wish you wouldn't do that.'

He wasn't awake. He turned in a full circle, eyes blank, moving without purpose. His bed hair stood up straight, just like his father's. I laid my empty mug quietly onto the table, careful to make no sudden movements. I'd done this a hundred times before. The young sleepwalker turned and pottered barefoot away from me, past Sacha's door, all the way to the other end of the balcony. He was wearing his Mr Men pyjamas, and his tufty head was level with the balustrade. There was a pile of leaves at the far end. His feet dragged through them with a long, swishing sound.

I sighed as I shook off the duvet, stretching my limbs. No rest for the wicked, indeed. I'd better take the little chap back to bed before the cold woke him. Kit might think I was a rotten mother, but I could at least manage a sleepwalking five-year-old.

I was edging around the table when I felt the reverberation of rapid steps. I heard the grinding of a bolt before the furthest door burst open with a harsh judder of twisted wood. An agitated figure thudded out and stood in the middle of the balcony, rocking. It had unnaturally black eyes, like pools of oil in a white face. Devil's eyes.

'Sacha,' I whispered, and laid a finger on my lips. 'Shh. Don't wake him up.'

She looked at me, then right through me. She was wearing a t-shirt and knickers. 'I know you're out here,' she yelled, shockingly loud. 'I hear you.'

I pride myself on being able to deal with difficult, angry clients; can't remember a time when calm handling and a cool head didn't defuse a situation. 'Sacha. Look at me,' I said clearly. 'I'm here.'

'I know you're there,' she snarled. As I took a step closer I realised that she was glaring into the distance, listening to a voice that wasn't mine. Her gaze was flickering fast from one side to the other, her head darting like a snake about to strike. 'Where are you? Come on! Show yourself.'

Close behind her, Finn moved among the leaves. Instantly, Sacha's eyes narrowed. She whirled around.

'Got you!' she hissed, and reached out for him.

I ran.

Oh, I ran. Time froze, as though the moment was crystallised, as though it would last forever. And it *will* last forever. I shall be running down that balcony for the rest of my life, and Sacha will be gripping her brother by his arms; she will be lifting him easily and holding him high in the air. She has the strength of ten men—how can she be so strong? I shall hear the pounding of my feet on the boards. I'll stretch out my hands, and scream.

But I'll always be too late. Finn will fall. He'll plunge headlong, tiny hands clutching at nothing.

So here's the question: what if your own daughter is a monster? Do you point and shout? She's an addict, a dealer, a thief. She's the devil who attacked your little son. I feel as though I'm cradling a ticking bomb.

Honesty isn't always the best policy, never mind what my mother says. Kit has a right to know what really happened to Finn, but I can't tell him. I really, truly can't. I feel as though I'll never love Sacha again or even look her in the eye. How can I expect him to? No, he'll leave me. He'll leave, and take the twins with him because they aren't safe near Sacha. The idea terrifies me because I can't bear to imagine life without Kit and my little boys. It would hardly be worth living.

What's more, if I blow the whistle those nice policemen will go straight out and arrest Sacha. They'll take her away. What will they charge her with—grievous bodily harm, attempted murder? Oh, and dealing in drugs, for good measure. Her life will be over, and so will Finn's and Charlie's. The boys are the real victims in all of this; the only ones who are completely innocent.

I'm alone, clutching that ticking bomb, and I mustn't drop it. If I drop it my family will be blown apart. If I can hold on, we all have the chance of a normal life.

So I tell Kit my story: how I sat on the sofa in the dark, waiting for him to come home. I describe how Finn wandered out of his door and climbed onto the rail as quick as a monkey.

'I ran,' I whisper. 'I ran, and I screamed at him. But he wouldn't wake up, it was like a nightmare. He just . . . toppled over the edge.' I can see it all, feel it all; I shudder at the monstrous thud. 'It's my fault. I wasn't quick enough.'

Kit covers my hand with his. 'It's not your fault.'

I hear voices, and glimpse Neil Sutherland's corrugated-iron hair. He's brought some sidekicks. They're in a huddle with a senior nurse.

I move closer to Kit. 'They think one of us did it on purpose.'

'They think *what*?'

'I've had a social worker trying to get a confession out of me. D'you remember when Finn came off his bike on New Year's Day?'

'Did he?' Kit's brow furrows. 'So he did.'

'It turns out his wrist was broken. It's healed now, but it showed up on an X-ray. And there are some bruises on his arm . . . they look like finger marks. So they've been getting their knickers in a twist. I mean, for God's sake, Kit! He's covered in bruises.'

'They think we've been abusing Finny?' Kit looks incredulous.

'They know you flew in yesterday, but I fibbed about it at first. I didn't want any awkward questions about why you came home and left again.'

He's on his feet, shock channelled into anger. 'Who do I speak to? Bring it on!'

'Calm down. You're being watched.'

'I don't give a fuck if I'm being watched.'

I put my arms around him, murmuring into his ear, 'They think one of us lost our rag and hurt Finn. So settle down, and stop behaving like a man who loses his rag easily.'

When Sutherland and his wing-men arrive, Kit collars them. 'Can you tell me what's going on here?'

'You're Dad, are you?' Sutherland is obviously used to agitated parents. He introduces himself, leans on the edge of a little basin and explains everything again. 'Finn arrived early this morning in a life-threatening condition—the helicopter team did a great job in keeping him stable until he got to us. He had a head injury and a ruptured spleen, both of which needed urgent surgical intervention. From an orthopaedic point of view, he got away with a fractured radius and ulna—least of his problems. We've just been discussing his progress and we're pleased, but he's still a very poorly boy.'

Kit has simmered down. After all, these people undoubtedly saved Finn's life. 'Thank you,' he says fervently. 'Thank you for what you did. Will he live normally without his spleen?'

'I'd say so. At the moment, I'm more concerned about the head injury.'

'And what's this about it not being an accident?'

Sutherland is unruffled. 'Whenever a child is injured we have to consider whether parenting fell short in some way. And there are features about Finn's presentation that raised concerns, so we consulted with the paediatric social worker.'

Kit points at me. 'Martha's never laid a finger on any of our kids, and she never would! Or am *I* chief suspect? If so, I checked into a motel in Westshore at about midnight last night. The bloke will remember me all right because he was in his dressing-gown.'

Sutherland's pager begins to bleep. 'It really would be best if you discussed this with Mrs Pohatu. Make contact with her tomorrow. Excuse me—I'm being paged.' And he is gone, marching through the swing doors with his squad.

'Why us?' Kit looks bewildered. 'What about all the truly abused kids who fall through the net? They get hurt time after time, live in abject misery, but nobody sounds the alarm and the poor little blighters wind up dead.'

We sit with Finn all evening. This is a ward on a knife edge, continually battling with death. Nobody relaxes, ever. And our Finn is here. Kit wants to hear every detail, yet again: the fall, the helicopter, my long vigil. He needs to understand exactly what each specialist has said. We talk around and around, promising one another with brittle airiness that Finn will be fine.

Finn doesn't look fine. There's no flicker, no sign that he is still inside the battered mannequin. He lies inert, plugged into his bank of machines.

Eventually, Kit asks about Sacha. I give him the barest facts: she's relapsed, given away her car, come home in a dreadful state.

He's holding Finn's hand between his own. 'Let's focus on this little guy. I can't think about anything else. Jesus, what else matters? Once this is all over we can worry about Sacha. We'll ask for professional help, do whatever it takes.'

I am only too happy to go along with his plan. I'm not capable of making life-changing decisions, either. My care, my will, my every thought and instinct is centred in Finn's survival. Nothing else exists.

'It's going to be all right,' says Kit, as though to reassure himself. 'He's a fighter.'

I close my eyes. A demon snatches up Finn's puny body—*got you!*—and hurls him out into the darkness. I'll never forgive her.

It's after ten when the senior nurse approaches us. 'I'd suggest you both go home and get some sleep,' she says firmly. 'Finn is stable. I promise we'll phone if there's any change at all.'

I'm aghast. 'Can't at least one of us stay?'

'Yes, you can. We won't throw you out. But look, you really should rest because you both look terrible. I know you were up all last night, Martha, and *you*—' she raises her eyebrows at Kit—'have only just flown in from Europe! You two have to look after yourselves. This little boy's recovery is going to be a long haul.'

Reluctantly, we obey. As we kiss Finn goodnight, Kit pulls something out of his pocket and lays it on the bedside cabinet.

'Charlie sent your Game Boy, friend.'

Thirty-seven

We leave Kit's car at the hospital and drive home together. Sacha runs out to meet us, tearing my door open.

'How is he?' She's breathing fast. I can hear the terror and love in her voice, but I can't bring myself to look into her eyes. I turn away, pretending to search for something on the back seat.

'He's all right,' I say shortly. 'Actually, no, he's not all right. He has a plate in his skull, no spleen and a broken arm. He could still die.' I want to shake her. I want to thrust my face close to hers and scream blue murder. *You did this. You did this.*

She bursts into stormy tears. Kit looks at me in astonishment. 'Mum's pretty stressed,' he soothes, walking around the car to comfort his step-daughter. 'Finny's doing well. He'll be playing football again before you know it.'

Tama and Bianka stand waiting for us at the kitchen door. 'Mum says she's thinking of you.' Bianka hugs me. 'If you want to stay at our place, save you driving so far . . . she says just to turn up.'

I'm touched by this message from one mother to another. We sit around the kitchen table, nursing mugs of tea. Charlie has fallen asleep in front of *Mary Poppins* and been carried up to bed. They tell me Ira was here earlier, but he's gone home.

'I can't believe it,' Sacha keeps muttering. 'Right outside my door.' She doesn't seem to be able to move on from this idea. She repeats it over and over, no matter what conversation the rest of us are having.

'Hey.' Kit taps her forearm, making her look at him. 'Listen, young lady. It wasn't your fault. Just get that into your head. Isn't that right, Martha?'

When Tama leaves, the rest of us begin to turn in. Bianka has already made up a mattress in Sacha's room, though I feel my daughter doesn't deserve such devotion. As I pass their door, Sacha calls out to me. My mind is fouled by an image of a fiend with devil's eyes, reaching for a tiny boy. It's like a film clip in my mind. It keeps replaying, over and over again.

'Where's Bianka?' I ask, looking around. The room has that familiar, ugly smell.

'Getting stuff from her car.'

'I'm going to bed,' I say, massaging my face. 'Haven't had any proper sleep for days, and I want to be up and off early tomorrow.'

She's sitting on the bed, picking at her arm. Her pillows have no covers, and the sheet lies in a heap on the floor. 'Last night was like a horror film.'

'You're right there.'

'I saw . . . I've never been so scared. I saw people.'

'People?'

'Crawling along the floor, whispering, like sort of human snakes. They had these weird eyes that gleamed. It was the freakiest night of my life.'

'Mine too.'

'And this morning—I just about died when I heard about Finn! It's like . . . nightmare meets reality. No more, Mum. No more. I never want to go through that again.' Sacha looks sickened. 'It was so dark.'

'We'll talk about it later.'

'I'm going to feel completely shit while I come off it. I feel completely shit right now. It's calling me already. It's calling me. Why can't I block my ears?'

'You tell me, Sacha. Why can't you?' I head for the door.

'I'm coming to see Finn tomorrow,' she says.

I stop. Hatred rises in my throat. I'm about to tell her that she can't see Finn ever again because she's a devil in human form, but when I turn around she's hunched on the edge of her bed, childishly round-eyed, squinting up at me with a mix of anxiety and trust. I know that look so very well, and I see no devil.

I wake at four. My mind is flitting like a fantail, never stopping, never resting. Kit sleeps beside me. He believed my story without question. He believed my lies. I can't bear it.

By four fifteen I've made a decision, once and for all. I'm going to tell the truth. Kit, Sacha, Finn and Charlie all have to know—how could I even *think* of covering up? I'll tell them, and they must deal with the appalling reality. Then, of course, we will go back to England.

By four thirty I've changed my mind. No. No, there is only misery down that road. I must keep my secret. Sacha is dismayed by her psychosis; she'll stay clean this time. If I can carry my bomb without dropping it, our family might—just might—be happy again. I even begin to hope we might stay here, in our own paradise.

By five I've changed my mind twice more. I can't think straight. I roll out of bed and pull on jeans, two sweaters and a pair of Kit's socks before padding down to the kitchen. Muffin is in her basket. When I lean to pat her, she stretches luxuriously and her tail flaps on the floor.

'Life's a bitch, Muffin,' I say. 'No offence.'

I try to phone Dad but he isn't in. Maybe he's away. I remember he said something about chairing a Rudolf Steiner conference sometime soon. In black loneliness, I try Lou's number. I get her answer phone, and don't leave a message.

Finally I stoke the stove and pull up a chair. Then I sit fretting, letting the warmth sink into my bones while Muffin clambers stiffly out of her basket and rests her head on my knee, eyes hidden by her schoolgirl fringe. When I hear the kitchen door inch open, I almost jump out of my skin.

'It's okay.' Bianka's low, smooth voice. 'Only me.'

'Jeepers, Bianka! I don't know how many more night-time horrors I can take.'

'Sorry.' The serene figure drags up a chair next to mine and sits down, wearing bed socks and a hoodie over her pyjamas. She's striking even in grungy nightclothes and without the blackberry lipstick. Her cheekbones are fine beneath the pale skin, her hair a dark gold—though a little frizzy this morning.

I squeeze her shoulder and get up to fill the kettle.

'Sacha kept me awake,' she says. 'Muttering and grinding her teeth.'

'Bless you for coming here yesterday. How did you know we were in trouble?'

She strokes Muffin's nose. 'Sacha hadn't spoken to me for weeks. Then yesterday morning—six o'clock?—I got this really weird call. She was in a state, going on about Finn and how these beings had come down from the hills to get her. It's meth psychosis, you know? I read about a guy who looked at trees, familiar trees that he saw every day, and thought they were people.' Bianka sits very still, her fingers resting on Muffin's ears. 'She said these creatures had come creeping along the balcony and into her room, whispering to her. She didn't remember much, but she remembered the fear. She was kind of delirious. When she woke up she wasn't in bed.'

'Where was she?'

'Sitting in her cupboard! She's no idea how she got there.' Bianka gets up and stands with her back to the stove, watching me. 'You know, it seems . . .'

I'm looking for teabags. 'Mm?'

There's a melancholy smile on the cupid's-bow lips. 'Well, you know, it just kind of strikes me as a bit of a coincidence. You've got Sacha, who's freaking about things on the balcony, and in the very same night you've got poor little Finn tumbling off it.' I freeze with my hand in the teabag jar. 'And then I noticed . . . I'm sorry, Martha . . . I noticed that her balcony door wasn't quite shut.'

I close my eyes for several seconds. Finally I make tea in two mugs, add milk and give one to Bianka. 'What would you do, if you were me?'

'I'd tell her. I wouldn't leave her with a hellish half-memory. She needs to face it head-on, or she'll relapse again.'

'She says she's finished with it.'

'Ever heard that before?'

I'm silenced.

'She means it,' says Bianka unhappily. 'She really does. But she's no longer in control. I've worked out her pattern: binge, crash, sleep, recover, binge. Every time she uses, she needs more and the crash is worse. All she can think about is that initial buzz, but all she's achieving is a deeper and deeper hell when she's coming down. I think they call it "chasing the dragon".'

'Chasing the dragon,' I muse. 'Chasing that beautiful moment.'

'It sounds a lot more romantic than it is.'

'Do you think you could forgive her, Bianka, if you were me?'

'Forgive her?' Bianka looks incredulous. 'Of course! You know it wasn't really Sacha on that balcony. She *worships* her little brothers. Her mind's been hijacked. But when it comes to forgiving herself . . . ooh, that's going to be harder. Much, much harder. I just hope she doesn't try to harm herself.'

It's still dark outside, but I catch the sleepy trill of a stirring bird. Another dawn. Another day to be faced. I dump my mug in the sink. 'I'll head out to the hospital. Kit's planning to bring Sacha and Charlie later. D'you think she'll make it, or has she totally crashed?'

'I'll get her into the car somehow. She needs to see Finn. Martha, please forgive her.'

I sigh. 'If you'd been there, on the balcony . . .'

'All the same, forgive her.'

'And you, Bianka? She's treated you so badly. Why are you here, sleeping on her floor?'

Bianka looks into her mug, swirling the tea. 'I was hiding in the instrument storeroom when Sacha auditioned for the orchestra. I couldn't face life that day, so I'd gone to ground. Then suddenly there was this sound . . . this beautiful sound. I'd never heard anything like it before. It wasn't just a schoolgirl playing. It was someone who knew and understood everything I'd ever felt. All the loneliness. All the grief. I sat on the floor, jammed between two cellos with tears pouring down my cheeks.' They're pouring down now, but Bianka lifts her head and smiles at me. 'That's the moment when I fell in love.'

It's after seven by the time I arrive at ICU. One of the nurses is just going off duty, and she lets me in.

'You're early,' she remarks, with friendly disapproval.

'How's Finn?'

'He's a little trooper. Actually, you're not his first visitor today. You've been pipped at the post.'

Perplexed, I stop in my tracks. 'But it's family only. And there's no other family who could visit.'

'Sure about that?'

'Quite sure.'

She raises her eyebrows. 'Finn's grandpa is here.'

'He can't be. It's physically impossible.'

'Well, he is.'

'No, really. Finn only has one grandpa, and he lives in England, and I don't think he even knows about the accident.'

'Really? Well, you'd better go and see.'

I sprint onto the ward. There's someone in the chair, a compact figure with his back to me. Lined hands are cradling Finn's. He must have heard my footsteps because he turns around.

It's like a miracle. I stop dead, staring into the face I know so well, the dark grey curls and keen eyes. Then he gets up and holds his arms out wide.

Why do our hearts finally overflow when we see someone we love? What is that about? I throw myself against him, and howl.

Thirty-eight

We sit side by side, Dad's arm around my shoulder. I feel dazed.

'Lay your hands on his chest,' says Dad. 'You'll feel your energy flow into him.'

I do what he says, and he's right: I have a sense that my life is somehow sustaining Finn. Wacky, my dad, but wise.

'I don't understand how you can be here,' I say. 'I think I must be dreaming, because this just isn't possible. I mean, it's only been thirty hours or so since the accident—that was midnight on Monday here, and it's now Wednesday morning. I hadn't even told you yet, and it takes thirty hours to get here from England. You *are* a witch doctor!'

'Well, it's a bit of a long story. And a strange one.'

'Go on, then.'

Dad sits back in the chair, stretching his legs. 'Very late on Sunday night, I had a visit from someone you don't much like. Someone you once said does *not* figure in Sacha's future. Who d'you think?'

'That leaves a pretty wide field. I'm narrow-minded and judgemental, according to Sacha.'

'Well . . . maybe you're not the most tolerant woman on the planet.'

'Get *on* with it!'

'My visitor was Ivan Jones, also known as Ivan Gnome. He said he didn't know where else to turn. He'd been on Facebook and Sacha was online. Hang on just a minute.' Dad has an overnight bag beside the chair. He rummages in it and finds an A4 sheet. 'This conversation starts with Ivan writing *hiya hows nz.* See? Ignore the grammar and spelling, it's hair-raising. The next line is Sacha, and so on.'

I read with growing nausea.

hiya hows nz

not gd

nt gd ?????????

na :/

aw sorry . . . wts up

in a house with ppl off their heads just lyng in sht think im going crzy

why u goin crazy

someones coming after me

??? whaaa

im freaking

u better go home

cant

why cant

ripped off my family

where r u

theyre coming for me fk

where r u!!!!!!!!!!

theyre coming

have you got your fone

yea

fn yr mum

think I wl die

fn ur mum plz !!!!!!!!

Sacha is offline.

'Dear Lord,' I breathe.

'As you can imagine, Ivan didn't like the sound of it. He tried ringing your place. No answer. So he got in his car and drove straight around to me—he'd been before, with Sacha. I didn't like the sound of it either.

I am aware that teenagers can be a little hysterical, but all the same . . . So I called you. No answer. Why don't you have an answer machine?'

'Never got round to it after we moved here. Kit reckons if it's important the person will call back.'

'Hmm. Well, I found Capeview's website and rang them, to be told that you were on leave. They wouldn't give me your mobile number. Actually, they weren't helpful at all.'

'Hang on. This would have been when?'

'About midnight on Sunday in the UK, so . . . um, Monday lunchtime here.'

Monday. I was driving around Napier on my own, searching.

Dad looks sheepish. 'Call me a busybody but I couldn't just do nothing! Anyway, I was bored, felt like an escapade. I've been looking for an excuse to come and see you. So I packed a bag, nipped down to Heathrow and grabbed the first flight I could. Via Kuala Lumpur. By crikey—it's a long way, isn't it?'

'Dad, you're crazy.'

'I know. By the time I'd got myself out of Auckland airport, it was too late to ring you people. I was feeling pretty good; had this idea I might surprise you. So I hired a car and drove to Napier—actually, that was gruelling. It took hours longer than I'd thought from the map. My car's a hairdryer on wheels, needed cardiac massage to get across the hills, but there were no hotels open so I just kept going. I phoned your place when I reached Napier. About six.'

'Six? You must have just missed me.'

'I had,' he agrees. 'A girl answered. The friend.'

'Bianka?'

'That's the one. Nice girl. I asked straightaway if Sacha was all right, and she said yes, she's asleep upstairs. So I felt like a silly old fool! Then she told me about Finn. So—' he spreads his arms—'here I am.'

I shake my head in admiration. 'You've been travelling for two days! You must feel like death.'

'Not too bad. I slept on the flights, and I've been taking some remedies.'

I hand back the bit of paper. 'She took his advice,' I say. 'She phoned me.'

'You see? Gnomes have their uses, after all.' Dad shoves the paper back in his bag and clasps my hands in his. 'Now. What on earth is all this about?'

I tell him everything. Well. Actually, no. Not quite everything. On the subject of Sacha's addiction, stealing and paranoia, I'm completely candid. It takes a lot to rattle my dad, but he's rattled.

Yet when it comes to a starry night on a balcony, I tell my kind, wise father a pack of lies. I'm all too good at it by now.

He sits for a long time with his hand on Finn's chest. Then he says something quite extraordinary. 'I know who Sacha's father is, of course.'

'You don't.' I'm sure of it. He can't possibly know—couldn't have known, all these years, and kept the secret. 'You certainly don't.'

'You had to balance the needs of an unborn person—Sacha—against that of others. At the time I'm sure it seemed the honourable course to take.'

I gape at him, feeling the telltale flush spread up my neck.

'I've pondered on it many times over the years,' he says. 'I've watched that little curly-haired delight of yours grow up into someone very special, and I've thought how proud he would be. Sometimes I've thought he has a right to know.'

'I'd rather not discuss this,' I say stiffly.

'But of course it's become more and more impossible—so many people's happiness at stake. Six people, since Theo was born.'

'I said I'd rather not—'

'It was a choice of evils. An unenviable choice. In the end, you chose to leave Sacha permanently fatherless. So she lost out. Have you lost out too, Martha, or did you prefer having that treasure all to yourself?'

I lean forward to stroke Finn's arm. Shame burns my face.

We were close friends, Philip and I, when we were young; the sort of mates who go out drinking and cry on one another's shoulders. One weekend Lou came to stay and I introduced them. She raved for days about his roguish smile, and he cornered me to talk about her lovely legs. It was a wild romance, and I wasn't jealous; well, not very. That summer Lou booked a holiday in Ibiza with a couple of girlfriends. Philip didn't want her to go, and they had a bust-up. She told him if he wasn't going to trust her, he could take a hike. So he took a hike, then came round to moan about it to me. He was petulant and lost, which is a pretty irresistible combination. We downed a bottle of scrumpy cider and one thing led to another.

Of course, the two of them made it up on the phone. By the time Louisa flew home, Philip and I were stretched on a rack of guilt. We had a pact: there would be (a) no repetition—ever; and (b) no confession—ever, under any circumstances. The event was expunged from history. Poor Philip was so overcome with remorse that he bought a whopping antique ring and proposed to Louisa in the Gatwick arrivals hall, to the cheers of about three hundred people all holding up signs saying things like AQUILA TOURS and HERTZ. She was in heaven. The two of them toured their families, showing off the ring and booking the church. Even Mum approved of Philip. When Lou asked me to be her bridesmaid she thanked me—*thanked* me!—for bringing him into her life. She said she'd never been so happy.

One morning as I lay in bed looking up at a crack in the ceiling, it hit me. Don't ask me how. I just knew, with a sick certainty, that I wasn't alone. It took me a fortnight to take the test, and another month to decide what to do about it. I fibbed about the due date, invented a one-night stand and fronted up at Lou's wedding in a maternity smock. I was my sister's bridesmaid, and pregnant with the groom's child. Not my most glorious moment.

Just once, very early on, Philip asked if the baby could possibly be his. I slapped his shoulder and told him not to be so bloody arrogant—how fertile did he think he was? I spun a complicated story about a tall chap called Simon who'd swung in and out of my life without leaving a forwarding address.

'Well,' said Philip, relieved. 'You know Louisa and I love you. If there's ever anything we can do . . .'

By the time my perfect daughter was born, people had stopped mentioning the father. He'd become a mythical creature. They wrote *Unknown* on the birth certificate. Sacha was mine. All mine.

'I know you very well, Martha,' says Dad. 'I was in the maternity unit when Lou and Philip came to visit. Everyone else was fixated on the new baby, but I was watching you. And I admired you, because I knew you were doing it for your sister.'

'*I* didn't admire me.'

'It also occurs to me that this might be one of the reasons you decided to emigrate. At any rate, a significant factor? Sacha was becoming more and more persistent. She'd started asking everyone, making wild guesses and stirring up old memories. I might not be the only person to have suspicions.'

'Dad,' I say faintly. 'Is there anything you *don't* know about me?'

'Twelve thousand miles is a long way to run.'

I sigh, looking at Finn. 'Not far enough.'

We're in the cafeteria when Kura Pohatu finds us. The white tresses are swirled into a regal bun today. I'm pretty offhand, but she seems thick-skinned. Has to be, I imagine.

When I introduce her to Dad, the social worker looks genuinely delighted. 'Will you stay in New Zealand for long, Mr Norris?'

'That depends,' he counters, pulling out a chair for her. 'Martha's told me all about your concerns. I think they're misplaced, but I applaud you for doing your job so thoroughly.'

She sits graciously, and turns to me. 'I hear Kit is home, Martha, and visited Finn last night.'

Her spies have told her, of course. Every nurse is an undercover agent. 'Yes, he did. He's planning to bring the other children in this morning.'

'Okay. Well, I have to tell you where we go from here.' She holds up two hands, palms towards me. 'Please. I want you to remember that I'm not here to make life difficult for you.'

'Go on.' I'm in that swing boat again.

She looks at Dad. 'The team has identified concerns and decided there should be further investigation. We need to be sure that Finn and the other children are not at risk of further harm.'

'What a waste of public money,' says Dad placidly.

'I'm actually employed by CYF,' continues Kura. 'That's Child, Youth and Family. I'm based at the hospital for half my working hours. Since I've already spent some time on this, I've been appointed lead social worker.'

'Is that good news or bad?' asks Dad.

'Good, I hope. I'll be working with a colleague. He'll talk again to the school, to the family doctor and maybe others. I'd like to meet the rest of the family. Finn obviously can't speak for himself just yet.'

'Just a minute.' I stare incredulously as what she's said sinks in. 'You want to talk to *Finn*?'

'If our initial screening doesn't eliminate this as accidental, he may be interviewed. Don't worry. It would be done very sensitively.'

'That's ludicrous, Kura! If he recovers—and I'd remind you that at the moment it's *if*—he won't remember a bloody thing.' I'm confident on this point. People with severe head injuries have amnesia about their accident, in my experience. 'Anyway, I've told you fifty times that he was *asleep*—he never woke up.'

'These incidents are not generally isolated. Any interview with Finn wouldn't focus only on the fall itself, but on the bigger picture. Look, I can see the idea distresses you. Shall we cross the bridge when we come to it?'

'I wish you'd leave us alone.' I reach for Dad's hand. 'There's a tiny scrap of a boy up there, hanging onto life by a thread. All we can think about right now—'

An incoherent cry of joy rings across the cafeteria. Dad leaps to his feet and turns to face a slender young woman as she hurls herself between the tables, knocking over a chair. Before we can blink, Sacha has careered into him, flinging her arms around his neck. 'Grandpa,' she sobs. 'Grandpa.'

'I've missed you,' says Dad. He encircles his granddaughter with both arms, almost lifting her off the ground. 'My beautiful, beautiful girl. I've missed you too much.'

Kura slips tactfully away. When she returns ten minutes later, Kit and Charlie have joined us too. The very sight of her grandfather seems to revive Sacha. She can't get close enough, sitting almost on top of him and butting her head into his shoulder.

Charlie is entrenched in his lap, clinging to his jersey like a baby koala bear. He keeps taking his grandfather's head in his hands and turning it to face his own. 'Talk to me, Grandpa,' he whines. 'Not them. *Me*.'

'A much-loved grandparent,' says Kura quietly.

*

We visit the intensive care unit in small groups. Sacha and Dad go up, followed by Kit, Charlie and me. We weren't sure whether Charlie ought to see Finn in such a distressing state, but he begged so frantically that we gave in. I think I was hoping for a miracle, like in the films: Finn would hear Charlie's voice and open those poor, bruised eyes, and say hello, and the doctor on duty would look astonished and say it's a first in medical history, he's out of danger, and we'd all sit on his bed and laugh during the closing credits.

The reality is pitiful. At first, Charlie tries to talk to his twin. Then he shouts and has to be shushed. Finally, desperate for some response, he offers to lend Finn his ultimate treasure—Blue Blanket. When even this sacrifice fails, he begins to roam angrily around the ward. We have to bring him away. He's troubled for the rest of the day, alternating between violence and white-faced silence.

Then Kura speaks to Kit in a family room. He tells me later that she cross-examined him about our row. He informed her that it was a private matter and he bloody well wasn't going to air his dirty laundry in her tumble dryer. All couples had their spats, he said, and we had plenty. Always had, always would. We were both strong characters and that made for a great partnership. If he had his time again, he'd marry me all over again.

She called the motel, whose manager bemusedly confirmed that at midnight on Monday, a Kit McNamara checked into a studio unit. Irish bloke—did she want his vehicle registration? Dark hair. Tired. Yes, it was documented. Yes, he was quite certain. How many Irishmen did she think came ringing his bell at midnight? What kind of an establishment did she think he was running there?'

'Bugger,' I moan, when Kit relays this conversation.

'*Bugger?*' He smiles tiredly. 'The heat's off. I'm in the clear.'

'Now she'll harry me instead. She'll think I lost my temper because you stormed out on me. The woman's like Sherlock bloody Holmes.'

'Ah, don't worry. You've nothing to hide.'

That's what he thinks, whispers Mum.

Thirty-nine

For a week we float in limbo between hospital and home, between hope and terror.

Sacha crashes after visiting Finn, curled tight and grey and dried-out in her room, like a dead spider. Ira and Tama return to their ordinary lives but kindling is magically chopped, the stove stoked, the lamb and the dog fed and cared for. Our phone rings all day—parents from the school, neighbours, all wanting to help; our kitchen groans with baking and casseroles, with get-well cards for Finn and toys for Charlie, many left by people I barely know.

Lillian, inevitably, makes a four-course banquet out of my absence from work. She reminds me that I've only just taken some leave. I remind her that my son is in the intensive care unit. She launches into a rant, but I accidentally cut her off in mid-sentence. Whoops. Must have pressed the button by mistake.

Keith calls five minutes later and forbids me to show so much as a toe at Capeview before Finn is safely on the road to recovery. Yes, of course they'll manage. Tsk tsk, do I think I'm indispensable? The next afternoon I arrive home from the hospital to find a vast bouquet of flowers on our doorstep, along with a card signed by everyone at work. Lillian's name is written in very small, repressed letters; but then she is a very small, repressed woman.

As I carry the flowers into the house, Dad holds out the phone. 'Your big sister for you.'

Dropping my burden in the sink, I take the receiver and muffle it against my chest. 'How's Sacha been?' I whisper to Dad.

'Poor lass seems to be in pain. I gave her some St John's wort.' Dad waggles his fingers, sketching a goodbye. 'I'm off to the hospital.'

I wave, then lift the phone to my ear. 'Louisa, for goodness' sake go back to bed! It must be five in the morning up there.'

'I'm coming over.' Lou's voice is brimming with emotion. 'I can be with you by the weekend.'

I smile down the line. 'I love you! But no, you can't. How will your children manage, poor motherless creatures?'

'Philip's found a nanny agency.'

'Thank you. And thanks to Philip, too. But Dad's here. Come another time, when we aren't in such chaos and can really show you around. You're going to fall in love with this place. You might even decide to stay!'

There's a fag-inhaling pause. 'But you'll be coming home, now this has happened.'

'Um . . . Actually, we aren't thinking that far ahead. At the moment we're just taking one day at a time.'

She sounds mystified. 'You need to come *home*.'

I look at the Capeview flowers in the sink, the cards and muffins and meals left for us. I look out into our garden, down our valley. I can smell the spring pasture. It occurs to me that we are already home. But I don't say so.

When Pamela and Jean return from their holiday, it takes half an hour for them to hear the news and arrive at the kitchen door. My heart lifts. 'Come in, come in! You're a sight for sore eyes,' I enthuse, flinging the door wide. 'They're all at the hospital. Just Charlie and me holding the fort.' I don't mention Sacha.

Pamela embraces me wordlessly. My friend seems distressed, her mouth set and her clothes less ordered than usual.

'How is he?' asks Jean, who is clutching a frozen lasagne.

'We're so lucky. They saved his life.' I've embarked on my story when

Charlie potters into the room, looking vacant and pressing Blue Blanket to one ear. The Colberts greet him with cries of affection. I thought he'd be pleased to see them, but he just holds his hands up to me like a weary toddler. I sit him on my lap at the table, while he regards the visitors with possum eyes.

I rub his back. 'Charlie's less than half a man without his twin. He wakes up every night and cries for him.'

'Indeed. They're a double act,' murmurs Jean.

Without a word, Charlie pokes his foot into Jean's comfortable stomach. When the Frenchman tickles his toes, he giggles silently behind his thumb. Pamela reaches out and strokes his silky curls as I tell the tale for the hundredth time: how Finn was walking in his sleep; how he suddenly climbed onto the balcony and toppled over. I have told and retold it so often that it has become reality—I can actually see it all quite clearly, happening in exactly the way I describe. It has become a part of our family history. It has become true.

Charlie takes out his thumb. 'Finn went in an 'elicopter.'

'We'll have to go and see him, won't we?' says Pamela. 'When he's a bit better.'

'I think he might be dead,' says Charlie. 'I talked to him and he didn't wake up.'

Pamela and Jean tut, and I clutch him closer. 'Finny's not dead, sweetheart. They've just made him sleep very deeply while he gets better.'

'He had a big pipe shoved up his nose. That would really really hurt. Someone should pull that out.'

My throat tightens. 'That's to help him breathe. It doesn't hurt.'

Charlie shrugs uncertainly. I can see his mind whirring, full of questions he's afraid to ask. 'So . . . no, I think he's probably dead. They cut his brains out.'

As they stand to leave, the Colberts offer babysitting and meals and lamb feeding. They promise to come back whenever we need them. They mean it.

'Odd thing.' Pamela hesitates, her hand on the doorknob. 'There's a message on our phone from someone at Child, Youth and Family.'

'Ah.'

'They want to talk to us about Finn's accident. But what's the point of that? We weren't even here.'

'They'd like to know if we're a dysfunctional family,' I say, uncomfortably aware that we are precisely that. 'You know, the sort who would grab their five-year-old and chuck him off a balcony.'

There's a chorus of scandalised tongue-clicking. Jean's eyebrows shoot right off the top of his head and hover in the air. 'Extraordinary!'

'Ooh!' His wife pushes up her sleeves, wearing her hungry seagull expression. 'I can't *wait* to call them back.'

On the fifth day, a team begins to wake Finn. They're at pains to explain that this might be a very slow process. He could be confused or agitated initially, and there may be false starts. If he seems too distressed they'll put him under again and wait until tomorrow. Kit and I are on tenterhooks.

'We might even have our Finn back by tonight,' says Kit hopefully, as we drive together to the hospital. He looks pinched and anxious, which is how I feel.

If he's still in there, I think, neurotically searching for wood to touch.

They varied the drugs last night, but begin to try to bring Finn to the surface at about midday. We've dug out the boys' Mr Men tape, and a play specialist comes along to help. She has the tape running quietly.

It's a slow process, all right. I see Finn's eyes open for the first time, just slits because they are still grossly swollen. He begins to wail, jerking his limbs and trying to tear at the line in his arm. He sounds like an animal in pain. I want to shout at them to stop, to leave him in peace.

Kit takes his hand. I can hear the urgency in his voice. 'C'mon, Finny. C'mon. *Please*, my friend. Come back.'

Finn makes an odd gargling sound. Then his eyes close, though his body is still tense. I think they've increased the anaesthetic just enough to put him under.

Sometime later, they try again. This time the eyes look blankly at me, at Kit, at the strangers who surround him. He doesn't seem to know us at all. We talk to him, talk gibberish, trying to sound calm and jovial, but he just doesn't register at all. It's deeply disturbing. Then his eyes close.

Making an excuse, I run out of the ward. I stumble blindly down the corridor, lock myself into a toilet and have a meltdown. By the time I return, the team have disappeared and a nurse is monitoring Finn's machinery.

'They reckon it's up to Finn now,' says Kit. 'They're going to do more tests and things tomorrow.'

As day wears into evening, sheer screaming panic begins to take hold of me. 'Perhaps his soul is already gone,' I whisper, and feel the answering pressure of Kit's hand in mine.

'Our boy's there all right,' he insists doggedly. 'I can hear him yelling in there. I can feel all that craziness and fun. I'm not moving. I'm going to sit right here in this chair until he comes back to me.'

Kit's passionate faith keeps me from collapse, but I can't hear Finn yelling, not at all. I imagine the years passing: Finn as an adolescent, a grown man; a thirty-year-old body, needing to be shaved and fed and have his toenails cut, but unable to die. An empty Finn, with no trace of the wicked smile and brilliant eyes.

At eight o'clock, Dad phones.

'No news,' I say unsteadily.

'Charlie is going to bed now. He's been quite upset. I wondered when you'll be coming home? You'll be needing to rest, yourselves.'

I say I'll call him back. Then I lean into Kit. We pinned such hopes on this day.

'Go on home,' Kit says, nuzzling my hair. 'Charlie's going to wake up in the night and he needs one of us there at least.'

'I want to stay with you. With Finn.'

Kit fumbles clumsily in his pocket and hands me the car keys. 'Go home and get some rest. Witch doctor's orders.'

It's awful, leaving my husband and son among the lights and buzzers and death. In the end Kit walks me to the door of ICU and more or less pushes me out. I drive home in a fog of horror and exhaustion. We're starting a different life, with a different Finn. I know the old Finn isn't coming back. He is lost.

Someone has written in the chapel book: *You bastard. Why create such brilliance if all along you were planning to destroy it?*

I stop by our letterbox at the sight of a misshapen parcel. Even in the starlight, I recognise Louisa's oversized handwriting. I open it in the kitchen where Dad is waiting for me.

'Slippers, books . . . posh colouring pencils . . . a magic set! My sister is amazing.' There's a card as well, signed by everyone including a rather revolting slobber mark from Thundering Theo. I leave it all on the table and slump over the stove, haunted by Finn's empty eyes.

'What's the worst that can happen?' asks Dad, resting a cup of tea beside me.

'Head injuries.' I blow out my cheeks. 'They're my Room 101; my greatest fear.'

'But the people you work with are bound to be at the higher end of the scale?'

'True. And a lot of them recover, though it can take years. But Dad, some never come back. I talk to the families and they say it just isn't the same person. They're mourning for the parent or wife or child they've lost forever.' I describe Gareth, the pilot, who is soon to be rehabilitated home to his grieving parents. 'I don't think he'll ever attain anything like normality. Thirty years old, and he's condemned to a twilight life.'

'Will his parents be able to manage?'

'They aren't young. They'll care for him until they drop, and then . . . well. There aren't many options.'

'The doctors are optimistic for Finn, though?'

'Ah, well. They're feeling pretty pleased with the way the trauma was managed—and yes, it was managed brilliantly. I can see that now, although I was in a flat spin at the time. Really impressive. But a success from *their* point of view could still be a tragedy from ours.'

'We'll soon know, either way.'

'It was horrible, Dad. He opened his eyes but there was nobody in there. The lights weren't . . .' I swallow a sob. 'Lights weren't on. I don't know if the lights will ever come on again.'

'He was always a bright little spark,' insists Dad. 'Such a clever look in those eyes, right from the day he was born! He'll come back, I'm sure.'

We sit by the stove until the early hours, talking about many things but always coming back to Finn. I ask how Sacha's been faring.

'Doing well.' Dad looks pleased. 'She got up today. We went for a stroll in the garden. I think she's coming right.'

Exhausted, I lean back in my chair and shut my eyes. 'For now.'

The minutes tick by. Muffin is delighted by our night-owl hours. She comes rolling out of her basket and leans against me. I've gone back to worrying about Finn when Dad speaks again.

'When do you plan to tell Philip and Sacha that they're father and daughter?'

'Um . . .' I'm flustered by the question. 'I don't know. Sometimes I've thought it would help, maybe she'd stop fretting and fantasising about her father, but all hell would break loose. Lou's a pretty emotional person.'

'But one day?'

'I hope so. When their children are grown up. It's like you said, Dad. There's so many people's happiness at stake.'

'Does Kit know?'

'Yes, Kit knows. I had a fit of conscience before our wedding. I swore him to secrecy.'

'I'm glad he's in the picture.' Dad looks shamefaced. 'I was a bit jealous when Kit first arrived on the scene.'

'You, jealous?' I can't imagine my father having such an ungenerous emotion.

He wags a finger. 'Not because of you; because of Sacha! I'd grown used to being the male figure in her life, and suddenly there was this funny, clever chap who seemed determined to be a father to her. And what's more, he was doing a pretty good job of it.'

I smile, remembering those early days. 'He was brave to take on Sacha.'

'He succeeded, though.' Muffin begins dribbling onto Dad's knee, and he manhandles her back into the basket. 'But all that matters now, tonight, is Finn. We'd both better get some shut-eye. How about an infusion of chamomile to help us sleep?'

I've been in bed ten minutes when Charlie appears, clutching Blue Blanket as he picks his way through the dark. I pull back the duvet and he clambers in. For the rest of the night I drift in and out of sleep, haunted by dreams of a soft-cheeked child with windblown curls, dragging his blanket, endlessly searching an alien landscape for a lost twin. I can hear his thin cries in the wilderness.

Horrible sounds shatter the weird desperation of my dream, vibrating and bellowing right next to my ear, sending my heartbeat way off the scale. I sit up with a yell, then realise my phone's receiving a text. The clock reads 5:25.

I turn on the light and reach for the phone. It takes me a few seconds to focus.

HES BACK!!!!! AWAKE AND TALKING

I screech. I scream the place down. I kiss Charlie—who isn't quite awake, despite my hullabaloo—then fall out of bed and stumble onto the landing. Dad shoots out of the spare bedroom, cannoning into me.

'Good news or bad?' he gasps, clutching at my arm.

I show him the message, and he dances a jig before hurtling into Sacha's room. 'He's awake!' I hear him switching on her light. 'Beautiful girl, your brother is awake! Now up you get. I want you in the car in five minutes. You hear me?

As he speaks, another text arrives: *Says get a move on and bring everyone.*

Other people's sons win the interschool cross-country. Other people's sons have a reading age of thirteen. Other people's sons are All Blacks in the making.

My son is awake and talking. It's a bloody miracle.

I didn't know Charlie could run so fast. Never seen him do it before.

Dad, Sacha and I have been in a tearing hurry since we got Kit's message, but Charlie is in another league altogether. He rolls off my bed, slides down the banister and piles into the car in his pyjamas. All the way to hospital he's mouthing some secret conversation to himself, jiggling legs betraying his agitation.

My phone goes off in the car, and Dad reads out the text. 'It's Kit. He says: *Asleep again, drugs still in system, doctors very happy though.*'

'No!' poor Charlie shrieks in panic, and then begins to wail broken-heartedly. '*No!* Don't let him go to sleep!'

Sitting next to him in the back seat, Sacha tries to soothe her brother. 'It's okay, buddy. He's not in a coma any more, just asleep.'

But Charlie doesn't believe her. He's inconsolable. I've barely parked before he's out, racing around the car in his pyjamas, ordering us all to come on come *on*, tugging at my hand as I lock the door and dragging me across the car park and into the building. Dad isn't as quick as he used to be. When we turn into the long corridor that leads to ICU Charlie drops my hand—he knows the way from here—and sprints for the finishing line. He's a man with a mission, and nothing is going to get in his way. The door to the unit is locked but to my astonishment he presses the buzzer and bangs the flat of his hand on the glass of the door. Someone must take pity on him, because a moment later the door opens a crack and he disappears inside.

Sacha breaks into a trot. 'D'you mind?' she calls over her shoulder.

'Go!' Dad waves her away, and she's off at the starter's pistol. 'Go, go!'

Dad and I have to ring the buzzer too, and it's several minutes before we're allowed in and round the corner to Finn's cubicle. Hearing eager chatter, we slide in quietly. Sacha is perched on the bed, cradling Finn's hand. Charlie's bouncing around on Kit's knee, talking, talking, talking. Between the three, still tangled in a mass of wires and tubes, lies a drowsy child with a shaved head and a plaster cast on one arm. A knitted pirate nestles under his ear.

Kit catches my eye and smiles. He looks weary and tearful and euphoric, all at the same time. His arms are full of Charlie.

'Then Bleater jumped right over the fence,' squeaks Charlie, who seems ready to explode with joy, 'and then she was a very naughty girl because do you know what she did? She went and ate up all Mum's pot plants, yum! And *then* she did a wee on the verandah, and it made a luverley waterfall'—he waves his arms—'all the way down the steps, tinkle—tinkle—tinkle!'

Finn giggles quietly. He seems to think for a moment, and I hold my breath. Then he speaks—not loud, but clear: 'Bleater should've peed on the lemon tree.'

Charlie is laughing uproariously when he spots Dad and me. He jumps off Kit's lap, pointing. 'Mum, he's not dead!'

'Hello, Finny.' I sit down on the bed, careful to avoid the wires.

The mutilated head swivels, and painfully bruised eyes regard me for several seconds. I have time to wonder whether he doesn't know who I am, whether he is terribly damaged after all. Then he holds out his good hand, reaching frantically as though trying to crawl into my arms. Finally he bursts into noisy tears.

The intensive care unit is a war zone, and the enemy is death itself. We later hear that at two o'clock that morning, a mother of three teenagers had succumbed to meningitis. But at five, a small boy began to wake.

Forty

By the time Finn moves into the child health unit, he's heartily bored of hospital. He has no idea how he got there although he stubbornly pretends to remember the helicopter ride. The children's ward is much jollier than ICU: bright colours and toys, and a hundred times more relaxed. Various doctors explain that although the signs are good, Finn isn't out of the woods. He'll need monitoring and follow-ups, and further surgery for the metal plate to be removed. For now though, it's enough that he is with us at all.

The staff do a wonderful job, but they have us under surveillance like monkeys in a cage, constantly monitoring how we behave and how the children react to us. I feel as though our every gesture, every word is being observed. Stopping to ask a question at the nurses' desk one time, I actually spot some notes: *Mum and Dad arrived 8 am with jigsaw puzzle. Greeted Finn appropriately. He seemed very pleased to see them.*

How nice, I think caustically. What a very generous observation.

Kura has hung around, of course. She plays Ludo with Charlie while I try to look nonchalant. She gets him talking. Bless him, the little chap is flattered by all the attention and tells her in numbingly minute detail all about his new green gumboots with crocodile faces on the toes. The social worker also speaks to Sacha in a family room, which is a terrifying half hour for me. I underestimated my daughter's ability to lie charmingly, though. They emerge, chatting about homework. Perhaps to Kura, Sacha is just a typical post-adolescent, profoundly upset about her little brother. She has no way of knowing that this sallow-skinned girl is no more than a ghost of the real person. Sacha's back at school but we're taking no chances. We deliver and collect her ourselves, and while there she's constantly guarded by Bianka. I can't imagine ever trusting her again.

As for Finn, he's pampered and spoiled for a fortnight, holding court to a constant stream of visitors. The Colberts come, bearing their sons' comic books; Destiny arrives with Harvey, who fills his face with Finn's leftover rice pudding. Ira brings Charlie along after school. Even Tama ventures in and spends an afternoon playing Snakes and Ladders. The lean figure looks supremely out of place, crammed onto a child's chair and moving a red plastic counter around a board. I've rarely seen him indoors before, nor without the hat.

'Social worker paid me a visit,' he says laconically.

My stomach drops. 'Oh.'

He rolls the dice without looking up. 'She asked how come I came over that night, so I told her you phoned after the accident. I also let her know what a nice family you are.'

'Thank you.'

'Well.' He moves his counter around the board, and his dark eyes meet mine. 'It's all true. But I think you've still got a problem to solve. A big problem.'

'I know.'

'Two and three makes five,' exults Finn. 'High five! You're goin' down the long snake, Tama. You're slidin' all the way to the bottom. *Wheee!*'

One evening, two police officers from the child protection team visit Patupaiarehe. They are a man and a woman, hunting in pairs like coyotes. The sight of their uniforms at the door makes me feel faint. I try—and fail—to look blasé. Following a policy of appeasement, Kit and I show them the boys' bedroom and then we all troop onto the balcony. The woman begins to take measurements and write them in her notebook.

'I couldn't see much,' I explain, for the zillionth time. 'It was dark. I'd left all the inside lights off so I could look at the stars. I was sitting way down there—see? Finn pottered to the rail—here—and then he was up and straight over. It happened in a flash.'

The man touches the handrail. 'They have to be built higher than this nowadays. It's in the building codes. Here.' He uses a tape measure to show us the new regulation height. 'This is where they need to be, see, as a minimum.'

Kit is pacing. He resents having to be polite to people who suspect us of trying to murder our child. 'Yes, we know.'

'A man's coming to fix cast-iron railings,' I explain. 'He's measured up. They'll actually be five centimetres higher than the regulations require. We've fitted deadlocks on all the French doors. Look—' I spread my arms, gazing from one officer to the other with innocent appeal—'it can't happen again.'

After two weeks, Kura comes to find us. Kit and I are deep in conversation with a junior doctor, but the social worker asks for a moment of our time. I see from her expression that she has something momentous to say.

We follow the swinging ponytail into a family room. I think we are both shaking.

'Take a seat,' says Kura, but we don't. We stand side by side, staring at her in terrified suspense. Kit takes my arm.

'Well, good news,' Kura announces. Her tone reminds me of the examiner telling me I'd passed my driving test. 'The investigation is concluded. A multi-disciplinary meeting was held yesterday. Both CYF and the police are satisfied that Finn's accident was just that—an accident. There was extensive discussion, but the team concluded that no child protection issue has been identified, and no further investigation is indicated. So we're out of your hair.'

'Oh, thank God,' I breathe. The blood seems to rush into my head. I sit down, literally dizzy with relief.

'An apology would be nice,' says Kit icily. I try to shush him, and he lays his hand on my shoulder.

'Kit.' Kura blinks at him. 'I hope you can understand why we had concerns?'

'Not really.' Kit's charm has been switched off. 'In heaven's name, woman! Can you not say sorry? This has been a nightmare for our family.

As though it wasn't enough to have our boy critically injured, we've been persecuted. Do you have the smallest idea how it feels to be called an abuser, Kura? Or don't you even care?'

'Of course I care.'

'She was doing her job, Kit,' I whisper, in the guilty knowledge that Kura was right to suspect something was amiss, right to investigate our family.

But Kit's in full flood, releasing all the nervous tension of the past fortnight. 'We've been spied on by everyone in this hospital—I reckon even the bloody cleaners were taking notes. Our neighbours and our doctor and our boys' teachers have been questioned, our name's been dragged right through the piggery. We've been living in terror that you might take our kids away! And now you have the brass neck to breeze in, all sweetness and light, and tell us we're in the clear. We've been innocent all along. Well, how about some acknowledgement that you made a disastrous error of judgement?'

'It wasn't personal,' insists Kura. 'If we don't act when there are indicators of abuse, we're vilified. And there were concerns. A child critically injured in the middle of the night, apparent finger bruises, a healed fracture that was never presented, parents who had a fight and then covered it up.'

'Only if you've a suspicious mind. I think maybe some of you people have been in this job too long. You see nastiness in every corner. You can't see the good any more.'

I'm ill at ease, but Kura isn't. She's heard it all before. She gives him a leaflet explaining the process we've just been through and what to do if we want to make a complaint. 'It's been a privilege to meet such a lovely family,' she says.

'You mean it's been a privilege to harass such a lovely family,' retorts Kit.

Kura merely smiles. 'How much longer can your father stay, Martha?'

'Only another week,' I say glumly.

'Grandpa will leave a hole in your life, won't he? But I know you've already made some good friends in the district. Really loyal friends, like Mr and Mrs Colbert and Finn's young teacher. Is there anything else you'd like to ask me at this stage? Now's your chance.'

We shake our heads. We want rid of her.

'Thank you,' I say.

At the door, she has a parting shot. 'You do need to get on with altering that balcony. And next time a child takes a nasty tumble off his bike, for goodness' sake get him to a doctor!'

Kit rolls his eyes at her departing back. 'If I ever see that woman again, it'll be too soon.'

I have to agree with him. The social worker hasn't made a disastrous error of judgement at all; quite the opposite. I genuinely like her as a person. I admire her acuity. No doubt colleagues respect, and grandchildren adore her. She's on the side of the angels, but all the same I never, ever want to see Kura Pohatu again.

Forty-one

We bring Finn home. I present the nurses in child health and ICU with boxes of locally made chocolates, and Charlie hands out some crumpled thank-you cards he's been working on for days. Finn's favourite nurse is on duty and she sees us to the door with smiles and hugs and admonitions not to fall off any more balconies. His plaster—actually dark green fibreglass—is smothered in graffiti. We pass the cafeteria and the chapel, and then Finn is out at last, free in the open air under a windblown sky.

Someone has written in the chapel book: *On the assumption that you made him well, THANK YOU! But tell me—what now?*

We drive up to Patupaiarehe in triumph. Dad comes trotting out of the kitchen door followed by Bianka, who's staying for the weekend.

'Here we are!' chants Kit, driving a little victory circuit under the walnut. 'The warrior returns.'

Finn talked all the way, but now he's looking pale and shaky. He fumbles to open the car door with his good hand. I think he's become institutionalised. Actually, we all have. Dad helps him out.

'Lucky you didn't break the ear-stroking arm,' says Charlie, who's been high as a kite since six this morning. He's on fire with happiness at his twin's return. 'Hey, come and see Bleater Brown! She's *this* big, now!'

'Careful,' I warn. 'Finn's got to take it very slowly. He can't rush around.'

'Okay.' In extravagant slow motion, Charlie leads his other half over to the lamb's pen. They lean on the fence like two old farmers, tickling Bleater's head and discussing the progress of their stock.

Bianka comes close to me. 'Martha, um—'

'Just a sec.' I'm distracted, lifting bags out of the car. 'Can you grab this for me, Bianka?'

At that moment, Finn looks around. 'Where's Sacha?'

'She'll be here in a minute,' says Dad quickly, with a glance at me. 'Shall we go and make Bleater a bottle?'

Something is very wrong. I stand bewildered, holding Finn's little backpack. Bianka takes my arm and leads me out of Kit's earshot. 'She's in the hut,' she whispers tersely.

I stare. 'Tell me she hasn't got hold of anything.'

'I'm so sorry! Look, I shadowed her all day, every day, until she was ready to punch me. But yesterday lunchtime I had to go and help a group of Year Nines with their history project . . . I got volunteered.' Bianka's mouth twists in regret.

'Yes?' I'm impatient. 'Go on.'

'She must've borrowed a phone, texted a dealer and met him outside school. That's all I can think of. I noticed her coming back, and she said she'd just nipped out to the dairy for a chocolate bar. But I could tell from the way she looked at me . . . you know?'

'Oh, yes. I know.' I can easily picture the new, deceitful Sacha. I know that creature all too well.

'She took some last night. I don't know how, I don't know when, but she was manic, up and down all night. I didn't want to spoil Finn's homecoming so I thought I'd just keep an eye on her, which was a stupid mistake because as soon as you'd gone this morning, she disappeared. It took me a while to find her in the smoko hut.'

'Okay.' Rage and sorrow and fear have been seething in me for months, and now they overflow. I know what I'm going to do. I begin to back away, ready to run. 'Have you spoken to her?'

Bianka shakes her head miserably. 'She wouldn't even open the door to your gorgeous dad. She went psycho. She—'

I don't need to hear any more. I sprint past the kitchen door and along the path to the hut. Its windows have been covered again, and the door is locked. I hammer on the flaky wood. Shards of paint fall away. 'Sacha!' I bellow.

There's clumsy movement inside, and the sound of something clattering; then a muttered 'get fucked'. It isn't a girl speaking. It's the voice of that horrible Sacha beast.

Resolve settles in me like icy water. It weighs me down and makes me cold. 'I won't get fucked,' I say, very clearly. 'It's time for you to listen. So listen carefully. Are you listening?'

A snarled obscenity.

'Do you know what really happened to Finn?'

Silence.

I lean my face close to the door, my lips almost touching it. 'I'll tell you. You thought creatures were coming to get you. Remember that, Sacha? They were creeping along the balcony and into your bedroom. You were scared out of your wits.'

'Shut up!' The voice is coarse. Ugly. 'Shut the fuck up.'

'All night long they were whispering. You saw their gleaming eyes, a face at the window, crawling things. And in the morning you weren't in bed, were you? No. You were sitting in your cupboard. How do you think you got there?'

I feel a powerful thud just in front of my face, followed by the smashing of glass. A bottle, I'm sure, hurled at the door. Then another. The old timber shivers at each impact.

I raise my voice. 'During the night, you heard something on the balcony. You ran out there. Remember, Sacha? Remember unlocking your door and running outside? Yes. I think you do.'

Another smash. The door buckles slightly.

'You caught a creature prowling around behind your door. You actually caught one! So what did you do? You hurled it over the rail.' I'm choking on my rage. It fills my chest. I have to breathe hard before my next words. 'That was Finn.'

I want her to taste my horror. I feel as though I'm slicing into this imposter with a sharp knife; I have to cut the real Sacha out of her. She must have run out of bottles to throw, because this time it sounds more like a kick. 'He's got no spleen,' I shriek, twisting the knife. 'He's got a broken arm and they had to dig two pieces of skull out of his brain. God knows what the future holds for him. And *you* did this to him!'

Volcanic pressure is building behind my forehead. I boot the door myself, kick it with all my fury. I kick five, ten times until it splinters and caves, and my foot goes through.

I hear the bolt drawing back. Sacha is standing in the doorway, her eyes black, her mouth open in a soundless scream.

'It's not true,' she wails. 'It's not true.'

'Oh yes, it is. I saw you do it. Shall I go and tell him? Shall I tell Finn how much his sister loves him?'

I see it in her eyes. The knowledge. The shock. Then she staggers back into the hut, pressing both arms over her face.

'Where is it?' I tear down the curtains and begin to ransack the room. I'm seriously considering whether to scatter petrol and set a match to this lair. I gather up a home-made pipe and lighters and tape and all the other bits of paraphernalia, and throw everything into her bin. 'I said, where is it?'

'I got it on credit. Just a point. It's all gone.'

'*Where is it?*'

She pulls one of the tiny bags from inside her bra. A few crystals; innocent, like rock salt. 'I shouldn't be on this earth,' she weeps, as I wash them down the plughole.

'No,' I say bitterly. 'You probably shouldn't.'

I hear footsteps outside. Dad stops at the door of the hut, taking in the scene in an instant. 'Finn's flaked out. He's asking for you, Martha.' He jerks his head back towards the house. 'Go on. Go and make him comfy, poor little man. Maybe I can help here.'

When I leave them, my father is sitting on the floor beside Sacha. He's doing what I haven't been able to do; what I think I may never again be able to do. He's put his arms around his granddaughter, and is telling her she is still loved.

*

When I look out of the kitchen window ten minutes later, Dad's car has gone. At lunchtime Finn asks for him and Sacha. I say they've gone for a walk, and Kit stares at me. After all, this is Finn's big homecoming day. Charlie and Dad spent yesterday evening making a cake and banners; the idea of anyone swanning off for a stroll is bound to raise an eyebrow.

After lunch, Finn falls asleep on the sofa. Charlie glues himself to his twin, warm and contented, squashed up close. Bianka sits nearby, reading a book. I know my time is running out. Well, let Kit tackle me. I've come to a decision.

He's loading the dishwasher when he finally asks the dreaded question. 'She's relapsed again, hasn't she?' he says quietly. When I nod, he slams the dishwasher door shut with his foot. '*Fuck*.'

'Kit.'

'*Stupid* girl,' he growls. 'Okay, okay. We've got to get help.'

'Kit.' I feel a cold sweat on my forehead, as though I'm about to be sick. I'm quivering at the top of a high diving board, gazing down, down, knowing I have to jump. This could be the end of everything.

'Get on to a counsellor,' he's saying. 'Tell them all about—'

I have to shout over him. 'Kit! Please listen.'

He stops talking. I shut my eyes for a second, and then I hurl myself off the board.

'She was paranoid,' I say. 'She thought there were evil beings stalking her. I think maybe it started months ago, the paranoia, but it got worse and worse. Sometimes she heard them whispering, even caught glimpses of them. They terrified her. Then one night, the night you came home from Dublin, she actually *caught* one lurking outside her bedroom door.'

Kit has turned to stone, the colour rapidly leaving his face.

'She knew it was one of her tormentors. She picked it up and she . . . she . . .'

'No. Jesus, Martha. *No*.'

I'm struggling to utter the terrible words. 'She threw him. She threw him off the balcony.' I bury my eyes in the palm of one hand, feeling tears run through my fingers. 'I wasn't quick enough.'

'You saw this happen?'

I step close to him, supplicating, trying to put my arms around his neck. 'I thought if I could only keep it to myself—'

'You thought you'd feed me a pack of lies! You thought you and I could live together for the next fifty years, whatever, and you'd be lying every second of it.'

'I didn't know whether you could forgive her.'

'Didn't you? No.' He throws my arms away from his neck and strides out of the room. A minute later, I hear a distant thud as the studio door slams.

I spend the next hour in a blank daze, lying on the floor by the stove with my hand on Muffin's warm back. Kit doesn't reappear. I imagine him hunched over a bottle, raging to himself. I don't blame him. His world has finally collapsed. His stepdaughter tried to kill his son, and his wife covered up for her. He must be wondering if there is anyone he can trust. I fear for us all.

The shadows are long on our lawn when I get a call from Dad. The line is faint.

'She's told me,' he says simply.

'Can you look her in the eye?'

'Who's going to cast the first stone, Martha? Not me, that's for sure.'

I sigh. 'I think Kit might.'

The line crackles. 'Look, come down to the beach. We're here. We need to talk to you.'

There's no sign of life from the studio, but Bianka says she'll keep an eye on the twins. They're both asleep now, piled in a soft heap on the sofa.

I find Dad's car near the school, in the spot where we parked the day we first came to Torutaniwha. It's a golden evening, just as that one was. Tussock grass shivers in a light breeze. I wander through the dunes, reliving the magic of that day. It's all over now. I wish I could wind back time and start again.

The beach is empty except for two familiar figures who sit close together among the rocks at the foot of Hinemoana's hill: a gaunt girl with bony arms, whose spray of curls seems to flow on the salt breeze;

and a wiry, grey-haired man whose eyes miss nothing. I love them both. I approach along the foreshore, my feet sinking with every step, the wind freshening around my ears. As I come closer I see that they're sharing a rock. They seem to be watching a party of gannets, soaring and diving beyond the breakers. Sacha has her head on Dad's shoulder, and his arm is around her.

He watches my approach with a tranquil smile. 'We came to ask her advice.'

I glance around, but we're alone. 'Ask who?'

'Hinemoana,' says Sacha jerkily, without lifting her head from Dad's shoulder. 'We thought she'd understand.'

I choose my own rock to sit on. It's covered in seaweed and little shells. Nearby, a hunting gannet plunges into the waves and reappears with a struggling fish in its beak.

Dad glances at the cliffs. 'Sacha thought of Hinemoana because she knows what it's like to be enchanted by evil. And she found her own way out.'

'We'll have to go back to England,' I say.

'And the boys?' persists Dad. 'And Kit? This is their true home. I've seen that for myself.'

'Kit doesn't have any choice. It's my job that got us the visas.'

'I don't want that!' Sacha must be coming down from her last smoke, whenever that was. She looks drained and edgy, but determined. 'I've done enough damage without making all of you leave Torutaniwha. It's the last thing I want. Look, Mum, I have to live with this for the rest of my life. I have to find a way to go on, knowing what I did to Finn. And just saying sorry is never, ever going to be enough.'

The temperature seems to drop abruptly, as the sun leaves the beach.

'The three of us have come up with a plan,' says Dad. 'Hinemoana had her say, too. At first Sacha felt that she didn't deserve to live, after what she did. She felt that there was only one way out.' He smiles at his granddaughter. 'But she will *not* drown herself here at Hinemoana's hill, no matter how poetic that might sound. She knows that she has a future—don't you, Sacha? She knows that her family want her to be made whole and well. She also knows that she can defeat this evil if she fights it with everything she's got, even if that means leaving the people she loves.'

'We *can* defeat it,' I insist desperately. 'We'll go to a doctor. We'll find a rehab place of some sort.'

Dad holds up a hand. 'Please listen, Martha. Listen to our plan.'

'I don't want to hear it!' I wail, pressing my hands to my ears.

'Mum.' Sacha slides from her rock and kneels in the sand in front of me. 'Just saying sorry isn't enough for *me*, this time. It can never be enough.'

So I listen, as the evening light softens Hinemoana's limestone face. I listen, and I argue. In the end, I can't fault the logic of their plan. It makes perfect sense. It gives us all a way out. But it's too much to bear.

Venus has risen as we begin to make our way back up the beach. The three of us don't speak much. We've made our decision. Even the waves are subdued.

'Look,' says Sacha, stopping to squint into the gloom. 'Someone's coming to meet us.'

Peering down the pale curve of the surf line, I make out a human shadow, a streak in the gunmetal twilight. He lopes steadily closer, hands in his pockets; no hint at all of a drunken stagger.

'It's Kit!' cries Sacha, and I hear her feet sinking in the wet sand as she runs. I'm about to follow when I feel a firm hand on my arm.

'They've a lot to talk about,' says Dad.

'She might need help! He's probably plastered.'

'He looks sober enough to me. Have a little faith, Martha.'

I watch Sacha's sprinting figure. 'Will you tell her about her father?' I ask.

'It's not my secret to tell.'

'But you'll be tempted.'

'*Kit* is her father.' Dad nods up the beach. 'Look.'

Ahead of us, the two silhouettes merge.

Forty-two

Six days. She has six days to pack, to organise, to say goodbye.

I try to put on a cheerful face. Really, I do try. I field anxious phone calls, assuring all enquirers that she just wants to finish her education in the UK—gosh, yes, she'll be back before we know it. I wash her clothes and organise the flights. Kit helps the boys to tape themselves telling jokes and singing their naughtiest songs, which they think might cheer her up when she's lonely.

Again and again, Dad tries to reassure me that we're doing the right thing. She'll live with him, in the bedroom that she's always used. She can go back to her old school, back to Lydia and her other friends, and simply start Year Twelve again. When I protest that we can't afford the fees, he smiles. He was going to leave Sacha a little money in his will. Well, he'll pay the school fees with it instead, and cheat the tax man.

But it doesn't help.

Every moment of every day is bathed in cold grief. Once the lights go out at night, we seem to drown in it. This time next week we'll have no Sacha. There will be emptiness and silence where she used to be. It feels almost like a death.

This time in five days, she'll be gone.

Four days.

Three.

Two.

It takes all her resolve to keep going through this crash. She forces herself to stay on the job, sorting through her possessions with gritted-teeth determination. There's a new certainty about her, as though—at last—she knows her enemy. On the final afternoon she telephones the Colberts and asks to visit. They're delighted to hear from her.

The river is too high to ford so she and I drive around to their place.

'Sure you want to do this, Sacha?' asks Kit, as we leave the house. 'You don't have to.'

'No more secrets.' Sacha begins to scratch her wrist, then balls her hands into nervous fists. 'That's rule number one.'

I'm not so sure. In fact, I'm dreading the next hour. Last night I dug out the newspaper article about Jean and his petition. *Those who are involved in the supply of this substance, and those who offend while under its influence, must be brought to justice and irrevocably removed from our streets.*

Unequivocal, you might say.

I've barely parked before Pamela and Jean come smiling out to meet us, kissing Sacha on both cheeks and exclaiming over how tired she looks. They've laid a pot of tea and blueberry muffins on a coffee table by the fire in their living room. It isn't a room they use much—generally they're to be found in their palatial kitchen or out on the glorious terrace—but today is obviously a special occasion. They've set out fine china teacups with gold edging. Above the fireplace, four brothers laugh together on a hillside.

'Sit down, sit down,' begs Jean, pulling out chairs. 'We're so pleased you've come. We didn't like to intrude at such a time. Your family will want to be left in peace, with Sacha and your father leaving so soon.'

'When will you be back?' asks Pamela, as she eases another log into the fire.

'I don't know,' says Sacha. She picks up a muffin, then lays it back on her plate. 'Look, Pamela . . . Jean. I can't eat your muffins. I can't accept any more of your kindness until I tell you something.'

Pamela is still fiddling with the fireguard but Jean leans closer, rubbing his hands amiably. 'A revelation! Go ahead.'

'Right.' Sacha glances at me, nervously tucking a curl behind her ear. 'Um, right. It's to do with why I'm leaving.'

And she tells them, with an honesty and humility that gives me hope. At first Pamela and Jean wear indulgent smiles, as though she's a small child reciting a poem; but as she continues to talk, the affection freezes on their faces. Pamela moves to sit on the arm of Jean's chair. He's leaning on one elbow, chewing his thumbnail and staring intently at Sacha while she tells them about her addiction, and the burglary, and Sibella's portrait. There's no hint of his usual good-natured humour.

As Sacha describes how she began to courier the drug, Jean's face actually seems to change texture. He looks like a different man. Any minute, I think, he's going to order us both out of the house. After all, he's heard the whining justifications of P addicts and their parents before. *It was the P that did it, the P changed her son . . . I hope he hangs himself in jail.*

It's when she comes to the night Finn fell that Sacha finally breaks down. Perhaps the hostile silence of her audience has unnerved her. She stops in mid-sentence and covers her face with her hands.

I rub her back, wishing we hadn't come. 'I owe you both an apology,' I say. 'I didn't tell you the truth.' Two horrified faces turn to me as I describe exactly what happened on the balcony.

Pamela takes Jean's hand. 'So the social workers were absolutely right,' she says dazedly. 'Finn didn't just fall. He was thrown.'

'I threw him,' whispers Sacha.

'You threw him.' Pamela blinks incredulously. 'And I gave them an earful. I told them you were the nicest family I'd ever met.'

'If you feel you must, you can phone the social services this minute,' I tell her. 'Or the police. Turn us in, I can't stop you. But Sacha is leaving New Zealand tomorrow and I have no idea when—or if—she will ever come back.'

The fire sparks and spits in the grate. Jean's eyes turn to the painting above the mantelpiece, and we all follow his gaze. Daniel smiles down at us, his face young and hopeful, hands around his little brother's shoulders. The next moment Sacha is on her feet, clumsily knocking the coffee table as she lurches sideways. A china cup tumbles to the floor, spraying tea in a long, dark streak across the carpet.

'I'll go,' she says, her voice high and quavering. 'I'm sorry. I'm sorry. I shouldn't be here . . . Mum, please can we just *go*?'

She heads blindly for the door. I'm stooping to pick up the fallen teacup when Jean levers himself from his chair. His eyes look hot and red-rimmed.

'No,' he roars.

Pamela's hand shoots out. She pulls her husband back by the shoulder. 'Let it go,' she hisses urgently. 'Wait until you've calmed down. You might say something you regret.'

Jean shakes her off. 'Sacha!' he shouts. His voice seems to rock the peaceful room. 'Don't you dare leave this house.'

Sacha halts in the doorway. She's beside herself, bent double with sobs, her arms tight around her stomach as though she has an agonising cramp. 'I just want to go,' she weeps. She's gasping for breath. 'Just want to . . . I'm so ashamed.'

Jean moves closer to her. I'm about to intervene when he holds out his arms and hugs her to his chest.

'I've never had a daughter.' He inhales, shutting his eyes. 'But if I had one, I hope she would be very much like you.'

Daybreak dilutes the darkness, and the early sun glints on the fuselage of a small aircraft. The rolling hills beyond the runway stretch forever and forever, painted and shaded like the backdrop to a play.

The seven of us left Patupaiarehe in a pewter dawn. It's September, just as it was when we first made our home there. Beside the drive the last daffodils waved farewell, like old friends.

The travellers have already checked in their bags. We're running out of time. Kit and Dad are talking about practicalities while Sacha and I press close together at a table. Her head is tilted onto my shoulder. She's wearing a pendant of carved pounamu around her neck; a present from Tama and Ira, made especially for her. She says she can feel their calm and strength in the warm greenstone.

Nearby, there's a kiosk. Two cheerful women stand chatting behind its counter. Commuters with briefcases are drinking coffee and reading newspapers. For those people, it's a normal day. I feel as though there will never again be a normal day.

The twins stomp around the polished floor, their hair sculpted into wild bed shapes, palms and noses pressed to the glass wall of the terminal as they watch the plane being refuelled. It will carry its precious cargo from Napier to Auckland, and by this afternoon they will have left New Zealand.

'There's Sacha's bag,' whimpers Charlie. He's holding Blue Blanket to his ear. 'That man just threw it down a hatch. Why are you going away, Sacha?'

Finn's arm is still in a sling, but his hair is already beginning to grow. 'You and Grandpa had both better be home in time for our birthday,' he growls fiercely.

'I'll be back soon,' says Sacha, and then she quickly turns away. There are bruised hollows beneath her eyes, and her skin has no bloom. I hold her thin frame against my chest and feel the tears burning holes in my eyelids. I can't let her go. I can't bear the thought of life without her.

The call comes too soon. I'm not ready. I'll never be ready.

'That's us,' mutters Dad, and feels in his pocket for boarding passes.

Panicked, Sacha and I cling together. Perhaps I can keep her with me if I hold tight enough. I feel Kit's hand on my shoulder. 'Martha,' he says gently. 'C'mon, you have to let go now.'

At last I give her up. She kneels on the floor, and her brothers clamber over her as other passengers file past. Then Kit rocks her in his arms.

'We're going to miss you like crazy,' he murmurs.

A girl stands slightly apart from our group, unwilling to intrude. She has wavy hair and arched eyebrows like a pre-war Hollywood film star, and her face is geisha pale. When we hear the final call, Sacha rushes to embrace her. This isn't the mascara-streaked hysteria of those classmates over a year ago. It's far more profound.

'I'll come back,' promises Sacha, wiping her friend's tears. 'I'll come back.'

The man at the gate looks at us, then at his watch. He holds out his hand for boarding passes. We're out of time.

Just as they're passing through the gate, Sacha stops dead, and turns around. Dad has taken her arm but she shakes him off and runs back to me, crying helplessly. I hold her face in my hands and kiss her, one last time.

Let her go, says my mother. There's compassion in her voice. *If you love her, let her go.*

'Go on,' I whisper to Sacha. 'It will be all right. Get well.'

I watch them hurry across the tarmac and up the metal steps. My father. My daughter. There's a fresh wind, and it dances in Sacha's hair. As she reaches the aircraft's door she looks back at us and waves frantically, then ducks her head and disappears. I notice Dad say something to the young cabin attendant, see her smile. Still smiling, she reaches out and shuts the door behind him.

Kit takes my hand, and we race up to the viewing platform and wait in thin sunshine, trying to work out which little round window has Sacha behind it. We pretend we can see her face. The aircraft begins to move, taxiing away from the terminal building. At the top of the runway it slowly turns, and its engines roar.

I'm waving. We're all waving. Bianka stands beside me, tears glinting on her cheekbones. I put my arm around her shoulders.

'She's not coming back,' she says. 'Not really.'

And that's when my heart finally breaks.

Sacha's plane sprints along the runway and into the air, and we wave still more desperately, with all our arms. We're crying out to our girl. We want her to see that we love her. We're waving as she becomes a speck over the crumpled blanket of hills. We are still waving as she disappears into skeins of light cirrus.

Hawke's Bay Today
Local News

Yesterday marked the anniversary of the death of Napier-born Daniel Colbert, who was murdered on the streets of Wellington ten years ago. It is a date which his parents used to dread. Last night, however, they marked it with the launch of the Daniel Colbert Conservation Trust. For Daniel's father, Jean Colbert, it was an occasion of new beginnings as some of the region's most talented musicians, together with local artist Kit McNamara, came together to create an evening of entertainment and hope.

'For the past decade I have focused too zealously on the cause of Daniel's death,' Mr Colbert told supporters who attended the concert in Napier's Century Theatre. 'My wife has been very patient! But now it is time to celebrate those things which made his life unique. He did not live to see his twenty-fourth birthday, but it is for those who loved and admired him to ensure that those twenty-three extraordinary years are not wasted on bitterness and mourning.

'Daniel was a devoted conservationist whose last project was the protection of the tara-iti, or fairy tern. One of his constant worries was that of funding. That is why Pamela and I have set up a trust in his name, to fund academic teams whose aim is to further the understanding and protection of New Zealand's unique fauna.'

Mr Colbert declared the Trust's first fundraising event a resounding success, thanks to the generosity of local performers. He warmly thanked celebrated Hawke's Bay artist Kit McNamara, whose work is currently on sale in Dublin and New York as well as Napier's Portside Gallery. Kit donated a series of paintings, each inspired by the landscape of Hawke's Bay. They excited considerable interest and were sold by auction during the course of the evening, raising over ten thousand dollars.

A highlight of the event was an atmospheric performance of Debussy's flute solo Syrinx *by nineteen-year-old British flautist Sacha Norris. The young musician's technical fluency and mature interpretation held her audience spellbound. Sacha is the stepdaughter of Kit McNamara, and has spent the past fortnight in Hawke's Bay visiting her family. It is likely to be her last such visit for some time: next week she will return to her home in the UK where she has gained a place to study medicine at Birmingham University, embarking on the long road to becoming a paediatrician.*

'I'd like to thank my family and friends for their incredible support and forgiveness,' she told the audience. 'I made some epic mistakes when I was younger, and hurt the people I most love. I also hurt myself. But they stood by me.'

Referring to a year she spent living with her family in the isolated coastal community of Torutaniwha, Sacha had this to say: 'Torutaniwha is a paradise, and my heart is still there with my parents and wonderful little brothers. I miss them every day. I learned a lot about myself in that year, and I'll never be the same person again.'

However, asked by the master of ceremonies whether she has plans to return permanently to New Zealand once qualified, Sacha looked doubtful. 'There are some people who can handle living in paradise, and some who can't. And you know what? I can't.'

Sacha dedicated her performance to Anita Varga, who died earlier this year, at the age of forty-five, after a long battle with cancer.